Dreamscapes

Tamara McKinley was born and raised in Australia. Adopted by her grandmother, she was eventually brought to England to finish her education. Tamara McKinley lives on the south coast of England, and writes full-time, but travels back to Australia frequently to visit her eldest son and do research for her books.

Also by Tamara McKinley

Matilda's Last Waltz
Jacaranda Vines
Windflowers
Summer Lightning
Undercurrents

Dreamscapes

Tamara McKinley

PIATKUS

Visit the Piatkus website!

Piatkus publishes a wide range of bestselling fiction and non-fiction, including books on health, mind, body & spirit, sex, self-help, cookery, biography and the paranormal.

If you want to:
- read descriptions of our popular titles
- buy our books over the Internet
- take advantage of our special offers
- enter our monthly competition
- learn more about your favourite Piatkus authors

VISIT OUR WEBSITE AT: www.piatkus.co.uk

All the characters ... al persons, living or

First published in Great Britain in 2005
by Judy Piatkus (Publishers) Ltd of
5 Windmill Street, London W1T 2JA
email: info@piatkus.co.uk

The moral right of the author has been asserted

A catalogue record for this book is available from the British Library

ISBN 0 7499 0733 9 (HB)
ISBN 0 7499 3600 2 (TPB)

Set in Times by
Action Publishing Technology Ltd, Gloucester

Printed and bound in Great Britain by
William Clowes Ltd, Beccles, Suffolk

Acknowledgements

To Liza Hobbs, mezzo-soprano, with grateful thanks for her expert advice and the time she spent helping me with all the research into the opera. The emails and the glasses of wine were really much appreciated. I apologise for any mistakes – they are my own.

To the Music Department Staff at Newlands School, Seaford, I give my thanks for lending me so many books from their library. They proved invaluable sources for my research into the operas I wanted to use in this work.

Thanks also to Gary and Karen Stidder for their generous gift of tickets to Glyndebourne so I could see how it was done in real life. My thanks to all of the above for teaching me so much, and giving me the chance to discover what has become a passion for the opera.

Chapter One

1921

It was the height of summer and the six painted wagons slowly trundled along the winding, narrow, dirt track which cut through the heart of the Australian Outback. Each wagon bore the legend, SUMMERS' MUSIC HALL, in bright red letters, and was pulled by a sure-footed shire-horse, whose chestnut coat and graceful plumed fetlocks gleamed in the sun. The troupe of travelling players had been together for over a year, and now they were heading for Charleville before turning north to spend the winter on the Queensland coast.

Velda Summers sat on the buckboard next to her husband, and tried to ease the nagging pain in her back. The jolt and sway of the wagon was making her feel nauseous, and she couldn't wait for the journey to be over. 'How far is it now?' she demanded.

Declan turned his head to look at her, his expression concerned. 'That's the fifth time you've asked me this morning,' he said in the warm Irish brogue so admired by his female audiences. 'Are you not well, my love?'

Velda put her hands over the burgeoning mound of her stomach. 'I think the baby's not liking all this jiggling about,' she said with a pout. 'And, frankly, Declan, neither am I.' She looked back at him through her lashes and tempered her petulance with a wan smile.

Declan's smile was indulgent, his dark hair flopping over his brow as the sun glinted in his brown eyes. 'We're almost there, darlin',' he murmured. 'Then you can rest while we get ready for the parade.'

1

Velda gave a great sigh to let him know she wasn't happy about it, and tried to find a more comfortable spot on the hard buckboard. She had no other option but to sit here and suffer, but even with a cushion rammed behind the small of her back, she couldn't ease the nagging ache. She tasted the dew of sweat on her top lip and pulled at her dress. The thin cotton shift was clinging to her, and despite the broad-brimmed hat she always wore to protect her face from the sun, she could feel the onset of a headache.

The heat of the Outback was all-encompassing. There was no escape, not even when they were sheltered from the fierce glare by surrounding trees. Flies and mosquitoes were drifting around them in clouds, and the eternal hiss and click of a million insects buzzed in her head. Her energy was sapped and she wilted like the pale green eucalyptus leaves that drooped overhead. How she missed the cool, misty mornings of her Irish home. The smell of rain on grass, the crashing of the sea against the black rocks and the pungent aroma of peat fires in the hearth.

'You're not regretting this, are you?' Declan asked as he slapped the reins over the shire's broad back in an attempt to quicken his pace.

Velda dismissed the treacherous thoughts of Ireland, for they came only in moments of weakness, and she knew she would follow her man to the ends of the earth – even if it was as hot as hell and twice as uncomfortable. She smiled at him as she saw the naked love for her in his eyes. 'Never,' she breathed. 'For how could I have let you come all this way alone?'

He seemed satisfied with her reply and, after kissing her cheek, turned his attention back to the vista that was opening out before them.

Velda looked at the empty miles of sun-bleached grass and blood-red earth and, despite her brave words, felt the return of the deep-seated fear that always lurked at the back of her mind. They were so far from civilisation – so very alone – what if something were to go wrong again? This Australia was an untamed place which instilled fear in even the most determined heart, and although she had Declan to protect and cherish her, there were moments when she wished with all her might they hadn't come here.

Tears blurred her vision and she bit her lip as she thought of the lonely little grave they had left behind a year ago. Her first baby

2

had come too fast and had not survived long enough to draw breath. They would probably never pass that way again, and her tiny son's resting place would be obliterated by the elements and the encroaching bush, until there was no sign he had ever existed.

She blinked back the tears, fighting to maintain a stoic disregard for the onset of loneliness and the yearning need for her mother. Her choice had been made and she'd married Declan, knowing she would never see the shores of Ireland again. For this had been their adventure, their search for a new life and perhaps even fame and fortune. It was too late now to regret anything.

The sun was high in the sky as the cavalcade entered the clearing in the bush and the troupe began to set up camp. Charleville was less than two miles away and they had to prepare for their Grand Parade. This would be their chance of drumming up business, of handing out fliers and giving the audience a taste of what was to come if they paid their twopenny entrance fee.

Declan lifted Velda from her high perch and gently set her on her feet. 'I've put some pillows and blankets under that tree,' he said. 'Go and rest while I try to knock some order into this company of rogues.'

Velda stroked his face, seeing the fear for her and their unborn child in his eyes.

'Did I ever tell you how much I love you?' she murmured, her earlier petulance forgotten.

'Many times, my darling,' he replied against her lips. 'But I will never tire of hearing you say it.'

They kissed, his embrace gentle as the baby moved between them. Then he was gone, striding into the circle of wagons, throwing orders to all who would listen, his rich, deep tones reverberating in the stillness of their bush surroundings.

'Blimey, 'e don't 'alf go on,' grumbled Poppy as she took Velda's arm.

Velda smiled as she eased her back. She and Poppy were both twenty-two, and the little Cockney dancer had become a good friend over the twelve months they'd been together. 'He just wants everything to be ready,' she murmured.

'Let's get you settled then. You look fair done in.'

Velda silently acknowledged she was out of sorts. 'I wish I had even half your energy, Poppy. Doesn't the heat ever get to you?'

The peroxide blonde hair shimmered in the sun and the freckles danced across her nose as she laughed. 'When you've lived through twenty winters in London you're only too pleased for a bit of warmth. Can't get enough of it.'

They picked their way over fallen branches and through the long, crisp grass to the trees overhanging the rivulet of water which meandered a tortuous path through the surrounding scrub and gurgled over shiny pebbles. With Poppy by her side, Declan's lilting, musical voice soothing her fears, and the close proximity of Charleville easing Velda's concerns, she could at last relax. This child would be born in a proper bed, with a doctor in attendance; they had the money, for these outback towns were starved of entertainment and the locals had come flocking to their performances.

She took off the broad-brimmed straw hat she'd decorated with silk roses and scarlet ribbons, and shook out her long black hair, leaving it to tumble almost to her waist. It was cooler here by the water, the sunlight dappled by the cascade of drooping eucalyptus branches. There would be no more performances from her until this baby was born, and it was lovely to sit idly by and let the others do all the work. Yet she couldn't quite dismiss the tug of longing to be with them, for she was a performer, a soprano, and she would miss not being on stage tonight, would miss the applause, the footlights and the excitement of playing to a new audience.

'I know what you're thinking,' muttered Poppy as she helped Velda get settled on the blankets. 'But you ain't gunna be on that stage for a while yet, so you might as well 'ave a kip and enjoy being a lady of leisure for a change.'

Velda squeezed her hand. 'Thanks, Pops.'

Poppy grinned, and without the usual thick make-up, she looked about sixteen. 'Better get on, or I'll 'ave yer old man yelling at me again.'

Velda watched her run back to the wagons, and smiled. Poppy was never still, and despite the skinny frame, seemed to possess the strength and stamina of a cart-horse. Declan had long since realised Poppy was a law unto herself and had given up trying to organise her.

Resting back on the pillows, she kicked off her shoes and dipped her feet in the icy water and watched the now familiar bustle of the camp as they prepared for the parade. Poppy was bossing the girls around as usual, her strident Cockney voice and raucous laughter echoing through the surrounding bush. The jugglers, musicians and acrobats were rehearsing and Max, the comedian and dog trainer, was sorting out his props. Patch, his little terrier snuffled in the long grass, tail whipping back and forth in excitement at all the different scents.

Velda smiled as Patch caught sight of her and ran, tongue lolling to be petted. With one black eye and another patch on his rump, he was aptly named. She patted his head and eventually pushed him away. He was too energetic for her today.

The wagons had been washed down, with water lifted in buckets from the stream, and now the green, red and yellow paintwork glittered in the sun. The white masks of comedy and tragedy gleamed like ghosts against the dark green paint, reminding the troupe they were following an ancient heritage – a heritage which had shifted and changed over the years – yet one that still enthralled those who played their part in it.

The horses had been fed and watered, then groomed until their chestnut coats and white manes gleamed in the sun. Feathered headdresses were fixed to their crown-pieces, brasses to the thick collars, and strings of tiny silver bells dangled from the scarlet blankets on their backs. Patch danced on his back legs, showing off his glittery ruff, his piratical patch giving him a raffish air as he sought admiration from each of the players.

There was an air of pent-up excitement among the men and women of the troupe as costumes were taken out of the trunks and brushed down. In this babble of chatter and laughter, top hats and shoes were polished, and feathery fans wafted to rid them of the dust that seemed to cling no matter how well they'd been packed. Heavy make-up was applied, frills and feathers adjusted and stockings checked for ladders. The props were inspected for any damage, and the fliers they'd had printed in the last town were divided up amongst the troupe to be handed out during the Grand Parade.

Velda eased her back against the cushions. The ache had ebbed into a niggle, and she was feeling drowsy, lulled by the dappled shadows and the chuckle of the water. It was bliss not to be in that wagon, not to be jolted and jarred and thrown about.

She sighed with sleepy contentment. The chorus girls chattered and bitched as they ruffled their brightly coloured skirts and jostled for a place in front of the one long mirror. Paste jewellery shot darts of fire in the sun, feathered headdresses swayed and dipped as they bent their heads and fought over lipsticks. They reminded her of the local birds, all bright plumage and squabbling tail-feathers, flitting here and there, never still.

The sharp rap of drums woke her and she sat up, startled. She hadn't meant to fall asleep, and by the look of things, the parade was ready to march into town.

'Stay here and rest,' said Declan as he squatted down beside her.

'Not on your life,' she insisted as she grabbed her shoes and struggled to her feet. She looked into his eyes, so loving, so kind, she couldn't resist kissing him. 'The show must go on, remember?' she teased. 'And as I've never missed a parade yet, I don't intend to start now.'

He looked uncertain, but she took the decision out of his hands by marching barefooted through the grass and clambering up into the wagon. The sleep had done her some good, and the pain had disappeared. Taking the reins, she looked down at him and grinned. 'It's showtime,' she said. 'Let's go.'

Charleville was a crossroads of the outback, with tracks that had been laid down by the early pioneers and explorers. The streets were broad and dusty, a leftover from the days of the great bullock droves when thirty oxen would pull the enormous drays loaded with bales of wool through the town on the way to the markets in Brisbane. It was a wealthy town with a hotel on every corner. These hotels catered to the needs of the stockmen and drovers who came with their mobs to the tiny Victorian station, where the animals would be sent east by train.

Surrounding the town were several hundred thousand acres of good grazing land and forests which were fed by a myriad number of underground streams and deep billabongs. Wool and beef were king and the Outlanders were rich after the Great War. Their money had provided wooden walkways and shops, two churches, a police station and a racecourse.

The finest of the hotels was the Coronas. Built to cater for the aristocracy of the Outback – the graziers – it was a graceful Victorian edifice with a shady verandah that overlooked the hitching posts and main thoroughfare. The dining room was panelled and beamed with the finest oak, the tables laid with snowy linen and polished silver beneath the crystal chandeliers which had been imported from France.

The reception hall was a hushed temple of comfortable chairs, tiffany lamps and highly polished floors. Upstairs, the luxurious bedrooms had their own bathrooms – an innovation which still caused wide-eyed awe amongst the locals – and opened out onto the broad balcony that ran the width of the hotel. From here, the graziers could sit in cane chairs in the shade, and smoke their cigars as they drank beer and whisky and looked down over the little town they were so proud to call their own. Several of these rooms were on permanent rental so these outback aristocrats and their families could come into town whenever they wished and be assured of a decent bed for the night.

The Coronas Hotel was a famous landmark, and the hall at the back of the hotel was a popular venue for parties and dances, and it was said by those not in the know, that it was often the scene of debauchery and loose morals. This hall was long and wide, with a stage at one end, and would be the travelling players' theatre for a few days.

They were now on the edge of town and Velda experienced the old familiar surge of adrenaline as she sat with the reins in her hands and waited for the signal to lead the parade down the main street. Runners had already been sent ahead to advertise their arrival, and the sense of energy and nervous excitement was rising to fever pitch as the horses sweated and tossed their plumes, Patch danced in circles, and the players adjusted their costumes and made ready.

Declan looked up at her and blew her a kiss before tugging at his tailed jacket and tweaking his bow-tie. With a signal to the musicians he led the procession into town. Drum and pipe, tambour, penny whistle, accordion and violin accompanied their slow, majestic advance. The horses stepped out, their great hoofs lifting the dust, their heads high as if they knew they were on show. The showgirls ruffled their skirts and showed shapely legs, the acrobats tumbled and cartwheeled in their white leotards, the jugglers threw balls and clubs and Declan's powerful baritone soared above it all in song.

The people of Charleville lined the street and watched in wonder as the children ran alongside the wagons and tried to catch the sweets Velda and the other drivers threw down to them. Men hung over the balconies and shouted ribald encouragement to the chorus girls, while the women admired the acrobats' muscles and fluttered

7

their handkerchiefs at Declan. The horses resting at the hitching posts propped and stamped at all the noise, and several dogs raced in and out of the parading feet, barking and snapping at the unusual sights and sounds. Patch snarled back, teeth bared, ready to see off these local intruders into his parade and show them he was no pushover despite the spangled ruff around his neck.

The cavalcade came to a standstill in the centre of town, and Declan climbed up to join Velda on the wagon. With a flourish of his top hat he silenced the music, and the crowds. 'Citizens of Charleville,' he boomed from his stance on the buckboard. 'It is our delicious design to declare our dedicated demonstrations for your delectation and delight.' He paused, for timing was all in this business. 'Our illustrious illusionist will illustrate his inimitable imagination and immeasurable insights into the mystic.'

Velda grinned as the oohs and aahs rippled through the watching townsfolk. Declan never failed to capture his audience with his tongue-twisting Master of Ceremonies act. No one would ever know how difficult it was to find the right words and string them together, and then deliver them with such wonderfully rolling aplomb.

As Declan stirred the audience into further rapturous applause, Velda gasped. The pain had suddenly returned, deeper now, like a vice around the lower half of her belly. Her hands trembled on the reins and she licked the sweat from her top lip. She could feel the rapid beat of her pulse, the lightness in her head and the overwhelming need to be out of the sun. She longed to lie down, yet she had to remain on the hard wooden seat in the debilitating glare of an Outback afternoon, for this was the only time they had to encourage people to part with their money. She was trapped; hemmed in by wagons and horses and people. She looked down at the others who were weaving in and out of the crowd as they passed out the flyers and balloons – it wouldn't be long now, she kept saying to herself, but oh, how the minutes seemed to drag.

Declan finally sat down to rapturous applause, and after a swift glance of concern at Velda, took the reins and led the procession to the wide entrance at the side of the Coronas Hotel. The cobbled yard echoed with the trundle of wagon wheels and the heavy clop of the horses' hoofs, but the sun was low enough in the sky to be hidden by the tall building, and for this Velda was grateful. She was sweating, her pulse racing as the deep pains tore through her and made her catch her breath. She leaned on Declan as he helped her down and led her into the cool of the hall.

'I should be getting the doctor,' he muttered as he and Poppy settled her in a nest of pillows in a corner.

She nodded. 'I'll feel better if you do,' she murmured. 'We don't want to risk losing this baby too.' She saw the pain flit in his eyes and forced a smile. 'It's probably only a false alarm, but it's best to make sure, don't you think?'

Declan hovered, obviously torn between his duty to his wife and the needs of the troupe who were beginning to argue amongst themselves.

Poppy folded her arms and looked down at her. 'You don't look right,' she stated. 'Better get the doc, mate, before she pops.'

'Declan's just going to find him,' Velda said with a firmness that sent her husband striding out of the hall. 'Clear off and sort those girls out, Poppy. They're fighting again.'

Poppy grimaced as she shrugged. 'So what else is new?' she said. 'Silly cows don't know when they're well off.'

Velda couldn't help but smile. Poppy called a spade a shovel and didn't give a damn for convention. 'Make us a cup of tea first, Pops. There's a mate.'

Poppy grinned, the freckles dancing across her nose. 'Righto. Won't be a tick.' She marched off, skirts swinging, heels tapping on the wooden floor, voice raised above the gabble of the other chorus girls as she ordered someone to find the kettle and primus stove amongst the bags and baskets.

Velda leaned back against the cushions and listened, eyes closed, as the dressing-rooms were lamented upon, the lavatory deplored, and space was fought for as boxes and baskets were unpacked. It was bliss to be out of the sun – to be lying down and apart from the chaos.

Declan eventually returned, his expression grim. 'The doctor's out of town,' he said, worry starkly etched in his eyes. 'But he's expected back at any minute.' He took her hand and raised it to his lips. 'It will be all right, darlin', I promise.'

The panic was rising. How could he be so certain? What if something were to go wrong? She felt the tears threaten and wanted to scream and shout and demand a doctor's help – yet she knew that histrionics would get her nowhere this time. She and Declan were helpless in the hands of fate.

9

'I'll be fine,' she said with as much firmness as she could muster under the circumstances. 'Go and sort out the troupe. Poppy will look after me.'

He kissed her cheek, hovered a moment more, then left her side as Poppy returned with her cup of tea.

'Where's the doc?' she asked, the concern darkening her blue eyes.

'Out of town,' Velda grimaced. 'I think it might have started for real this time, Pops.' She grabbed Poppy's hand. 'Run back to the hotel and see if he's on his way, or if there's anyone else who can help. But don't tell Declan until we know for sure this isn't a false alarm. I don't want him worrying any more.'

'If you say so,' Poppy replied, looking unconvinced.

Velda nodded firmly. 'Dec's got enough on his plate – and you've seen how he is, Pops. He hasn't a clue and will only panic.'

Poppy plumped the cushions and turned away. Velda sipped her tea, and as the minutes passed, she began to feel a bit of a fraud. The pains had stopped as suddenly as they had started, and apart from feeling wrung out, there really wasn't much wrong with her. Still, she thought, it would do no harm to have a doctor nearby in case things went all of a rush again.

Poppy returned some time later, flushed and sweating. 'The doc's still out somewhere, but he's expected back tonight,' she said breathlessly. 'I 'ad to run all the bloody way through the town to his 'ouse, but 'is missus is real nice and she says she'll send 'im over the minute 'e's back.'

Velda digested this news and realised there was little she could do about it. At least the pains had stopped and they weren't in the middle of nowhere, she reasoned. This time, she stood a better chance of delivering a live baby. Deciding she'd had enough of sitting around, and despite Poppy's protests, she hauled herself to her feet. 'Time I got to work,' she said firmly. 'Can't be sitting around here when there's so much to do, and I need to get my mind occupied by something else.'

Declan turned from hanging the stage curtains. 'You'll stay there,' he said firmly. 'There's nothing for you to do but look after yourself and our baby.'

Velda argued her point, but it didn't sound convincing even to her, and when Declan refused to listen she sank gratefully back into the nest of cushions. Yet, despite feeling pampered and at ease, it was with growing frustration that she watched the familiar routines of setting up for the show. She should have been helping with the props and the costume baskets – should have been stringing up the curtains and sweeping the stage – instead of which, she was lying here feeling as fat and indolent as a well-fed cat.

At last the hall was ready. The hotel's plush seats were placed in orderly rows and the red velvet curtains they'd found in a cupboard backstage looked grand against the pristine white paint of the hall. The footlights were a marvel of invention, already in place and linked to the hotel's power supply which came from an enormous generator out the back – so much more sophisticated than the old gaslights they were used to.

With everything in place, Declan and two of the other men turned their attention to his special rostrum. This was an old pulpit, found during the renovation of a country church and bought for a song – literally – for Declan had given a solo performance of his favourite arias to the circle of delighted women who were in charge of church funds, and who were only too willing to let him have the old pulpit in return.

This edifice had been cushioned with kapok and covered with the deepest red velvet. Thick gold braid had been stitched decoratively onto the velvet and great tassels dangled from the sides. Once it was heaved into place on the edge of the stage, Declan would use it to introduce the acts and entertain the audience, his gavel at the ready, his convoluted script word-perfect.

Velda's anxiety grew as there was no further word on the doctor's progress. Yet there was nothing she could do about it, and when she was finally allowed to move from her nest of cushions and was made comfortable backstage in an ancient wicker chair, she kept her mind occupied by mediating in arguments, helping to tie laces and, with her friend Poppy, generally keep the peace.

Night fell swiftly in the Outback, and lights were switched on as the excitement grew and their audience began to trickle in to take their seats. The orchestra was small, but skilled, and with the combined efforts of the accordion, the drum, piano and the violin, they soon had their audience clapping along in time to their favourite tunes.

Velda had helped as best she could in the dressing-room – a tight squeeze with so many people jostling for elbow-room – and had fixed broken fans, stitched laddered stockings, sorted out fights

11

amongst the girls and generally tried to keep order. Now she was tired, the pain having returned in unrelenting waves which threatened to overwhelm her. Yet she knew she must keep going and not let anyone see how bad it was – the show had to go on and the players must not be distracted. If the worst came to the worst, then she'd slip out during the performance and get help in the hotel, for Poppy had assured her the doctor was on his way.

The excited buzz of conversation grew as the lights dimmed and the curtains were pulled back to reveal Poppy and the five other dancing girls doing their high-kicks. The rest of the troupe was waiting in the wings. The show had begun.

Velda was finally alone in the dressing-room and she listened to the music, and the thud of the dancers' feet on the wooden stage. She could smell the dust of the hall, the pungent odour of camphor and greasepaint and the perfume of the women in the audience. Her heightened senses picked out a bum note played by the violinist, the missed cue by the leading chorus girl who should have come in two chords earlier, and the slap of the ceiling fan which stirred the humid air to little effect.

Declan's voice reverberated to the rafters as he did his speech from the Scottish play, and Velda sank back in the wicker chair gasping with the pain. It was a vice, squeezing ever more strongly, taking her breath away, leaving her in a void where no sound could be heard, nothing could be seen or experienced but the core of agony.

The fear was deep and unremitting. She should have gone to the hotel earlier and asked for help – should have heeded her body's warnings and not put her unborn child at risk for the sake of a performance. She tried to call out, but the audience was laughing and clapping and her voice was lost. Breathing sharp, shallow breaths, she struggled to her feet and edged her way from the stifling room into the narrow corridor which led to the wings. If she could catch someone's attention, then she would be all right, she kept telling herself. If not, then she would just have to get on with it alone and hope she could reach the hotel in time.

'Stupid,' she gasped. 'How stupid not to get help sooner.'

The girls came running off the stage and nearly knocked her over. 'Velda?' Poppy caught her arm and just managed to keep her on her feet.

'It's started,' Velda hissed. 'Go and get help. Quickly.'

Poppy took charge as she always did in moments of crisis. She

12

was a sensible girl, with very little talent, but with stunning good looks, a superb figure and sweet nature. She glared at the other five girls and started whispering rapid instructions. One of them ran out into the darkness heading for the hotel, and the others helped Velda back into the dressing-room. A makeshift bed was laid out on the floor, using old curtains, pillows and pilfered sheets Poppy had hidden in her costume basket.

Velda knew Poppy had the acquisitive nature of a magpie and was past caring where the sheets had come from. The pain was deeper now, coming in wave after wave. Her waters had broken and she knew she must give birth soon. As she sweated and strained and waited for news of the doctor's arrival, she could hear Declan introducing Max and his little dog. The sound of his voice soothed her a little and she struggled to keep her cries soft so they wouldn't spoil his performance. She could do this, she told herself. She could do this without him.

'Where's the doctor?' she gasped as she held on to Poppy's hand.

'He's still up country,' replied Poppy, her usually cheerful face stern with worry. 'It's a good thing I 'elped me mum with all 'er sprogs, so I knows what to do. Come on Velda. Just tell me when you're ready for the big one, and we'll have this little bugger born in no time.'

Velda gathered all her remaining energy and with one great heave, felt her child slither from her. Falling back against the makeshift bed, she had only one thought. 'Is it breathing?' she asked as Poppy cut the cord and swiftly bundled it into a towel.

As if in reply, the baby let out a lusty yell and waved its fists in the air, kicking tiny, chubby legs in protest at being so rudely disturbed. The protest didn't stop as Poppy washed and cleaned and tidied up.

Velda's tears were hot on her cheeks as she reached for her child. The pain and fear were forgotten as she held the wriggling, protesting little being in her arms and looked down with a heart-swell of such emotion she would have been hard pressed to describe it.

The thunder of feet down the passageway heralded Declan's arrival. 'I heard a baby crying,' he said as he fell to his knees and gathered his wife and child into his embrace. 'My darling, darling girl. Why didn't you tell me?'

13

'And stop the show?' She grinned. 'Never – we have a tradition to keep, remember?'

Declan gently took the baby from her and cradled it in his arms. 'Then the tradition must be properly fulfilled,' he said, the tears sparkling in his eyes and running unheeded down his handsome face.

Velda knew what he was going to do, and struggled to her feet. Waving away all protests from the girls, she took his arm and, leaning heavily against him, walked with him back into the wings. With a nod of encouragement, she slumped against the solid old walls of the country hall and watched as Declan strode out on to the stage. Without a doubt, she thought, I belong with this man – and now we are complete.

'Ladies and gentlemen,' boomed Declan as he stood in the footlights and held the tightly wrapped baby up to show the audience. 'I give you Catriona Summers. The new star of Summers' Music Hall.'

Chapter Two

'Kitty, will you be hurrying up, girl? We're leaving.'

Catriona, startled from her day-dreams, looked up at her mother and blinked. She had been so lost in the beauty of her surroundings she had forgotten everything else. 'Do we have to go, Mam?' she asked. 'I like it here.'

Velda Summers gave her a swift hug, enveloping her in slender arms and the fragrance of her flowery perfume. 'I know, *acushla,* but we have to move on.' She drew back and held Catriona at arm's length as she smiled. 'We'll come this way again, Kitty. But you know how it is.'

Catriona sighed. She'd been born in the dusty dressing-room of a country hall during one of their performances. Her cradle had been a costume basket, her home a brightly decorated wagon, her life – all ten years of it – spent following the dirt tracks that crisscrossed the great Australian Outback.

Another town meant another show – an endless circle of tramping the tracks, of rehearsals and costume fittings – of being regarded by the townspeople as an outsider, a gypsy. Her friends were the men and women of the troupe – her education overseen by her Da, who made her learn great reams of Shakespeare and expected her to perform them on stage once she was old enough to understand the importance of playing to an audience.

She'd been born to the smell of greasepaint and sweat and the travelling life, but every now and then she longed for peace, for silence and the chance to remain in one place for more than a few days without the accompanying racket of showgirls and artistes. The idea of school, of friends her own age was enticing, but she knew it was only a dream for, as her parents had often told her, people such as them were not meant to live a commonplace kind of life – she was a star of the stage, and necessarily stood apart from mere mortals.

Catriona looked into the violet eyes with their thick black lashes and wished she could tell her mother her thoughts. Yet she knew that if she did, Velda would dismiss them as childish day-dreams, the wish for something not yet experienced that would only disappoint if it was tried. 'When will we come back?' she persisted.

Velda shrugged her elegant shoulders. 'Soon,' she murmured, her thoughts obviously elsewhere. She reached for Catriona's hand. 'Come on. Or the wagons will be leaving without us.'

Catriona stepped to one side, avoiding the outstretched hand. She wanted to look one last time at the homestead which nestled deep in the great valley below her. Sheltered by stands of eucalyptus, and surrounded by outbuildings, it looked cosy and welcoming – looked like home.

The Great Dividing Range was a purple smudge on the horizon, the sky was clear, and as she stood on the stony outcrop overlooking the valley, she could hear the sound of rushing water coming from the nearby falls. Horses and cattle cropped at the long, yellow grass below her, the white fences stark in the sunlight. There was smoke coming from the chimney and a line of washing flapped in the warm breeze. She took a deep breath, fighting the tears that suddenly blurred her vision, and vowed that one day she would come back and never leave.

She turned reluctantly away and followed her mother over the tumble of rocks and through the bush into the clearing where they had made camp the previous night. Sniffing back the tears and the disappointment, she swiftly helped her mother to finish loading the wagon.

Declan Summers had already backed Jupiter, the lovely shire, into the traces and, with his black hair flopping in his eyes, was tightening the thick leather straps. 'Kitty, me darling,' he boomed. 'I thought you'd deserted us.'

She grinned as she heaved the last of the baskets into the back of the wagon. 'Not yet, Da,' she replied.

He strode across the clearing, flung his arm over her shoulder and squeezed her close as he kissed the top of her head. 'It's glad I am that day's far off,' he declared. 'For what would I be doing without my best girl by my side?'

16

Catriona grinned as she buried her face in his shirt and breathed in the delicious aroma that was her father. Sharp-scented soap, tobacco smoke and hair oil – they were the very essence of the man she adored and although it had made her parents sad, at this moment she was glad they'd had no more children.

Declan finally released her and, turning to look at the others in the travelling troupe of players, he strode into the centre of the encampment. '"Let us then, be up and doing,"' he boomed. '"With a heart for any fate; Still achieving, still pursuing."'

Catriona was all too familiar with her da's favourite Longfellow quotation. He said it each time they set out for a new town. Yet his voice never failed to send a shiver of excitement through her, for it somehow reinforced the adventure of their lives and momentarily swept away the longing to be still.

There were only four wagons now and Catriona sat between her parents on the buckboard of the leading wagon as the slow procession left the encampment. The troupe was her family – an ever-changing, but depleted, family of men and women who shared her parents' passion for everything theatrical. There were jugglers and musicians, singers, dancers, fire-eaters and acrobats – each of them willing to play many parts for the chance to shine in their particular skills.

Catriona settled down for the journey, the pride in her family warming her soul. Da could sing and recite and work the audience into a frenzy with his complicated and clever introductions to the acts. Mam was a soprano, the real star of the show, and the only one who didn't have to join in the chorus or help the conjurer.

Catriona had learned very early on that she was expected to do her part in entertaining the audiences, and although she sometimes felt sick at the thought of going on stage, she'd learned the dances Poppy had taught her and could now, after much practice, get a decent tune out of the old piano that was strapped to the back of the rear wagon. Yet the thing she loved best was to sing along to the records she played on the heavy wind-up gramophone – and although most of the songs were from the operas and in foreign languages, Mam had explained enough of the stories behind the operas for her to understand the passion behind the music. It was her burning ambition to follow in Mam's footsteps and take centre stage as a soprano.

Catriona's thoughts drifted and she yawned as the sway and jolt

17

of the wagon took them further into the hinterland. She hadn't had much sleep the night before, having been kept awake by the heated debate over whether or not to trade in the horse-drawn wagons for motorised trucks. It was 1931, and although times were harder than ever before because of the Depression, they were falling behind the times, and in her father's opinion they were in danger of being mistaken for circus people – a completely different class of entertainer all together.

The argument had raged around the camp-fire far into the night, and Catriona, curled up in blankets in the back of the wagon, could see logic in both sides of the debate. A truck would make the journeys faster, but would be more expensive to maintain than the horses. The old way had a charm about it, but the inconveniences they had to withstand would still be there, for they still wouldn't be able to afford more than a tent to sleep in.

There were few secrets in such a tight community, and Catriona knew the takings were down, the acts were getting stale and the troupe was in danger of diminishing further as each week passed and another act left to try their luck elsewhere. It was getting harder to fill even the smallest hall, for people just didn't have the money to spend on entertainment. The Great Depression had a lot to answer for.

The jolt of the wagon brought her back to the present and Catriona glanced over her shoulder hoping for one last glimpse of the magical valley. But it was out of sight, behind the trees and the rocky incline, and she had only the vibrant images in her head to keep the dream alive that she would return one day.

They reached the outskirts of Lightning Ridge the following afternoon and set up camp in a clearing. There was no theatre here, so tomorrow's performance would take place in the open. But they didn't expect to do very well, for they had learned on their travels that the opal miners were a poor lot and feeling the pinch – just like everyone else.

Lightning Ridge was an isolated community of makeshift dwellings made out of canvas, old kerosene cans and anything else that was found lying around the place. There were mules and horses and a strange collection of carts surrounding each deep pit. Mullocky heaps littered the ground, and the air was sharp with the sound of rusting wheels and pulleys bringing the dirt and silica up from below ground. This was a world of men, of hope and shattered dreams – a world of suspicious glances and sullen faces that watched as the troupe settled beneath the trees some distance away from the main mining area.

Catriona helped with the horses before turning her hand to unpacking the costumes and rehearsing the latest song and dance routine Poppy had devised for her. It was a strange place, this Lightning Ridge, she thought as she went through the familiar steps and tried to concentrate. It smelled funny too, but Da had said that was because of the sulphur pools that lay so green and mysterious amongst the ironstone rocks. There were no rivers here, no billabongs or creeks – just scrub and bare rock with tufts of spiny grass clinging to life amongst the cracks and fissures. Yet, looking beyond Poppy out over the valley, Catriona could see miles of empty grassland, with wildflowers adding a dash of vibrant colour to the soft green of the stands of trees and dark red of the earth.

'Kitty. Keep yer mind on yer feet,' said Poppy crossly. 'That's the third time you've done the wrong step.'

Catriona was sick of practising. She knew the steps and would perform them properly when it came to the show. For now she wanted to be free – to run along the ridges and explore the sulphur pools. She folded her arms and pouted. 'I'm fed up,' she said.

Poppy hooked her hair behind her ears. The abundant shock of peroxide blonde had been recently cropped into a fashionable bob which had been permed into corrugated ridges, the fringe flopping into the blue eyes. 'Don't expect it'll matter much, anyways,' she sighed. 'This place ain't exactly the Windmill.'

Catriona loved hearing about the London theatres and knew how easy it was to get Poppy sidetracked. 'Did you ever dance there?' she asked, giving up all pretence of rehearsing. She perched on a nearby rock and grimaced at the leathery taste as she drank from the water-bag.

Poppy grinned and mopped the sweat from her face. 'Of course,' she replied as she perched next to Catriona and took a swig from the bag. 'But only once. The manager found out I'd lied about me age.' Her grin was wide. 'I was a big girl even then, if you know what I mean.' She cupped her generous bosom in her hands and gave it a jiggle. 'But someone sneaked to the manager that I was only fifteen and 'e sent me packing.' She pulled a face. 'They 'ad rules, you see, and I was supposed to be at school, not prancing about in me knickers in front of a load of men.'

19

Catriona's eyes widened. 'In your knickers?' she breathed. 'You mean you had no clothes on?'

Poppy tipped her head back and laughed. 'That's right, me duck. Bare as a baby's bum – well, the top-half anyways. There were only a few feathers and spangles between me and pneumonia. You'd never believe 'ow cold those dressing-rooms were, and the draught on stage was something awful – fair whistled up yer ...' She seemed to realise how young her audience was and fell silent. 'They was good days,' she murmured finally.

Catriona tried to imagine Poppy in feathers and knickers, prancing up and down a big stage. She bit her lip, holding back on the giggle that was threatening – for surely this was just one of her tall stories? 'You don't regret coming out here, though, do you, Poppy?'

'I'm thirty-two years old, luv, 'course I've got some regrets, and this bloody place is just too big and empty for a girl to handle.' She looked around her before gazing back at Catriona and sighing. 'Reckon it'll soon be time for me to go back to the cities, luv. Getting a bit old for all this.' She waved a slender arm which seemed to encompass their isolated surroundings. 'I ain't never goin' to set the world alight. And if I don't watch it, I'll be too old to get a man and have babies.'

Catriona felt a lump rise in her throat. Poppy had been a part of her life – had helped her come into the world and become her closest friend. She was like another mother as well as her best friend, and the thought of her leaving was unbearable. 'You're not really leaving, are you, Poppy?' Her voice was plaintive, echoing her emotions.

The blue eyes were distant as they gazed out over the miles of empty land. 'We all got to make difficult decisions, luv, and I ain't never gunna find my Prince Charmin' out 'ere.' Then Poppy put her arm around Catriona and gave her a cuddle. 'No worries, darling,' she said, her Cockney accent still as strong as ever after her years in Australia. 'I ain't gunna leave without warning you first.'

Catriona nestled in the warm embrace. Poppy was so dear, and she couldn't imagine life without her. 'I don't want you to go,' she mumbled. 'I won't let you.'

Poppy held her away and looked deeply into her eyes. 'I need something more than this, Kitty,' she said softly. 'I want an 'ome, a man and babies.' She gave a harsh cough of laughter. 'And I ain't gunna get one traipsing about the back of beyond in a flaming wagon.'

Catriona shivered. Poppy sounded as if she really meant to leave. 'But where will you go? What will you do without us?'

Poppy stood and ran her hands down the thin cotton dress that barely covered her knees. 'I'll manage,' she said with a sigh. 'I've been managing since I was your age – so there's no need to worry about me.' She held out her hand and drew Catriona to her feet. 'Time to rehearse once more before your da gets back and tears us both off a strip for wasting time. Come on.'

Catriona saw a new purpose in the way Poppy walked. A new determination in her manner as they went through the routine, and as the day progressed, she began to see that Poppy had to be allowed to choose how she lived her life. She was being selfish in wanting her to stay, she realised. Yet it was hard to think of her somewhere else – hard to come to terms with the fact her family was rapidly being depleted.

Declan returned from the miners' camp where he'd been handing out the fliers. He was accompanied by a stranger. A tall, fair-haired man in a top hat, carrying a silver-topped cane, the stranger had a pleasant smile on his handsome face as he was introduced to the gathered troupe.

'This is Francis Kane,' Declan explained. 'He's going to show us where to collect fresh water.'

'Good afternoon, fellow travellers.' He swept off his hat with a flourish before turning to Velda. 'Francis Albert Kane at your service, dear lady.' The stranger bowed low over her hand and kissed the air above her fingers.

'Kane's an actor,' explained Declan to the bemused gathering.

'Alas, dear boy, I've been caught by the fever of the opals in these less than salubrious surroundings and my career has faltered.' He settled the fine top hat once more on his fair head. 'How I yearn to tread the boards again.'

'If you don't mind hard work, simple food and very little pay, you're welcome to join us,' offered Declan.

'Dear boy.' Kane stood with his hands clasped over his heart long enough to ensure he held centre stage in the circle of players. 'It would be an honour.'

Catriona watched him. Not only were his ways flowery and

21

over-enthusiastic, he spoke in an accent she'd never heard before. It was as if he was trying to talk with his mouth full of plums.

Poppy must have read her thoughts, for she leaned towards her and hissed behind her hand. 'He's a Pom. And a toff at that, unless I'm mistaken.'

'He's funny,' giggled Catriona.

Poppy looked towards the newcomer, her expression thoughtful. 'There's something ain't right, though. What's a bloke like 'im doin' out 'ere?' She shook her head. 'Reckon 'e needs watching – and that's a fact.'

Catriona shrugged. Poppy was always suspicious of new people joining the troupe, and she liked the way this man was making everyone laugh. 'If Da likes him, then that's good enough for me,' she said.

Poppy shrugged. 'He might sound like an actor, but there ain't no one I know dresses like that – especially out 'ere.'

Catriona grimaced. She was bored with this conversation. 'It's up to Da. I'm going for a walk,' she muttered. 'Catch you later.'

She clambered down the steep incline to the valley floor and began to hunt for berries in the tangled bushes that grew beneath the slender trees. She watched in delight as the brightly coloured birds squabbled and swooped and jostled for purchase on the overhanging branches. They reminded her of Poppy and the chorus girls who shared a wagon, for they wore brightly coloured plumage even when off the stage, and never stopped chattering and complaining.

She carried the berries back to camp and helped to finish preparing the last of the vegetables before tipping them into the large pot of goat stew that was simmering over the camp-fire. Along with the damper bread and potatoes baking in the ashes, they would eat well tonight. This area abounded with feral goats, and the song-and-dance man had caught three. The other two had been skinned and salted and were now hanging in the back of his wagon.

Da was still off somewhere with Mr Kane, and Mam was settling down to do some mending while the light was still good. The horses had been hobbled and were cropping at the poor grass under the wilting stands of trees. The camp was strangely quiet, with most of the occupants preparing for their performance the following day. Even Poppy and the girls were busy sorting their costumes, their voices muted for once as an air of hopelessness hung over then all.

Catriona was an only child, brought up among adults who treated her as they treated one another – yet she rarely felt the need for other children's companionship. She was a quick learner, an avid reader and day-dreamer. Poppy was her closest friend, even though she was the same age as her mother, and she'd learned a lot about life from her during their long, whispered conversations in the back of the wagon. Some of it surprising, some of it rather shocking, but always related in such a humorous way Catriona could only laugh and suppose it was all tall tales. Yet she enjoyed her own company best and seeing everyone else occupied, she decided to fetch a blanket and her book and slip away again and find a sheltered, private hollow where she could read in peace.

Leaving the camp, she found a quiet spot beneath a spreading tree that was out of sight of everyone. Stripping down to her knickers, she kicked off her shoes and socks and lay on the blanket and watched the dappled shadows drift over her naked chest and stomach. A breath of air sifted into the hiding place, making it wonderfully cool after the heat of the long day, and she stretched and yawned with pleasure. Now she knew how cats felt when they were contented.

Her imagination grew. If this had been water, she would be a mermaid, with a long silvery tail which she'd use to carry her to the dark green, cool depths of the ocean. She'd never seen an ocean, except in story books, but Da had told her what it was like and she could imagine how it must be.

Sensing she was no longer alone she was startled from her day-dreams.

The silhouette of a man stood close to her on the bank, the sun at his back, masking his features. It was an unfamiliar silhouette and it made her shiver.

Catriona instinctively sat up and curled her arms around her knees. 'Who are you?' she demanded as she squinted into the sun. 'And what are doing here?'

'The name's Francis Albert Kane.' His words rolled from one to another in the rich, rounded tones she'd heard back in the camp. 'Actor and raconteur of the English stage at your service, *mademoiselle.*' He bowed from the waist, his top hat flourished in the same expansive gesture he'd used before.

Despite his friendly demeanour, she felt uneasy. The years of dressing and undressing in front of the others had erased any shyness, but lately she'd become aware of changes within her body – and her nakedness in front of this stranger made her blush. 'Turn your back while I get dressed,' she ordered.

He picked up the cotton dress and handed it to her before he turned away and regarded the view. 'Haste thee nymph, and bring with thee jest and youthful jollity.'

Catriona regarded his back as she quickly pulled the dress over her head. He was tall like her father and, she guessed, of a similar age. But, apart from the obvious need to quote poetry at any opportunity, and the theatrical way he had of talking, there the likeness ended. She went to stand beside him and looked up into his face. He was fair and blue-eyed, with a neat moustache and goatee beard, and as Catriona studied him, she realised his suit looked new and his shoes were polished. Poppy was right. It was strange attire for an opal miner, even if he was a resting actor.

He returned her scrutiny, his expression masking his thoughts from her. 'Adieu, kind friend, adieu. I can no longer stay with you. I'll hang my harp on a weeping willow tree, and may the world go well with thee.'

She watched him walk away, his shoulders square, his back straight, the walking stick swinging from an elegant hand that had seen little hard labour. He was an enigma – an intriguing one – but it wouldn't be wise to trust him, for there was indeed something about Francis Albert Kane that didn't add up.

Everything was ready for tomorrow's performance and the camp had settled down to sleep. The wagon was long and fairly narrow, with a bed that pulled down each night taking up most of the width at the front. Catriona slept at the far end on a mattress surrounded by costume baskets and boxes. Beneath the wagon was a deep recess where the props and cooking utensils were stored, and above them, suspended from the wooden roof in muslin bags were the wigs and masks, too precious to pack away.

Velda snuggled up to Declan, it was cold at night out here in the high ironstone ridges, and she was grateful for his warmth beneath the blankets. Yet, as tired as she was, she couldn't sleep. Her mind was churning with worry over their future, and even the arrival of such an august personality as Kane hadn't brought hope. There was a two-pronged attack on their way of life. Not only was the Depression slowly killing them – draining them of energy and enthusiasm – the moving pictures had arrived, offering images of comedy and drama that were impossible to mirror on stage. It seemed that no one wanted to visit the Music Hall anymore.

She lay there in the darkness, her head cushioned by Declan's arm, his fingers gently caressing her shoulder. There had been endless discussions as to what to do for the best, but it seemed there was only one answer. To give up the travelling life. To try and find work in the city theatres – even if it meant going into Vaudeville. She shuddered. No self-respecting artiste would stoop so low, and she'd rather sweep the streets than get into the company of common strippers and off-colour comedians.

As always, Declan seemed to sense her thoughts. 'We'll find a way,' he whispered. 'Perhaps Mr Kane's arrival will be the start of better things.'

Mindful of Catriona sleeping at the other end of the wagon, she kept her voice to a murmur. 'Mr Kane's certainly very entertaining,' she agreed. 'It's been a long time since we've laughed so much.'

He must have heard the doubt in her voice, for he pulled her to him and kissed her forehead. 'He's a born raconteur. I don't know why he ever left the stage.'

Velda shifted in his embrace and pulled the blanket up to her chin. She could see the panoply of stars through the chink in the heavy curtains at the end of the wagon and hear the wind in the trees. 'What's his story?' she asked when she'd settled again.

Declan chuckled. 'They all have one, don't they?'

He was silent for a moment and Velda wondered what he was thinking. A lot of the men and women who had travelled with them over the past eleven years had done so because they were escaping something – or someone. It was a fact that a lot of the players had secrets and it was accepted and not questioned, as long as they proved their worth and didn't bring disgrace to the company. But Kane was different, and Velda was finding it hard to place him.

'We had a long talk when we went to fetch the water from the sheep station. He's from England, of course, with an accent like that he couldn't be from anywhere else.' Velda heard the smile in his voice. 'He came out here several years ago with a touring company and when he was offered a place with a Sydney theatrical company, he stayed. He's worked in all the best theatres, lucky beggar.'

25

Velda shifted in his arms and looked at him. 'Then why is he in Lightning Ridge?'

Declan shrugged. 'It's like he said. He got the mining bug and decided to try his luck. By all accounts he did well in the goldfields, and thought he'd come here and see if his luck held.'

'So why does he want to join us?' Velda persisted. 'If he's got money why doesn't he go back to the city?'

'I didn't ask him. You know the rules, Velda. A man is entitled to privacy – we never pry.'

Velda was far from satisfied. 'Poppy doesn't trust him,' she muttered. 'And neither do I. He's not one of us.'

Declan shifted on to his elbow and looked down at her. 'He's an actor – and even has the theatre programmes to prove it. But the best thing about him is that he has money in the bank and will not be asking for wages all the time he is with us.'

Velda stared at him. 'And you don't think that's just a little too convenient?'

Declan rested back on the pillows and pulled the blanket up to his ears as he turned on to his side. 'It suits our purpose for the moment,' he mumbled into the kapok. 'You shouldn't be so suspicious, Velda. The man has a right to lead his life in any way he wishes, it's not for us to question his motives.'

Velda was far from satisfied, but she had to bow to Declan's decision. Perhaps Kane would indeed prove a blessing – but her instincts told her otherwise.

The show was scheduled to begin at eleven o'clock in the morning. The stage was a square of flattened earth, the audience would sit on blankets in a semi-circle before it. Sheets of tarpaulin and old velvet curtains hung from surrounding trees to give the impression of wings. Declan's pulpit looked shabby in the bright sunlight as it stood to one side, and the old piano which was standing in the back of a wagon was out of tune, but the depleted cast, despite their gloomy mood, were dressed and made up, ready to perform.

The time ticked away and Catriona watched her father check his pocket-watch a dozen times before the first of their audience trickled in. They were a strange sight, these men who lived on The Ridge. Thin to the point of emaciation, their ragged clothes bore the dirt and sweat of their work in the deep opal mines that pitted the ironstone Ridge. Their hair was long and unkempt, their beards

26

straggling down to their chests looking for all the world as if they'd never seen sight of soap and water. They came in ones and twos, their eyes downcast and suspicious as they paid their pennies and took their places.

'Bloody hell,' muttered Poppy. 'I seen more life in a bloody corpse.'

'Then, my dear, we must liven them up.' Kane smiled and twirled his walking stick. 'I've already done my part by selling them the last of my beer, so come on girls, show them what you can do.' He looked across at Declan who nodded to the pianist.

At the first note the three girls ruffled their skirts and with wild whoops they danced on to the stage and began their routine of high kicks and twirls.

Catriona glanced at the miners. The sight of the girls had indeed dragged them from their stupor, and one or two of them were clapping in time and grinning. Kane's supply of beer had already been snapped up, and this was adding to their enthusiasm. As long as things didn't get out of hand, she thought. She'd seen what happened when the audience was drunk before, and didn't want to witness it again. Things had turned nasty and fighting had broken out, and Da had had to wade in and rescue some of the girls.

When the girls finished dancing Declan introduced Max and his little dog. There were jeers of derision and calls for the girls to return. Max left the stage halfway through his act and left the jugglers and acrobats to take his place. But the audience would not be appeased. The drink was beginning to take its hold, and they didn't want to watch the song and dance man, neither did they want to listen to Velda and her voice was drowned by whistles and shouts and ribald comments.

She came off stage and took Catriona's hand. 'You won't be going on stage today,' she said urgently. 'It might turn nasty. When your da's finished his recitation, he's putting the girls on again. We're to load up and be ready to leave the minute they're finished.'

Catriona helped her mother pack up the wagon and draw Jupiter back between the traces. Velda hid the meagre takings in a tin and bundled it in between the folds of the costumes she'd already packed, then she climbed up on the buckboard and took the reins. 'Get inside,' she ordered. 'And don't come out until I say so.'

Catriona sat in the back of the wagon and peeked through the

27

curtains. The girls were back on stage, but apart from Kane and Da, the other players had quietly packed up and returned to their wagons. Da's pulpit was being hefted onto the back of a wagon, the two men struggling with the weight, sweating from the heat and exertion as the girls drew out their performance to play for time. Dust was kicked up by their feet as they swung round, their skirts lifting enough to give the watching miners a glimpse of shapely thigh and well-turned calf. Whistles and cheers encouraged them on and on, and Poppy darted anxious glances across at Declan, waiting for the signal to leave the stage and run.

Declan looked around him and saw all was ready. With a nod to Kane, the two men strode forward onto the earthen stage. This was the cue the girls had been waiting for and they swiftly left for the wagons. Declan tried to restore order as the mood turned ugly and the miners got to their feet, cursing and shouting that they'd been cheated out of their money.

Catriona watched, her pulse racing, her mouth dry as the men formed an angry phalanx around her father and Kane. Then Kane raised a hand and the glitter of silver sparkled in the air. As one the men began to scrabble in the dirt, fighting and jostling to retrieve the coins.

Unseen and unheeded, the two men made their escape. Kane to his fine chestnut gelding, Declan to the safety of the buckboard. 'Go,' he shouted above the noise. 'Go before they realise what we've done.'

Catriona was thrown to the floor of the wagon as Velda slapped the reins across Jupiter's broad back and the big horse broke into a gallop. The costume basket scratched her arm and she felt the bruising thud of something hard hit her leg, but the thrill of it all, mixed with the fear they might be caught meant she felt little pain. And yet, as the hectic flight eventually slowed to a more leisurely and sedate plod along the Outback track, she realised her way of life was indeed coming to an end. It was no longer a case of if it would happen, but how soon.

Chapter Three

There was a sense of defeat hanging over them as the two wagons rolled along the wide dirt road which ran through the tiny settlement of Goondiwindi and disappeared beyond the horizon. Goondiwindi was an Aboriginal name – it meant the resting place of the birds – yet Catriona wondered if the troupe would ever find a resting place where they were welcome. With the advent of talking pictures, and the lure of the bright lights of the cities, the troupe had dwindled further during the months following the disaster of Lightning Ridge. They could no longer compete with the marvel of the flickering screen that brought a whole new, exciting world to the Outback people and the audiences numbered so few it was hardly worth the effort to unpack and rehearse.

Catriona sat between her parents and tried hard to lift her spirits by finding something hopeful in the random collection of ramshackle buildings that made up Goondiwindi. The Victorian Customs House looked fine enough, but its appearance was incongruous against the dusty shacks which passed for shops and feed-stores. A wooden church stood in a weed-strewn yard, its timbers weathered, the windows boarded up. The only sign of life seemed to come from the hotel where, by the sound of breaking glass and much shouting, there was a fight in progress.

She heard her father sigh as he brought the horse to a standstill. 'It'll be right, Da,' she said with forced cheerfulness – the deep-seated hope that she was to be proved right making her voice unsteady. 'If there's a hotel, then at least we've got a chance of an audience.'

Declan Summers' eyes were dark with worry, his brow creased in a frown as he watched the brawl spill through the hotel doors

29

and out into the street. He steadied Jupiter as he shied from the violent scuffle, and coaxed him across the street to the water trough and out of harm's way. 'There's nothing here for us,' he said almost to himself. 'Look at the posters. The moving pictures are due to arrive tomorrow. They won't want to be spending their money on us.'

'That's defeatist talk, and I won't be having it,' retorted Velda. 'We need the money to get to the coast, so we have to persuade them we're worth a few pennies.' She climbed down from the wagon, brushed the dust from her dress and tucked a few stray wisps of hair back into the knot at her nape. 'Are you coming with me, Declan, or do you propose to sit up there all day?'

Declan's smile was wan, but he seemed to gather strength from her unusual burst of determination and his shoulders weren't quite as slumped as he joined his wife in the dusty street. 'Would it not be better to let them finish fighting first?' he enquired as he collected his top hat and dusted it down with scant enthusiasm.

'Not at all,' she said firmly. 'What they need is a wake-up call. Don't you agree, Mr Kane?' She looked up at the Englishman who was still astride his dusty horse, silently pleading with him to take charge.

'Indeed, Mrs Summers,' he replied, his eyes squinted against the sun as he watched the half-dozen men wrestling and throwing punches. He turned in the saddle after a swift glance at Declan. 'Poppy. Break out the drum and anything else you can get a tune out of. It's time to let this godforsaken place know we've arrived.'

Poppy grimaced. 'Righto,' she replied. 'But I ain't getting down off this wagon until the dust settles.'

Kane handed out the penny whistles and the tambourines and propped the big bass drum on the buckdboard in front of Catriona. 'Let's see how hard you can hit that,' he encouraged with a smile.

Catriona grinned as she beat the drum enthusiastically. She'd learned to like Mr Kane during the past six months. He made her laugh, and his stories were so enthralling she would sit for hours listening to him, forgetting the time and the work to be done. Mam and Da seemed to like him too, and as they relied on him even more now the troupe was so depleted, she had pushed aside her doubts and Poppy's obvious dislike of the man, and decided to make up her own mind about him.

At the sound of the ragged music, the fighting came to a

30

confused halt. The hotel doors were flung open and bleary eyes rounded in astonishment at the sight and sound of the remnants of Summers' Music Hall.

Catriona watched as Kane shook the tambourine and made his horse prance in circles among the bewildered men who only a moment before had been beating seven bells out of each other, and who now scurried away from the flashing hoofs. She grinned as she continued beating the drum, for Poppy had decided to join in the fun and was now doing the can-can, skirts lifted high, long legs and jewelled headdress flashing in the sun. It never ceased to amaze Catriona at the speed with which Poppy could slip into costume, for only minutes before she'd been wearing a cotton dress and sensible shoes.

Max carried the ageing Patch as Kane led the way, coaxing his horse up the wooden steps and through the hotel door, stooping to avoid the overhead beam. Catriona jumped down from the wagon and steadied the old man as he shuffled after Kane. Max was well past retirement age, and so was Patch, but Catriona knew she and the others were his only family and none of them had had the heart to leave him to the mercies of any of the old folks' homes they'd passed during their travels. The women stayed outside the hotel bar – it was an unwritten law that no female should enter the hallowed grounds of such a male-orientated den of iniquity – but they stood in the doorway, their worries for the future momentarily forgotten as they watched the fun.

Kane brought his horse to a standstill at the bar. 'For the price of a glass of beer, we bring you entertainment,' he said into the stunned silence. 'For these few coppers we will bring you the delights of Paris and the Moulin Rouge,' he swept his arm out to indicate Poppy who was standing in the doorway and ruffling her skirts. 'The delights of The Bard.' Declan bowed. 'And the Song-bird of the South, Velda Summers.' Velda dipped a curtsy, her cheeks reddening beneath the impudent stares of the men in the bar.

The silence was profound, the tableau before Catriona frozen in this one moment of time which would decide their fate. Kane's horse shifted and snorted and lifted its tail as it deposited a pile of steaming dung on the dusty floor.

The collective trance was broken as the circle of men stepped back. 'You'll clean up that flamin' mess, mate, and clear off out

31

of it,' shouted the red-faced barman. 'Bringin' flamin' horses in 'ere. Whatever next?'

Poppy pushed through the door and, disregarding the horrified glares, flounced up to the bar. 'That's lucky mate,' she said, chucking the barman under the chin. 'In fact, this is your lucky day all round. Now, 'ow's about giving us a chance to entertain you?' She turned and flashed a grin at the astonished audience. 'Looks like you could do with something to cheer you all up, and it won't cost more than a few pennies.'

'Flamin' gypsies,' muttered the barman. 'Worse than flamin' Abos.' He folded his arms over his chest. 'I ain't having no painted tarts prancing about in my hotel. Clean that up and get out, before I set me dogs on the lot of yer.'

'I ain't no tart,' shouted Poppy. 'I'm a theatrical.'

The barman leaned over the bar, his fat red face close to Poppy's. 'Whatever you choose to call yerself, it still comes down to the same thing. If it's whoring you're after, then we can come to some arrangement – otherwise you can clear off with the others.'

Catriona saw the spirit go out of Poppy, and it was in that moment she realised they had reached rock-bottom. For Poppy could always find something to smile about, could always dredge up the energy to give an argument or wheedle her way in or out of things. This time she was struck dumb, and Catriona could see the tears glisten on her rouged cheeks as she turned and fled.

The noise had brought the rest of the townspeople onto the wooden boardwalk. Their muttering grew like the hum of a swarm of angry bees as they watched the travellers clean up. Catriona was shielded closely by her parents, but she knew she would never forget the suspicion in the townspeople's eyes, or the censorship in their expressions as they silently parted to allow the troupe to leave the hotel. She could feel their animosity like a knife in her back as she climbed onto the wagon, and for the first time in her life she felt fear.

The first clod of dirt hit the side of the wagon. It was followed by many more as the muttering turned to shouts of derision and the local dogs snapped and growled at the horses' heels.

Declan's face was grim as he slapped the reins and they trundled out of town, and Velda was silent as she hugged Catriona to her side. Kane no longer laughed and joked as he rode alongside, and

Poppy sat next to the trembling Max in the other wagon, her face ashen, all spirit dowsed by the harsh reality of what they had become.

It was a sad little troupe that finally set up camp two hours later. In desultory silence they sat around the fire and ate the last of the damper bread and golden syrup which they washed down with billy tea. Catriona looked at the faces, each of them closed to her, their thoughts and emotions shut away.

Max was staring into the flames, his gaze bleak as he held the grey-muzzled terrier in his trembling arms. Patch licked the old man's face, but his gesture was not acknowledged, his sympathy lost in the mire of the old man's sense of hopelessness. Poppy's make-up was streaked with her tears, her shoulders hunched beneath the heavy woollen shawl as she clasped her knees and rocked back and forth. The gaudy dress glittered coldly in the light of the flames, the feathered head-dress drooping sadly over her eyes. This was a defeated Poppy – a Poppy who couldn't even dredge up the energy to wash her face or change into something more comfortable.

Kane smoked a cheroot, the firelight glinting on the ruby ring he wore on his little finger, his eyes narrowed in contemplation as he stared into the darkness. Catriona wondered what he was thinking, for although she had come to like him, Kane was still a puzzle. He had been with them for months, and although he'd told them many a tale, he'd never revealed any clear details of his life before he'd joined the troupe – had never explained why he'd chosen to live like this when he could have afforded better.

As Catriona watched him, she experienced a pang of fright. Kane might have been tight-lipped and secretive about his past, but he was never mean, and his money had seen them out of many a crisis. What if he decided to leave them? What would they do then? Catriona bit her lip, knowing she had to encourage him to stay. But how? She looked at her parents, hoping for inspiration.

Velda and Declan sat on a fallen branch, their hands entwined, their shoulders resting against each other, and Catriona felt a strange and unwelcome sense of isolation wash over her. For their very togetherness was exclusive. It was as if they no longer needed her – or even noticed she was there. She shivered as she looked out at the great darkness beyond the camp-fire. She had never feared the darkness before, but tonight was different. Things had

33

changed, and she knew without a doubt that life, as she had known it, would never be the same again. For the heart had gone out of the troupe – the very essence of who they were had been obliterated in the shame of what had happened in Goondiwindi.

There was a reluctance to leave the warm glow of the camp-fire – it was as if it offered the only comfort on such a bleak night. Catriona finally went to check on the horses, patting both of them, resting her cheek on the warm, dusty coats as they cropped at the grass. They would move on tomorrow, and the next day as well as the day after – a seemingly never-ending journey to nowhere. Catriona sighed as she turned away and headed for the wagon. Bit by bit her life was falling apart, but as long as she had Mam and Da, surely they would survive?

Yet, despite the disasters that had beset them, hope still flickered. Toowoomba lay on the edge of the Great Dividing Range. According to Declan, the town was the gateway to the fertile Darling Downs, and still an important staging-point for the cattle drovers who came from the great grazing lands to the west. They had high hopes of earning some money in Toowoomba, for it was a large town, with gracious buildings, several churches and a railway station.

'There's no point in putting on a parade,' said Declan, as he stood, hands deep in his pockets next to the wagon. 'There are so few of us now, we'd just look ridiculous.'

Catriona and Poppy still had nightmares about Goondiwindi, and they both shuddered.

Kane, as usual, came up with a solution. 'I have been to the Post Office and picked up my money,' he said cheerfully. 'And have taken the liberty of hiring a small hall for tonight. If we quickly draw some fliers, we can hand them out. There are sure to be some takers in a well-set-up place like this.'

Velda looked up at Kane, her eyes bright with unshed tears. 'What would we do without you, Mr Kane?' she said, her voice husky. 'You're so generous. So kind.'

Kane put his arms around Catriona and her mother and hugged them close. 'I am only doing what I can to help, dear lady,' he said. He smiled down at Catriona. 'We can't let this young, sweet little thing go to bed hungry, now can we?'

Poppy snorted and Catriona blushed. She'd never been called a 'young, sweet thing' before and didn't quite know how to take

Kane's rather flowery compliments in the glare of Poppy's scorn.

Declan got down from the wagon, his eyes dark with pain. 'It should be me seeing to my family's welfare,' he growled. 'But I thank you, Kane.' Declan shook the Englishman's hand, his shoulders stiff with pride.

Catriona eased from Kane's embrace and watched the three adults. She was aware of the strong, underlying emotions that laced through the conversation – yet couldn't identify them fully, for there were things peculiar to adults that she was too young to understand. She knew only that her father hated taking what he termed as charity from Kane, and he would have refused it if only he'd been able to afford to do so. His pride was broken.

Her mam was simply grateful, relieved that the next few hours could be survived, and that there was someone strong to make all the decisions – for Velda, despite her determination to remain cheerful in the face of disaster, was a woman who found life much easier when she didn't have to think for herself. She had always leaned on Declan for advice and support – now she had turned to Kane who appeared the stronger of the two men.

They slowly made their way through town, marvelling at the trucks and cars that lined the streets and sent great clouds of dust into the sky from beneath their wheels. Toowoomba was certainly a town of riches, and even the people wore smart clothes as they walked along the boardwalks and did their shopping.

Velda sighed with longing over the hats and gloves and shoes, so smart, so very up to date – so out of her reach. Catriona wished she could have gone into a shop and bought her mam a lovely hat, but with only a few pennies in the tin, the wish could not be fulfilled.

The hall was a long, narrow wooden building which was in a sad state of repair and obviously neglected in favour of the new hall in the centre of town. Situated next to the station, it was veiled in the soot that came from the steam-engines. The paint had peeled, the stage curtains were rotting from age and mildew, and the single, filthy window was glued fast with water-swollen timbers that were covered in black mould. There was a raised platform at one end of the hall, and a stack of aged chairs piled up to one side. The floor hadn't been swept in months and there was evidence of nesting rodents in the corners and on the overhead rafters.

Yet there were surprises. The electricity worked, so they had lights and a ceiling fan. There was a lavatory out the back that was eventually coaxed into flushing, and a tap with cold running water to wash in.

Declan and Kane went into town to hand out the hastily drawn fliers. The women found brooms and mops and old rags and set to work. Their cotton dresses were soon soaked in sweat, the white collars grubby from the dust and accumulated filth of years of neglect. Hands were reddened and knees became ingrained with dirt as they scrubbed the floor. Hair tumbled from pins and stuck to their sweating faces as they wrestled to bring down the heavy velvet curtains so they could be shaken free of their dust and re-hung. And all the while Max and his little dog sat in a corner and dreamed away the afternoon.

Catriona kept glancing across at him. She was worried, for Max didn't seem to understand where he was, and when she'd gone across to him earlier and asked him if he wanted a cuppa, he'd looked at her as if she was a stranger. He sat there in a strange sort of trance, humming to himself and Patch, and then every so often he would look up and smile and ask if it was time for tea.

'Poor old bugger's losing his mind,' whispered Poppy as they finally stacked away the cleaning things and headed for the tap. 'He ain't been right since Goondiwindi.'

Catriona and Velda looked back into the hall. 'He's just old,' said Velda.

Poppy finished soaping her hair and shoved her head under the flow of water. She emerged with face and hair streaming. 'I'm with him all day,' she replied as rubbed the towel over her head. 'He's forgotten who I am, you know. Keeps asking me my name, and whether tea's ready yet and has 'e 'ad 'is breakfast.' She dried her face and handed over the shared towel. 'It ain't fair to keep 'im travelling no more,' she muttered.

'There's nowhere else for him to go,' said Velda with a frown of worry as she took her turn at the tap. 'The homes won't take him all the while he's got Patch, and they've been together so long it would be an awful thing to separate them.'

The three of them finished their ablutions in silence. With all their worries and concerns, Max's rapid deterioration was the hardest to come to terms with.

The show had been different to any other. Instead of performing

36

separately, Catriona's parents had formed a duo and sung in harmony. Poppy had gone down into the audience to flirt light-heartedly with the male patrons as she sang some of the naughty songs she'd learned so long ago in London. Kane's monologue had been greeted with laughter and applause, his slightly off-colour jokes taken with good heart. Even Max had stirred from his dream-like state, and with his baggy suit and squashed hat, had led the ruffed Patch through his weary paces. It had been a bravura perfor-mance, and they had watched with tears in their eyes as the old man and his dog shuffled through the act and received polite, but sympathetic applause.

Catriona's nerves had kicked in – this would be the first time on stage alone. The pink taffeta dress was too tight, too short and too childish, but it was all she had to wear. Yet, once the gramophone had been wound up and the music began, the nerves took flight and she forgot the discomfort of the dress and lost herself in the aria. She came off stage, flushed and elated, for she knew she'd done well tonight. The audience had enjoyed her singing, and had even called for more. The show had been a success, giving her hope for their future, so what did it matter if the puffed sleeves of her dress bit into her arm, or the skirt barely skimmed her knees – she had performed her first solo – she finally felt like a star.

The hall slowly emptied and the money was counted. There was enough to see them on the next leg of their journey north-east. They changed into their everyday clothes and went to the nearest hotel where they treated themselves to a feast of meat and potatoes and fresh vegetables all served up in a thick, rich gravy. For pudding there had been tinned fruit and lashings of creamy yellow custard.

Even Max enjoyed his meal, hiding the terrier beneath the folds of his voluminous coat and surreptitiously feeding him scraps when the hotelier's wife wasn't looking. Sated and content, the troupe slowly made their way back to the paddock behind the hall where they had left the horses and two wagons.

'You're very quiet, Poppy,' said Catriona as they strolled arm in arm down the moonlit dirt track. 'I'd have thought you'd have been pleased about the way the show went tonight.'

Poppy pulled her cardigan across her chest and shivered. It was cold in the Outback at night, and her clothes were thin and worn. 'I ain't got no enthusiasm for it any more,' she said quietly. 'Not after Goondiwindi.'

'It'll all come right, you'll see,' said Catriona. 'Goondiwindi was just a bad town. A couple more nights like tonight and you'll soon be your old self.'

'Nah.' Poppy came to a standstill as the others caught up with them. 'I've 'ad it, luv. I ain't ever goin' to be anything else but a third-rate chorus girl, and I'm gettin' too old to be prancing about in frilly knickers. It's time I found something else to do.'

'You can't,' breathed Velda. 'What am I to do without you, Poppy? Please.' She stretched out a hand and laid it on Poppy's arm. 'Please reconsider.'

'Poppy don't go,' cried Catriona as she threw her arms around Poppy's waist and clung to her. The tears were hot, the fear of losing her only true friend almost too much to bear. 'It'll get better, you'll see,' she pleaded, the tears running down her face and soaking Poppy's cardigan. 'They loved you tonight. They always love you no matter what.' She pulled away and looked with beseeching eyes into Poppy's face. 'I love you too,' she sobbed. 'Please don't leave me.'

Poppy's voice was rough with emotion as she held Catriona's hands and looked down into her face. 'And I'll always love you, Kitty. But it's time for me to move on. Time for all of us to find something better than this. It's the end, Kitty. We all know that.'

'But where will you go?' asked Velda, the tears evident in her voice. 'What will you do?'

'I'll find work somewhere,' she replied, releasing her hold of Catriona's hands. 'Perhaps in a hotel, or a shop. There's bound to be something in Brisbane, or one of the cities on the coast.'

'But you'll be on your own,' wept Catriona.

'I been on me own before,' she murmured. 'I'll manage.'

'Have I had me dinner yet?' said the frail voice.

As if relieved to be breaking the tension, Poppy linked arms with Max and steered him towards the second wagon. 'Yes,' she said firmly. 'Now it's time for you and Patch to go to sleep.'

'I'm not sleepy,' the old man grumbled. 'And who are you? Why are you talking to me like that?'

'It's me, Poppy,' she explained carefully as she kept him on the move. 'And if you're very good, I'll let you have the last biscuit out of the tin.'

'Oh, God,' breathed Velda. 'I can't bear it. Poor Max. Poor Poppy.'

Catriona watched her friend walk away into the night with the old man shuffling along beside her. 'We're going to lose both of them, aren't we, Mam?' she sobbed.

Velda's arm around her shoulders was little comfort, her words merely enforcing the awful pain that had lodged around her heart. 'Max is old and bewildered,' she explained. 'He'll be better off in a home where he can be looked after properly. Perhaps we can find somewhere that will take Patch as well.'

'And Poppy? What about Poppy?' Catriona persisted.

'Poppy's a grown woman, Kitty. She has to make her own decisions about her future.' Velda turned Catriona to face her, and gently wiped away the tears. 'We all know it's the end, Kitty, despite how well it went tonight. Why prolong the agony by refusing to acknowledge that?'

'She could still come with us until she finds something else to do,' said Catriona stubbornly.

Velda shook her head, her expression sad. 'She's had enough,' she explained softly. 'There's a station here, and a train that will take her to the coast where she's a good chance of finding better paid work. Don't begrudge her that, Kitty. Don't make her feel guilty or ashamed because she has to leave. It doesn't mean she's stopped loving you – doesn't mean she won't miss you just as much as you'll miss her.'

Catriona blinked away the fresh tears. 'But I'll never see her again,' she sniffed.

'Goodbyes are a part of life, my darling,' said her mother with a smile. 'We are all on a journey, and will meet many people on our way. Some we will know for many years, some only fleetingly. We will make friends and enemies as we go through life. But each and every one of those people will touch us – will give us something that, hopefully, will enrich our lives or bring us a deeper understanding of the world we are living in and why we are who we are.'

Catriona thought about that, and although she didn't really understand all her mother was saying, she did feel comforted by it.

Max's querulous voice drifted into the night as Poppy tried to settle him down to sleep, and Catriona huddled beneath the heavy blankets, her thoughts racing. There had to be some way of persuading Poppy to stay – but how? She looked out at the night sky, so clear, so studded with stars the light from them gilded the surrounding paddock and the horses, making them look like a scene from a fantasy tale. If only Poppy would stay until they reached the coast, then they could all find work together and not have to be parted.

'We'll have to sell the other horse and wagon,' murmured Declan to his wife as they lay close together at the other end of the wagon.

Catriona tensed as she listened in to their quiet conversation.

'Kane might prefer to use it instead of that old tent,' replied Velda. 'Besides, there's Max. Where would he sleep? There's no room in here as it is.'

'We need the money, darling,' he murmured. 'Kane and Max will have to share the tent until we can find a suitable place to leave Max.'

'But I thought we had enough to see us through for a while?' Velda's voice was sharp with concern.

'If Poppy is determined to leave, then she must be paid what she's owed. She'll need money for train fare, food, and lodgings. It won't leave us much, and there's no guarantee we'll have another night like tonight.'

'Oh, Declan,' Velda's sigh was a sob of anguish. 'Has it really come to this? Surely Mr Kane will buy the wagon once he realises how broke we are?'

There was a long silence. 'Mr Kane has been generous to a fault over the months he's been with us,' Declan said finally. 'And although I'm grateful to him, we must not rely so heavily on him to bail us out of trouble. I am still head of this family – of this troupe, what's left of it – and I will decide what is to be done.' There was a pause. 'The wagon and horse will have to go, along with any props and costumes we can sell off. We won't be needing them.'

'But what about Catriona?' whispered her mother fiercely. 'She's the voice of an angel, you only had to listen to the applause tonight, and see the audience's faces when she sang to know she's a bright future ahead of her. We can't just give up.'

'Catriona's eleven years old, and still a child,' he replied softly. 'Who knows what will happen to her voice when she reaches puberty? But we can't afford to speculate, to risk surviving on the few pennies we're bringing in. We must sell what we can and move on.'

'Where to?' sobbed Velda. 'What's to become of us?'

'Cairns,' he said firmly. 'Kane has contacts there who might help us to find work. He's already sent a letter to an old friend of his who's got a hotel somewhere up there. We just have to hope he has something for us all.'

Catriona buried her head beneath the blankets, the tears hot as they rolled down her face and soaked the kapok pillow. She loved singing – loved the way her voice soared in harmony with her mother's as they rehearsed – loved the passion of the beautiful arias she'd learned from the scratched records her father had collected and which she played on the wind-up gramophone. Now it seemed that all her dreams were to be shattered.

As the moon waned and the stars slowly lost their brilliance, Catriona struggled to come to terms with what this bleak future might hold.

Dawn came to Toowoomba and Catriona was the first to rise. She clambered down from the wagon, her eyes bleary from lack of sleep, her spirits low despite the beauty of her surroundings. Remnants of mist clung to the tops of the trees and capped the soft undulations of the surrounding hills, and the dew sparkled in the long grass. In the distance she could hear the cackle of a kook-aburra, and this sound would normally have cheered her, but this morning she was too downhearted to even raise a smile. A flock of rosellas and galahs clattered from a nearby tree and rose in a cloud of bright colour into the pale sky with shrieks of alarm as she walked barefooted through the wet grass to where the horses were still dozing.

Kane's flashy gelding snorted and tossed his head when he discovered she hadn't brought him a carrot, but the old shires, Jupiter and Mars, stood placidly in the early morning sunlight as she stroked their sturdy necks and told them her troubles. Both horses had been a part of her life from her earliest memory. She'd learned to ride on their broad backs, had groomed them and fed them and looked after them as special members of her extended family. Now Mars was to be sold. It was all too much to bear, and mindless of the dew soaking the hem of her nightdress and chilling her feet, Catriona buried her face in the long mane and wept bitter tears.

'You'll catch your death,' said the quiet voice behind her.

Catriona whirled around. She'd been so deep in thought she hadn't heard his approach. 'Will you buy Mars and the wagon, Mr

41

Kane?' she said with breathless entreaty. 'We need the money, you see, and I couldn't bear to leave Mars behind, and the wagon will be so much more comfortable than your old tent.' She finally ran out of breath.

Kane's long riding boots swished through the grass as he strode forward and patted the shire's broad nose. 'Regrettably, my dear, I have no need of another horse, and my tent is sufficient.' He sighed. 'It's always sad to say goodbye to old friends, but Mars has earned his rest, don't you think?'

Catriona looked up into the handsome face. Kane's hair glinted gold in the rising sun, his eyes were very blue in his tanned face, and he'd recently trimmed his moustache and goatee. There seemed to be genuine sadness in his expression and she felt another onslaught of tears threatening.

'Don't cry, little one,' he said gently as his fingers traced the tracks of her tears down her cheeks. 'Be glad for Mars that he'll have a fine stable to live in, and lots of grass to eat. And for Poppy too. She's got a great adventure ahead of her – just as we have.'

Catriona sniffed and ducked her chin. She knew he was making sense, but at this very moment she didn't feel like being glad for anyone.

'Come, child. Your feet must be freezing.'

Catriona was about to argue when she was swept up into his arms and held tightly against his chest. She lay in his embrace, too surprised to protest as he looked down at her and smiled. She could feel the rapid beat of his heart against her side, could feel the strength of his arms and the roughness of the tweed jacket against her cheek as he held her close. His breath was shallow, the air of it tainted with tobacco smoke as he dropped a fleeting kiss on her brow. His eyes, she noticed were very blue and seemed to delve right to her very core as he looked down at her. She pushed against his chest, suddenly shy and awkward. 'I can walk,' she said firmly. 'I'm not a baby.'

'Why walk when you can be carried?' asked Kane with a laugh. 'I'll wager Cleopatra never walked anywhere. Don't you like to be treated like a queen?' He didn't wait for a reply, and began to carry her back to the wagons. 'Let's see what we can find for m'lady's breakfast,' he murmured.

It was a solemn affair, for they all knew this was the last meal they would have together. Even Max seemed to have caught the desultory mood and ate his meal in silence before returning to his bed in the second wagon. It was agreed he should be allowed to rest while they said goodbye to Poppy, for he didn't really have much of a grip on reality and there was no point in distressing him further.

The station was a long Victorian edifice with a corrugated-iron roof and wooden lace-work running between the posts of the broad verandah. From the neatly swept platform there was a clear view of the rails which ran far into the distance in both directions. To the east, lay Brisbane and the coast. To the west was channel country, where millions of acres were home to the vast cattle herds of Queensland's Outback. A train was waiting, smoke billowed from the stack and steam hissed between the great iron wheels. Horses were being loaded at the back, and a large consignment of cattle was being coaxed up the ramps of the cattle-trucks. A few passengers stood waiting to board, huddled into little groups on the platform, or standing alone, staring along the rails and the empty miles they would soon cross to their destination.

Catriona sat among the baskets of costumes and watched as her father handed Poppy the ticket and the rest of her wages. Her tears blinded her as she tried to stamp the image of her friend into her mind so she would never forget her. Poppy was dressed in a smart, sprigged cotton dress that had buttons down the front and white collar and arm-cuffs. A thin white belt was around her waist, and she wore a jaunty, homemade hat on her freshly washed hair, gloves on her hands and highly polished, low-heeled shoes with a strap that buttoned across the instep. She had never seen Poppy look so smart – or so different. It was as if by making the decision to leave, Poppy had shed the frills and flounces and become ordinary and colourless – had changed into a stranger – the distance between her past and her future already widening.

Catriona clambered down from the wagon and stood in silent anguish as her friend said goodbye to the others. She blinked away the tears and did her best to look stoic as Poppy enfolded her in a warm embrace.

'Come on, luv,' Poppy coaxed into her hair. 'No tears, there's my girl.'

'I don't want to say goodbye,' sniffed Catriona as she pulled from the embrace and looked into Poppy's eyes.

'Neither do I,' murmured Poppy, her voice unsteady, her blue

43

eyes strangely bright. 'That's why I'm going now before you get me crying too.'

Catriona saw Kane and the others watching, and had a brilliant flash of inspiration. She caught Poppy's arm as she turned away. 'If you married Mr Kane, then you wouldn't have to leave, or find a job, or anything.' She smiled in delight at how clever she was to find such a wonderful last-minute solution. 'You could stay with us and have babies, and I'd help to look after them.' She looked into her friend's face, her delight vanquished by what she saw there.

Poppy didn't seem at all thrilled with the idea – in fact she looked shocked. She glanced across at Kane before turning back to Catriona. 'He ain't my type,' she said firmly. 'And I certainly ain't 'is.' She hesitated as if she wanted to say more, but instead gave Catriona a swift peck on the cheek. 'Nice try, darlin', but I gotta be goin' or I'll miss me train. I've left some of me dresses for you. They're a bit washed-out, but they'll fit you better than your old stuff. Take care of yourself, and one day I just know I'll see your name up in lights.' She blew a final kiss to all of them and hurried through the station door and out of sight.

Catriona knew she was behaving like a baby, but she couldn't help it. She pulled away from her mother's restraining hand and raced across the dirt road, heedless of an approaching truck, to the station. The shadows were deep in the ticket hall, and her hurried footsteps echoed in the silence. The platform was cool in the shade of the sloping roof – and deserted but for the guard who was waving his flag. It was as if Poppy had been swallowed up by the great iron beast that belched smoke and steam.

Catriona ran along the platform, looking into the carriages. She wanted one last chance to say goodbye. One last chance to see her again before she was gone from her life for ever. But it was not to be. With a snort of smoke and a hiss of steam the great wheels began to turn. Jolting and clanking, the carriages rocking, they gathered pace and drew the great iron train into the searing bright-ness. She stood on the deserted platform and watched as it chugged along the silvery rails until the last carriage was a mere speck in the distance. The mournful wail of its hooter echoed across the deserted grasslands – a final, sad farewell to Toowoomba and those it had left behind.

Mars stood patiently beside Jupiter, his great plumed feet spread

44

sturdily in the dirt. He tossed his head in welcome and nuzzled her hair as Catriona leaned her cheek against him and groomed him for the last time. It was to be a day of goodbyes, and Catriona's heart was breaking.

'This is Mr Mallings,' said Velda softly as she put her arm around Catriona. 'He's going to give Mars a good home.'

'Too right, darlin',' said the ruddy-faced stranger as he tipped his hat. He reached out a calloused hand and slapped the shire's strong neck in appreciation. 'He's a fine old horse, so he is, and I've acres of paddock for him to keep down.' He bent from the waist so his face was on a level with Catriona's. 'You'll always be welcome to visit him, should you be passing this way again, and I promise he'll not want for anything.'

Catriona stood aside and watched as Mars plodded away with his new owner. He didn't look back, didn't seem to realise he would never again pull a Music Hall Wagon. She sniffed back the tears and gave a shaky laugh as Jupiter nuzzled her shoulder. It was as if he was commiserating with her, for he too was losing a lifelong friend.

'We'd better get back to camp,' muttered Velda. 'Max shouldn't be left on his own for too long, and there's a travelling salesman coming to look at the other wagon.'

The day progressed, each minute seeming to drag like an hour. The salesman bought the second wagon and Max's few possessions were stowed away in the almost empty storage box beneath the first. The costume baskets were bought by a woman who owned a millinery shop in the main street. She would use them to store the bales of material. The piano had long since given in to termite and worm and had fallen apart months ago, left behind as they'd had moved on. Most of the costumes were already gone, the stock depleted as each member of the troupe left for new horizons, and the few pieces that remained were sold for pennies or burned. The once grand pulpit was riddled with worm, the velvet covering and tassels moth-eaten, mildewed and worthless.

Declan and Kane dug a pit and filled it with all the rubbish. The pulpit from which Declan had performed for so many years was the last addition. It burned merrily, and soon there was nothing left but a pile of smouldering ashes.

Despite her own pain, Catriona realised she wasn't the only one who was suffering. Da's face was haggard and drawn as he stirred

45

the cold ashes with the toe of his boot. Mam bustled back and forth, her face set, her eyes determinedly dry as she kept up a brittle chatter. Yet her anguish could be seen in the trembling of her hands and in the dark shadows that bruised the flesh beneath her eyes. Even Kane's usually cheerful face was sombre as he moved around the remains of the camp and quietly saw to the confused Max.

The five of them left Toowoomba in silence. None of them looked back.

Several days later they camped among the bunya and pine and the extensive rainforests of the Bunya Mountains. It was a good place to rest – a perfect spot to explore and refresh the spirit – for there were orchids in the forest, and swathes of wildflowers to be picked from among the tangled roots and fallen branches of the trees. Rock wallabies and kangaroos grazed in the grassland and a profusion of colourful birds flitted and chattered overhead, their noise bringing life to the dark and mysterious forests.

Catriona and her parents climbed the great craggy hills and gasped in wonder at the magnificent views of the grasslands and the green canopy of the forest below them. Vast waterfalls tumbled down the ancient walls of the mountains and filled swiftly flowing rivers which raced headlong towards the coast. The earth was red and fertile, and in the fields surrounding Kingaroy they could see the flourishing peanut and bean crops that brought wealth to the farming community.

They returned to camp, pleasantly weary from their long hike in the hills, and were met by an obviously agitated Kane. He glanced at Catriona before taking Declan by the arm and leading him out of earshot.

Catriona saw her father blanch, saw his anxious glance over his shoulder and the silent message telegraphed to Mam who was standing beside her. 'What's happening, Mam?' she asked fearfully.

'Stay there,' Velda ordered sharply. 'Make yourself useful by putting the billy on to boil. We could all do with a cup of tea.' She moved swiftly away and joined the two men, then, after a hurried conference, they walked over to the tent that had been set up beneath a towering fern.

Catriona shivered. She knew what had happened. Leaving the billycan by the side of the smouldering fire, she slowly approached the tent.

Velda emerged, her face grey with distress. She looked at Catriona, the rebuke dying on her lips as the first tear slowly ran down her cheek. 'He's gone to sleep, darling,' she said gruffly. 'Max has come to the end of his travelling. He's finally at rest, poor old man.' She covered her face with her hands and wept.

Catriona had never seen death before, and although she was fearful of what she might find, she blinked away her tears and looked through the opening in the canvas. How peaceful he looked, she thought with surprise. It was as if he slept, the lines of care and worry erased in that dreamless, endless sleep from which he would never return.

Her attention was caught by Patch. The little terrier was curled at Max's side, ears drooping, eyes filled with liquid sadness as he looked up at her. She hesitantly stepped into the tent which was lit by the green glow of the surrounding forest, and approached the still figure that was being so closely guarded by his terrier.

Patch growled, his hackles rising, ears pricked. Every fibre of his being was warning Catriona to leave him alone – to stay away and leave his master in peace.

'Come away, darling,' muttered Velda. 'This is no place for you.'

'But we can't leave Patch here,' she protested.

'He'll come out when he's hungry,' muttered Velda. She led Catriona outside and dropped the canvas flap over the opening. 'I want you to make the tea while I prepare Max. Your father has gone into Kingaroy to find a priest, and I need you to do as I say.'

Catriona wanted to ask what 'preparing Max' entailed, but the look on her mother's face was enough to silence her. The tears were blinding as she went in search of more dry wood for the camp-fire, and once she had coaxed the flames into a blaze, she perched on a fallen log and stared sadly into them.

Kane finally managed to grab hold of Patch's scruff and haul him out of the tent. He found a length of rope and firmly attached it to his collar at one end, and tied it around the bole of a tree at the other. Patch, defeated and confused, lay with his nose on his paws, and whimpered. Yet he still seemed to prefer to grieve alone, for when anyone approached him he barred his teeth and snarled.

The priest arrived just as the sun was dipping behind the trees. He was a tall, thin man with a weather-beaten face and a kind smile. His horse was lathered in sweat from the swift ride out from Kingaroy, and Catriona led it to the little stream so it could have a drink whilst the priest went into the tent.

Patch sprung to his feet and strained against his tether as Kane and Da carried the still bundle to the deep hole they'd dug earlier. Velda took pity on him, and with a tight fist around the makeshift leash, she had to fight to keep control as he pulled and strained to reach his master.

Catriona stood beside her mother as Max was carefully lowered into the ground. He was wearing his stage costume, she noticed, and one of his old blankets had been wrapped around him as if to shield him from the cold of that dark red earth which would soon cover him. She shivered as the priest conducted the short service, and blinked away the tears as the earth slowly filled that great, deep hole and took Max away from them.

Patch whined and scrabbled as a rough crucifix was hammered into the ground, and Max's jaunty hat was placed on top of it. The green feathers were faded, the braid worn, but it was a poignant reminder of the man who had entertained so many people over the years.

Velda was thanking the priest when Patch finally managed to escape. He scrabbled up the soft mound of earth and sniffed the wooden cross. He whined as he inspected the hat and searched for Max. Then, with a sigh of infinite sadness, he settled down, chin on paws, to wait for him to return.

Father Michael must have seen the distress on her face, for he turned to Catriona and took her hand. 'He has to mourn, just like the rest of us,' he said in the soft Irish brogue that had never been erased over the years of living in Australia. 'I've seen it before. There's none so faithful as a dog – he is indeed man's best friend.'

'But we can't leave him here,' she sobbed. 'Who will feed him and look after him?'

The priest smiled. 'I'll come every day and make sure he's all right,' he promised. 'And when he's tired of sitting out here alone, I'll take him home with me.'

'You promise you won't forget him?'

He nodded. 'We're all God's creatures, Catriona, and even the care of a little dog is watched over by Our Lord. I would be failing Him as well as you if I didn't keep my promise.'

*

They broke camp early the morning after the burial. Patch was still curled up on the mound of earth waiting for Max. Catriona tried to coax him away with a chicken bone, but he refused. She stroked his head and he licked her fingers, his eyes sad as he made no move to follow her back to the wagon.

Jupiter was backed into the traces, Kane was astride his prancing gelding, and Catriona was squashed on the buckboard between her parents. She couldn't help but glance back as they left the clearing. The mound of earth already looked forlorn, and the tears ran down her face at the thought of leaving them both behind.

'It's a peaceful place to rest,' murmured Velda as she dabbed away Catriona's tears with a scrap of handkerchief. 'Surely God must have touched this land to make it so beautiful? Look at the waterfall, Kitty. See how it splashes and roars, and listen to how the air is full of birdsong.' She put her arm around Catriona and held her close as Declan's fingers gripped the reins and steered Jupiter along the winding tracks. 'It's always a mistake to look back, *acushla*,' she said softly. 'And Patch will be looked after. The priest is an honourable man.'

Catriona knuckled away the tears and tried to appreciate the splendour of her surroundings that only yesterday had awed and excited her. Yet all she could think about was that sunny glade, the dark forest and the lonely grave with its sad little guardian. She hoped with all her heart the priest would keep his word.

Yet it was to be many years before Catriona could return to that wooded glade and learn that indeed the priest had kept his promise. Patch had spent his final years in the priest's home, and at the end, had been buried alongside Max, the master he had always loved.

Chapter Four

The days turned to weeks as they headed north, and yet another blow befell them. Kane's money had gone. He returned from his visit to the town, his face ashen, the newspaper clutched tightly in his hands. His investments had disappeared along with the main stockholders of the shipping company he'd been so certain was a safe deposit for his hard-earned cash. From now on he would have to rely on the small amounts deposited in the Post Office by his family back in England. It was a bitter blow – one that swept away his cheerful demeanour and made him surly and silent.

Bunyip Station sprawled over thousands of square acres in the heart of the Queensland Outback, and there was work to be had if a man could stand the heat and the flies and the unremitting loneliness of sinking posts and repairing fences. Because of the rains through the winter, the grass was lush and plentiful, the sheep fat and thickly fleeced. Now it was high summer – shearing time – with many mouths to feed. Velda and Catriona took on the task of managing the vast kitchen for the four weeks the shearers would be on the property.

The homestead was a long, low building sheltered from the sun by trees – the kitchen was situated close to the shearing sheds, the corrugated-iron roof shimmering in a heat haze. The noise from the sheds was constant, with animals complaining, men swearing and the angry buzz of the electric shears ripping through the torpid heat. Flies hovered in relentless clouds and the heat didn't even wane after the sun went down, merely made it almost impossible to sleep.

Catriona's world consisted of mounds of potatoes and vegetables to be peeled and prepared for the cooking pot. When she wasn't doing that, she was helping with the washing up. The heat was like a furnace in that iron-clad kitchen, the ovens glowing from dawn to dusk. Three meals a day for over a hundred men was a task almost beyond Velda, but despite the long hours and the gruelling heat, they made it to the end of the month.

'You done good,' said the owner as he handed them their wages. 'Reckon you might come back next year?'

Catriona looked at her mother, so pale and bedraggled, so wrung out by the heat of that awful kitchen. Velda shook her head. 'We'll not be coming this way again,' she said quietly before turning away. When they were out of earshot, she took Catriona's hand. 'I feel as if I've been released from prison,' she sighed. 'Surely there's an easier way to make a living?'

'We've got lots of money to see us through for a while,' replied Catriona as they joined Da and Kane.

Velda handed over her wages to Declan. 'Guard it with your life,' she muttered. 'I never want to do that again.'

As they trundled further north, the heat and humidity increased. Even the lightest clothes felt heavy and were soon soaked in sweat. Biting insects left their marks on bare arms and legs and the flies hovered in great clouds around their faces. At night the heat stifled them in a blanket of humidity, the large, ugly cane toads kept up a constant racket and the deep rumble of thunder and sharp forks of lightning startled them from uneasy sleep.

The rolling grasslands gave way to mile upon mile of verdant green cane fields that swept from the purple-headed mountains almost to the sparkling ribbon of sea that edged the horizon. The cane stood taller than a man, in regimented lines that dipped and swayed in the hot wind. Catriona shivered as they jolted along beside the rusting tracks of the cane railway towards Bundaberg and the smoking chimney-stacks of the refineries, for this northern country was like an impenetrable jungle, dark and unforgiving, with unseen predators she suspected were waiting to catch the unwary.

While the men went into the refinery to see if there was any work to be had, Velda and Catriona made their way to the deserted shore. Shallow dunes tumbled down to a beach that was so wide it disappeared north and south over the horizon. The scent of pine and eucalyptus overrode the sickly sweet aroma of the smoke coming from the refinery's chimneys, and the few clumps of spiny

51

grass clung tightly to their sandy anchors as they rustled in the breeze.

Catriona stood on the dune and stared in amazement. The sea stretched before her in a glittering feast of the brightest, clearest blue she had ever seen. Sailboats dipped and tossed in the frothy waves, their sails gleaming in the sun. Yet it was the sheer breadth of the ocean that took her breath away, for never, even in her wildest imagination, could she have expected this. With shrieks of delight, she and Velda pulled off their shoes and raced across the soft, warm sand to the ripples of water lapping the shore.

'The water's warm,' she breathed in awe. Holding up the hem of her dress, she ventured further, laughing as the little waves splashed her thighs and caressed her ankles. She watched the white seabirds hover and swoop above her, heard their mournful cries, and breathed in the clean, salty air that drifted back to her on the warm breeze. This was a magical place – a place where she felt anything was possible if you wished hard enough.

'Can we stay a while?' she begged Velda.

Velda splashed in the water, her face content, the lines not so deeply carved at the side of her mouth or around her violet eyes. 'If your da and Mr Kane can find work,' she said. Then she grinned as she unpinned her glorious hair, shook it out, and let it blow freely in the wind. 'But I'm sure we could all do with a rest. So why not?'

Catriona watched her mother open her arms and lift her face to the sun. She looked so young, so carefree despite the tendrils of grey that now sparked in the dark hair, and for the first time in a long while, Catriona began to feel the weight of sorrow lift from her shoulders. She stretched out her own arms and embraced the warmth of the sun, spinning around and around until she was giddy and her black hair fell in a tumble over her shoulders. For this one joyous moment she could forget everything and just be a child again.

There was no work in the refinery, and Da and Mr Kane were forced to seek employment with the cane growers. It was a rough, tough and unforgiving man's world, and very few women were courageous enough to withstand it – so there was no work for Catriona and Velda.

The work in the cane fields was something only done by the

toughest breed of men, who worked hard and lived hard and, when Sunday came around, fought and drank hard. Mate-ship was everything; to be the 'gun-cutter', the fastest cutter in the team, was an ambition they all envied and strived for. Fights broke out on a regular basis, and the teams of cutters formed almost medieval tribes and territories which they guarded and protected jealously.

These men lived in long, dilapidated shacks that were perched on poles above the canopy of the surrounding rainforest. They were old before their time, burned by the sun, bowed by the heat, their faces etched with lines of exhaustion. They wore torn singlets and baggy shorts, with thick socks and heavy boots to protect their ankles. To a man they shared the dream of one day owning their own cane plantation, and were single-minded in their quest to earn the vast sums of money that could be had if their day's tally beat the one before.

Yet these ambitions were soon forgotten as they drank away their hard-earned money at the weekend – for cane cutting was thirsty work, and if a man didn't drink he wasn't a mate, wasn't a part of the tribe.

The interminable heat and humidity, combined with the constant attack by mosquitoes and flies, sapped the remains of their strength. Yet these men knew no other life; had no desire to leave the familiarity of this masculine world where a man was judged by his strength and his tenacity, to explore what else there was outside the cane fields. Many suffered from Weils, dysentery and malaria, but they still kept going, for the lure of the money to be made was a fever of its own.

Working in the steamy, fly-blown heat from sunup to sundown Da and Mr Kane laboured with machetes. They were slashed by the razor-sharp cane and lived in fear of the enormous rats that scuttled around their feet – one bite from those deadly teeth would mean sickness, maybe even death. Their soft hands were soon covered in blisters, their clothes soaked in sweat, hanging from their sunburned, mosquito-ravaged bodies in rags. The filth from the cane and the back-burning streaked their skins, ingraining the dirt so well that not even a swim could dislodge it. It was back-breaking work, made worse by the jeers of the men who lived in this hell and seemed to relish it.

Velda and Catriona bathed their wounds and smeared them with ointment, but there was nothing they could do about the red-rimmed eyes, the sunburn and the bites, and the bone-weariness that had them falling asleep over their meagre supper every night. Even Kane seemed to have lost his spirit, and no longer regaled them with the outrageous stories that usually had Catriona laughing until her sides hurt.

Within two weeks, Velda had had enough. The site they'd chosen for the wagon was in a good spot, high above the cane fields on the flat mesa of a nearby hill. The air was slightly cooler, the river fast-flowing, and the flies and mosquitoes didn't worry them as much. But she could see what life in the cane-fields was doing to her husband, and didn't like the way he was slowly being drawn into this twilight world.

She looked at the two men who were drooping wearily over their cups of tea and made a decision. 'We're leaving this hell-hole,' she declared. 'You'll be picking up your wages in the morning, and then we're off. I'll not let either of you kill yourselves anymore.'

'But it's good money, Velda,' Declan protested. 'Another week and I'll be bringing home an extra couple of quid. In a month I'll be earning more than ever.'

'Another week and you'll be dead,' she snapped. 'We leave tomorrow, Declan. And that's final.'

Catriona had never heard her mother talk to him like that before, and she might have protested if she hadn't seen the fleeting look of gratitude in her father's eyes. It was the depths of his weariness and lack of self-worth that stooped his shoulders and made him give in to her demands – and it was only as she watched him shuffle from the camp and climb into the wagon, that she realised why Mam had taken the decision out of his hands. He was too proud to admit he couldn't cope, too sick at heart to voice his fear that this was all he could do to feed his family.

Her heart ached as she watched him collapse on the mattress. He would be asleep in an instant – but perhaps now he could dream easier knowing he wouldn't have to go into the fields again tomorrow.

She looked at Kane, and saw that he too had acquiesced to her Mam's demands. The cane had to be a terrible thing if it could do that to two such strong men, she decided. And although she would be sorry to leave the ocean and the beach, anything had to be better than seeing them so beaten and defeated.

*

The next day dawned brightly, but there were thick clouds coming in from the mountains which soon brought a refreshing coolness to the hillside. Da and Kane had gone to the cutters' camp for their wages, and Catriona was helping her mother pack up in readiness for leaving.

'Can we go to the beach, Mam?' she asked as the last box was stowed away and the fire was stamped out and covered with earth.

Velda smiled, but it was a weary smile as she knuckled back the wisps of sweat-dampened hair from her eyes. 'We'll wait for your Da,' she replied. 'I'm thinking the men would like a dip in the sea to refresh them before our journey.'

With the week's wages hidden away, they took the horses and wagon down to the beach for the last time. Catriona was too impatient to wait for the adults, and she ran into the sea, splashing the water so it rose in droplets of diamonds. She scooped the salty water in her hands and washed her face and her arms. It soothed the bites and washed away the dirt, and she wished she could strip off her clothes and immerse herself in the freshness of it.

As the adults splashed and laughed in the water, Catriona hunted for shells, and watched in fascination as a tiny crab scuttled across the hard, wet shore, leaving a beaded trail of sand in its wake before swiftly burying itself at the edge of the waves.

Tired of the game, and wanting to drink in this glorious scene, she stared out at the expanse of incredible blue. She had to shield her eyes, for the light on the water was blinding as the sun streamed down between the gathering clouds. Shadows of those clouds raced across the surface of the water, turning the turquoise to a dark green that was now laced with white as the gulls swooped and screamed overhead.

She turned to Kane who had come to stand beside her at the water's edge. 'It's a bonzer place,' she sighed. 'I wish we didn't have to leave.'

He put his arm around her and gave her a swift hug. 'We all have to move on, my dear,' he said. 'And the sea is just as beautiful in Cairns.'

She looked up at the sky. The wind was freshening and the clouds were thicker now, bringing an eerie twilight to the world. She shivered, wrapping her arms tightly around her waist. 'It's getting cold,' she said.

'We're in for a tropical storm,' muttered Kane as he shielded his eyes and looked out to sea. 'And if my memory serves me right, the rain will come down very heavily. We'd better get the wagon off this sand, or we'll be bogged down.'

'But it's summer,' protested Catriona. 'It doesn't rain in the summer.'

'Not much in the south,' admitted Kane as he looked down at her and smiled. 'But up here in the north it's the rainy season – what the locals call, the Wet. Rivers flood, roads get washed away, lightning strikes and thunder booms.' He put a finger beneath her chin and looked deep into her eyes. 'But there's no need to worry, Catriona,' he said quietly. 'I'll see no harm comes to you.'

Catriona eased from his touch. 'My Da will protect me,' she said firmly. 'Anyway, I'm not a baby to be scared of silly old storms.'

'Of course you're not,' he said thoughtfully as he regarded the damp cotton dress that clung so tightly to her. 'In fact you've become quite grown up.' His thumb brushed the dimple in her chin. 'How old are you now? I forget.'

'I'm eleven,' 'she said, pulling away from that caressing thumb, feeling uneasy beneath his close scrutiny. She folded her arms over her tiny, burgeoning breasts, suddenly aware of how the wet cotton was clinging to them. 'And old enough not to be treated like a kid.'

'How very right you are,' muttered Kane, his eyes thoughtful as he looked down at her.

The sun was soon hidden behind the rolling black clouds that raced in from the mountains. A cool wind whipped the surrounding palm trees and ferns, making them dance and clatter as the wagon and horses made their way along the dirt tracks that led through the hinterland. By leaving the coast they had hoped to by-pass the storm – or at least find shelter from it – but there was to be no escape.

The rain began to fall. Softly at first, with a slow drip, drip, drip on the roof of the wagon, that was quite pleasant to listen to. But all too soon it turned into a rapid tattoo which muffled and deadened all other sound. It beat against the surrounding trees and bounced off the hardened earth, pummelling it into muddy submission. The great, grey curtain of water enclosed the little group and blotted out their surroundings, bringing night where there had been day as it hammered all beneath it.

Catriona and her parents huddled against the onslaught, the lightweight waterproofs no match for the sheer ferocity of the rain. Jupiter dipped his head, his sodden mane clinging to his streaming neck as he splashed through the mud. He had to work harder now, for the wagon-wheels were becoming bogged down. Kane, dressed in a stockman's thick waterproof coat that covered him from neck to foot, sat astride his own horse, chin tucked into his collar as the water poured in rivers from the brim of his bush hat.

'Get into the back,' shouted Declan, his voice almost drowned out by the thunder of the rain. 'Before you catch your deaths.'

Catriona and Velda clambered over the buckboard and through the narrow doors into the relative safety of the wagon. They towelled their hair and swiftly changed into dry clothes. It was impossible to talk, for the small space was echoing with the sledge-hammer blows of the rain on the roof.

Catriona sat on the kapok mattress and, with one of the narrow doors ajar, kept watch on her Da. His shoulders were hunched, his clothes soaked through as he tried to keep a firm grip on the slick reins. The cabbage-leaf hat that had been woven by one of the Chinese coolies back on the cane fields was drooping, the water sliding off it in miniature waterfalls.

From her high vantage point behind the buckboard, she could see the broad palm leaves being bent beneath the weight of the rain, and noticed that the stream they had been following was swelled and now rushed over the dark red rocks that had so recently been high and dry.

Catriona snuggled up to her mother as they peered out at this watery world of twilight. She felt warm and safe in this cocoon that was home – contented to be a child again in her mother's arms as she laughed at the antics of the birds.

The galahs and rosellas were hanging upside down, spreading their feathers, squawking and squabbling as they rid themselves of ticks and lice. The white cockatoos fanned their sulphur yellow combs and shouted abuse as they flapped their wings and fought for purchase on the slippery branches. Kookaburras fluffed their feathers and sank their beaks into their chests, their chortling muted by the sheer volume of the rain.

Catriona shivered with anticipation as she heard the thunder approach. The rumble was deep-throated, penetrating the all-encompassing thud of the rain. Sheets of brilliant light illuminated the surrounding bush, bringing into sharp relief the towering black

57

boulders that stood like sentinels amongst the trees. She had a healthy respect for storms, but she didn't fear them. They were as much a part of her life as the heat and the dust – and this one promised to be a beaut.

The growl of the thunder was deeper now, coming closer. The lightning flashed broad sheets of blazing white across the racing, purple clouds, turning the rain into a sparkling curtain. The dark, red earth clung to his sturdy feet as Jupiter gamely plodded through the widening puddles and the hurrying, scurrying rivulets of water that streamed from the hills and swept across the parched land.

The crash of thunder rocked the earth beneath them as their world was illuminated by a fork of lightning that spat and hissed and ripped through the sky to hit a nearby tree. With a rifle-crack, the timber exploded into a pillar of flame.

Jupiter reared up onto his hind legs, pawing the air, screaming in terror.

Declan shouted as the wagon pitched and rolled and he fought to maintain his balance.

Catriona and Velda were tossed about, their sharp cries lost in the mayhem of the storm as they crashed against the wooden sides and jarred elbows and knees on the hard floor.

Kane clung on to the saddle and shortened the reins as the gelding reared and danced on his toes. The animal weaved in a tight circle, ears flat, eyes rolling in terror as it tried to rid himself of the man on his back and escape the sights and sounds of a world gone mad.

Jagged forks of lightning split the sky as the thunder crashed and boomed overhead. The pillar of flame burned brightly in the gloom, reaching out hungry tongues to lap at the nearby kindling of fallen branches and dry leaves which lay sheltered beneath the overhanging trees. With the dexterity of a snake it slithered through the undergrowth and climbed the frail, white bark of the sheltered saplings and began to feed.

Jupiter fought the restraints of the traces – fought the reins and the man who held them. His great front feet hit the earth with a shuddering crash – dug in – and in his terror, his mighty strength propelled him in a headlong rush down the muddy track.

Declan clung to the reins, his feet jammed against the front board to give him greater purchase. He could barely see, could barely feel the reins in his cold, wet fingers. Struggling to maintain his balance, he shouted to Kane. But his voice was lost in the doomsday booms of thunder.

Jupiter shook his head and raced for cover, his great legs stretching into a lumbering gallop along the muddy track. He wanted to escape and was heedless of the wagon that bounced along behind him like a child's toy.

The boulder was at the side of the track. It was big and jagged and right in their path. The ironclad wheel hit it with a juddering blow that sent shockwaves through the wagon.

Declan was tossed into the air. Flung like a rag doll into the rain, he landed heavily against another boulder, his bones snapping like twigs.

Catriona screamed as she too was thrown off balance. She landed on the wagon floor with a thud and felt something sharp stab her wrist. Velda was clinging to the wooden door at the front of the wagon, screaming for Kane to do something as the wagon careered out of control.

With a shouted curse, Kane kicked his horse into obedience and forced the animal to catch up with the terrified Jupiter. Leaning across, he judged the distance and swiftly grabbed the driving reins, pulling on them with all his might as he was dragged from the saddle and hauled unceremoniously through the mud.

Free at last, the gelding bolted.

Jupiter was an old horse and not built for such a headlong flight. He resisted the persistent drag on the reins and shook his head, but soon realised he'd never be rid of the weight of the crippled wagon, or the man who held on so grimly. He finally ran out of steam and came to a trembling standstill, his great sides heaving from the effort.

Velda was out of the wagon and running back down the track.

Catriona's wrist was a circle of throbbing fire. She saw the glimmer of bone pushing through bloody skin and her stomach clenched as the bile rose in her throat. Determined to be with her father she swallowed and took deep breaths as she cradled her arm and clambered down into the mud. Black clouds filled her head and threatened to overcome her as she tried to run – but she fought against them, pushing herself to hurry to her father's side.

Declan lay still, his face grey as the rain splashed his closed eyelids and streamed down his cheeks. Velda knelt in the mud beside him and took his hand. Her hair had come loose from its pins and lay in a wet

59

mass down her back and over her shoulders. Her dress clung to her, showing the knots in her spine and the sharpness of her hip-bones as she swiftly ran her hands over his body.

Catriona sank into the mud. She felt sick from the pain of her wrist – sick with the anxiety of what had happened to Da. 'He's not dead, is he?' she asked fearfully. She had to repeat the question for her mother hadn't heard her over the thunder of the rain.

Velda shook her head. 'No, but he's hurt badly,' she shouted back. 'Fetch me a blanket, and that little bottle of brandy from my basket,' she ordered.

Catriona stood up. The agony tore through her and the black clouds filled her head again and blotted out the scene before her. She tried to call out, tried to fight them, but this time they would not be denied. As she felt her legs buckle and the ground rise up to meet her, she heard her mother scream.

Catriona felt the chill needles of rain on her face and opened her eyes. She was confused. Why was she lying in the mud? Where was she, and what was that searing, throbbing agony burning in her wrist?

She blinked against the deluge of water and realised Kane was bending over her, his hands delving in the mud beneath her, lifting her up. Her feeble protests were ignored as he held her close and swiftly carried her through the rain to the canvas shelter that had been strung beneath the trees. Then she remembered. 'Da,' she cried out, wriggling to be free. 'Where's Da?'

'Keep still,' Kane shouted above the downpour. 'He's all right.'

Catriona squirmed and wriggled until he was forced to set her down. She splashed her way through the mud and, with her throbbing arm curved against her chest, she almost fell into the shelter.

Da was lying on a blanket, his head resting on a pillow stained with his blood. It spread across the cotton like the hideous, dark red flowers that bloomed around his ankle and his ribs. His face was ashen, his eyes were closed. The only signs of life were the rapid rise and fall of his chest and the strangulated gurgle as he struggled to breathe.

Velda left his side and swiftly gathered Catriona into her arms and gently examined her wrist. She pulled a long silk scarf from her voluminous carpet-bag, made a neat sling for the damaged wrist and eased Catriona down on to the blanket next to her father.

60

She put her mouth close to Catriona's ear so she could hear what she was saying.

'It's a good thing you fainted,' she said. 'Kane managed to put the bone back in place while you were out, and it was only his quick thinking which stopped you from bleeding to death.'

Catriona eyed her wrist. A strip of cotton had been bound just below her elbow, a sturdy stick keeping the material so tight, her arm throbbed. There was another strip of cotton around her wrist, fixed with a large safety pin. Thankfully there was no blood and no glimmer of bone to make her feel giddy again.

She reached for the stick and her mother pushed her hand away. 'Leave it,' she ordered. 'It's there to stop the blood flowing.'

'What about Da?' she asked, as she looked at the spreading blossoms on his clothes. 'Why can't you stop him bleeding too?'

Kane finished tying splints to Declan's shattered leg, and rested back on his haunches. 'The bandages won't hold,' he said. 'I can't put enough pressure on them.' He checked the bandage around Declan's midriff and stood up. 'We have to get them both to a doctor, and quick,' he shouted above the thunder. 'Come on Velda, you'll have to help me fix the wheel.'

Catriona lay next to her father, her small hand in his as he struggled for breath and fought to stay alive. The tears mingled with the remnants of the rain on her face as she watched her mother and Mr Kane splash through the mud, their heads bowed by the weight of the rain. Mam's dress was soaked, it clung to her legs as the mud captured her shoes and tore them from her feet. Kane, better equipped to cope with the weather, strode out in his long waxed drover's coat, his boots squelching in the mud.

She looked across at her father. He was making strange gurgling sounds in his throat, and there was a bubble of bloody mucus at the corner of his mouth. She gripped his hand, trying to instil some of her own youthful energy into him as encouragement. He must not be allowed to die.

The world was grey outside the canvas cover, and the two figures battling with the wagon looked so small and vulnerable Catriona wished she could help. But it would be impossible, for the pain was taking over again – drumming through her in tortuous waves – bringing the blackness and the welcome oblivion. She held on to Da's hand and let them take her over.

*

Francis Kane hammered in the last nail and with Velda's help, managed to get the wheel back on the axle before fixing the hub over the top of it. He was sweating inside the heavy coat, and his discomfort was aggravated by the icy rainwater teeming down his neck from his hat.

His hand slipped, the head of the nail neatly slicing a deep gash in the fleshy part of his palm. He swore softly and quickly wrapped the wound in a none-too-clean handkerchief. This was a god-awful country, he thought grimly as he splashed through the mud to the canvas shelter. The sun boiled and burned, the humidity smothered and the rain threatened to drown him. What the hell did he think he was doing here? He should have left them months ago, gone off on his own and found something better to do with his life than this.

He stood for a moment and looked down at the injured man and his daughter. The questions were rhetorical – he already knew the answers. There was no other life, no other choices; his money was gone, he was doomed to remain in this exile for as long as his family paid him to be here.

He scooped the child into his arms and carried her back to the wagon. Settling her on the kapok mattress, he covered her with a dry blanket. Squatting back on his haunches he looked at the pale little face, and with a gentle finger, traced the curve of her cheek. She looked so innocent, so fragile – like a china doll, and he couldn't resist lightly placing his lips on her hot little forehead.

'Mr Kane. Hurry. We have to hurry.'

With a grunt of impatience he turned at the sound of Velda's voice and climbed back into the rain. He strode through the mud, mourning for his expensive riding boots that were no doubt ruined. He struggled to mask his bad temper by plastering on a smile of concern as he found Velda shivering with cold and fear in the shelter, and was sickened by the look of gratitude she gave him as he once again took charge. If only she didn't rely on him so much – if only he'd had the will-power to leave with the others. A surge of anger tore through him and he pushed it away – it was too late now, the die was cast.

'Take one end of the blanket, and I'll take the other. But try not to jolt him.'

Declan was no lightweight and they struggled to carry him on the blanket through the rain and the mud to the wagon. It was impossible to lift him inside in this way, so Francis took the man in his arms and as gently as he could hoisted him up and onto the mattress beside his daughter.

He still ached from his time in the cane fields, and the effort of mending the wheel and carrying Declan had exhausted him. He rested his hands on his knees and tried to catch his breath as Velda clambered up into the back of the wagon and tended to her wounded. He glared out at the rain. At least it had put the bush fire out, he thought grimly. But that was about the only good thing about it.

He straightened as he heard the thud of hoofs. The gelding had decided to return, no doubt more afraid of being alone than with company during the storm. Halfwitted beast, he thought as he swiftly caught the reins and gentled him. That was the trouble with highly bred horses, didn't know when they were well off. If he'd been such a beast, he'd be long gone by now, he mused as he tied the reins firmly to the rear of the wagon.

'We have to go now, Mr Kane,' shouted Velda from the wagon. 'Declan's getting worse.'

He tipped his hat, his smile almost a grimace as he ducked his head and headed for the buckboard. Climbing up, he grabbed the reins and slapped them across the broad back of the shire. It was time Velda was made to understand he wasn't her lackey – time to assert his position and review his plans.

The thunder crashed and rumbled as the lightning ripped through the sky and the rain teemed down in a never-ending sheet of grey. The sound of the rain on the roof was a thunder in itself, drowning out all other sound, enclosing them in the small space like prisoners trapped in a cell.

Catriona was shivering with the cold despite the blanket. Her dress clung to her and her hair stuck to her face in damp tendrils that dripped icy water down her neck and soaked the pillow. She could hear Kane cursing as poor Jupiter struggled to pull them through the swirling, watery mud, and wondered how long it would take to return to Bundaberg. It felt as if she'd already spent hours in the back of the wagon – she longed to escape the narrow confinements of her home.

She lay on the mattress next to her father and tried not to whimper when the agony in her wrist became almost too much to bear. She kept her gaze firmly fixed on Declan's face as they were

63

jolted and bumped over the rough track they had so recently come along. He too was in terrible pain. She could see it in the greyness of his face, and in the deep hollows at his cheeks and temple – could hear the keening in his throat as each jolt, each roll and jerk of the wagon sent shock waves of agony through him.

Velda sat between them, but most of her concern was for Declan. She tried to soothe him with her voice, tried to make him comfortable by stroking his brow and wiping away the sweat and the blood from his face. She bent over him, her sodden dress clinging to her slender frame, her hair tangled wetly into a rough knot at the nape of her neck as her tears traced tracks through the grime on her face.

Catriona experienced a warm rush of love for her mother, and yearned to be held, to be comforted – but she knew she was being selfish, for Da needed her more. She drifted in and out of the darkness, coming awake only when her father cried out, or the jolting sent a stab of pain through her wrist.

She opened her eyes as she felt the hands lifting her out of the wagon. She looked for her father. He was gone.

'Don't fret,' said Kane as he carried her through the rain and into the long wooden house that was almost hidden by overhanging trees. 'He's with the doctor.'

'He's all right, isn't he?' she asked through the feverish haze that seemed to have taken her over. 'He will be all right?'

'Let's get you fixed up, and then you can go and see him for yourself,' he replied as he carried her into a room at the back of the building.

The country hospital sprawled amongst the trees on the very edge of Bundaberg. Constructed and financed by the owners of the cane plantations, it was well equipped, efficiently run, and served the widespread community that surrounded it. Cane cutting was dangerous, and the men were always getting sick or injured, so the two doctors and three nurses were kept busy.

The building consisted of a large ward for the cutters, two sidewards for the women and children and a small operating theatre. A wide verandah ran along the front of the building, sheltered by the sloping corrugated-iron roof that was almost smothered in bougainvillea – this was a favourite spot for the convalescents who would sit in the cane chairs and yarn as they smoked their cigarettes and passed the time until they were released back into the fields.

As Catriona surfaced from a deep sleep, she discovered several things at once. Her arm was firmly smothered in a white plaster, and didn't hurt any more. She was lying in a proper bed, tucked in with crisp sheets, a soft pillow beneath her head. She snuggled down, relishing the delicious feeling of being clean and comfortable as she took in her surroundings.

She was alone in the small room, but through the open door she could see and hear the bustle of a busy hospital. To Catriona it was a haven of clean sheets, clean smells and friendly faces. There were flowers on the window-sills, bright curtains and bedspreads and polished floors. The nurses looked lovely in their winged caps and starched aprons, and she wondered how they managed to keep them so stiff and white.

As the fog of sleep left her, she realised she'd forgotten about her father. She struggled to sit up and throw off the sheets, but the giddiness made her feel sick and she slumped back into the pillows. She had to find him – had to see that he was all right. Where was Mam? She needed Mam.

As if she'd heard the silent, desperate plea, Velda appeared in the doorway.

Catriona's initial relief and pleasure in seeing her mother was immediately swept away. Velda's face was ashen, the cheekbones high and sharply carved, the eyes shadowed. She seemed to have shrunk, to have aged, and she leaned heavily on Mr Kane as he helped her into the chair beside Catriona's bed.

'Mam?' Her voice wavered as the tears blurred her vision. She was frightened – more frightened than she'd ever been.

Velda took her hands. Her fingers were cold, her voice low, the words almost indistinct as she told Catriona her father was dead. 'He was so brave,' she sobbed. 'But the injuries were too serious. The doctors did what they could, but it was too late.'

Catriona was numb. The tears flowed down her face, and the breath was trapped in her throat as she stared at her mother and tried to make sense of what she was saying. It couldn't be, she thought. There had to be a mistake. Da was strong – he was still a young man – of course he wasn't dead.

Velda blew her nose and dabbed her tears with a sodden scrap of handkerchief. 'I shouldn't have moved him,' she murmured. 'I should

65

never have moved him, let alone made him go through that awful journey back here.' She broke down, her sobs raking her slender body as she buried her face in her hands and gave vent to her anguish.

'What else could we have done?' asked Kane as he stood beside her and put his hand on her shoulder. 'Come, my dear. You mustn't blame yourself.'

Velda lifted a tear-swollen face to him. 'But I do,' she wailed. 'I do.'

Catriona looked from her mother to Mr Kane. The lump in her throat was threatening to choke her, and as the dreadful clamour of reality swirled in her head, she gave in to the knowledge that indeed her da was gone. She would never see him again. Would never hear his voice, or feel his arms around her – would never sit beside him and listen to his stories as he held the reins and steered Jupiter through the Outback.

She began to cry, raging at her mother for letting him die. Raging at her father for leaving her. Raging at Kane for making him take the awful journey here. She shrugged off Velda's hand. Scorned Kane's quiet attempts to calm her. She hated him – hated them both. She just wanted her da.

The sharp prick of a needle in her arm closed her eyes and swept her into a place where there was no pain, no anguish – just a void of eternal darkness.

When she woke, her head felt as if it was filled with cotton wool, and for an instant she had no memory of what had happened. Then she saw her mother and Kane, sitting by her bed, watching her. 'I want to see him,' she said.

Velda reached out and took her hand. 'That's not possible, my *mavourneen,*' she murmured, her eyes dark with pain. 'We buried him two days ago. He's with the angels now, God love his soul.'

Catriona lay back against the pillows, stunned and confused. 'How can that be?' she whispered. 'We only came here today.'

Kane left his chair and sat on the bed. The mattress dipped beneath his weight as he leaned over her and gently brushed away the tendrils of hair from her face. 'You've been a very sick little girl,' he said quietly. 'The fever was severe and the doctor thought it best to let you sleep for as long as possible. We've been here almost a week.'

Her eyes widened and she looked at her mother for

confirmation. How could she lose a whole week? How could she be so ill she hadn't known that her father was dead? Surely, even in the depths of a fever she should have realised he'd left her?

Velda came and stood at Kane's side. 'He's right, darling,' she said. 'You've been very sick and I was afraid I would lose you too.' She gave Catriona a watery smile as she took her hands and held them. 'Your da never woke up. He didn't suffer at the end.'

Catriona couldn't find the words to express all the terrible emotions that were tearing through her.

Velda tucked Catriona's hands beneath the sheet and stepped back from the bed. 'The doctor says you can leave here tomorrow, my darling. You've made a good recovery, and he says you're well enough to travel again.'

Catriona stared at the two of them. She didn't want to leave. Didn't want to go anywhere without her da. How could Mam suggest such a thing? She blinked and tried to concentrate on what Mr Kane was saying.

'I will take care of you both now,' he said as he stood and put his arm around Velda's narrow waist. 'We leave for Cairns tomorrow.'

Catriona didn't like the way Mr Kane held her mother, or the way Velda was looking up at him as if her life depended upon him. 'I don't want to go to Cairns,' she said stubbornly. 'Why can't we stay here?'

Kane pulled Velda close and murmured something in her ear, and with a sad smile to Catriona, she left the room. He came back to the bed and the mattress dipped again beneath his weight. 'Your mother is heartbroken, and I don't believe you wish to cause her further anguish,' he said softly. He stroked back the hair from her cheek. 'I think you know how difficult it would be for her to stay here, so be a good girl – if not for me – then for your mother.'

His words might have been softly spoken, but Catriona heard the steely determination underlying them, and knew without a doubt Kane meant to take charge. 'I am good,' she sniffed. 'I just want my da.'

He took her hand and held it on his lap. 'Of course you're a good girl,' he murmured. 'But we can't stay here any longer.' He smiled. 'The horses and wagon have already been sold,' he said. 'I have bought train tickets for us to leave here tomorrow for Cairns where I have been offered work.' His very blue gaze was steady as he traced the outline of her face with his fingers. 'From now on, Catriona, I will take care of you.'

67

Chapter Five

Velda couldn't bear to visit the cemetery again. She'd cried so many tears she was exhausted as well as frightened. Without Declan what would become of her and Catriona? How would they manage – how would she cope with finding work and shelter when she had so little experience of life outside the travelling troupe?

Catriona listened to the muttered, frantic words and realised her mother was so wrapped up in her own fearful misery, she barely noticed that Catriona was suffering too. Velda seemed to lean on Kane more and more, physically as well as mentally – allowing him to make all the decisions, clinging to him as though she was drowning in a storm. It was as if she didn't care any more about herself, or her daughter. She moved like a ghost, her animation gone, her energy depleted. She'd given up on life – given up caring.

Catriona helped settle her mother in the station waiting-room, and made sure she was comfortable with a book while they went to pay their last respects to Declan. As Catriona turned in the doorway she saw the book resting unopened on her mother's lap, her fingers plucking at the pages as she stared into space. With a heavy heart, Catriona eased her arm in the sling and followed Kane to the cemetery.

She couldn't afford flowers, so she picked some Kangaroo Paw and wild daisies on the way. It was a pretty cemetery, if such things could be termed 'pretty', she thought, as she took in their surroundings. The grass had been recently cut, and the trees were full of birds – it was a quiet, peaceful place, and, in her childish way, she hoped he'd be at rest here. Placing the already wilting flowers on the freshly turned earth, she looked at the crude wooden cross and said goodbye to him.

*

They arrived in Cairns on New Year's Day, 1933. Catriona was hot, thirsty and tired. Her clothes were filthy from the soot and smuts from the engine, and she longed for a bath and a proper meal.

It had been a long journey from Bundaberg, the train slow, the waiting at various isolated stations interminable. Food had consisted of bread and mutton and endless cups of tea. Their sleeping quarters were the hard benches they sat on and they watched, with little interest, as the scenery rolled out majestically beside them in a never-changing blur of green cane fields, green palms and green ferns.

She stepped down from the train and helped her mother and Kane unload their bags and boxes. Velda was thinner than ever, her face wan and her sweat-stained clothes grubby from the long journey. She had hardly spoken since leaving Bundaberg, had made no effort to comfort Catriona, or even acknowledge her presence. Now she stood on the platform, the hatboxes dangling from her fingers as she stared ahead like a bewildered child.

Catriona struggled to carry the heavy bag. Her wrist had yet to heal properly and she couldn't lift even the lightest weight.

Kane took the bag from her and gathered up the others. 'I'll set them aside in the porter's lodge,' he murmured. 'We'll come back for them when I've organised some transport.' He smiled down at her and handed over the water-bottle. 'You look thirsty and tired,' he said kindly. 'It won't be long before we get to the hotel.'

'Is it very far, Mr Kane?' she asked, ashamed at the childish whine in her voice.

He smiled and shook his head. 'Not really,' he said. 'But the journey will be more pleasant, the heat slightly more tolerable for you and your mother, for we're going up there, into the mountains.'

Catriona looked across the vast, empty valley to the line of protective, pine-clad mountains that seemed to dominate the little town. Threatening dark clouds were drifting over the top of them, throwing black shadows over the pine trees and promising a deluge of rain. Yet the heat down here in the valley was almost intolerable. It seemed to insinuate itself around her, enfolding her in a damp, heavy blanket that sapped the last of her strength.

'Can't we rest here for a while?' she asked plaintively.

'We don't have the funds to idle about in Cairns,' replied Kane as he dumped the bags and signed the porter's chit. 'Neither can we afford the train fare up into the mountains, or the hire of a car – which is why I have to find us cheap transport. But your mother will find it easier to rest up there – it's cool and quiet, the perfect place to recuperate.'

He reined in his obvious impatience and gave her a hug. 'You're a big girl now, Kitty,' he murmured into her hair. 'Chin up.'

Catriona leaned into his embrace. She no longer felt disloyal to her father by embracing Mr Kane, for the Englishman could never take his place in her heart – yet he was all she had left to cling to. With Velda overwhelmed by her loss, his strength and kindness had been her saviour. They had spent many hours playing cards and talking – the long nights huddled together for warmth on those hard wooden seats as the train rattled and jolted over the rails – and she finally realised she'd come to rely on him as much as her mother did. For they had no money, no home or work, not even a relative to provide food or shelter – without him they would have been lost.

Kane released her and strode over to Velda. 'Come, my dear,' he said as he took her arm. 'We must find transport for the next leg of our journey.'

Velda looked back at him, her face expressionless, eyes dull with her loss. She moved as he moved, drifting along beside him like a wraith as he led her into the searing heat of the noonday sun.

Cairns wasn't very big, just a random collection of white wooden houses scattered amongst the palm trees, a couple of hotels and several churches. The bustling docks were busy with vast lorries unloading their cargoes into the cane ships, and the board-walks offered shade to those who wandered along them looking into the few shops. Catriona found the beach disappointing – the tide was way out, leaving mud-flats behind that were a haven only for the sea birds and waders.

There was little time to linger and no money to sit in the shade and drink cool lemonade, for Kane had found someone to take them up into the tablelands.

Herbert Allchorn was a strange and rather frightening individual, who had a horse and cart. His clothes hung about him in layers like dirty laundry, his boots were cracked and held together with string, and his hat was so stained with sweat and dirt that it was hard to see what colour it had once been.

He was not a man for lengthy conversation, and he glared out at

70

them from the shadows of his hat-brim, his bloodshot eyes missing nothing as Kane loaded up the bags and boxes and helped Velda settle on the wooden seat. He spat tobacco juice, wiped his mouth on his filthy sleeve and climbed up onto the driving seat. With a sharp crack of the whip, they were on their way.

Catriona sat in the back of the cart opposite Kane and her mother. The sway and roll was as familiar as breathing, and it made her ache with longing for the old days – for Da and the players, for Poppy and Max and the darling shires. Yet, as the sun bore down on them and the horse began the long trek towards the mountains, she knew that those days were gone forever.

Herbert Allchorn sat hunched on the driving seat, his hat pulled over his eyes as he stared between his horse's ears. He had nothing to say, no comment to make on their surroundings, and Catriona wrinkled her nose at the smell emanating from him. It appeared that Mr Allchom was a stranger to soap and water.

The clouds veiled the sun, bringing a welcome coolness to the day as they slowly trundled up the steep, winding dirt track that would lead them onto the Tablelands. The air was full of the sibilant chatter of thousands of insects. Pine trees threw dark shadows, vines clambered in among the enormous ferns and bright tropical flowers as the birds flitted and fussed and called their piping tunes. Deep, frightening ravines opened up beside her and she didn't dare look down into their endless fall from the track – yet, looking beyond the ravines the valley below was sprawled out in the sun, the glitter of the ocean so bright it almost hurt her eyes.

They passed a waterfall that tumbled down the shiny black rocks and raced away through the ravines to the rivers below. A railway line had been carved out of these rocks, and with an echoing hoot, the little train belched smoke and clattered away through a tunnel and out of sight.

Catriona saw glimpses of neat wooden houses perched precariously on poles amongst the trees and gasped at the sight of a whistling kite as it hovered in the air searching for prey. Tiny rock wallabies watched them pass, and a large red kangaroo bounced in front of them and bounded with consummate ease down into the ravine.

If she hadn't been so sad, she might have found this place magical – but as it was, she couldn't dredge up any enthusiasm at all. She just wanted the journey to come to an end, so she could sleep and forget.

Kuranda was a tiny settlement which had sprung up since the building of the railway. It consisted of a few log cabins, one or two neat little cottages, a pub, and a sprawling Aboriginal community which was almost hidden by the trees. The sun broke through the canopy of surrounding rainforest and Catriona gasped. The forest was lush and green and rampant with tropical colour. It was all around them, dark, green and cool, the exotic flowers and birds bringing a wonderful vibrancy to the whole area.

The carter flicked a lazy switch over the horse's back and they trundled away from Kuranda and into the heart of the Atherton Tablelands. It was good farming land, the soil rich, the rainfall plentiful, and obviously a popular spot to breed cattle. Dense rainforests surrounded them, offering glimpses of crater-lakes, ancient tumbles of dark rock, and magnificent waterfalls.

With his hat pulled low over his beetling brows, Herbert Allchorn kept up his morose silence as the horse pulled the wagon along the rutted tracks to the little town of Atherton.

Velda was curled up on the other bench and had fallen asleep, unaware and uncaring of her surroundings. Catriona leaned against Mr Kane's broad shoulder, drowsy with the heat, grateful for his comfort, but unlike her mother, too curious to sleep.

This land of the far north was different to anything she had seen before. The rainforests were a tangle of gigantic ferns, elegant trees and dark, mysterious creepers that weaved through the broad, glossy green leaves of plants she couldn't put a name to. Bright flowers competed with bright birds and the air was sibilant with the hiss and saw of insects.

Once out of the cool shadows of the rainforest they were soon travelling through pasture-land that stretched endlessly into the dancing heat-haze. Cattle grazed in contentment on the rich grass that sprouted from earth so red it was a shock to the eye. Waterfalls splashed into pools from black, glistening rocks, and palm trees stretched their long straight trunks to the sky as if in competition with the sugar-refineries' chimneys.

These chimneys belched grey smoke that was heavily laden with the sickly scent of molasses – it filled the atmosphere, insinuating itself in her clothes and on her skin, and when she licked her lips she thought she could taste its cloying sweetness mingled with the dust on her tongue.

'I sent a telegram two days ago to say we were coming,'

murmured Kane as he rested his chin on the top of her head. 'Hopefully someone will be there to meet us.'

Catriona snuggled against him, glad of his presence in the absence of any communication from Velda. 'I just hope they have a comfortable bed,' she said through a yawn. 'I'm so tired, and it'll be good not to be on the move any more.'

Kane squeezed her shoulder and ran his fingers lightly over her bare arm. 'Won't be long now,' he promised.

With the refineries behind them they approached a vast logging camp which was stacked high with sweetly resinous timber. The scent of it was less cloying than the molasses, with a sharp, citrus tang that seemed to cut through the air and cleanse it. This logging camp stood on the edge of a small settlement which consisted of one broad street, a few houses, a church and two hotels.

Herbert Allchorn slapped the reins over the horse's back and they plodded through the little town and out the other side where they were once again plunged into the welcoming cool, green shadows of a rainforest. As they rounded the long, curving bend in the track, Catriona caught her first glimpse of her new home.

The iron gates looked forbidding, and as Kane clambered down from the wagon and thrust them open, she couldn't help but notice how darkly the shadows from the surrounding forest fell across the gravelled driveway. She shivered and pulled her cardigan over her shoulders. It was as if that darkness was reaching out to her with its icy fingers, probing deeply, chasing away the heat of the sun.

'Where are we?' Velda sat up, blinking sleepily as she adjusted her hat and straightened her dress.

'Petersburg Park,' said Kane. 'Your new home.' He talked softly to Allchorn and then began to walk quickly up the driveway.

Allchorn spat into the dirt, the reins held loosely in his hands as the horse cropped the grass.

'Why are we waiting?' asked Catriona. She had shaken off the gloomy thoughts and decided she was merely tired and out of sorts – her imagination was playing tricks on her, that was all. Now she was eager to catch sight of the house. Eager to begin this new adventure.

Allchorn shrugged. 'Just following orders,' he grumbled.

Catriona frowned. Why should Mr Kane want to go to the house alone?

After what seemed like an age, Allchorn slapped the reins over the rump of the horse and they were trundling down the gravelled driveway.

Catriona sat forward, impatient to see the house. And there it was. The stone walls looked warm in the sunlight that pierced the surrounding forest, and the turrets and towers were beckoning her to explore them. Her eyes widened as she took it all in. If it hadn't been for the collection of very grand cars parked in the semi-circle in front of the house, and the presence of several smartly dressed people sitting on the lawn taking afternoon tea, it could have been a fairy tale castle. She would be like Rapunzel – the only thing missing was a Prince on a white horse.

She looked at her mother for some sign of animation or curiosity – but Velda merely stared ahead, her face expressionless as they trundled on.

Catriona refused to be downhearted despite her mother's obvious indifference to where she was, for, as they slowly advanced towards the house she realised that not only was she going to live in a castle – there was indeed a Prince to go with it. He was standing on the steps by the great stone pillars, his white suit gleaming against the dark front doors. Even from this distance Catriona could see he was tall and dark and handsome, with a neat beard and moustache. He was a bit old for a prince – about the same age as Mr Kane, but his broad smile was welcoming as the two men greeted each other.

'Welcome, welcome,' he said, his voice rich with a rolling, rather exotic accent Catriona couldn't place. 'Kane, my old friend,' he boomed with much backslapping. 'How good to see you again after so long.'

Mr Kane appeared to be just as delighted at the reunion. The two men clasped hands and slapped each other enthusiastically on the shoulder as they exchanged greetings and tried to outdo each other in their eagerness to swap news.

Allchorn drew the wagon to a halt, and Catriona saw the handsome man frown as he caught sight of her and her mother – noticed the swift, questioning look he shot Mr Kane before his smile was once more in place and he was removing his hat in readiness to greet them.

Catriona followed Velda down from the wagon and was suddenly uneasy as she stood there waiting for Mr Kane to make the introductions. The stranger was looking at her with a curious expression on his face, his dark eyes thoughtful beneath the heavy

74

brows that were drawn together in a frown.

'This is Demetri Yvchenkov,' said Kane. 'Formerly of St Petersburg in Russia – now a very rich citizen of Australia.' He chucked Catriona under the chin and winked. 'Don't frown so, Kitty. He won't eat you.' He grinned back at his friend. 'Demetri might look and sound fierce, but he's our benefactor, the owner of this stately pile.'

Catriona's hand was swamped in the Russian's large paw, and as she looked up into dark, questioning eyes she was overwhelmed with an unusual shyness. He was very tall, his shoulders broad, his brows heavy and dark above his penetrating eyes; but his smile was warm, his handshake firm, and that went some way towards reassuring her. She bobbed a curtsy and he sketched a bow before turning to Velda and lightly kissing the air above her gloved fingers.

'You are a man of great surprises, Kane,' he murmured as he looked deeply into Velda's eyes before releasing her hand. 'To have such a wife and daughter is to be blessed.'

Kane's reply was a bark of humourless laughter. 'Good grief, Demetri,' he protested. 'I'm not the marrying kind, you know that. Circumstances have meant we are merely travellers sharing the hardships of this wild and untamed land.' He slapped Demetri on the back. 'You know how it is, old boy. Needs must when the devil drives, and all that, eh?'

Catriona felt a jolt of shock. How easily he'd dismissed them – how swiftly he'd relegated them to insignificant travelling companions. What would happen to them if this enormous Russian decided they couldn't stay?

She glanced at her mother, but Velda didn't appear to be listening. She was standing in the hot sun, staring up at the towers and turrets of this extraordinary house, her face devoid of any expression. Catriona reached for her hand, holding on tightly as she turned her attention back to the two men.

Demetri looked thoughtful as he adjusted his Panama hat. 'Is it that you are hoping they will work for me also?' he asked. 'Or are they wishing to stay for only a short while before moving on?'

Kane seem unfazed and totally at ease with the situation. 'Velda and Catriona are alone in the world, Demetri, and I have taken them under my wing, so to speak.' He slapped Demetri's shoulder in an attempt at being jovial. 'You said you wanted help with this place, and here we are, at your service.'

Demetri tugged thoughtfully at his neat beard as he eyed Velda and Catriona. 'We need to discuss this, Kane,' he murmured, his words almost indistinct. Then he seemed to realise Catriona was listening to this exchange, and visibly brightened – once more the welcoming host. 'But the ladies must come in out of this heat and see my palace.' He threw open the doors and signalled for them to follow him into the coolness of the great hall.

Catriona was struck by the grandness of it all. The wide, sweeping staircase, the intricate plaster moulding on the ceiling, the flowers and paintings and the crystal chandelier were a delight to the eye. There was the scent of flowers and furniture polish in the air, and the temptations of open doors just asking to be explored.

'I see your guests have arrived, sir. And there is *a person* outside with a *cart.*'

Catriona turned and saw a woman of sour countenance. Dressed in black, the dress encircled the scrawny neck and fell almost to her thin ankles. Her hair was an indeterminate brown and pulled tightly away from her face into a thin knot. Her hands were clasped at her waist as the grey eyes swept over them.

'Edith,' boomed Demetri. 'This is Kane, who I was telling you about, and this is Velda and Catriona.'

She nodded in silence, the animosity emanating from her like a dark cloud.

'Tea in my private drawing room, I am thinking. The lady is tired.'

The grey eyes swept over Velda and the thin mouth tightened into a hard line. 'Will the *lady* be staying, sir?'

'Of course, of course,' he rumbled, obviously preferring to ignore Edith's scarcely veiled insult. 'She and her daughter are in my care for as long as they wish. Any friend of Kane's is a friend of mine.' He smiled down at Catriona and winked. 'And bring some cordial for Catriona, and some of those lovely little cakes Cook made this morning.'

'As you wish, sir.' She turned away and seemed to melt silently into the doorway that was almost hidden by the wood panelling.

Demetri laughed and slapped Kane on the shoulder. 'Better pay off the carter. He seems to offend the sensibilities of Edith.'

Kane slipped away to see to the carter and the luggage, and Demetri led the way into his private drawing room. 'Do not be minding Edith,' he said. 'She is spinster lady and not an happy woman – but she is good housekeeper.'

76

Catriona stared in amazement at the rich carpet on the polished floor, the rows of books lining the walls and the vast chandelier that sparkled in the late afternoon gloom. It was obviously a man's room, for the furniture was large and comfortable and there were no frills at the windows, just plain drops of velvet tied back with heavy silken ropes.

As they settled into the comfortable velvet chairs Edith returned with a maid and set out the tea on a heavy oak table that Demetri obviously used as a desk. The maid reminded Catriona of Poppy. She was slender and fair, with a friendly smile which she shot at Catriona when the sour-faced old woman wasn't looking. The short black dress and perky white apron and cap suited her, and Catriona smiled back, thinking how Poppy would have loved this place. Yet it was the great silver urn now being placed in the centre of the table that really held her attention. It was a vast, ornate thing, etched with cherubs and vines and what looked like grapes.

Demetri must have noticed her awe at such a sight, for he leaned towards her, his voice muted. 'It is a samovar,' he explained. 'In Russia this is the only way to make the tea.' He looked across at Kane who had returned from seeing to Allchorn and was now sprawled languidly in a deep armchair smoking a cigar. 'Not like the English with their mean little china pots, and their warm milk,' he said with a smile. 'To drink the tea as in Russia, it is correct to have it with lemon.'

He dismissed Edith and the maid and handed her the fine bone china cup and saucer. 'Try it, little one. Is good but there is cordial if you would prefer.'

Catriona sipped the tea. It was hot and fragrant and like no other tea she'd had before. Feeling a little easier in his presence, she dared to ask him the question that had been in her mind since their arrival. 'What kind of work will we have to do?'

He smiled back at her, the humour bright in his dark eyes. 'None at all,' he replied. 'You and your mama are my guests. I, Demetri, am a man of my word.'

She looked across at Velda who was sipping tea from the delicate cup and staring around her. 'But we can't expect to do nothing,' she said hesitantly.

Demetri set down the cup that looked too small for his great hand and rested back in the chair. 'Why not? You are alone in the world are you not? You have no one to look after you. You must rest here and grow strong again – is a good place to heal the wounds of the past.'

Catriona looked back at him and realised this man understood. Perhaps he too had suffered a terrible loss, and this magical place had brought him solace. 'You're very kind,' she said shyly.

'Not at all,' he boomed. 'And now Mr Kane has arrived and the guests have finally found us way up here, I can begin to see my dream take shape.'

'Why do you need Mr Kane? Are you going to have a theatre here?'

He laughed, tilting his head back and opening his mouth wide. 'It is not Mr Kane's experience on the stage that I require, little one,' he said eventually. 'But his class, his English quality.'

'Seems a strange sort of thing to want,' she murmured as she looked from the Russian to Kane. 'You are very rich. Why not run the hotel yourself?' She realised she was being too bold with this fascinating stranger, and swiftly busied herself with the cup and saucer. However, his next words reassured her.

'You see my beautiful house, my expensive clothes – but under all this, I am poor Russian peasant, little one. I have no family – they were killed in the pogroms – so I must make new life for myself in this great country.'

Catriona looked up at him and he smiled broadly, showing the glint of gold in his teeth. 'I know only work with my hands. I make my money from the gold that is lying in the earth of this generous new country of mine, but I have no education, no English manners for making rich guests comfortable in my castle.'

'Well, I think that's silly,' replied Catriona firmly. 'I bet you've got lots of interesting stories to tell, and I'm sure your guests would love to hear them.'

He laughed again, an uninhibited, open-mouthed roar that lifted to the rafters and made Velda's teacup tremble in its saucer. 'I like you, little one,' he said once he'd contained his laughter and wiped his eyes on a vast handkerchief. 'You are like Russian – you speak your mind.' He grinned at her, his voice low. 'One day I will tell you how I find my gold, and show you the mysteries of turning it into money.'

Catriona was no longer shy of him. 'I'd like that very much,' she said.

He nodded, his mouth pursed in thought. 'How would you like to see my palace, Catriona?'

'I'd love to,' she breathed with childlike enthusiasm.

'Come then. We will leave the others here and explore.'

The entrance hall was bustling with porters carrying expensive looking suitcases and bags belonging to the new arrivals who had driven up here in shining motors that stood outside in the sun. The women wore pretty dresses with full skirts, their feet clad in high-heeled shoes with peep toes. Jaunty hats perched on their neat heads, and jewellery sparkled at their throats and ears. The men with them wore smart suits of dark material, with silk ties and polished brogues, brushed hats carried in hands that looked as if they'd never done a day's labour. Maids sped to and fro carrying tea-trays and linen, and Edith stood behind the reception desk orchestrating the entire mêlée, snapping orders to maids and porters, handing out keys and simpering at the male guests.

Catriona was shamefully aware of her hand-me-down dress and scuffed shoes. 'They all look very rich,' she whispered to the Russian.

'They are,' he whispered back. 'That's why I build hotel. To help them spend their money.'

She grinned up at him. He was teasing her, for she had realised immediately that this house, this hotel meant far more to Demetri than a way of making money.

Demetri signalled to a porter and their luggage was collected and carried up the broad stairs and out of sight. 'I cannot show you all of the house,' he murmured. 'We have people staying in most of the guest rooms. But there are many more places to explore.' He held out his hand. 'Come, little one. Let me show you my palace.'

There were so many rooms, so many corridors and hallways that Catriona soon lost her bearings, and was convinced she would never learn how to find her way back to the grand entrance hall. Yet the house was beautiful, with rich carpets and gilded mirrors, secret doorways and stairs leading up to the towers where the view spread all the way down to the sea, and down into cellars that were mysteriously dark and cool and housed rack upon rack of wine bottles. The kitchen was vast with a row of ranges and spits and copper pots hanging from the rafters. Cook was a big fat woman with rosy cheeks and a jolly smile who was busy rolling out pastry and throwing orders at the scullery maids who were about Catriona's age. Mr Kane had not been exaggerating, she realised. Demetri was indeed very rich and no expense had been spared in realising his dream.

They returned to the drawing room to find that Velda was dozing and Kane was engrossed in a newspaper. Catriona was disappointed. She longed to tell her mother all that she'd seen and her excitement dwindled as she realised her mother didn't actually care where she was.

Demetri once again seemed to understand. 'For now, is time for you to go to your rooms and rest after your long journey. Your mother is not well, I think.'

Catriona at once felt guilty. Poor Mam was in no fit state to care one way or another what happened to them – she'd been selfish to feel such excitement. 'My da died only a few weeks ago,' she said softly. 'Mam isn't over it yet.'

'And you, little one? Are you over it?' His gaze was steady, the kindness visible in his soft brown eyes.

'Not really,' she admitted. 'But Mr Kane has been very kind. I don't know how we would have managed without him.'

Demetri nodded as he tugged his beard. 'Mr Kane was right to bring you here, little one. From now on you – and your mother – will be safe in my home. I, Demetri will see to that.'

Catriona smiled her thanks and crossed the room to Velda. 'Come on, Mam,' she said softly. 'It's been a long day and you look as if you need a rest.'

Velda opened her eyes, blinked and shook off her hand before rising from her chair. She stood before Demetri and looked at him squarely for the first time. 'Thank you,' she said simply before drifting out of the room and up the broad flight of stairs.

Catriona hurried after her, for Demetri had showed her where they would sleep and she was eager to share her excitement with her mother in the hope that some of it would rub off on her. The top floor echoed with their footsteps. There were no carpets up here, just bare boards in the narrow corridor that had a line of doors on either side.

'We're in the servants' quarters,' muttered Velda as she stepped into her allocated room and sank down onto the narrow bed. 'Oh, God,' she groaned. 'What's to become of us?' She buried her face in her hands and wept.

Catriona sat beside her and put her arm around her waist. 'We'll be right, Mam,' she said with bolstered confidence. 'Demetri seems nice and he's promised to see us right.' She leaned her cheek against Velda's shoulder. 'At least we've got a proper roof over our heads and lovely beds to sleep in.'

Velda groaned and eased her hand from Catriona's grip. 'That it should come to this,' she sobbed. 'Charity, that's what it is. Charity. We have no say in what will happen to us.' Turning her back on Catriona, she sank against the pillows, drew up her knees and curled into a ball of misery, her face buried in the crisp linen.

'Mam?' Catriona touched her shoulder, but her hand was shrugged away. 'Leave me,' Velda sobbed. 'I want Declan. Only Declan.'

Catriona wanted him too, but even at her tender age she knew that all the wishing in the world wouldn't bring him back. She sat there in isolation, wanting so badly to share her own grief with her mother, for she could feel the ache of her loss, could feel the tears gathering tightly in her throat and yearned to be able to release them.

The moments passed and she realised with awful clarity that Velda had neither the will, nor the energy to deal with her daughter's grief, for she was incapable of coping with her own. With dull acceptance, Catriona quietly left the room.

Her own room was just down the hall and exactly the same as Velda's. Long and narrow, with a bare floor and white walls, it was in sharp contrast to the highly coloured and cramped wagon she'd lived in all her life. The bed was narrow too, the brass polished to gleaming perfection against the snow white of the linen.

Catriona sat down, feeling the soft mattress cushion her against the coiled metal springs and the thickness of the pillows beckoning her to rest against them. She ran her hands over the crisp whiteness, almost afraid of marking its perfection. It would be her first real experience of having a room of her own. She felt a thrill of excitement course through her, and was impatient for night to fall.

Resisting the lure of the pillows and soft mattress, Catriona sat on the edge of the bed and took in the rest of the room. A small cupboard at one side of the bed held an imposing china chamber pot, and there was a chest of drawers jammed in the other side. A painting of a rather fierce woman in old-fashioned clothes glared down from the wall opposite, and there was a bowl and jug on a marble-topped table beneath the single window. Coloured hooks had been fixed on the back of the door, towels had been folded in a neat pile next to the bowl, and there was a hairbrush and comb on the top of the chest of drawers. Demetri had thought of everything.

The window was high, and Catriona pulled the wooden chair across the floor and stood on it to look out at the view. She sighed with disappointment. All she could see were the grey slates of the roof, the corner of one of the chimneys, and the tops of the trees in the surrounding rainforest.

Having unpacked her few clothes and stored them in the drawers and on the hooks, she placed her books on the top and tried to make the place more welcoming by draping a colourful shawl over the bed. Once she'd placed the family photographs on the bedside cupboard and stacked her father's record collection alongside the wind-up gramophone on the floor, she felt it was at last beginning to look like home.

Catriona sat on the bed, wondering what to do next. It was still daylight, and although she was tired, she didn't want to waste the day by sleeping. Neither did she want to stay up here when there were so many places to explore.

She moved restlessly around the room, debating her options. She could explore the towers at leisure now Mr Kane and Demetri were downstairs, or she could go out into the grounds and wander for a while. Her stomach rumbled reminding her she hadn't eaten more than a sandwich and a tiny cake since early that morning. The kitchen would be a good place to start, and she didn't think Demetri would mind if she asked cook for something to keep her going until tea.

Leaving her room she listened at her mother's door. Velda was no longer sobbing, and Catriona suspected she was asleep. Turning away, she hurried down the stairs. If she remembered rightly, the kitchen was through the door in the panelling of the entrance hall and down a long, tiled corridor. Her mouth was already watering at the thought of bread and cheese and perhaps a little pickle.

She suddenly became aware of the different mood of the raised voices coming from Demetri's private rooms. Guests and maids who'd been milling in the hall had stopped and were listening unashamedly at the exchange. This was no enthusiastic relating of news, she realised as she faltered uncertainly on the landing. This was a furious row.

She stood there, hands gripping the banisters as she tried to decide what to do for the best. She knew she shouldn't be listening, but, like the others below, she couldn't help it.

The voices were so loud and angry, she wouldn't have been

surprised to learn they could be heard in Cairns.

'You should have told me,' shouted Demetri.

'Why?' yelled Kane. 'What difference does it make?'

'It make lot of difference.'

'We had a deal, and it's none of your damn business,' stormed Kane. 'Watch your mouth, Demetri, or you'll be sorry.'

'Sorry?' Demetri's voice rose to a roar. 'You dare to threaten me, Kane? Is you will be sorry.'

'We had a deal,' shouted Kane. 'What's changed?'

'Deal is off,' yelled Demetri. 'You know why – so don't insult me by asking.' His voice dropped several decibels, but his words were still distinct. 'Always you lie. You say you change – but you do not.'

Catriona gripped the highly polished banister, frozen by their raging – frightened for the consequences. And even though the voices were softer now, the words indistinct, she could feel their menace and was frightened by the violence that had erupted between the two men she had thought were friends.

Without warning, the door to the drawing room crashed against the wall, breaking the tableau of interested guests and servants who swiftly got out of the way.

Catriona let go of the banister and cringed in the shadows of the upper flight of stairs, her hands covering her mouth, smothering the sharp hiss of her breath.

Demetri stormed out of the drawing room, his boot-heels rapping against the marble floor as he crossed the hall and slammed his way through the door that led to the kitchens.

Kane emerged from the drawing room and with an almost insolent nonchalance, leaned against the door jamb and lit a cigar. Yet, as he stared across the hall to where Demetri had disappeared, his eyes were arctic, his face etched in cold relief as if from marble.

From her vantage point at the top of the stairs Catriona began to tremble. She had never seen this side of Mr Kane – he frightened her.

Chapter Six

There was no sign of Demetri at dinner time, and Velda and Catriona hesitated in the hallway wondering where they should go.

'Dinner will be served in Mr Yvchenkov's dining room,' muttered Edith, glaring at Velda. 'It wouldn't be proper for you to eat with the guests.'

Velda's violet eyes stared back at her, her expression enigmatic. 'Why the hostility?' she asked.

Edith shrugged. 'Some people should know their place,' she muttered.

Velda would not be put off by her rudeness, and her voice was steady and cool as she replied. 'And what place is that, exactly?'

Edith sniffed as she looked at the faded cotton dress, the scuffed shoes and lack of stockings. 'Neither fish nor fowl,' she snapped. 'This is a high-class establishment. I don't know why he gives you houseroom.'

Velda's high cheek-bones flushed, and Catriona didn't know if it was with anger or shame. 'You seem to have a very high opinion of yourself, Edith,' she said coldly. 'But you are a servant – whereas my daughter and I are Demetri's guests. You would do well to remember that.' She lifted her chin and swept with all the imperiousness of a queen into Demetri's quarters, leaving Edith in the hall, mouth open like a landed trout.

Catriona stared at her mother in amazement. She had never seen Velda so cold and in command before – yet, as the door closed behind them, the veneer fell away and Velda sank onto a chair and dipped her chin. 'Is this to be the way of it?' she sighed. 'Scorned, treated like dirt by women like that because we must take charity?'

'You were brilliant, Mam,' breathed Catriona. 'She wouldn't

dare talk to you like that if Demetri was around, and I reckon she'll give you a wide berth from now on.'

Kane entered the room and sat down just as the maid brought in the tureen of soup and basket of freshly baked bread. 'Cook says to ring when you've finished that, and I'll bring the main course.' She pointed at the rope bell-pull by the door and left.

Catriona eagerly began to eat. The soup was hot and steaming and full of vegetables and bits of ham. It was delicious.

Velda stirred the soup around and around with her spoon, ate a couple of mouthfuls and left it. She picked up the bread roll and began to crumble it in her fingers as she stared out through the windows to the garden beyond. 'I wonder where our host is,' she said without emotion.

Kane stirred the soup and added salt and pepper. 'He's gone out to his shed,' he muttered. 'Seems he prefers his own company to ours.'

'What does he do in his shed?' asked Catriona.

'Who knows,' Kane shrugged. 'Probably messing around with his chemicals and gloating over his gold.' His voice was tight, the bitterness sharp.

Catriona eyed him thoughtfully. Kane ate his soup, his napkin tucked into the crisp white collar of his shirt. He was looking very smart, she noticed. With a clean, pressed suit, highly polished shoes, new shirt and silk tie. There was a handkerchief to match the tie, drooping from the breast pocket of his jacket, and the gold chain of a watch dangled across the embroidered waistcoat. Yet he didn't seem to be in a better mood. The argument with Demetri obviously still rankled.

He seemed to become aware of her scrutiny. 'Demetri lent me a few items to be going along with,' he said. 'I have to be properly dressed when I deal with the guests.'

Catriona still had that furious row at the back of her mind, and was intrigued to learn what it had all been about, but she knew that now was not the time to question him. 'What does Demetri want you to do?' she asked instead.

'I will be a master of ceremony,' he said as he finished the soup and leaned back in his chair. 'I will organise picnics and parties, card games and entertainment for the guests. I will arrange hunting parties for the men and tea parties for the women. I will iron out any problems that may arise and ensure they have a pleasant stay.

85

In short, I will be in charge of this rabble Demetri calls staff.'

'Does Edith know that?' She grinned, knowing the question was cheeky, but unable to resist asking.

Kane sighed. 'Poor Edith. With those looks and unfortunate manner, she will never get what she wants. One almost feels sorry for her.'

Catriona eyed him. He didn't look the least bit sorry for Edith, but he did seem to have some insight as to why she'd been such a cow to Mam. 'What does she want? Surely she has everything here?'

Kane rose to pull the cord and summon the maid. 'Everything but the man she pines for,' he replied. 'Alas, Demetri does not see her as the wife she longs to be, so instead of mistress, she must remain servant.'

'Poor Edith,' muttered Catriona. 'No wonder she's so sour.' She leaned back and waited as the maid took away their bowls and set the large plates of roast meat and vegetables before them. Cheese and biscuits and a bowl of fruit would be their dessert. Catriona had never seen such food before, or in such quantities and she tucked in. The meat was tender, the gravy thick and tasty, the vegetables fresh and crisp, oozing in butter. The Depression was obviously over, at least for the people who lived in this house. 'Try and eat something Mam,' she coaxed as Velda once again played with her food.

'I'm going to bed,' she said as she pushed the plate away and stood. 'Goodnight, Mr Kane, goodnight, Catriona.' She brushed her lips lightly over Catriona's hair and drifted out of the room.

'It will take your poor mother some time to come to terms with her loss,' said Kane as he speared a square of cheese and helped himself to butter and biscuits. 'But sooner or later she will have to realise she can't rely on Demetri's generosity for ever.'

'You mean we'll have to leave?' Catriona's pulse began to race and all the pleasure she'd gained from the food was lost.

'That depends,' he said thoughtfully through the cheese.

Catriona waited. Perhaps now she would learn about the row he'd had with Demetri earlier.

'Demetri is a wealthy man, who made his fortune in the gold-fields. He came here over twenty-five years ago when his family was killed in the pogroms back in Russia. He had nothing to lose and everything to gain.' Kane waved his knife in the air. 'This was

86

his dream, and it seems he has achieved it.'

He ate another biscuit and stared out of the window into the darkness of the garden. 'But one must never forget that Demetri is a man used to working with his hands. He's a peasant, with a peasant's mentality. He does not always keep his word.'

Catriona sat in silence, confused at the conflicting thoughts and emotions his words conjured up.

Kane finished eating, brushed the crumbs from his moustache and beard and pushed away from the table. He walked to the sideboard and poured a glass of port before lighting a cigar. 'It was agreed I would take up this post on the understanding we shared the profits. It was also agreed we would be partners in his next mining venture. Demetri has reneged on his promises, and I am to be merely his factotum. The man is not a gentleman.'

Catriona could see the tightly reined anger in Kane, and wondered how it was she saw the Russian in such a different light.

Kane must have noticed her reluctance to believe him, for he smiled and patted her hand. 'I don't wish to frighten you, my dear,' he said softly. 'Of course I will do all in my power to keep you and your mother here. But Demetri cannot be trusted. He's a liar and a thief and capable of great violence. It would be better if you were never alone with him.'

'He wouldn't hurt me,' she protested. 'He's not like that.'

Kane placed his hand over hers and smiled. 'My dear, let my experience of life and men such as Demetri guide you. He may seem friendly, but believe me, there is another side to him which I hope you never have to see.' He paused for a moment and then seemed to come to a decision. 'Demetri once killed a man,' he said softly, his fingers tightening on her hand. 'It was back in the days when we were in the gold-fields, and he had to leave quickly before the police arrived.'

Catriona stared up at him as he stood and threw the napkin on the table. 'Come my dear. It's time you were in bed, and I have work to do.' He put his arm lightly around her shoulders and brushed his warm lips over her forehead. 'Sleep well,' he murmured as she walked away from him.

Catriona climbed the stairs and listened outside her mother's door. There was no sound, so she carried on down the corridor and went into her room. Sitting on the bed, she brushed out her long dark hair, before plaiting it in preparation for sleep.

Having turned down the covers she pulled the faded cotton night-dress over her head, slipped between the cool linen sheets and turned out the light. Yet, as she lay there in the darkness staring at the moon which hovered outside her window, she found sleep elusive. Her thoughts were jumbled. Demetri had seemed so nice, so friendly and kind, and he'd been generous to a fault. So why did Kane portray him as an ogre? Had he really killed a man? Was he dangerous? The images didn't match up. It seemed to Catriona that Kane was a bitter man, and that bitterness had stemmed from the row she'd overheard earlier. Perhaps she would never know the real reason behind that furious argument, but she was determined to decide for herself whether to trust Demetri or not.

The land surrounding Demetri's palace had been manicured and tidied by an ancient gardener and his two young apprentices. There were shady arbours for the guests to sit in out of the fierce sun, tables and chairs and umbrellas dotted about the terraced lawns, and in one corner there were croquet hoops set out should anyone wish to play. Stone steps led the way down to the river where turtles and fish hid beneath the water lilies and herons tried their luck along with the fishermen. The tennis court and swimming pool were popular, and even at a distance, Catriona could hear the calls and laughter and the clink of glasses as the barman poured drinks at the garden bar.

Catriona had come to explore after having a splendid breakfast in the kitchen. Cook had presented her with a plate of sizzling eggs and bacon and one of the younger maids had sat with her over a cup of tea and regaled her with gossip concerning Edith and her unrequited love for Demetri. They had giggled and chattered and lost track of time until Cook, looking stern, had ordered fifteen-year-old Phoebe to get on with her work. Phoebe had left with a wink, and it looked to Catriona as if she'd made a friend of a similar age for the first time.

Now she peeked through the trees at the men and women who sat on long chairs in the sun, and who seemed to have little to worry them but the depth of their tan and the chill of their chosen tipple. On the driveway the chauffeurs were polishing the elegant cars, giving her a cheery 'G'day' as they gossiped and discussed the day's race meeting.

Catriona wandered around the outside of the house taking it all in. This was a world she never knew existed; a world in which money was spent without thought, clothes worn with the carelessness of people who knew someone else would pick them up, launder them and put them away again. How very different it all was to the life she had known. Poppy would have been in her element here, she thought sadly. How she would have loved the clothes, the jewellery, the flash cars and the mounds of wonderful food. She wished she'd stayed with the troupe – wished that Poppy could have shared this with her.

She returned from her wanderings to the garden behind Demetri's apartments at the back of the hotel. Velda was sitting in a cane chair, an umbrella shielding her from the sun, a drink in a long glass on a table beside her, and a book in her lap. Catriona didn't disturb her, for she appeared to be sleeping.

Despite the hustle and bustle and all the wonderful sights and sounds of the hotel, Catriona preferred the tranquillity of this back garden. It was shielded from the guests by a stand of trees and an ornate wooden fence, the grass sweeping away to become immersed in the lush greenery of the surrounding rainforest. With a broad lawn and formal flower-beds it was a peaceful haven – a place of contemplation and rest where she hoped her mother would find some benefit.

'Good morning, little one. I hope you slept well?'

Remembering Kane's warning of the previous night, she looked up at Demetri warily. 'Yes thank you,' she replied. 'It was lovely having a room to myself for a change.'

He looked down at her and smiled. His dark hair shone almost blue in the sunlight, his brown eyes touched with gold. His dress was less formal than yesterday, she realised, for the suit had been exchanged for baggy trousers that had obviously seen much use, a check shirt and heavy boots. 'I too like to be alone,' he admitted. 'Is good to have place to think – to be oneself.'

'Then why did you build the hotel?' she asked in amazement.

'I have money to spend. It has always been my dream to have such a place.' He grinned, but his eyes were remorseful. 'Sometimes to wish for something is enough. For when it becomes real it is perhaps not as what one imagined.'

He was talking in riddles and she frowned.

'That is why I ask Mr Kane to come,' he explained. 'He has the education, the English voice and manners my guests understand.'

89

He looked down at his boots. 'I am a peasant, a man of little education. I have nothing in common with these people with their fancy cars and clothes and strange ways.'

Catriona grinned up at him. She liked Demetri, and despite Kane's bitter tirade against him, she knew instinctively she would come to no harm with him. They walked together across the lawn and into the rainforest where he named every flower, shrub and climbing vine. He reached into his pocket and pulled out seeds and breadcrumbs and when he whistled the rosellas and parakeets flew down from the trees and fed from his hand.

'Come,' he said finally. 'I will show you where I spend most of my time.'

She followed him willingly back through the bush and into the distant corner of the garden. The shed stood in the shadows of the trees, surrounded by wildflowers and long grass. 'No one comes here any more,' he told her as he fetched the large key from under the rock by the door and turned it in the lock. 'This was the outhouse and laundry once upon a time, and when I make this old house into my palace, there was no need for it any longer.' He opened the door and stood back to let her go in.

Catriona gasped as she stepped inside. It was dark, but not gloomy, and smelled of hot metal and strange potions. Dusty bottles stood on shelves with names inscribed on them that she couldn't pronounce. There was a wood-stove in the far corner beside which sat a large cauldron and several odd-looking spoons that were surely meant for a giant. There were ragged old tents and ancient boots, shovels and spades and picks and wheelbarrows filling every available space. A giant wooden sieve leaned against the wall and an old desk was covered in books and papers and odd bits of wire and metal.

'I keep everything here in case I want to go prospecting again. You Australians call it going walkabout, but I prefer to think of it as time to gather myself up again and be my own man, the true Demetri.' He saw her puzzlement and laughed. 'I like being a rich man, little one, but I am a gypsy at heart, a Russian gypsy, with the open road in my veins.'

Catriona could understand that; after all, she reasoned, she'd spent her entire life, all twelve years of it tramping the tracks. It would indeed seem peculiar to be settled in one place for more than a few days.

90

'What do you do in here?' she asked as she looked around at the strange tools and the cauldron.

'I make things,' he said with a mysterious air. 'Come, I show you.'

He settled her on a rickety chair and hastened over to the wood-stove. Having stoked the fire to a roaring blaze he lifted the great ladle and put something in it. 'Watch now, Catriona. It's magic.'

She came to stand beside him. The gold sizzled in the ladle sending a strange smell into the air. She watched as he carefully poured the liquid into a metal mould. Within moments he had a finely wrought gold ring in the palm of his hand. It was as if Merlin himself stood at her shoulder.

'I make something for you one day,' he promised. 'You would like that?'

'Please.' She knew her eyes were shining and her cheeks were aglow not only from the heat of the fire.

'Then it will be,' he promised. 'Now, you must go, for I hear your mother calling.' He looked down at her with fondness and the hint of a tear in his eye. 'You remind me very much of my darling Irina,' he said sadly.

'Who was Irina?'

'My daughter,' he said as he took a large handkerchief from his pocket and lustily blew his nose. 'But she is dead, like my wife, mother and father and my brothers. The Cossacks come to my village and kill all – all. I was away, hunting for food in the forest. It was winter, deep snow. I return to find death and blood where once there was warmth and love. I never go back.'

Catriona could feel the tears well and blinked them away. She took his large hand and squeezed the fingers. There were no words to say to him that would ease his pain, but she hoped her touch might console him a little.

'Then I come to this great country and find gold,' he said with a watery smile. 'Wealth will never heal the pain of losing Irina and Lara, but it gives me a life I could never hope for in Russia. Here is freedom, the chance to live as I wish.'

Catriona smiled up at him as she heard her mother calling for her. 'I have to go. It's time for my singing practice, and if nothing else, it seems to keep Mam focussed.'

He raised his bushy eyebrows. 'So? It is I think the only thing

91

she cares about; of course you must use my piano. It is in my apartments. Feel free to use it at any time.'

As the weeks carried on into months Catriona settled into her new way of life. She had made firm friends with Phoebe. Yet the little maid worked long hours and as she lived with her parents on the other side of Atherton, they rarely had a chance to do much together but snatch a few moments during the hectic days. Phoebe was also in the throes of first love and every spare minute was spent rushing out into the garden to flirt and giggle with one of the young garden apprentices.

The hotel was full, and apart from the glowering presence of Edith Powell, her new life was beginning to take shape. She had grown to like Demetri more and more. He was the father she'd lost, the grandfather she'd never had, and she realised they found in one another a bond that filled the aching void in their hearts. He might have been an uneducated Russian émigré, but he was a true friend, who never seemed to mind how many hours he spent with her. He taught her the names of the trees and the birds, showed her the secret places where the wombats slept with their young, took her deep into the forest where they would sit and watch the wallabies and their joeys feed. But the most exciting thing of all was when he turned the nuggets of gold into a fiery liquid, and then fashioned it into exquisite jewellery.

Demetri had also taken Velda under his protective wing. Each morning he would sit with her in the garden and talk to her, his deep voice a rumble in the warm stillness. Yet, despite his care, Velda had grown even thinner during the past months. She kept away from Edith and the patrons of the hotel and moved around the garden and Demetri's apartments like a wraith, her face as pale as paper. At night Catriona would hear her sobbing herself to sleep and it broke her heart. She longed to comfort her and be comforted – longed for Velda to notice that she too was hurting. But apart from the morning singing lessons, Velda's days were spent in an almost dream-like state, her nights in tears – she didn't appear to have the energy or time to notice her daughter needed more than singing lessons to help her through her loss.

Catriona's relationship with Kane had changed. It was a subtle change, one that had happened so slowly over the months she'd hardly noticed it. Where once she'd accepted his embraces, his innocent kisses on her brow, his hand on her arm or at her waist, she realised she was uncomfortable with his touch and uneasy with his over-familiarity. And yet he seemed to offer sympathy and support where her mother had failed, and had offered solace and quiet friendship as he had always done. Perhaps it was the changes within herself that made her uneasy with him, for he had done nothing specific to warrant this sense of something not being quite right.

It was a few weeks before her thirteenth birthday and Velda had, as usual, gone to bed early, leaving her alone with Kane in Demetri's drawing room. Catriona was bored with the book she'd been reading, and had set it aside to go and stand at the window. She loved looking out into the garden, for the fireflies danced in the bushes like tiny fairies.

'Come and sit with me and tell me about your day,' Kane drawled. He reached out his hand.

Catriona turned from the window with reluctance.

'What's the matter?' He grinned. 'Surely you don't begrudge me a few minutes of your day? I remember a time when you were always running to me with tales of what you'd been up to.'

She remembered those times out on the tracks, when she'd sought out his company. Remembered how good he'd been to her and Mam during those awful days after Da's death. It made her feel foolish standing there and she took the proffered hand.

He grasped it and before she realised what was happening, he had pulled her on to his lap.

'I'm too big to sit on your knee,' she protested, her face hot with embarrassment.

'Nonsense,' he said as he drew her closer. 'You're only a little thing. Weigh less than a sparrow despite all the food you've been putting away.' His fingers roamed up her arm to the capped sleeve of her dress. 'So, what have you been up to all day?'

'This and that,' she muttered. She tried not to move, but she was hot and uncomfortable in his embrace. She wasn't a little girl any more, she would be thirteen in a matter of weeks, and she knew instinctively that it wasn't seemly to be in such a position. She could smell the cigar smoke on his breath mingled with the port he'd been drinking, and could feel the rapid drum of his pulse against her bare arm. She didn't know what to do or say, how to express the tide of emotions that swept through her.

93

'Flirting with the gardener's boy with Phoebe, I suspect,' he said softly as he nuzzled her ear. 'You want to be careful, or you'll get a bad reputation.' His fingers brushed against the buds of her breasts and traced a line at her throat.

'I've got to go,' she said all in a rush as she tried to pull away from him. 'Mam will wonder where I am.'

'Give us a kiss goodnight then,' he murmured, his grip relentless on her waist.

Catriona hesitated. If she did as he asked he would let her go, perhaps a peck on the cheek would satisfy him.

He swiftly turned his head and returned her kiss, his lips crushing hers, his fingers tight on the back of her neck as his other hand swept beneath the hem of her dress to her underwear.

She shoved away from him and stood up. Her legs were trembling and she was finding it hard to breathe. She wiped her mouth on the back of her hand. 'You shouldn't have done that,' she spluttered.

His blue eyes widened. 'What's this?' he said with a snort of laughter. 'I thought we were friends?'

She shook her head. She didn't have the words to explain her feelings; was confused and frightened and suddenly terribly shy in the light of his easy dismissal of her protest. And yet something told her his actions tonight were a precursor of something more unpleasant and that he was enjoying her discomfort. She hurried from the room to the sound of him chuckling over his port and went in search of her mother. She would understand her predicament and would know what to do.

Velda was in bed, the light casting a warm glow over the frosty white sheets that covered her thin frame. 'Go to bed, Kitty. I'm tired,' she murmured with a sigh.

'Mam,' she began, the tears making her voice rough. 'Mam, there's something I need to talk to you about.'

Velda sighed and sat up, pulling the sheet to her chin, barely disguising the sharp bones of her chest. 'What is it now, Catriona?'

'It's Mr Kane,' she replied, determined to have her say. 'I don't like him.'

'Why ever not?' Velda's violet eyes widened.

Catriona searched for the right way to express her feelings, but she was so confused and unsure of exactly what to say it came out all wrong. 'He treats me like a little girl,' she said finally.

94

'Is that all?' Velda's words were impatient. 'Perhaps that's because you are,' she said flatly. 'Go to bed, Catriona. It's too late for tantrums.'

'I'm not a kid,' she retorted. 'And I don't like it when he ...'

'Go to bed, Catriona,' her mother repeated. 'Kane's a good man. He loves you like a daughter and would be horrified to think you didn't like him after all he's done for us.'

'He's not my father,' Catriona snapped. 'And I don't care if he knows I don't like him. He's, he's ...' She faltered beneath the cold glare of those violet eyes.

Velda sighed and slid back down the pillows. 'For goodness sake, Catriona, it's late and I promised Demetri I'd join him early in the morning for a walk. Stop being dramatic and calm down. No doubt it's your hormones playing up – you're of an age for things to have started, but we'll talk about all that tomorrow.'

'But ...'

Velda cut her off. 'Goodnight,' she said firmly.

Catriona hovered.

Velda sighed. 'You want to thank your lucky stars you have a roof over your head and a comfortable bed to sleep in. Perhaps you should remember who made all that possible.'

'Demetri made it possible,' Catriona snapped. 'It's his hotel, not Mr Kane's.'

Velda turned over on to her side and switched off the light, leaving Catriona standing in the doorway mute with misery and frustration.

Chapter Seven

Christmas had come and gone and now they were into the new year of 1934. Edith Powell stood at the window and watched Demetri take the Irish gypsy's arm as they crossed the lawn and went into the rainforest. The anger and frustration were mixed with despair, for her long-held dreams of having Demetri to herself were shattered. He barely had the time to talk to her any more; it was as if she'd become a part of the fabric of this hotel – invisible.

She clenched her fists as he opened the umbrella to shield the woman from the sun, and her mouth curved in a sneer. That Irish bitch had snared him from right under her nose. She'd come here, all doe-eyed and mournful, her precocious brat in tow, and Demetri, soft-hearted and kind to a fault, had fallen for it. It wasn't fair. None of it was fair. Life had treated her cruelly and she knew she'd become bitter and ugly because of it.

She dipped her head and sighed, no longer able to watch them. Her fiancé had been killed in the Great War and she'd nursed her parents to the end of their lives. With so many of the young men of her generation killed on the battlefields of Europe she had become a spinster, to be derided and talked about and, worst of all, pitied. The opportunity to work for Demetri had come as a thrilling proposition. He was single, handsome and rich, and as his new building rose on the hillside, she had looked after him, making sure he ate properly and that his clothes were always clean and neat. She had been easily persuaded to take on the enormous task of overseeing the running of his hotel, because she loved him and thought that by easing his workload, he would see her as a woman rather than a housekeeper and realise how good they would be together.

Yet, kind as he was, she knew she meant little to him, and the thought of her lonely little cottage on the outskirts of Atherton made her depressed. Where once it had been a haven, it was now the place where she spent each night plagued by dreams of Demetri. Did he sleep with the gypsy? Did he run his fingers through that long dark hair and kiss her face? Oh, how she longed for his touch, for the sound of his voice soft in her ear, his hands upon her body, bringing the life and warmth she could only imagine to her parched soul.

'How very touching. I'm sure Demetri is delighted you take such careful interest in his affairs.'

Edith whirled round, her face flushed with embarrassment. 'I came in here to change the flowers,' she said, aware that her voice was too high, the words garbled.

His fair eyebrow lifted and his blue eyes were mocking. 'I'm sure you did,' he said dismissively. 'But rather than snooping, you would be better occupied with the details for Catriona's birthday party.'

Edith gritted her teeth. She despised Kane. His very Englishness grated on her and made her yearn to lash out and claw his supercilious face. But years of reining in her emotions wouldn't allow her to do that and she clasped her hands tightly at her waist. 'There will be tea and an iced cake in here on the afternoon,' she said stiffly.

'I think not,' he drawled. 'Her mother and Demetri are planning something on a far grander scale. I have already organised a dance band, and there will be a formal dinner with champagne to toast the occasion.'

'She's only a child,' Edith gasped. 'Far too young for that sort of extravagance.'

'Demetri has ordered it.' Kane towered over her, his tone giving her no choice but to acquiesce. 'Please make sure Cook is prepared and the stores ordered. The hotel will be full that night and I want nothing left to chance.'

Edith was quivering with rage. 'You mean that gypsy brat is having her party out there amongst the guests?' she hissed. 'I suppose her tart of a mother thinks she can lord it over me as well, making me run around after her doing all the work?' She was finding it hard to breathe. 'I won't have it,' she snapped finally.

He looked down at her, the scorn clear in his expression. 'I'd be careful, Edith. One of these days your jealous tongue will get you into trouble. You of all people should remember you are only a servant here. You will obey orders or get out.'

Edith bit her lip. She knew she'd gone too far, but his threat to sack her had come as a terrible blow. She glared up at him and, without another word, left the room.

Velda let Demetri settle her into the garden chair. It was pleasant out here in the fresh air away from the noise of the hotel and Demetri was very kind, but she wanted to be alone.

'Are all the arrangements for Catriona's party in progress?' he asked, the rolling consonants and lilt of his accent deeply tuneful in the still air.

'I suppose so,' she replied as she stared out over the lawn. 'I've done the dress, the rest is up to Edith and Mr Kane.'

'I will leave you,' he said, sketching a bow. 'I have things to do now. Will you be all right here on your own?'

She nodded, her thoughts distant, his presence almost immediately forgotten. A great weariness settled upon her and she closed her eyes. It was as if the world had tilted somehow and she'd been left suspended somewhere above it, out of reach of reality, lost in a haze of sorrow and confusion. The days dragged one into another until they blurred into nothing. She wanted Declan, needed him, yearned for his familiar touch and soothing voice. How she missed him.

The tears seeped between her lids and rolled unheeded down her face. Demetri, for all his kindness, was not Declan. This preposterous hotel was a million miles from the painted wagon and the life they had led together. If only she had the money to return to Ireland, to home and family and the soft rain on the gentle hills. Yet she was trapped – at the mercy of Demetri's charity.

She blinked and dabbed at the tears with a handkerchief. If only she didn't feel so exhausted all the time; it made her unable to think, to put things into perspective and take charge of her life again. Apart from the few hours she spent coaching Catriona, she felt as if she was drifting on a great tide, with no anchor and no port of call. Perhaps it had something to do with the drink Mr Kane gave her every evening before she went to bed? She shook her head. That was absurd. Mr Kane had told her it would help her sleep, but he'd assured her it would do no harm.

Leaning back in the chair she gazed unseeing over the garden. Christmas had passed in a haze of lights and noise and endless parties in the ballroom. Not that she'd attended such things, she couldn't face them. Now it was January and Catriona would soon be thirteen. She gave a great sigh. She didn't understand her daughter any more. It was as if a great chasm had opened up between them, with no point of reference, no understanding or even a hint of the closeness they had once shared. She'd turned surly and rude and bad-tempered, and at the first hint of criticism would slam doors and behave in the most appalling manner. Catriona might be almost thirteen, but since coming here to the hotel she'd been behaving like a petulant five-year-old, and if only Velda had the strength and energy, she would have given her daughter a smacked behind.

Velda closed her eyes, but deep in the back of her confused and weary thoughts she wondered if perhaps she was to blame for her daughter's behaviour. She had tried to share her grief, but had found it impossible. Had tried to offer what solace she could, but had found her energy depleted by her own tears. How could a child understand what she was going through? Catriona was resilient, as all children were. She'd grow out of it, and it wasn't as if she was alone. She had Demetri and Mr Kane to look after her. She sighed as the weariness fogged her mind. It was all too much to think about.

It was the eve of her birthday, and despite Kane's increasing over-familiarity, and his almost blatant attempts to catch her alone so he could kiss and fondle her, Catriona was excited at the thought of her party. She had been in the kitchen to watch Cook ice her cake and put the finishing touches to the trays of canapés that would be handed out with the drinks before dinner. There were meats to be roasted and vegetables to prepare and the kitchen was a bustle of industry.

Catriona had asked if Phoebe could join in the celebrations, but had met with refusal at every turn. Phoebe was a maid, she would be working that night. Catriona hated the thought of Phoebe missing out, and couldn't understand why there had to be a distinction between them. It wasn't fair. Yet her spirits didn't remain low for long, and after supper that night, she hurried down to Demetri's shed. He'd promised her a surprise, and she was longing to find out what it was.

'For you,' he said as he held out a velvet box. 'I hope you like.'

99

Catriona pressed the tiny catch and the lid flew open to reveal a necklace. The chain was finely wrought, and the golden circles that made up the pendant winked in the light of the lamp he'd lit on his desk. 'It's beautiful,' she breathed.

He lifted it from the box and let it dangle before her. 'I make it,' he said proudly as he showed her the interwoven rings of gold. 'These are the circles of life, each band a different colour and type of gold. They represent our different worlds and the way our lives have come together as we travel on our separate journeys. I make one for me also,' he said with a smile. 'To remind me of the little one who is my friend.'

She held up her hair so he could fasten it around her neck, and her fingers caressed the warm, glowing gold that rested over her heart. Throwing her arms around Demetri's broad waist she gave him a hug. 'It's a beautiful present,' she said against the barrel of his chest. 'I will treasure it always.'

He gently released her grip and held her away from him. 'If I ever have another daughter,' he said softly. 'I would hope she is like you.' He smiled and patted her shoulder with a sudden awkwardness. 'It is time for you to be in your bed, Kitty. You have a birthday tomorrow.'

Catriona smiled up at him. 'My first grown-up party,' she breathed. 'Mam says I can have my hair up especially, and there'll be dancing and everything.'

He tipped back his leonine head and roared with laughter. 'So young, and in such a hurry to grow up,' he spluttered finally. 'Kitty, Kitty,' he said as he shook his head. 'I hope you have a wonderful birthday.'

There was something in his tone that made her study him more closely. 'You are coming to my party, aren't you?' she demanded. 'You promised.'

'I know,' he sighed, his hands deep in his voluminous pockets. 'But I am not at ease in the company of such people. It is better, I think, that I stay here.'

'You promised,' she said stubbornly, her arms folded, the tears already threatening to spill. 'It's your hotel, you can do what you like.'

'I like to stay here in my shed,' he said firmly. 'These people who stay in my hotel will not be easy with my rough ways. The party will be a success without me getting in the way, and you can come and tell me all about it afterwards.'

The disappointment was sharp, but even as she protested, she had come to understand that unlike Kane, he didn't enjoy the company of strangers. She fell silent, her thoughts churning. Demetri was her friend and there were things she wanted to say to him – secret things involving Kane that had been troubling her for some time. Yet, even as she opened her mouth to speak, she knew she didn't have the courage to confide in him, to trust he would believe her. For if she did tell him, the consequences could destroy them all.

'I'd really like you to come,' she said softly, the pleading clear in her eyes, the underlying message pounding in her head so loudly she was certain he must hear it.

'No more,' he protested gently. 'Go to the house. I will see you tomorrow.'

Catriona stepped reluctantly out into the warm, sultry darkness. There were fireflies in the shrubs, and the saw of crickets came from the grass. The surrounding rainforest was dark and mysterious, and she could see the moon and the stars above the clearing. It was a magical night, but she was hardly touched by it as she looked down the broad expanse of lawn to the house. The lights were on in every window and she could hear the piano music drifting into the garden as the guests drank their cocktails in the bar and played cards in the sitting-room. She could imagine how it would be with no lights and no music, the empty rooms echoing in the silence. She shivered as if touched by icy fingers.

She turned to wave to Demetri as he stood in the doorway of his workshop. The light was behind him, streaming from the bare bulb above his bench, throwing his face into shadows, reducing him to a solid silhouette. Something made her run back to him and plant a kiss on his stubbled cheek before she turned away and headed for the house. But the moment for confidences was over – she was on her own.

'There you are,' said Kane as she entered the side door into the entrance hall. 'Where have you been? It's past your bedtime.'

'Out,' she muttered, sidling past him as she headed for the staircase.

His hand was firm on her bare arm as he stayed her escape. 'You've been with Demetri again, haven't you?' he hissed. 'What have you been up to down there in that shed of his?'

She pulled away from him, rubbing her arm where the marks of his fingers still showed on her skin. 'None of your business,' she retorted.

'It is my business,' he said softly as he glanced at the drawing-room door. 'And I don't need to remind you that your mother and I have expressly forbidden you to spend so much time with him.'

'Mam's barely spoken to me for months,' she countered. 'And probably doesn't care where the hell I am as long as it's not in her way. It's only you who makes the bloody rules around here – and we know why that is, don't we?'

'Mind your mouth,' he snapped. 'I won't have you talk to me like that.'

She began to edge away, her bravado suddenly deserting her. 'I'll talk to you in any way I please,' she muttered. 'You're not my father.'

'I'm the nearest thing you've got, and you'll do as I tell you,' he said crossly as he took a step towards her.

She stepped back; the stairs were behind her. 'Where's Mam?' she demanded.

His eyes were very blue, his face cold, expression inscrutable. 'She doesn't want to be disturbed,' he said. 'She's not at all well and the last thing she needs is you upsetting her.' He took another step towards her, his face set, eyes hard and determined. 'Velda is very sick, Catriona, her mind is fragile and the slightest upset could tip her over the edge.'

Catriona looked up at him, unwilling to believe him, yet knowing he was probably right. Mam had changed in the last few months, and the difference in her was frightening. She was about to reply when a group of guests clattered into the hall and demanded Mr Kane's attention. With a sigh of relief, Catriona raced up the stairs. He would be busy for hours yet, and regardless of how bad her mother was feeling, she needed to talk to her.

The topmost landing was silent, the doors closed with no lights showing beneath them. Catriona tiptoed along to her mother's room and listened at the door. There was no sound on the other side, so she carefully turned the handle and peeked in.

Velda was lying in the bed staring at the ceiling, the glow of the moon falling across her weary face and illuminating her eyes. 'What do you want, Catriona?' Her voice was sharp with the edge of impatience as she pulled the covers more firnly over her shoulders. 'I told Mr Kane I didn't want to be disturbed.'

Catriona shut the door behind her and approached the bed. 'I just came in to say goodnight,' she began.

'So? Now you've said it, you can go.'

'Why are you being like this, Mam? What have I done wrong?' Catriona stood beside the bed, the tears once more filling her eyes, yet she was determined not to let them fall, determined to remain calm in the face of her mother's hostility.

Velda sighed and reached for the tumbler on the table beside the bed. Having taken a sip she replaced it and leaned against the pillows. 'You've barely spoken to me for weeks,' she said finally, her voice low, the petulant whine now all too familiar. 'And when you do, you're insolent and thoroughly unpleasant. Mr Kane and I are at our wits' end to know what to do with you.'

'Mr Kane should mind his own bloody business,' snapped Catriona.

'That's exactly the sort of thing I'm talking about,' sighed Velda. 'How dare you use such language? Mr Kane is right. You should be kept apart from that Russian, if this is the sort of behaviour he encourages.'

'This has nothing to do with Demetri,' stormed Catriona. 'Mr Kane is just poisoning you against him. Can't you see that?'

Velda's eyes were fogged with weariness, her expression without emotion as she regarded Catriona. 'I see a wilful child who has turned into a morose, bad-tempered, foul-mouthed young girl, and if the plans for your party weren't already in place, I would cancel the whole thing. Go to your room, Catriona.'

The tears were streaming down her face, the words coming out in a sob. 'I don't want to,' she sobbed. 'I don't like it in there.'

'Don't be ridiculous,' snapped Velda. 'It's a lovely room, you ungrateful girl.'

Catriona thought of the nights Kane had come into her room and sat on her bed. Of the long, silent minutes that seemed to stretch into hours as he regarded her in silence before forcing her to kiss him on the mouth. 'Can't I stay with you tonight, Mam? Like when we were in the wagon? We could snuggle up and talk about the old times, and . . .' She was pleading now, desperate for her mother to see beyond the words and the tears to the heart of her unhappiness.

Velda remained untouched by this show of emotion. She slid back down the bed beneath the covers. 'You're far too old to be

103

sharing my bed,' she said. 'And I need my sleep. It's a busy day tomorrow as you very well know.'

'Please, Mam,' Catriona reached out a hand but it was ignored. She perched on the edge of the bed, making the mattress dip. Smearing back the tears from her face she made a concerted effort to remain calm. The time had come to tell her mother everything. 'I'm sorry, Mam,' she murmured. 'I don't mean to be rude and disobedient, really I don't. But there's things I . . .'

'Enough, Catriona,' snapped Velda, pushing her away. 'You've apologised before and there's been precious little change in your attitude. If your father was here he'd be breaking his heart.'

'If my father was here he'd bloody well listen to me,' yelled Catriona as she stood up.

'Get out.' Velda pointed at the door. 'And don't come back until you mend your ways. You're not too big for a slap, my girl. Goodness knows you've been deserving one for months.'

Catriona clenched her jaw as she strode back to the door and reached for the handle. 'You're a selfish bitch,' she spat. 'You've done bloody nothing but whinge and whine and carry on as if you're the only one in mourning. You don't care about me – just your bloody self.' She took a breath, shocked at her own venom and the rough vocabulary that had come so easily to her tongue, but at least it had got a reaction from her mother for once. She turned the handle and stood in the doorway, her face suffused with rage as she noted her stunned expression. 'Well, I hurt too. I'm lonely and scared and one of these days you'll be sorry you didn't listen to me.' She slammed the door as hard as she could and ran down the hall to her room and slammed that door too. Flinging herself onto the bed she buried her face in the pillow and gave in to a storm of tears.

The next morning she awoke with a pounding headache and eyelids so puffed from tears she could barely see through them. Not wanting to traipse down the hall to the bathroom, she poured cold water from the jug into the bowl and washed, scrubbing herself clean with a flannel until her skin was red and tingling. Kane's visits to her room, and the touch of his hands always made her feel dirty.

As she dressed, she caught sight of herself in the small mirror, and she stared at her reflection noting how deeply all this was affecting her. It was there in her eyes, in the droop of her mouth and the pallor of her skin, but the damage was deeper than that, she acknowledged. It had touched her soul, darkening it into something that was slowly dying inside her. 'How can Mam not see?' she breathed. She stared at her reflection, but the answering silence was profound. She turned away and ran out of the room.

'As there is a great deal to be done today, you can help by being useful for a change,' said Edith as Catriona wandered into the kitchen.

'Can't I unwrap just one present?' she asked, seeing the pile on the dresser.

'Tonight,' said Edith sternly, her tone brooking any argument. 'Help the maids clear the dining room.'

Catriona wanted to go and see Demetri, but Edith seemed determined to keep her busy, and she spent the rest of the day at her beck and call, clearing rooms, helping with the food and the flowers and laying the tables.

It was to be a grand affair, celebrating not only her birthday, but the end of the hotel's first, and very successful season. The gardeners had brought in vines and flowers which had been interwoven with ribbon and laced all the way up through the spindles of the oak banisters. More greenery decorated the great marble fireplace in the hall, and long pale candles were set firmly in amongst the leaves. The dining room was to be lit by hundreds of candles, each table dressed in the finest linen, the silver cutlery and crystal glasses polished to perfection. Flowers were arranged on each table, and in great bouquets around the downstairs rooms. The scent of them filled the house and made Catriona's head throb – all she really wanted to do was go into the garden to get some fresh air and see Demetri.

Yet Edith still found jobs for her, and as the day wore on Catriona realised Demetri was keeping away from the chaos. Kane had also disappeared and that was strange, for usually he would have been barking orders and getting in everyone's way. Velda was nowhere to be found. She wasn't in her room or in Demetri's apartments. It was a puzzle, but then Mam's behaviour lately had been odd to say the least, and perhaps she had only gone into Cairns to have her hair done.

A three-piece band set up their instruments in the corner of the drawing room and the carpet was pulled back and the floor polished and chalked ready for the dancing. In the kitchens there was the delicious smell of baking bread and roasting meat. Fresh vegetables were being prepared and sauces mixed by the fat cook who came up each day from the nearby town. Then of course there was the cake – a magnificent tower of white icing and sugared flowers, topped off with even more candles.

Taking advantage of the lull at tea-time, Catriona decided she had to confide in Demetri before Kane took things further. He was her only real friend, and maybe when he'd heard what she had to say he would do something to help. She'd been stupid not to trust him.

She came out of the kitchen and noticed how dark it had become. The rain had been falling all day and the sky was thick with black clouds. She grabbed a raincoat from a peg by the front door and was just pulling it on when a voice stopped her.

'Where do you think you're going?'

Catriona froze as Kane emerged from the shadows of the deep chair he'd been sitting in by the ornate hall fireplace. 'I'm going to see Demetri.' Her voice sounded breathless and high.

'I don't think so,' he replied, cupping her elbow with his hand.

She yanked her arm from his clutches. 'You can't stop me,' she hissed.

'What's so important you see him now?' he asked, unfazed by her fury.

'I'm going to tell him what you're doing to me,' she retorted. 'I've already told Mam.'

His fair brows lifted and his eyes glinted in the light from the crystal chandelier. 'And what did Velda have to say?' His voice was smooth and mocking and sent a chill through her.

She shook her head, unwilling to tell him her mother had taken no notice – had barely listened on the occasions she'd tried to broach the subject.

'So,' he said softly. 'Your mother doesn't believe you. And what is there to tell Demetri? Eh?' He lifted her chin with his fingers, forcing her to look him in the eyes. 'That the man who has looked after you and your family for over a year has dared to kiss his daughter? That I take the time and trouble to tuck you in bed at night?'

'I'm not your daughter, and no Da kisses their daughter like that – or touches her like you do.' Her voice rose as his fingers tight-ened on her chin.

'Shut up and listen, Catriona.' His voice was like a gunshot and

106

she obeyed instantly, the fear stilling her tongue. 'Your mother is a sick woman. On the edge of reason. I am her saviour and you are just a little girl. She won't believe you today, tomorrow or ever.' He fell silent, allowing his words to drip remorselessly into her mind. 'As for Demetri. He's a murderer. If you go running to him with your lies you will have blood on your hands.'

'I don't believe you,' she muttered. 'You're making this up.'

He ignored her interruption. 'He's a dangerous man, Catriona. He has killed once already – he will have no compunction about doing it again.'

She stared back at him through her tears, as transfixed as a rabbit in the stare of a snake.

'Your mother is in danger of losing her mind. What would it do to her if your lies killed me and put Demetri in gaol? You would end up with no home, no one to look after you. With Demetri in prison waiting for the hangman, the hotel would be closed up and you would be sent packing and your mother would spend her last days in an asylum for the mentally disturbed.'

She saw the iron will in his eyes, the firmness in the set of his mouth and felt the tight grasp of his fingers on her jawbone. She was a prisoner, with nowhere to go, nowhere to hide and with no one to help her. 'They aren't lies,' she whispered. 'I know what you're up to.'

'Innocent kisses and caresses.' He released her and stood back. 'A fatherly interest in your welfare. Hardly worth a mention, let alone these histrionics.' He folded his arms and looked down at her. 'You have a vivid imagination, but then I suppose that can't be helped considering the life you've led. Now go and find something to do to help Edith, and we'll hear no more of it.'

Catriona eased away from him and flew up the stairs. She knew what she knew. Kane had kissed her and touched her, had come into her room at night and made it obvious he was planning to take things further. These were not signs of fatherly affection, but something darker, more unpleasant and deeply disturbing.

She raced into the bathroom and shot the bolt, then fell sobbing onto the tiled floor. If only her mother had listened to her. If only she could see what was happening. But Kane was right, Mam was seriously troubled – and she didn't want to be the cause of any more anguish for her. She would have to find Demetri. He was her only chance.

She finally dragged a brush through her hair and splashed cold water on her face before returning to the warmth and friendliness of the kitchen. There was still no sign of Mam, and she felt safer with Cook than on her own and Kane rarely came in here.

At six o'clock her mother sent a message downstairs. It was time for her to get ready. She opened the door to her room and found Velda waiting for her. There was the new dress laid out on the bed, with shoes and stockings and delicate underwear to go with it.

'Get dressed and I'll do your hair before you go down,' she said as she wandered out of the room.

Catriona looked at the finery laid out on her bed. She touched the silky underwear and the laced petticoat, and admired the gown Velda had spent so many hours sewing. It was the loveliest pale green satin, with delicate straps, a tight bodice, and a froth of matching net for the skirt.

She stepped into it, feeling its coolness on her skin as she fastened the tiny buttons at her side. The skirts rustled as she walked up and down the room in the satin pumps Velda had dyed to match the dress. Despite the heartache, a thrill of excitement ran through her as she danced around the narrow room. Her mother did care after all, for why else would she have gone to all this trouble.

She went swiftly to Velda's room and tapped on the door. Her mother was sitting on the bed, as pale and as languid as the lilies in the vases downstairs. 'It's a lovely dress, Mam. Thank you,' she murmured.

Velda gave no sign she'd heard her and began to sort through her bag of brushes and make-up. When she'd finished, Catriona looked in amazement at her reflection. The dark, lustrous hair had been twisted into an elegant chignon, and decorated with a single white camellia. Velda had touched her lips with lipstick and added a delicate dusting of powder to her face. Mascara darkened her lashes, and a hint of rouge enhanced the shape of her cheek-bones.

'If you were older,' said Velda studying her thoughtfully. 'I would have lent you my necklace and earrings. But I see you have a pendant already. Where did it come from?'

'It was a present from Demetri,' she replied. Catriona kissed her cheek, careful not to smudge her mother's make-up. 'Thanks for everything, Mam,' she said softly.

Velda ran her hands down her slender hips. The dark red satin enhanced her pale skin and dark hair to perfection, but she was too thin and the shadows were like bruises beneath her lovely eyes. 'You don't deserve it,' she said gruffly. 'But you're only thirteen once, so I could hardly ignore such an important milestone.'

Catriona watched as she finished the drink in the tumbler that always seemed to be beside her mother's bed, picked up a glittering shawl and pulled it around her shoulders. Velda had never before mingled with the guests and Catriona could see it was taking a great effort for her to pluck up the energy to do so tonight.

Velda hesitated in the doorway. 'Catriona, there's something . . .'

'Come on birthday girl.' The shout had come from below. 'The champagne's getting warm.'

'What is it, Mam?' There was something even stranger about her mother this evening, but Catriona put it down to nerves.

Velda shook her head and took a deep breath. 'It doesn't matter,' she muttered. 'Come on, we'd better go down.'

Catriona felt the nervous flutter in her stomach as she reached the final landing. It was such a special night, surely nothing bad would happen to spoil it?

The hall was crowded with guests, some strangers, some familiar, the staff lined up along the wall, outside the door to the kitchens. As she began the long descent, their animated conversation stopped and they turned to watch her. She slowly made her way down the stairs, the skirts rustling around her ankles, the tight bodice making it difficult to breathe. It was stage fright all over again – only it seemed as if it had been years since she'd made such a dramatic entrance.

The waiting guests began to applaud and the staff shouted out 'Happy Birthday'. She laughed and clapped her hands in delight as she sketched a curtsy. Then her spirits sank and all the joy of the occasion was swept away in the realisation that Mr Kane was waiting for her at the bottom of the stairs. He was looking up at her, a strange and all-too-familiar gleam in his eyes as he reached out to help her and her mother down the last step.

'Happy birthday,' he murmured in her ear.

Catriona saw her mother tuck her hand in the crook of his arm and was forced to follow her lead as he escorted them both into the drawing room for pre-dinner drinks and tiny canapés. Phoebe gave her a wink as she carried the vast silver tray around the room and

Catriona searched among the faces for Demetri. He was late – surely he hadn't meant it when he said he wouldn't be coming?

The party moved into the dining room. The food was probably delicious, but squeezed as she was between her mother and Mr Kane, she barely tasted it, for she was aware of the pressure of his thigh and the seemingly innocent brush of his arm against her breast as he reached for his glass.

Velda appeared more animated than she had for months and actually allowed her to have a little watered-down wine to go with the dessert. Then it was time to cut the cake and open her presents. She tore the wrapping off and untied ribbons and expressed her genuine delight in the strings of beads, the shawls and gloves and books the guests and staff had given her. She had never had so many presents in her life, and if it hadn't been for Kane watching her every move, this would have been the most wonderful birthday ever.

The orchestra started to play as they entered the drawing room. The carpet had been rolled back, the chairs placed around the room. She stiffened as Mr Kane encircled her waist and led her on to the floor to begin the first waltz. Her feet refused to obey her and she stumbled against him. She could feel the heat of his hands and the pressure of his fingers on the small of her back as he held her tightly. His cologne was strong and she could smell his freshly laundered shirt and the carnation in his button-hole.

'You look very grown-up,' he murmured as the music and the chatter swirled around them, cutting them off as surely as an island by the tide. 'But I prefer you without all that powder and paint – makes you look like a tart.'

Stung by his insult she tried to escape his tight embrace, but he smiled and whirled her around the floor, completely in charge, and determined to remain so.

When the music stopped she managed to escape, but was immediately swept away in a fast foxtrot by one of the younger guests, and if it hadn't been for Kane's ominous presence, she might have actually begun to enjoy herself.

The night was spent avoiding him. She caught glimpses of him dancing with the single ladies and with her mother, but she knew he was watching her every move – knew he was waiting to snare her into another dance so he could press her tightly to him. He seemed to get some kind of perverse pleasure out of it – knowing she couldn't

110

escape, couldn't make a fuss in front of all these people.

As the night wore on, and he returned again and again to dance with her, she decided it was time to tell Velda what had been going on. But this time she would make her listen, force her if she had to – surely even in the depths of whatever illness ailed her, she would take notice and do something to protect her?

She swiftly looked around and saw Velda sitting with another woman at the far end of the room. Kane was dancing with an animated brunette, so he was occupied for now. Catriona shook her head as someone asked her to dance and began to weave her way through the others. 'Mam,' she said.

'I'm talking, Catriona. Don't interrupt.'

'Mam,' she said more firmly. 'It's important. Very important.'

Velda made her excuses to the other woman and stood. 'It had better be,' she said grimly. 'That was very rude.'

Catriona grabbed her mother's hand and began to pull her, protesting, towards the door. 'Mam, it's about K ...' She got no further, for there he was, at her side, his eyes arctic.

'There you are, Velda,' he said smoothly, capturing her hand. 'I think it's time, don't you?'

Velda looked up at him, her eyes dull, her expression confused. 'Catriona was just about to ...'

'I'm sure Catriona can wait just one more minute. This is important.' He glanced at Catriona, his eyes bright with some kind of malicious humour she didn't understand. 'Come, my dear.'

Catriona watched him tuck Velda's hand into the crook of his arm and lead her into the centre of the dance-floor. With a nod to the bandmaster, the music stopped and the dancers slowly came to a halt. The waitresses came in with trays of glasses filled with what looked suspiciously like champagne. A hush fell over the drawing room and Catriona realised Kane was probably going to make a speech about the successful season. It would be an excellent time to make her escape and go and see Demetri.

'I have an announcement to make,' boomed Kane in his best stage-voice.

Catriona began to edge towards the door.

'Not only are we celebrating a very successful year at the Petersburg, and the thirteenth birthday of the delightful Catriona.' There was a ripple of applause and Catriona blushed as all eyes turned her way. 'But also the happy news that this wonderful lady, Velda

111

Summers, has agreed to become my wife.'

Catriona froze. Kane looked across the room, his gaze alight with victory as he raised his glass. The shouts of congratulations galvanised her into action and regardless of the curious stares, she raced out of the room and into the hallway. She didn't stop until she had reached the garden.

It was a sultry night. The soft, drenching rains had started earlier in the day, which had enhanced the heat and humidity and soaked the lawn. Kicking off her shoes, she lifted her skirts and ran across the lawn to the shelter of the overhanging roof of the workshop. She could barely see for her tears, could hardly catch her breath as the sheer horror of what she'd heard began to really sink in.

Demetri's shed was in darkness, and there was no reply when she rapped heavily on the door. She looked over her shoulder. The doors to the drawing room were open, the lights and the sound of the party spilling into the darkness as the rain grew heavier and more determined. There was no sign she had been followed or that Kane had come looking for her.

She sheltered under the overhanging roof and knocked again, louder this time. 'Demetri?' she called. 'Are you in there? Demetri? Please. I need you.'

There was no reply. No answering light or movement from behind the door. Catriona turned the handle, found it was unlocked, and stepped inside. Perhaps he'd fallen asleep, he was always working in here through the night and often used to bed down on the sacks in the corner.

But as she lit the lamp she looked around in shock. The shed had been stripped of the mining tools and the old clothes and tents. The desk was bare, the cauldron gone along with the ladles and boxes of nuggets. It was as if Demetri had simply vanished.

'He left late last night,' said the voice at her shoulder.

Catriona whirled to face him, pulse jumping, the breath caught in her throat. 'He couldn't have done,' she protested. 'He would have told me.'

Kane smiled as he stepped into the shelter of the hut and selected a cigar from the leather case he always carried in his top pocket. 'He told me to tell you he was sorry, but he couldn't stay any longer.'

'But why?' it was a wail of despair.

'His dream didn't turn out the way he thought it would,' said

112

Kane as he put a match to his cigar. Having lit it satisfactorily, he held it between his teeth at the corner of his mouth. 'Demetri missed the cut and thrust of the gold-fields. He hated the noise and the upheaval of this place and wanted to return to the solitude of the outback diggings.'

'He wouldn't have gone without telling me,' she said with the stubborn logic of a thirteen-year-old who couldn't accept that her one and only friend had deserted her when she needed him most.

Kane took the cigar from his mouth, studied the burning tip before flicking ash onto the dirt floor. 'He knew you'd be upset, and he didn't want to have to choose between you and the lure of the gold he knew was still waiting for him out there.' He waved his arm in the vague direction of the west. 'He's gone back to the Territory,' he said softly. 'It's where he feels at home.'

'But this is his home. He was happy here.'

He sighed. 'Catriona, don't be childish. He was a man who liked to be free – a gypsy, like your father. He could never be happy in one place for very long. That's why he's gone.' He stared back at the house. 'Ask your mother if you don't believe me,' he said.

'Mam knew?' This was an even crueller blow. 'Will he come back?' Catriona stepped out of the shed, heedless of the rain ruining her dress and drenching her hair. She had to get away from him; had to find Mam and make her listen.

'Of course,' replied Kane in his matter-of-fact way. 'But only when he's ready to – until then you'll just have to accept it is what he wants.' His smile didn't touch his eyes.

Catriona was blinded by her tears. 'You can't marry Mam,' she blurted out. 'You just can't.'

'Too late,' he said with a smirk. 'We got married this morning.'

She gaped, blinking in disbelief. 'How? When? Why didn't Mam tell me?'

He shrugged with a nonchalance that made her want to scream. 'She thought it would be a nice surprise for your birthday.'

She turned from him and fled back across the lawn. She could barely see where she was going as the rain hammered the grass into submission. She was remembering her mother's words as they were about to go downstairs. Why didn't she tell me? Why?

Avoiding the lights and the noise of her birthday party, she slammed through the back door and raced up the stairs to the top of the house. She didn't want to see her mother ever again. She had betrayed her. Passing the closed door of her bedroom she stumbled up the stairs to the tower, and sank to the floor beneath the window, giving in to the loneliness and fear that had been locked inside her for so long.

Kane found her there in the darkness, and as he raped her for the first time, Catriona realised her childhood was over.

Chapter Eight

Edith felt the glow of happiness warm her through and through as she turned from the celebrations in the drawing room and walked back to the chaos in the kitchen. The gypsy and Kane were married – Demetri was still a free man. Perhaps now he would finally notice her. She poured a glass of champagne into the delicate flute and carried it into her little office behind the kitchen. Closing the door, she sank into the leather chair behind her desk and raised her glass. 'To the future,' she breathed. 'To you and me, Demetri.' The champagne was cold, the bubbles fizzing on her tongue.

It had been a long and tiring day, but the thrill of realising she was to have a second chance of persuading Demetri to appreciate all she could do for him was more potent than any champagne. She settled back in the chair and thought about that extraordinary announcement. It had come as a surprise to everyone, but the brat's reaction was interesting.

She sipped her champagne and thought about how Catriona had fled from the room her face ashen, her eyes wild. The kid obviously wasn't pleased, but perhaps, now she had Kane as a step-father she would be taught some manners. Never in her life had she heard such language, or seen such tantrums – but then what could one expect from a gypsy? She snorted. They were a rough lot and no mistake, and the kid had been powdered and painted like a miniature version of her mother. 'Spoilt brat,' she hissed. 'Who in their right mind would give a party like that for a thirteen year old?'

Edith thought of her own childhood, the meagre presents, the shoddy clothes and shoes, the birthday teas that had consisted of bread and jam and a small sponge cake. The unfairness of it all made the champagne taste sour and she put down her glass, her gaze settling on the account books spread out on her desk.

She hadn't had a chance to go through them thoroughly but, on her fleeting inspection earlier, she had been puzzled. The figures seemed to balance, and yet there were irregularities in the way cash had been handled, and unexplained rises in some of the wages that she hadn't been consulted over. If Kane was up to no good, then it would be the perfect ammunition to get him fired.

Taking another sip of the champagne, Edith sat there deep in contemplation. She would take the books home with her tonight and go through them thoroughly. If, as she suspected, Kane had been skimming off the profits, she would take her findings to Demetri. It would be the perfect revenge she needed to get rid of Kane, the gypsy and her brat. She put the glass down on the desk, picked up the heavy books and locked them in the wall-safe. Returning the key to the chain she wore at her thin waist, she finished the glass of champagne and left the office.

The party was breaking up as the rain hammered against the windows and drummed on the gravel drive. A lot of guests had been invited up from Cairns, and they had scampered out beneath umbrellas and coats to their cars. There were murmurs among those staying the night that perhaps they should leave tomorrow. The weather could be notorious up here in Tablelands, with roads washed away and landslips making it impossible to escape, and they seemed reluctant to risk being stranded here for what could be weeks. The party mood waned and Edith was kept busy behind the reception desk, making out bills and taking money in readiness for tomorrow's exodus.

As the hotel guests disappeared upstairs to their rooms and the maids finished clearing up, Edith wandered through the halls and drawing rooms checking that all was as it should be. The maids and boot-boys, the porters and waiters all lived out, and because Demetri was such a generous employer, they had the use of a small charabanc to get them home. Cook had her own little car – of which Edith was very jealous, for she had only a bicycle – and had left the hotel as soon as dinner was over. Cook lived in Kuranda with her husband and six children and didn't spend a moment longer than she had to in the hotel, preferring the warmth and comfort of her own home.

As the lights were turned off and the hotel became silent, Edith went back to the kitchen. Demetri would be hungry, so she would prepare him a plate of supper and take it to him in his apartment before she left. As she forked cold meat onto the plate and sliced bread, she wondered why he hadn't come to the party. It was strange, because he seemed genuinely to like the brat, though she couldn't understand why. Shrugging off her thoughts, she laid a tray and carried it across the hall. With a gentle tap on the door, she balanced the tray on her hip and turned the handle.

The apartment rooms were dark and silent, the curtains still drawn back from the windows. Perhaps he was asleep. She put the tray down on the table and tiptoed to the bedroom door. Demetri usually snored loud enough to rattle the windows, but tonight there was silence. With a frown, she gently eased the door open and looked in. The bed had not been slept in. Clucking with concern, she picked up the tray and headed back into the hall. He must have fallen asleep in his shed, and it was too wet and dark for her to find her way there. She put the plate in the larder and fetched the account books and a raincoat from her office. Pulling a waterproof hat over her head and galoshes onto her feet, she wrapped the books up in an old raincoat she found in Cook's locker, and stepped out into the teeming rain. With the account books in the basket, her head bent against the onslaught, she began the long pedal home.

The next day barely dawned, for the clouds were low and dark, blotting out the sun.

Edith arrived cold and shivering at the hotel and leaned her bike against the wall. She was exhausted, for the journey the night before had given her a chill and she'd been up all night examining the books. Yet, despite feeling wrung out and not at all well, she had the proof that Kane was stealing money from Demetri. He'd been clever, but not clever enough to pull the wool over her eyes, she thought as she shed the raincoat and galoshes and hugged the precious account books tightly to her narrow chest.

She walked into the kitchen and froze. It was dark and deserted despite the heat coming from the cooking ranges and the lingering aroma of frying bacon. Flicking a switch, she realised there was no electricity. Hurrying out into the reception hall, she found Kane behind her desk, surrounded by guests clamouring for his attention. Candlelight and lamps flickered shadows on the walls as the rain once again began to rattle against the windows. There were only two porters, she noticed, both of them looking harassed and none too happy at getting soaked every time they had to carry the bags and cases out to the waiting cars.

'Where have you been?' Kane hissed as she joined him behind the desk.

She ignored him and began to sort out the chaos. It wasn't until the last guest had driven away that she had time to sit down and catch her breath. There was a pain in her chest and she was burning with fever. All she really wanted to do was get home and go to bed. Yet she had to see Demetri.

Kane had disappeared and the porters had been told to go home. Demetri's apartment was as she'd found it the night before. Edith dragged the sodden coat back on and picked up the precious books. Her galoshes splashed through the muddy grass as the wind picked up and battered her wet coat against her legs. She bent her head and struggled through the rain and the wind to the shelter of the shed's overhanging roof. The door was open, swinging back and forth, banging against the frame.

'Demetri?' Her voice was almost lost in the slash of the rain amongst the leaves and the creaking of the ancient branches overhead.

The shed was empty, the tools gone. There were no signs of Demetri at all, for even his books and papers had been cleared away. She stood in the doorway, the account books clutched to her chest, the fever burning her skin and making her eyes ache. Yet through the fever her mind was working with sluggish determination. Something wasn't right. She closed the door and locked it, returning the key to its usual place beneath a large stone.

The hotel was silent, the shadows deep in the corners flickering with the dancing flames of the candles which had been left to burn. She placed the books on the hall table and blew some of the candles out. They were in danger of setting the hotel on fire. Shivering, she pulled off the raincoat and hat and listened to the silence. Her breath seemed to echo in the stillness, the sickly sweet perfume of lilies and roses reminding her of funerals. The great stone walls seemed to close in on her and she could feel the chill of the marble beneath her feet.

'You might as well go home, Edith.'

She looked up, startled out of her dark thoughts. Kane was standing

118

on the stairs looking down at her. He moved like a cat, she realised, slinking in and out of shadows, his eyes missing nothing. 'Where's Demetri?' Her voice was sharp with an unexplained fear.

'Gone,' he said flatly as he came down the last few steps and stood before her.

'Gone? Where to? And why?'

'Back to the Territory,' he said calmly.

Edith shook her head in bewilderment. 'He would have said something. Would have told me,' she murmured, her mind fogged with the fever that was raging through her. She looked up at him in bewilderment. 'Why now, when the hotel is doing so well? Surely ...'

She didn't get to finish her rambling speech for Kane interrupted. 'He asked me to give you this,' he said, his voice unusually soft and kind. 'He couldn't write it himself, but dictated to me what he wanted to say.' He smiled down at her, and turned his back. 'I expect you'd like a few moments alone to read it,' he said.

Edith heard his echoing footsteps as he walked away and sank down into the chair that stood by the great empty marble fireplace. With trembling fingers she opened the letter.

My dear Edith,

You have been a good friend, and I thank you for your loyalty and kindness. My dream would not have been possible without your help and I want you to know that I understand how much you have given of yourself to me.

Edith smiled, the tears streaming down her face as she read the words she'd so longed to hear from his lips.

I know you wished for more, but it was not possible, and I am sorry if these words cause you distress. But Lara was my wife and there is only room for her in my heart. Forgive me for leaving you this way, but it is for the best. The call of the open road is too strong to resist and I am going to seek my future there. Take care of my dream Edith, for there is no one else I trust more. I will return some day, but I cannot promise when, and until that day I entrust my dream to you.

Goodbye dear friend,
Demetri

The scrawl at the bottom of the page had been made by an uneducated man who could neither read nor write and she could see how carefully he'd formed the letters of his name. Dear, kind, sweet Demetri. He hadn't forgotten her after all. She folded the letter again and carefully put it back in the envelope. She would treasure it always.

Kane's footsteps echoed once again and he reappeared in the grand hall. 'I'm sorry if you're distressed,' he said kindly. 'Demetri thought it best to go while everyone was busy. He hated a fuss, but then you knew that, didn't you?'

She nodded, too miserable to speak.

'Go home, Edith. The hotel is empty and I've cancelled all the bookings for the next few days because the forecast predicts flash-floods and landslides if this rain keeps up. There's nothing for you to do here, and you look tired and unwell.'

His unexpected kindness merely made her feel worse and she couldn't seem to stop crying.

'I've asked the gardener to take you home in his utility. You can't possibly cycle all the way to the other side of town.'

She looked at him in mute misery as he helped her on with her coat and galoshes and held her arm as he helped her into the utility. 'I'll send a message to you when things are better,' he said through the window. 'Take care of yourself, Edith.'

Edith slumped back into the uncomfortable seat and stared through the streaming windows. It wasn't until she had changed out of her wet clothes and was sitting by her lonely little fire that she realised she'd left the account books behind.

Over the next few weeks the rain was unrelenting, driving down in great, endless grey sheets through the day and night. Never before had the Atherton Tablelands seen so much water. It rushed down the hills, filled the rivers and streams and sent the falls thundering into the valleys. Roads were washed away, earth slipped and shifted bringing down trees to block tracks and crash through the roofs of some of the isolated houses. Telegraph poles were brought down, effectively shutting off the community from the outside world until the repair teams could be sent out. Even the little railway had been closed – it was too dangerous and some of the track had been washed away. And on the very outskirts of Atherton, the hotel in the rainforest had become an island.

Velda shifted in the bed unable to sleep. The constant sound of the rain on the roof made her head ache and she wished she hadn't poured her usual nightcap down the sink. Kane had brought it in as he always did, and for the past couple of days she'd thrown it away. She had decided she didn't need it any more, and she found to her amazement that, without it, her mind seemed clearer, more focussed and she felt more able to put her life and circumstances in order.

Her marriage to Kane had been one of convenience. He'd persuaded her it wouldn't be seemly to live under the same roof, and that Demetri had worried it might harm the hotel's business if it was thought they were living in sin. At first she'd been horrified by his suggestion, but as the weeks had gone on and it became clear that indeed she was thought of as his mistress by Edith and the rest of the staff, she realised he was right. She didn't love him – she could never love anyone as much as she'd loved Declan – but he was kind and thoughtful, and had been so patient during those awful months of mourning that it would have been churlish to refuse. Besides, she'd reasoned, she was in her mid thirties, with no money, no permanent home and no real work. She had few choices left to her. At least marriage to Kane would bring her some semblance of respectability.

And then there was Catriona. She needed a father – needed to have a firm hand to guide her – for since coming here she had run wild. She was rude, disobedient and inclined to tantrums, and her unfortunate habit of using the swear words she learned during their travelling time was beginning to grate on everyone. Her lovely, sweet daughter had become a surly, unpleasant presence and she had hoped Kane's influence would make her change her ways.

Velda climbed out of bed and, without bothering to light the lamp, went to stand at the window. Despite the darkness and the rain, it was hot, the humidity high even at night. The windows had been thrown open, the mesh screens the only barrier to mosquitoes and flying, stinging, biting insects that swarmed out of the sodden forest. There was no breeze, no lifting of the heavy blanket of humidity and as the tropical rain continued to fall she felt trapped and restless. Her marriage was a sham she was willing to uphold for as long as necessary if it meant Catriona grew out of this awful phase and realised she now had a solid family behind her. Demetri's sudden departure hadn't helped the situation of course,

121

but Catriona was old enough now to get over her childish disappointments and knuckle down to some serious work on her singing.

Velda stared out of the window, wondering where Kane was. He was still a mystery, giving little of himself away despite their marriage. She had been dreading the more intimate side of things on her wedding night, for Declan had been a gentle but exciting lover. To her surprise and relief Kane rarely came to her bed, and when he did his love-making was swift and mechanical as if he was fulfilling a duty. She had soon come to suspect Poppy had been correct when she'd said Kane was homosexual.

Velda's lips curved in a smile. That hadn't been quite the way Poppy had expressed it, she remembered. She'd called him a nancy boy, a poofter. She reached for the hairbrush and began to stroke it through her long hair. There was more grey in it now and its style was out of fashion, but it seemed to her it was the only thing that tied her still to Declan, for he had loved to run his fingers through it.

She stilled as she heard footsteps outside her door. Not tonight, she breathed. Please don't turn that handle. She waited, her gaze fixed to the glimmer of brass, watching for it to dip as Kane came in. The footsteps moved on, almost silent on the bare floorboards but for the occasional scuff and groan of the wood.

Velda climbed back into bed, relieved at the reprieve, but her thoughts were troubled. Catriona had come to her a few days ago and the child hadn't looked right – she'd grown thin and pale and there were shadows under her eyes that Velda hadn't noticed before. She'd been in one of her foul moods and they'd ended up having the most terrible row.

Velda rubbed her forehead as she tried to remember what it had been about. But her mind had been fogged by the drink she'd had, and she'd found it difficult to focus on what her daughter was trying to tell her. She stilled as the hazy memory of that confrontation returned. Catriona had definitely been trying to tell her something important – but what was it? She shook her head. She knew only that Catriona had slammed out of the room calling her vile names.

As she lay there in the darkness she realised she had been unfair on the child. She'd been so wrapped up in her own misery that she'd ignored her daughter's pain, had pushed her away and isolated herself in her own feeling of helplessness. Of course

Catriona had needed her. Of course she was in pain after losing her da. How could she, her mother have been so blind? Now her lovely girl had turned into a little virago and it was all her fault.

Velda bit her lip. She had failed Catriona, had failed in her role as a mother. Why had she allowed herself to be drawn into the twilight world her nightly drink offered? It made her thoughts sluggish, her perception dull and blurred her focus on what was happening around her. She threw back the sheet and clambered out of bed. She would go and see Catriona and try to put things right and make amends for her neglect.

The long passageway was dark. The electricity had failed right at the beginning of the rain storms and because the generator had run out of oil, they'd had to rely on candles, the old wood-burning cooking range and kerosene lamps. Velda hesitated, then decided not to light a candle, she could see well enough and Catriona's room was only a short walk to the end of the corridor.

Her bare feet made little noise on the floorboards, her slight weight not even making them creak. She approached Catriona's door and was pleased to see a light glimmering beneath it. She was still awake.

Velda was about to reach for the handle when she heard a noise on the other side of the door. She stilled, the hairs on the back of her neck lifting as she heard it again, tried to deny it and finally realised she'd not been mistaken. With her heart thudding against her ribs and her fingers trembling on the handle, she quietly opened the door.

The scene before her was captured in all its horror by the light from the lantern which stood on the chest of drawers. Velda froze.

Catriona was naked, her eyes tightly shut, the tears squeezing between the lids. Her sobs were muffled by the large hand that was over her mouth. Kane was on top of her, his shadow rising and falling on the wall beside him as the bed-springs creaked their ghastly rhythm.

Velda felt the blood drain from her face as she gasped at the sheer horror of what she was seeing.

Catriona opened her eyes and fixed her pain-filled gaze on her mother in silent, desperate entreaty.

As Kane continued to rape her daughter, Velda moved without thought. She snatched up the heavy candlestick on the bedside table.

Kane finally heard her and lifted his head.

He wasn't quick enough and Velda swung the candlestick with all the strength her hatred gave her and dealt him a glancing blow to the temple. As he slumped over her daughter's naked body and his blood spattered over the sheets, Catriona began to scream.

Velda was blinded by a red haze of rage and vengeance. She wanted him dead. He was worse than any animal. Filthy, filthy, dirty, disgusting. He had to die – had to be smashed to a pulp and made to pay for what he was and what he was doing.

Catriona screamed as she lay trapped beneath him. She screamed until the sound rang through the house and blotted out the thunder of rain. The high, terrified release of all her fears echoed again and again as her mother's arm rose and fell with unrelenting fury. His blood drenched the sheets and stuck to her flesh. His face was smashed to a bloody gore that was soon unrecognisably human.

Velda's hatred kept her going. Her daughter's screams were reverberating in her skull as she smashed the life out of the animal that had abused her baby. She swung the candlestick into his ribs, his legs, his back – wanting to leave her hatred in every mark she left on his flesh.

Catriona scrambled from beneath him and cringed against the brass bed-head as the blood flew and the dull thud of the candlestick continued. She screamed as she tried to smear away his gore from her body. Screamed for the carnage to stop. He was dead. He couldn't harm her any more.

But Velda was like the grim reaper. Catriona could see the bones beneath the flesh of her face, the dark sockets of her wild, crazed eyes. She hadn't realised Velda possessed such strength, or that she was capable of so much hate.

Velda finally emerged from the scarlet haze and dropped the candlestick. With one swift step she gathered up her daughter in her arms and carried her out of the room. Then, with the door shut behind them she sank to the hall floor. She held Catriona with all the strength she had left, sobbing and pleading with her to forgive her for not listening, for not seeing what had been happening over the past weeks. Her voice was broken as she rocked her child in her arms and soothed the screams to sobs. Held her as the trembling stilled and when the child was calmer, she carried her to the bathroom. The water was cold, but with gentle, loving hands she washed away the blood before wrapping her in a big towel and taking her to her own bed.

124

They lay huddled together beneath the blankets, holding tightly to one another as they shivered and trembled with the shock of what had happened that night. Yet neither of them could shake off the image of Kane's battered and bloody corpse in the other room.

Velda lay there staring into the darkness, overwhelmed by the sheer ferocity and power she'd been capable of. Yet the knowledge of what she'd done – and the brutality with which she'd punished him – had brought her to the very edge of reason. Almost bankrupt of spirit she struggled to fight off the rip-tide of emotion that was surging through her. She had to remain coldly detached, had to keep strong and determined for Catriona's sake. For the body must be moved, must be hidden.

Catriona eventually quietened, her breathing becoming deeper and more even as sleep took her over. Velda eased her arm from beneath her and edged out of the bed. Standing in the gloom she shivered despite the all-pervasive humidity. The night's work was far from over.

She pulled on a thick sweater over her bloodied nightgown and shoved her feet into an old pair of shoes. With a glance across to the bed, she hoped Catriona would remain asleep until it was over. Then, tiptoeing to the door she quickly left the room.

The lamp was still alight and the flickering shadows made the scene even more macabre. She closed her eyes and took a deep breath, then, before she could give herself time to think about what she was doing, she covered him in the blanket and wound him in the bloodied sheets. It was easier now she couldn't see him, but as she grasped hold of his feet and tugged, he hit the floor with a sickening, wet thud. She gagged at the smell of blood and had to stop a moment to regain her icy composure. She had to do this – had to finish what she'd started.

She was panting now, the cold sweat soaking her nightdress as she dragged the burden across the room. It would take the rest of the night to get him downstairs and out into the garden. Did she have the strength? Would the tenuous hold on reality remain with her long enough for her to bury him? She didn't know. All she could do was keep going.

'Let me help, Mam.' Catriona was standing beside her in a thick skirt and sweater she'd taken from Velda's wardrobe. Her face was ashen, her expression set in cold determination.

Velda gave a sharp cry of distress. 'Go back to bed,' she ordered. 'You shouldn't be here.'

125

Catriona shook her head and silently grasped two corners of the sheet and wound them into a knot. 'Take his feet,' she commanded softly. 'It'll be easier with two of us.'

Velda looked at her daughter and saw the strength of spirit in her and the maturity that her ordeal had given her. She nodded and they struggled with the dead weight of their burden and slowly descended the stairs. The silence of the hotel seemed to close in on them as they reached the grand hall and made their way to the front door. They rested for a moment, their rapid breaths sharp in the stillness.

'We'll have to bury him,' said Catriona as she stared down at the bundle. 'Demetri's shed's the best place. No one ever goes there.'

Velda shivered as she nodded. Catriona seemed to have taken charge with a maturity way beyond her tender years, and although it didn't feel right, she was glad to have someone else make the decisions. She was rapidly losing all sense of reality, and as the nightmare continued she wondered how long it would be before she gave in to madness.

They struggled outside, the dead-weight between them growing heavier as the rain hammered down and the gravel slipped and slid beneath their feet. The lawn was sodden, the mud clinging to their shoes as they tripped and stumbled to the far corner of the garden where the shed loomed darkly amongst the trees. The sky was lightening, but dawn was masked in black clouds that hung thickly in the grey sky.

Having found the key beneath the rock, Catriona opened the door and they dragged the body inside. She lit the lamp. 'I'll have to go to the gardener's shed and get a spade,' she said.

'Don't leave me,' cried Velda, her voice high with fear.

'I have to, Mam.' Catriona was so calm – too calm – her voice level and without emotion. 'Move the desk and clear a space over in that corner. I'll be back before you know it.'

Velda watched her run out into the rain. She sniffed back the tears, and ignoring the gruesome bundle on the floor began to clear a space.

Catriona returned with two spades and they began to dig. The earth was solid, flattened down over the years by trampling feet and heavy machinery. The sweat was cold on their skin as they worked in silence, their breath coming in sharp puffs of agony as the earth slowly gave in to their efforts. As they finally dropped their spades and stood at the side of the deep hole, the sky had lightened to a watery grey and the torrent of rain had become a soft fall.

Catriona looked at her mother, and together they rolled the body into the hole. She moved to the shelves where Demetri kept his bottles and selected the one that was marked NITROHYDROCHLORIC ACID. Twisting off the stopper, she poured it over the shrouded remains. There was a hiss and the stench of burning flesh as the acid set to work. Her face showed no emotion and her hand was steady as she calmly replaced the stopper and returned the bottle to the shelf.

They covered the body in the earth, tamping it down with the backs of the spades until it was as flat as the rest. With the desk once more in place, the shed look undisturbed. They closed the door and Catriona locked it, returning the key to its hiding place. She put the spades back in the gardener's shed and arm in arm with Velda, they splashed their way to the house.

As the rain continued to fall and the house remained isolated on the tablelands, Catriona realised Kane had been right about Velda. She was indeed a tortured soul, the events of that night pushing her very close to the edge of reason. There had been a madness in her eyes as she'd bludgeoned Kane that had frightened Catriona, and now, as they waited in that echoing mansion for the rains to peter out, the same madness showed itself in her manic energy. It was as if by working in feverish silence she could blank out what had happened here. She refused to talk to Catriona about him – asked no questions or showed the slightest inclination to know how long the abuse had lasted. She had become a silent, driven stranger, and Catriona could only watch as Velda cleaned and polished and washed, scrubbing the floor in the bedroom until her nails were broken and her hands were raw from the lye soap.

Catriona's emotions were running high as well. She had helped to kill a man – had helped to bury him. She needed her mother's love, her consolation, her reassurance that everything would be all right and that they could once again share a loving relationship. But after those few hours of closeness Velda single-mindedly refused to give in to what she saw as weakness. She became hell-bent on erasing all signs of Kane – almost manic in her desire to

127

wash away the memories of what had happened so she could pretend it never had. And yet Catriona had seen her running down to the shed every day, had watched as she unlocked the door and stood on the threshold staring at the place they had buried him. It was as if she had to reassure herself it hadn't been a bad dream – that the murder was real – and then she would return to the house and spend long minutes washing and scrubbing at her hands.

Kane's room had been stripped bare. His stash of money was tucked away in Velda's case along with his cuff-links, gold watch and chain, the gold nugget that had once topped his cane, and the ruby ring which had dropped from his finger during the attack. The rest of his belongings were burned in the great hearth of the hall fireplace, and Catriona watched the flames with little emotion. Kane was dead. He would never hurt her again. Yet the nightmares still haunted her – and the memories would remain with her for as long as Velda refused to acknowledge what had happened here.

Chapter Nine

Edith had read Demetri's letter so many times the folds had worn and the paper was in danger of disintegrating. Although it had been written in Kane's flourishing hand, Demetri's words had kept her company through the long days and nights, for in the silence of her little cottage she could almost hear his voice. Despite the cough that wouldn't go away, she had been comfortable during the deluge, for the larder was well stocked and the hotel gardener had made sure she had plenty of chopped wood for the fire. Yet she was impatient to return to the hotel, for Demetri had charged her with its care, and she couldn't bear the thought of Kane and his woman living there and perhaps making changes.

The rains petered out and the work-crews began the mammoth task of clearing fallen trees, replacing telegraph poles and shoring up the landslides. At last the track was open. Edith took her bicycle out of the woodshed and headed off to the hotel. The track was still muddy, rough with stones that had been washed down from the hills and, fearing a puncture, she walked most of the way. Out of breath and exhausted from the long journey and nagging cough, she at last reached the impressive iron gates.

As she wheeled her bicycle along the driveway, she noted the weeds that had sprung up in the earth where the gravel had been washed away. Several of the larger shrubs on either side had been broken by a falling palm tree, and the sodden grass was overgrown and littered with branches and leaves. The stone lions which stood proudly guarding the imposing front door were already patched with lichen and the flower-beds had been hammered into submission by the sheer force of the rain. She clucked in despair. It didn't take long in the tropics for the work of men to be undone. Nature was already trying to reclaim its foothold on Demetri's dream.

She left her bicycle at the kitchen door as she had always done, and went in. The kitchen smelled musty and the range was cold. There were dirty plates and cups and cutlery in the sink and the whole room had an air of disuse about it. She walked through into the hall. The silence reproached her and she stood for a moment and listened. Nothing moved and the only sound was the sigh and creak of the great house. She eyed the fireplace and saw the ashes, but they too were cold. A layer of dust dulled the reception desk and table and the flowers were dead in the vases.

'Hello,' she called. Her voice echoed in the walls and up into the rafters. There was no reply and she frowned. She called again, louder this time, her shout terminated abruptly by a fit of coughing. Still there was no answer. Hurrying through the downstairs rooms she saw yet more evidence of neglect. The beautiful carpets hadn't been cleaned for weeks and there was already evidence of mould on the curtains and tapestries. Dust covered everything in a thick layer and as she went from room to room she felt a rising anger. Kane and his woman had lived out the Wet in indolence. It would take an army of servants and weeks of labour to get the hotel back into shape.

She climbed the stairs, calling as she went. The sound of her voice echoed back, almost mocking her as she checked all the guest bedrooms and finally reached the servants' landing. These rooms were empty too, and judging by the musty smell, had been for some time. She checked the drawers and cupboards but there was no sign of Kane, the woman or the brat. She stood on the landing and gnawed her thumb. Instead of feeling elated that she had the hotel to herself, something about their disappearance bothered her. Returning to the downstairs rooms she quickly discovered what it was.

Demetri's apartment appeared undisturbed, but as she wandered through the rooms she began to notice the gaps. A pair of silver candlesticks was missing, along with three of his little gold snuff boxes and the silver-backed hairbrushes from the dressing table. As she took a more careful tour around the public rooms she saw that a small painting had been taken from the wall, and several silver salvers were missing from the sideboard in the dining room.

She felt the anger rise further and her footsteps rang out on the marble floor as she hurried back to her little office behind the kitchen. The account books were nowhere to be seen, but that was hardly surprising – Kane would have destroyed them the minute she'd left the house. Yet, as she opened up the wall-safe, she was in for a surprise. For there, wrapped in sacking was the picture, the hairbrushes and two of the silver salvers. None of it made any sense, and Edith sat there in her office for a long while before coming to a decision. Pulling on her coat, she returned to her bicycle and headed back down the driveway. Harold Bradley must be informed immediately.

Harold Bradley tidied up his desk, then stood with his back to the blazing fire and warmed his broad behind. He was a contented man. He had a good job in the police force that didn't involve a great deal of detective work, for crime was a rarity amongst these hard-working farming people and when the occasional skirmish broke out in the pub on a Saturday night a few hours in the lock-up was all that was needed to sober the offender up and send him packing. There was a little cottage that went with the job, and his wife was a cheerful woman who had given him a son and three daughters. All in all, he counted himself lucky. He rocked back and forth, the squeak of his police issue boots a pleasant accompaniment to the crackle of the fire. Taking his pipe from his pocket he began to fill it with tobacco.

The knock on the door startled him. 'Come in.'

Edith Powell looked flustered, her eyes bright, her cheeks unusually flushed. She was dressed, as always, in rusty black, the overcoat almost swamping her skinny frame. No one knew how old she was, but he guessed she was the wrong side of fifty. 'What can I do for you, luv?' he asked in his friendly way. He didn't like Edith very much, but he felt sorry for her. Some women were born to be spinsters and Edith was a typical example.

'I need to report a theft,' she said as she sat down on the hard chair in front of his desk. 'And I know who did it too,' she added sharply.

He raised an eyebrow. 'Sounds serious,' he rumbled, looking down at the pinched little face. He brushed his luxuriant moustache with a finger and sat down. 'You'd better tell me all about it.'

Harold leaned back in his chair, thumbs in waistcoat pockets as he listened to the rambling tale. There probably had been a theft in the hotel, but Edith's concerns were deeper than that, he

131

realised. She had set her cap at Demetri from the moment he'd arrived on the Tablelands. She was a woman scorned and now Demetri had shot through she was determined to lay the blame on someone. But a woman scorned was a ruddy nuisance as far as he was concerned, and the sooner he got rid of Edith the better.

He stroked his moustache between thumb and finger as she rambled on, and he heard the bitterness in her voice as she described Kane and Velda and the child. She obviously hated them all, but her jealousy of Velda was almost painful to witness. 'So, what do you want me to do, Miss Powell?' he asked finally.

'I want you to find Demetri,' she demanded. 'And I want you to hunt down that Mr Kane and arrest him for theft and fraud.' She stifled a cough with her hand.

Harold stared back at her thoughtfully. 'But you say you no longer have the account books, Miss Powell,' he said. 'And without them you have no proof. As for Demetri, he's probably out in the middle of the Territory somewhere. It will be impossible to find him.'

'What about the missing silver?' she demanded.

'There's no proof that Kane or the woman took it,' he said. 'After all, you've already found some of it. The rest might have been put away for safe-keeping during the Wet.'

'I demand you find Kane and bring him in,' she spluttered, her hands tightly clasped in her lap.

Communications were poor at the best of times, and because of the flooding they were even worse. 'There isn't much I can do,' he said. 'I can put out a message on the two-way radio, but I don't hold out much hope of finding him. They could be miles away by now.'

'Then find Demetri,' she said, close to tears. 'He has to know what's happened.'

Harold handed her a large clean handkerchief. 'Fair go, Miss Powell. I'll do my best, but I wouldn't keep your hopes up. He's probably down a mine somewhere in the Never-Never, or tramping the tracks and out of communication with the rest of the country. You know how he is, Miss Powell. He's a drifter.'

She blew her nose and tucked the handkerchief in her pocket as she nodded. 'What shall I do?' she said finally.

'Go back to the hotel and get it cleaned up,' he said kindly as he stood and came around the desk. He helped her to her feet.

'Demetri trusted you to look after it, and I'm sure you're very capable of running it until he returns.'

Edith was overtaken by a fit of coughing and she pulled the handkerchief from her pocket and covered her mouth. 'I haven't been well,' she said finally. 'I don't think I could manage on my own.' She raised fevered eyes to Harold. 'You must find Demetri,' she pleaded.

Harold bit down on his impatience. 'Then close it up and keep an eye on it,' he said. 'I'll write up a report of what you've told me and set the wheels in motion to find Kane and Demetri.'

He watched her leave on that old bone-shaker of a bike and closed the door. She obviously wasn't well, and riding that bike was doing her no favours. He shrugged and returned to his desk. After a long moment's thought, he picked up a pen, checked the nib and began to laboriously fill in a report of their conversation. It would do little good, he realised, but the force expected everything to be written down, and if Demetri did return at least it would prove he'd done something.

Catriona and Velda had left the hotel within days of the murder. They carried a bag each – it was all they could manage. Kane's disappearance would have to be explained, and they had decided to tell anyone who asked, that he'd shot through because he had another, better job down south and they were on their way to join him.

The rains had calmed enough for them to make the long, tortuous walk across the Tablelands to Kuranda. From there they began the winding descent to Cairns by foot. The little steam train was still not in service, but it was better not to be seen and questioned, and they avoided the work-crews who were labouring to replace the tracks and clear the paths. By the time they reached the city they were exhausted.

Velda forced one foot in front of the other, determined to keep her fragile hold on reality. They had to escape, had to begin again. Perhaps, when they reached Brisbane they could put the horror behind them and start a new life. Catriona hadn't wanted to take Kane's secret cache of money. She'd said it made her feel as if she was taking payment for her services; made her feel dirty. But Velda had to be practical. They would need the money for food and lodgings as well as travelling expenses. Blood money or not, it would see them through until she found work.

From Caims they caught a bus to Townsville. It was cheaper than the train and took three times as long. The bus was a big white charabanc, at least it had started out white many years before. Now it was pitted with rust, the windows so heat-blasted it was difficult to see through them. The damn thing wheezed and groaned and creaked and amazed everyone at its ability to keep going. There were ten passengers and they all had to get out on a regular basis to wait for the engine to cool and for the driver to top up the radiator. It became almost a game, and Velda noticed how Catriona's spirits lifted as she chattered with the others and shared their tea and sandwiches. Yet her own spirits were dulled, her thoughts returning constantly to that dark, wet night. It seemed that no matter how far she ran, she would never escape.

They caught another bus in Mackay, and then a train for the rest of the journey. Velda found a little house to rent in Brisbane's southern suburbs, and persuaded the owner of a wool exporter to give her a job. It seemed her plans for the future were coming to fruition – but she was worried about Catriona. The child was sickly, her animation dulled, her spirits low as she wandered around the cottage and spent most of the day in bed. Velda tried not to be impatient with her, but she was tired from the long hours at work and didn't appreciate coming home to a wan and tearful Catriona.

'I need to see a doctor,' she said that morning. They had been in Brisbane for two months and the sickness and terrible pain in her back hadn't eased up.

'Doctors cost money,' snapped Velda. 'I'll get something from the pharmacy.'

Catriona shook her head. 'The pain won't go away, Mam, and there's blood when I pee.'

Velda realised she had to do something. 'If the doctor has to examine you, he'll know what's been going on,' she muttered.

'I don't care,' stormed Catriona. 'I'm in pain, Mam.'

They went to a surgery on the other side of town and Velda gave a false name and address. The doctor was a middle-aged man who listened carefully to Catriona's catalogue of symptoms before examining her.

Catriona squeezed her eyes shut as he poked and prodded. It reminded her of Kane, and she had to fight to stop screaming at him to stop. When he'd finished he gruffly told her to dress.

'Mrs Simmons,' he began, his expression cold with disgust. 'Not only has your daughter contracted an extremely unpleasant urinary tract infection, but she is also at least four months pregnant.'

The stunned silence was finally broken by the sound of Catriona's sobs. Velda's shock made it almost impossible to hear the rest of what he was saying. Kane's legacy lived on. Dear God in Heaven, were they never to be free of him? And Catrionas, what of her? She was only thirteen. What was all this doing to her?

The doctor made out a prescription. 'Due to her age, I suggest she is admitted immediately to the home for wayward girls,' he said coldly.

'We'll not be needing that,' Velda snapped as she plucked the prescription from his hand and stood up. 'My daughter's suffered enough without being called wayward.' She grabbed Catriona's hand and swiftly left the surgery.

On the long journey back to the house in the suburbs, Catriona tried to accept the terrible news. Thank goodness they weren't going back to that doctor. She hadn't liked him, and his instant assumption that she was wayward had made her feel sick and deeply ashamed. She looked across at Velda as they sat in the bus. They had barely spoken since leaving the surgery and although she yearned for comfort, she knew Velda would maintain her icy silence. Their relationship had never recovered from that awful night, despite what they had shared. Perhaps it would never again return to the way it had once been, for they were scratchy with one another, always walking on eggshells, fearful of saying or doing something which could be interpreted as a slight or accusation.

Catriona regarded her mother's profile as she stared straight ahead. Her expression gave nothing away, but Catriona knew she had to be dealing with her own demons. For since that night, Velda had become distant, hard and driven, her ambition to see Catriona succeed on the stage where she'd failed was now an obsession. They had moved around each other in that little house, never quite managing to say what they were really thinking. Emotions were tightly harnessed, Kane was never mentioned. Now this. The cruellest blow of all.

The wide suburban street was lined with palm trees that clattered and rustled in the breeze which came from the sea. Each little wooden house was painted white, with two windows and a door at the front and at the back, and resembled boxes rather than houses. A narrow verandah with a curving iron roof offered shelter from the sun, and the small front garden was neat behind the white picket fence. There was one bedroom, a kitchen that doubled up as a lounge, and a miniscule bathroom. The wattle tree had been planted too close to the back of the house, and the golden rain of its blossom shifted and sighed against the window of the bedroom Catriona shared with her mother.

It was late afternoon four months later, and Catriona was stretched out on the bed in her petticoat, attempting to garner relief from the heat. The ceiling fan hummed above her and the window was open so any breeze could come through the fly-screen. She lay there staring at the fan, her vast stomach blocking out the view of her feet. Her ankles were swollen and she was feeling uncomfortable. The baby had been kicking all day, as if impatient to be born, and Catriona winced as a particularly sharp little knee or elbow prodded her in the ribs.

She put her hands over the mound of her stomach, as if by touching it she could calm the growing baby inside her. This baby was a part of her now and she was longing for it to be born so she could hold it and love it. She began to sing a gentle lullaby, her soft voice drifting into the sweltering, sticky heat as her thoughts turned to the things she'd bought today and hidden in the bottom of her suitcase.

'What on earth do you think you're doing?' Velda came into the room and began to strip off the smart suit and white blouse she always wore to work.

'I'm singing to my baby,' Catriona replied dreamily.

Velda kicked off the peep-toed shoes and peeled off her stockings before pulling on a cotton wrap and sinking down onto the bed. 'It's not your baby, Kitty,' she said with a weary and rather impatient sigh. 'There's no point in getting sentimental about it because the minute it's born it's going to be adopted.'

'It *is* my baby,' she retorted as she struggled to sit up. 'And I don't want it to be adopted.' She edged off the bed and stood before her mother. 'In fact,' she said firmly. 'I won't let you give it away.'

'Don't be absurd,' snapped Velda. 'You're carrying Kane's bastard, and the sooner it's out of our lives the better.'

Catriona had had this argument with her mother before, but as the months had dragged on and the baby had grown, she'd realised she had begun to love it. It didn't matter any longer how it had come to be – it was – and she was determined to keep it. 'It's a little baby, Mam,' she said hotly. 'And it's mine. I love it. I'm going to keep it.'

Velda glared at her and stood up. 'You're still a child yourself,' she said firmly. 'And have no say in the matter. The kid goes the minute it's born, and that's final.' She wrapped the cotton dressing-gown around her thin frame and left the room, slamming the door behind her.

Catriona put her hands over the swell of her belly, the tears running down her face. 'Don't worry, little baby,' she whispered. 'I'm your mummy, not her, and I'll make sure she doesn't take you away.'

She went into labour two weeks later. It was long and painful and the doctors at the hospital looked worried. She was too young, too slightly built, there could be complications. Catriona, alone in the hospital room that smelled strange and glared too whitely in the bright lights, was terrified, not only at what was happening to her, but for her unborn child. Mam was still determined to have it adopted, but she was equally determined, and told everyone that came near her she wanted to keep it.

The tiny little girl was finally born and Catriona reached out her arms to hold her. The nurse bundled her into a blanket and glared down at Catriona. 'Perhaps this will be a lesson to you, young lady,' she said with a sniff of disapproval.

'I want my baby,' screamed Catriona. 'Give her to me.' She begged and sobbed, and tried to clamber out of bed, but the straps holding her feet imprisoned her. Her pleading was to no avail. The nurse whisked the tiny bundle out of the room, and all Catriona saw of her baby was a wisp of black hair peeking above the blanket.

Velda was permitted to visit for a few minutes later that day. Her face was ashen, her mouth set in a determined line as she sat by the bed and took Catriona's hand. 'You have to understand I'm doing all this for you,' she said firmly. 'It's no good crying and making yourself ill, what's done is done.'

'But I love her,' sobbed Catriona. 'Please let me at least hold her.'

Velda sat back in the chair. 'An illegitimate child is a disgrace. Society will not accept her or you, should you keep her. She will blight your life and your career, and although you played no willing part in her creation, society will tar you with the same brush.'

137

'Where is she?' Catriona's voice was a whisper.

'Safe,' she replied.

'I'll make the doctors and nurses tell me where,' she muttered. 'They can't just take my baby away and hide her.'

'They already have,' said Velda. 'It's over, Catriona.'

'How could you be so cruel?' Catriona stared at her with eyes filled with tears.

Velda fiddled with her handbag and gloves, and after a long moment of silence seemed to come to a decision. 'There are a great many things for which I'm ashamed,' she said finally. 'I should have known what Kane was doing, should have been a better mother so you could have confided in me. I cannot forgive myself for that, and probably never will.' She took a deep breath. 'But to keep his baby? Never. It would be a constant reminder and I couldn't bear it.' She took Catriona's hand, her expression softened by the anguish she was obviously feeling. 'You're thirteen, with your whole life ahead of you. Let her go, Kitty.'

Two weeks later they had packed their bags and were on the road again. Velda had made the decision to settle in Sydney.

Catriona sat next to her mother in the train and stared out of the window. She would never forget that wisp of dark hair peeking from the blanket, and she knew she would think about her always, wondering if she was safe and well and happy. For now, she would have to find a way to live with what had happened. It wouldn't be easy, but there were few options open to her. Velda seemed determined to have her way and all she could do was obey her mother and wait until she was old enough to begin the search for her baby.

Doris Fairfax ran a tight ship. She was the widow of a sea captain, and the owner of a boarding-house in the back streets of Sydney. The death of her husband had come shortly before the onset of the Great Depression, and although times were hard, Doris had been determined to maintain standards of cleanliness and respectability. She had chosen her lodgers carefully, and now, as prosperity once again seemed to be on the horizon, she was looking forward to a comfortable retirement in a few years time.

She was a plump little woman, well past her prime, with a penchant for flowery dresses, large earrings and lots of jangling bracelets. Once a month the house stank of the peroxide she used to bleach her hair brassy blonde, and it was whispered that she had enough cosmetics to stock a shop. Her constant companion was a rotund and bad-tempered Pekinese dog called Mr Woo, which snarled and wheezed and was likely to take a sharp nip out of an unwary hand or ankle.

Doris lived on the ground floor where she could watch the front door and those of her neighbours. She had strict rules about female visitors, and in the cosiness of her over-furnished and much-frilled sitting room, she could keep an eye on the comings and goings of her male lodgers. She was delighted with the arrival of Catriona and her mother, and was only too happy to accompany the child on the piano when she was practising her complicated songs and running through those endless scales her mother made her practice. Yet she was concerned at the stillness in the young girl, at the lack of emotion between mother and daughter. Doris had been around the block enough times to realise they were harbouring a secret, but as curious as she was, she decided not to pry. They were clean and respectable and obviously worked long hours in that hotel – why rock the boat when they had proved over the past year to be such good tenants?

Like the owner, the boarding house had seen better, more youthful days. It stood three storeys high, cheek-by-jowl with its neighbours in a long, dilapidated terrace that climbed up a steep hill and afforded a good view of the city from the attic windows. The rooms were cheaply furnished, but clean, and the five lodgers shared a single bathroom and ate their breakfast and evening meal downstairs the comfortable kitchen.

Catriona leaned on the window-sill and looked out over the roofs to the city. It was a clear, cold winter afternoon and she could just make out the blue glimmer of the harbour. Yet, in this quiet moment she thought she could detect the hues of the Outback in the far distance, and could catch the scent of eucalyptus and pine and the dry, dusty aroma of dirt tracks. How she missed the freedom of the tracks, the sound of a wagon rattling over the ruts as the plod of the shires took them further and further into the wilderness.

'Hurry up, Kitty,' said Velda as she bustled about the room gathering up their coats and hats. 'We'll be late, and it's a long walk.'

Catriona turned from the window and watched her mother moving about the small room they shared. Velda now lived her life

139

almost in silence, as if afraid to speak in case once started she wouldn't be able to stop. Yet she was always on the move – rushing here and there, never still, as if she was trying to escape something – trying to cheat time. She was too thin, her face lacked animation and her eyes were dull, and although she moved swiftly with her customary grace, Catriona could see the tension in her thin frame.

'There's plenty of time, Mam,' she said softly. 'We aren't due to start our shift until six.'

'I want to get there early tonight,' she replied as she put on her hat and applied lipstick to her pale mouth.

Catriona shoved her feet into low-heeled pumps, pulled on the thin coat and reached for her hat. It was old and battered despite the cotton flowers she'd sewn onto the band, but it would have to do. There was little enough money coming in, without wasting it on luxuries. 'We won't get paid extra, so why bother?' she asked as she searched for her scarf and gloves.

'I've got something to discuss with the owner,' said Velda mysteriously. 'And the best time to do that is before the evening rush.'

Catriona watched as Velda tugged the counterpanes straight on the narrow single beds and smoothed the pillows before turning to the dressing table to tidy the few bits and pieces that lay strewn across it. Always tidying, fidgeting, smoothing and adjusting, Velda was driven. 'What's so important it can't wait?' Catriona asked.

'I'll tell you later,' said Velda as she snatched up the cheap handbag and headed for the door.

Catriona realised she wouldn't get anything more from her, and yearned for the easy way they'd once had with each other. The companionship and love they had once shared had been cast aside for an almost formal co-habitation. Yet the years since her father's death had changed both of them, and Catriona knew this state of affairs would remain as it was. For Velda's way of coping with tragedy had been to withdraw, and Catriona had been forced to put her own fears and nightmares aside and try to face the future with hope: for without hope there was nothing.

She looked back at the room they'd shared for almost a year and checked that the gas fire was out and the windows locked. It was a small room divided from the other half of the attic by a partition

140

wall, and space was at a premium with the two beds, a hefty wardrobe, chest of drawers and a dressing-table filling every available inch. This claustrophobic space could never be home but it provided shelter, and that was all that mattered. She slammed the door and ran down the stairs to catch up with Velda.

Doris was, as usual, sitting in her over-stuffed chair by the window, and Catriona waved to her as they hurried down the hill towards the city. She liked Doris, and had spent many happy hours listening to the stories of her youth and the adventures of her seafaring husband. They were a welcome relief after Velda's long silences.

Sydney was bustling and noisy from the trams that rattled down the centre of the broad main streets. Men and women hurried along the pavements, bundled against the crisp winter afternoon in coats and scarves. The Depression had hit Sydney, just as it had rocked the rest of the world, and its effect could still be seen in the many boarded-up windows and neglected buildings that had once been profitable business establishments.

And yet there was evidence that the bad times were coming to an end. Some of the businesses that had scraped survival were now taking on new employees, factories had begun to return to production and the hotels were at last beginning to fill again. Not everyone had lost their fortunes; in fact, for the canny few, it was a boom period, and the black market in cheap property, cheap labour and cheap liquor thrived.

The Hyde Hotel stood squarely in Macquarie Street. It had once been a rich man's mansion, with elegant verandahs and manicured Italianate gardens, but the owner had gone bankrupt and it had fallen into disrepair. After his suicide, the beautiful old house had been sold at auction for a pittance. Robert Thomas, the new owner, had an eye for the main chance. He pooled together the resources of his widespread family and went into business, with ambitions for making this the best hotel in the city. He was already well on the way to seeing that dream realised, for the hotel was always full, the dining room busy, and the newly refurbished cocktail lounge had become a popular meeting place for Sydney's elite.

Catriona followed her mother along the side of the hotel to the staff entrance. She hung up her coat and hat, pulled off her gloves and scarf, and reached for the black dress, white apron and cap she had to wear in the dining room.

141

Her mother's hand stilled her. 'Don't get changed yet,' she said. 'Come with me.'

Catriona frowned. Her mother was acting very strangely, and there seemed to be a pent-up excitement about her – an animation that had been missing for too long. 'What's all this about, Mam?' she demanded as she was pulled into the staff cloakroom and steered towards the brightly lit mirror above the line of basins.

Velda pulled one of her dresses from the voluminous bag she was carrying. 'Put this on,' she ordered. 'Then I'll see to your hair and make-up.'

Catriona became aware that her mouth was open. She snapped it shut and looked at the dress her mother had thrust at her. It was Velda's favourite, and her best, a memento of the early days when she could afford such things. 'I'm not doing anything until you tell me what this is about,' she said stubbornly.

'You'll do as I say and get a move on,' snapped Velda as she tugged Catriona's sweater over her head and began to unfasten the button on her skirt. 'Mr Thomas is waiting, and you have to give a good impression of yourself.'

'I've already got a job waiting tables,' said Catriona as she stepped out of her skirt, lifted her arms and felt the soft chiffon drift down and over her body. It was cool and rustling, skimming over her hips and finishing above her knees in handkerchief points.

'You weren't meant to be a waitress,' Velda snapped as she flourished a hairbrush. 'You have a voice, a voice that should be heard, and Mr Thomas is a man of influence. He has the contacts, and will help get you noticed if this audition goes well.'

Catriona stood in silent terror before her mother as Velda brushed her long dark hair and fixed it into an elegant chignon. She saw the determination in Velda's eyes, in the set of her mouth and in the quick, sure strokes as she applied powder, lipstick and mascara. There was no point in arguing when her Mam was like this.

'There,' Velda said with a nod of satisfaction. 'Look in the mirror. Tell me what you see.'

Catriona turned and found a stranger staring back at her. 'I see a woman,' she breathed.

'Precisely,' muttered Velda as she fixed a string of beads around Catriona's neck and clipped on matching earrings. 'A beautiful young woman.' She took Catriona's arms in her cold hands and

142

turned her to face her. 'Mr Thomas has an important man with him this evening, Catriona,' she said fiercely. 'Show him just how talented you are, and the world will be your oyster.'

Catriona stared at her mother in horror. It was as if Velda was putting her up for sale.

'Don't look at me like that,' she snapped. 'I haven't spent my time coaching you for it all to come to nothing.' She tugged the strap over Catriona's slender shoulder and nodded with satisfaction. 'Come on. We mustn't keep him waiting.'

Catriona's mouth was dry with terror as Velda grabbed her hand and pulled her down the long corridor towards the basement lounge. It had been years since her last stage performance, and although she had practised every day, she was so nervous she felt quite ill and was convinced she wouldn't be able to utter a note.

The basement lounge ran the full length and breadth of the hotel. It was sumptuously decorated in black and white, with the odd splash of deep scarlet in the banquettes and chair cushions. Lit by a vast chandelier that was reflected in a multitude of mirrors, it was a glaring stage-setting, the likes of which Catriona had never seen.

The floor was highly polished, the small tables and gilt chairs by the dance floor looked inviting, and the velvet banquettes set around the walls offered an intimacy for those who wished a degree of privacy. A piano stood to one side of the tiny stage which had a backdrop of black velvet that had been stitched with crystals to catch the light and give the impression of a night sky.

Catriona froze in the doorway as she saw the man sitting at the piano, and the two men who had risen to greet them. She couldn't do this. She was too young, too inexperienced, just too scared. She wanted to run, to turn away and hide in the labyrinth of corridors. But it was too late. Mr Thomas was shaking her mother's hand, was introducing his friend, his voice coming to her as if from the depths of the sea in a muffled, incomprehensible monotone.

She realised she was being closely watched by the second man, and as she looked into his face the fear began to ebb. He had kind brown eyes and sandy hair and his smile was encouraging.

'Peter Keary,' he said as he took her hand. 'Delighted to meet you.'

Catriona looked up at him, her smile hesitant. He was handsome, but old, at least thirty. What did he expect of her?

'And just how old are you, Catriona?' he asked.

'Eighteen,' interrupted Velda. 'Come along, Catriona. We've kept these gentlemen waiting long enough.'

Before Catriona could protest at the lie, Velda bustled her across the dance floor to the piano, and, pulling out some sheet music she gave it to the pianist with detailed instructions. Mam had obviously been planning this for a while – the aria from *La Bohème* had been her practice piece for weeks. She glanced back over her shoulder. Mr Keary and Mr Thomas were seated at a banquette, their cigar smoke drifting above their heads as they talked quietly to one another. 'I can't sing opera here,' she whispered feverishly.

'You can, and you will,' hissed her mother.

'But I'm only fifteen,' Catriona protested. 'I'm not even allowed in this sort of place.'

'Who said anything about singing in a cocktail bar?' snapped Velda as her fingers tightened around Catriona's arm. 'This is an audition for Mr Keary. He runs the best theatrical agency in the city,' she hissed with a flush of excitement colouring her face. 'Now get on that stage and show him what you're made of.'

Catriona was propelled forward by a sharp nudge in the small of her back. She stood there in the bright lights, almost frozen with fear. Then she heard the first bars of the beautiful aria and her terror ebbed away. She closed her eyes, centring her thoughts on the music and what it meant to her, and as she began to sing she was transported into the world of the tragic Mimi and her lover, the poet Rodolfo.

As the final notes drifted into silence, Catriona stepped back from the edge of the stage and dipped her chin. The sad, sweet story of the tragic lovers, and the passion needed to sing the aria echoed something deep within her. Yet it was draining – had her performance been good enough?

The silence grew and she finally looked up. Surely it hadn't been that bad? As she was about to flee the stage she saw Peter Keary rise slowly to his feet. With incredulous wonder she saw the tears glistening on his cheeks as he moved across the dance floor and captured her hands.

'Beautiful,' he breathed. 'Incredible to find such understanding and depth in one so young.' He held her away from him as he looked at her. 'You are the perfect Mimi,' he breathed. 'Small, frail – it's as if Puccini wrote his opera just for you.'

144

'So you'll represent her then?' Velda was immediately at her side, ready to do business.

'When she turns eighteen,' he murmured, his brown eyes shining with humour as he wiped his damp cheeks with a snowy handkerchief.

Velda protested and he waved away her lies. 'She's too young,' he murmured as he looked into Catriona's eyes and smiled. 'Her voice might be mature, but there's a long way to go if this young lady's potential is to be fully realised.'

Catriona was warmed by the lilt of his soft Irish voice. It reminded her of Da. She smiled back at him, for here was someone who understood what the opera meant to her, someone who had seen beyond the child and discovered the strength of her passion for the music. 'So, what now?' she asked shyly, the excitement making her tremble.

'It's back to school for you, Catriona,' he murmured. 'A special school where you will learn all there is to know about singing.'

'We can't afford special schools,' snapped Velda. 'Catriona needs to work.'

'I will pay,' he replied with a firmness that belied argument.

'And what exactly do you want in return?' Velda stood before him, arms tightly folded around her skinny waist, her expression arctic.

'I expect nothing until she has graduated. Then I will represent her.' He smiled then, took Catriona's hand and bowed low over her fingers. 'I will make you famous, Catriona Summers. And one day, we will conquer the world.'

Chapter Ten

Catriona arrived at the Conservatorium in a high state of tension and excitement. At last she would be going to a real school. At last she would mix with other people her own age. Yet she was fearful. What if Peter Keary had been mistaken and they didn't think her voice was good enough? What if she didn't fit in? She was very aware of her cheap coat and dress, of the scuffed shoes she'd whitened earlier. Her gloves were darned and her hat homemade; surely they would take one look at her and decide she wasn't right for them?

Peter seemed to read her thoughts, for he gently took her elbow and steered her to the back of the building. 'You look lovely,' he assured her. 'And once we get you through this audition, I'll take you shopping.'

'I don't need you to buy me clothes,' she said gruffly.

'Let's call it a loan,' he replied with airy nonchalance. 'For once they hear you sing, they can't fail to make you a star.'

Catriona's confidence wasn't as high. 'Who will be at this audition?' she asked as they reached the door.

'John and Aida, of course, are the principal tutors and much respected in the world of opera, the principal of the Conservatorium and the board of directors, but don't be frightened of them. Think of them as just another audience, and with your background that should be easy enough.'

Catriona had a fleeting memory of Lightning Ridge and Goondiwindi. She shivered as they entered the long, dark corridor and the door slammed behind them.

'Listen,' said Peter.

They stood in the gloom, and Catriona lifted her chin. She could hear music, lovely music: a piano concerto drifting through the sound of sopranos, contraltos and baritones going through their warming-up exercises. Her pulse began to race. Soon, if all went well, she would be a part of this. The nervous excitement made her mouth dry.

Peter smiled as he led her into a large room that was empty but for a grand piano and embroidered stool. 'You will have an hour to warm up. I'll come and fetch you when it's time.'

Catriona took off her hat and gloves and shed her coat. The room was warm, the heat coming from heavy radiators that stood against the white walls. Long, elegant windows looked out over a walled garden, and in the distance she could see the rooftops of the houses up in the hills. She carefully folded her coat and put it on the windowsill along with her hat and gloves. Walking over to the piano, she ran her fingers over the smooth, polished wood before touching the keys. The tone was wonderful, clear and resonant – so different from the old piano she'd learned on – even better than the one in Demetri's hotel.

She pushed away the thought of Demetri. That was her old life, and if she was to survive her new one, then it was time to concentrate. She ran her fingers over the keys. Remembering her mother's hours of tuition, she sat down and began to play. Her fingers were clumsy at first, but as she heard the sounds of others practising, she grew in confidence. As she began to go through the scales, her voice gathered strength until it echoed up to the high ceiling.

It seemed only minutes later when Peter opened the door. 'It's time,' he said.

She followed him up the stairs to another great room. This one had the same long, elegant windows, but was far from empty. A long table had been set up at one end, and there were ten people sitting behind it. At the other end of the room was a stout woman sitting at a piano. Catriona bobbed a curtsy to the adjudicators. She could hardly breathe and her hands were moist as she clutched them behind her back. Peter had taken a chair to one side of the room and he nodded at her in encouragement.

'How old are you, my dear?' asked the bearded gentlemen who sat in the centre of the ten judges. He peered at her over his half-moon spectacles.

'Fifteen and a half, sir,' she replied, her voice breaking with nerves.

He leaned aside and spoke quietly to the woman beside him before returning his gaze to her. 'And what are you going to sing for us?'

'"Mi chiamano Mimi,"' she replied. 'From Puccini's *La Bohème*.' She blushed as the panel smiled at one another. Of course they knew what opera it was from, how stupid she was. She turned and walked over to the piano, her legs trembling with panic, her thoughts flying in all directions. She couldn't remember the words, had forgotten the phrasing and even the first bars of music. If only Mam had come with her.

Then she caught the smile of the pianist, and saw her encouraging nod. The woman's hands hovered over the keys and Catriona took a deep breath. The words came back to her and she was soon lost in Mimi's world of embroidered flowers which transports the consumptive girl out of her narrow room into the fields and meadows outside the Latin Quarter of Paris.

As the last note died the elderly gentleman spoke again. 'Thank you, my dear. Would you please wait outside?'

Catriona glanced across at Peter. Had she failed? Were they going to turn her down? She looked back at the ten people behind the table. They were deep in hushed conversation and it looked as if they had already forgotten her.

Peter led her from the room and sat her down on a chair in the broad corridor. 'It won't be long,' he said softly. 'But they have a lot to discuss. This is a vast enterprise and there are very few scholarships for students who cannot afford the fees. They have to be certain they make the right decision, for you weren't the only one being auditioned today.'

Catriona finally became aware of other young people waiting in that corridor. There were several boys and three other girls – some of them held instruments, others held sheets of music. All of them looked pale and drawn, and as terrified as she was. She caught the eye of the girl opposite – a pretty girl with fair hair and blue eyes, wearing a dress that must have cost a fortune – and smiled. The girl regarded her coldly and after a swift, appraising glance over Catriona's shabby clothes, looked away. But the boy with the violin next to her grinned, and that made her feel a little better.

'Are they all wanting a scholarship?' she whispered to Peter. Some of the others didn't look as if they were poor, especially the blonde girl.

He shook his head. 'It's the beginning of a new year,' he replied softly. 'They are choosing this year's intake from other academies and musical establishments.'

The waiting seemed to go on for ever as one by one the students were called back into the room. She could tell if they had been successful or not by their expressions when they returned to the corridor. The blonde girl strode out, a triumphant gleam in her eye as she picked up her expensive coat and slipped it around her shoulders. With a sneering glance at Catriona, she swung her hips as she walked along the corridor, then broke into a run as she raced down the stairs.

Catriona heard her name and she stood up. 'Wish me luck,' she breathed.

'You don't need it,' he said. 'But you have it anyway.'

She walked into the room and stood before the table. The bespectacled gentleman sifted through the papers in front of him. 'You are very young,' he began, and her spirits fell. 'But there are possibilities here which are rather marvellous. Your voice is untutored, and the tone is unequal. Yet you have made a tremendous impression on the panel. The mood was imaginative and stirred the soul, while the rough beauty of your voice shone out like a beacon.' He eyed her over his spectacles. 'You are a true soprano, Catriona. With a most artistic perception of what the music conveys.'

Catriona didn't dare move, couldn't have stirred an inch she was so tense.

'Therefore, Catriona, we are willing to offer you a full scholarship for three years. Term begins in two weeks time.'

Catriona could finally breathe. The air escaped in a long, drawn-out sigh. 'Thank you,' she murmured.

'We expect great things of you, Catriona. I hope you will not let us down.'

'Never,' she breathed. 'Thank you, thank you.' She wanted to kiss each and every one of them, but knew that such behaviour would be frowned upon, so she hurried from the room and threw her arms around Peter Keary instead. 'I've got it,' she said through her tears and laughter.

'Told you,' he replied as he hugged her. 'Come on. We've got some shopping to do, and after that I'll treat you to a slap-up tea.'

The tall, cool-eyed blonde girl was called Emily Harris. She was

149

the daughter of a wealthy beef exporter and had the most beautiful contralto voice. Catriona thought she was terribly sophisticated and envied her beautiful clothes, but Emily was a bitch, and she caused Catriona a great deal of hurt in the first few months at the Academy.

Catriona would arrive each day having walked from the boarding-house in the hills. Emily would be dropped off by her mother in a sleek car. At first, Catriona had tried to make friends with her; she was a sociable person and unused to hostility, especially when there appeared to be no reason for it. But her advances of friendship were snubbed, and Catriona had to accept that Emily considered herself, at eighteen, to be far too grand.

Coming out of the music room one morning, she saw Emily and two other girls giggling behind their hands. They had obviously been talking about her for they fell silent and watched her with almost greedy anticipation. 'G'day,' she said brightly. 'How 'ya goin'?'

'Will you listen to that,' drawled Emily who'd had the benefits of a private education in England. 'The standards of this place must have dropped. Fancy letting a gypsy in.' She turned to the others, and in a stage whisper, said. 'Her mother works as a waitress. Can you believe it?'

Catriona reddened as the girls giggled. She'd had this kind of treatment from Emily before and she knew her pernicious gossip would one day reach the tutors. Well, she decided, she wouldn't stand for it any longer. 'I heard you still have that break between your head and chest registers,' she said coldly. 'You want to watch out,' she warned. 'End of term exams are next week, and you could find yourself out on your ear.'

'Common little guttersnipe,' hissed Emily. 'What does she know?'

Catriona watched the girls stroll away arm in arm. Her comment had hit its mark, for Emily was aware of the insecurity of her voice between the two octaves of bottom G to top G, and the glint in those blue eyes had revealed she was still struggling to cure it.

Catriona walked slowly down the corridor after them. Emily and her coterie of friends were welcome to each other. There were boys and girls at the Academy who were friendly and kind and although she had a wealth of life experience that the others couldn't even imagine, she was beginning to make friends and settle in.

The days passed one after the other, every minute filled with music lessons, voice coaching and tutorials. They pored over books illustrated with photographs of the great names of the opera world – Ludwig and Malwina Schnorr von Carolsfeld, Rosa Ponselle, and of course Dame Nellie Melba – and discussed stage-sets and costumes and the different interpretations of the great operas. Catriona, having such a good grounding in stagecraft, dancing and singing, optimised her advantage and threw herself wholeheartedly into the lessons. Even her piano playing had advanced in leaps and bounds.

As the first year drew to a close, she had studied most of the older Italian arias, as well as the songs of Purcell, and Handel and excerpts from the *Choral Cantatas*. Her tutors were now concentrating on building a repertoire for her, for soon she would take part in the soirées the Academy held once a term.

Catriona enjoyed the camaraderie of the other students and loved joining in when they gathered in the drawing room after lessons. This was their time to relax from the strictures of their education; to play popular songs on their instruments, to sing together, their voices rising in harmony so sweet it sent Catriona home each night to that crowded little room with a sense of fulfilment.

Velda still worked in the hotel, but her demeanour hadn't changed despite Catriona's successes. She remained silent and stern, her wiry body constantly on the move, her hands always restless. Yet she demanded Catriona told her about each day, about what she'd learned, and what she'd achieved. It was as if she'd given up on her own life and was living through her daughter.

The Academy staged many performances for the public. They were show-cases for their best students, and there was great rivalry among them to take part. Catriona was the youngest there, and so had to be content with minor roles and the occasional duet. But as the second year ended and her voice strengthened and matured, she was finally given the chance to perform her first solo in public.

Her aria was from Act I of Purcell's *Dido and Aeneas*. The song, a magnificent expression of sorrow, had to be delivered in a dignified and restrained manner as befitted the Queen of Carthage. Yet it had to be worthy of the tragedy it foreshadowed and at no point could it belie the conflict implied in its final words, 'Peace and I are strangers grown.'

Catriona waited in the wings as her friend Bobby finished his violin solo. The music soared to the rafters of that great stage, swept through the curtains and overhangings and deep into her soul. He was a wonderful musician, and she'd liked him from the moment he'd winked at her after her first audition.

He came off the stage, flushed with pleasure. 'Good luck,' he whispered. 'You look gorgeous, by the way.'

She grinned back at him. The dress was gold and it clung to her like a second skin. The cape of gossamer lace sparkled with thousands of sequins, and the paste jewellery sparked in the overhead lights. Her hair had grown to her waist, and today it had been piled high and fixed with glittering pins. She felt regal and as she was introduced, she took a deep breath and walked confidently onto the stage. This was her moment to shine.

The music began and her voice filled the auditorium with its purity and sadness. She held the audience in thrall as she portrayed the tragic Queen of Carthage, and when the last note drifted away there was a stunned silence.

As she bowed low she was deafened by the storm of applause. People were standing now, calling for more, clapping and cheering. She bowed again, overwhelmed at their response, and unsure what to do next. They had been forcibly reminded that time was of the essence and no performer was to do an encore. But Catriona came from a theatrical family and it was hard to fight the instinct to sing again.

The Principal of the Academy came on stage to join her and present her with a bouquet of flowers. 'Well done,' he said beneath the roar of the audience. 'How does it feel to be a star?'

'Wonderful,' she breathed as she looked down into the audience and saw her mother sitting in the front row next to Peter. Velda's hands were tightly clasped to her narrow chest, her eyes glistening with tears. The pride in her expression said more than all the applause and Catriona could feel her own tears well in her eyes, for without Velda's determination and steadfast belief in her, she would never have come so far.

There had been rumours of war over the months before Catriona turned eighteen. Several short weeks later war was finally declared in Europe. The Academy was buzzing with the news, the radio was on constantly, the talk always about the German advances and the part Australia would be expected to play.

She noticed how the boys listened avidly to the news from Europe, how they talked of going away to fight, to join up and show the world Australia was a proud country full of brave men willing to fight a just cause. Catriona listened and didn't dare voice her loathing for such talk. Her da had told her about the Great War and the carnage in the fields of France – how could anyone wish to take part in such a terrible thing?

'They're so young,' she said to Peter that evening. She and Velda had joined him for a late supper in a smart restaurant just down from the Sydney Town Hall. 'Bobby seems determined to throw in his music and join up. Nothing I say will persuade him otherwise.'

'He's a young man,' replied Peter as he put down his knife and fork. 'If it wasn't for my weak chest, I'd join up too.' He saw their surprise. 'I contracted pleurisy as a child. The slightest chill and my lungs seize up and I'm in bed for days.'

'Thank goodness,' breathed Catriona. 'I couldn't bear to lose you as well as Bobby.'

He eyed her thoughtfully. 'It seems this young man occupies your thoughts a great deal. I hope there's nothing serious between you. You are on the brink of a fine career; you haven't time for that sort of nonsense.'

Catriona blushed. Bobby had kissed her the night of her triumphant first performance. It had been a soft night, she remembered, as they'd stood outside the Academy theatre and looked up at the stars. His kiss had come as no surprise – he'd been angling for one for ages – but she'd been warmed at how tender he'd been, how hesitant. Yet she'd gently pulled away when his hands threatened to crush her to him – she wasn't ready for that kind of intimacy again.

'Catriona would never do anything to damage her career,' said Velda as she gave up on the food and pushed the plate away. 'She's worked too hard and too long for it. We both have.'

To Catriona it sounded like a veiled threat to remember the sacrifices they had both made to get this far. The warmth of the restaurant closed in on her, smothering all joy she'd garnered from a pleasant evening. The memory of her child kept her focussed – for once she was established she could begin her search – and yet she was fully aware it could take years.

*

153

Catriona graduated from the Academy with the highest honours, and Peter set about arranging a busy concert schedule for her. It would be impossible to launch her international career while the war was on in Europe, but he was determined to do as much as he could within Australia. There were no theatres large enough to stage a full opera, and apart from the Town Hall in Sydney and the Conservatorium, there were only the concert halls and oratories big enough to stage solo performances.

Catriona was deeply saddened by Bobby's enlistment into the army, and she'd skipped rehearsals that morning to wave goodbye to him on the station platform. Peter found her in tears and he put his arm around her shoulders as they walked back to his car. 'He'll come back,' he said.

'But he's my friend,' she sobbed, dabbing at her face with his handkerchief. 'I'm going to miss him terribly.'

'Oh, dear,' he sighed. 'So that's the way of it.'

'What do you mean?'

He took the handkerchief and gently wiped away the tears that were still streaming down her face. 'First love is always the hardest,' he murmured.

She looked at him in amazement. 'I don't love him. He's a friend, a very dear friend. I can't believe he was stupid enough to fall for all that old propaganda and warmongering.' She snatched the hankie back and blew her nose.

He didn't start the car, merely sat back and watched her.

'What?' He was beginning to make her feel uncomfortable.

'I was just wondering how you feel about me,' he said softly.

Catriona blushed beneath his scrutiny. She adored him. He was her mentor, her Svengali. His dark eyes and gentle Irish brogue reminded her of Da, and despite the fact he was almost twenty years older than her, she couldn't imagine life without him. 'I think you know,' she whispered.

His finger softly traced the curves of her cheekbones and came to rest in the dimple at her chin. 'I've loved you since the moment I saw you in that ridiculous cocktail bar. You were beautiful then, but now you are truly the most glorious of women.'

She felt as if she was drowning in his eyes.

'Will you marry me, Catriona?'

'You'll have to ask Mam,' she whispered.

He laughed, tilting back his head and filling the car with the

154

sound. 'Of course,' he said finally. 'I forgot how young you still are.' He grew serious. 'You have a maturity about you that is way beyond your years and yet at times you are like a child. Are you sure you can marry an old man like me, Kitty? I will be forty soon, and I'm not the fittest of men. You could have your pick of any man in Australia . . .'

She silenced his protest by putting her finger to his lips. 'Then I pick you,' she murmured.

He crushed her to him and kissed her, and she responded, ready and willing to trust this man with her life, her career and her heart.

Velda gave her consent and they were married in the Catholic Church in Macquarie Street. Catriona's dress was a gossamer confection of lace and silk, and she carried a bouquet of the palest yellow roses. There was no time for a honeymoon, her busy schedule didn't permit it, and Peter had to travel to Melbourne to be with one of his other clients. Yet Catriona was happier and more content than she had been for years. They had the rest of their lives to be together, and soon, very soon she would begin the search for her baby.

The thought of the child she'd given away was the only shadow on her horizon. She should have told Peter right from the start, in fact, she should have told him the moment he proposed. But it had never seemed to be the right time for such a confession, and she suspected it was her own fear of his reaction that kept her silent. Now, after six months of blissful marriage she made the decision to tell him. It would take courage, but she was confident enough in Peter's love to believe he would understand.

Their rented apartment was on the ground floor of an elegant Victorian mansion which backed onto Hyde Park, and was a short walk down into Sydney's main shopping area. The rooms were big, the ceilings high and the sun poured in through the long bay windows. Catriona had enjoyed shopping for furniture and curtains and was blissfully happy. Her career was blossoming, her marriage was a success, and her husband was a kind and patient lover. It was as if he'd understood her fears even though she had never voiced them, and his lovemaking was always gentle.

Catriona hadn't been this content for years and she rushed back from rehearsals to change her clothes and prepare a special dinner. Peter's agency had gone from strength to strength, his reputation growing in stature as he represented some of the best theatricals in Australia. Her career was beginning to take off too, and at last she felt confident enough to speak out. The time had come to tell Peter about her baby.

'It'll be all right,' she kept muttering as she laid the table and lit the candles. 'Peter loves me. He'll understand, and help me to find her.'

They sat close to one another in the candle-lit room, and talked softly of their day as they ate the steak and fried potatoes Catriona had so carefully cooked and fretted over. The wine was white and crisp and cold, the crystal glasses glittering and sparking in the light from the candles. As she poured the coffee her engagement ring flashed and the deep lustre of her wedding ring shone warmly against her skin. The time had come.

'Peter?' she began.

'Mmm?' He was cutting a slice of cheese.

'Peter, there's something I've got to tell you.'

He put down the knife and wiped his mouth on a linen napkin. 'Sounds terribly serious, my little Kitty Keary,' he said with a twinkle in his eye. 'Come on then, what have you done? Overspent on the housekeeping again, bought a new frock?'

'It's a bit more serious than that, my darling, and I want you to listen very carefully.' She took a sip of wine to calm her nerves and, with her eyes downcast, began to tell him about Kane and her lost child.

Peter remained silent all through the story, moving only to pick up his glass of wine and sip from it.

Encouraged, Catriona rushed through the rest of her tale. 'Now we're married,' she finished breathlessly. 'I can find my baby and bring her home. We can bring her up together. We can be a proper family.' She finally lifted her gaze to his face and froze.

Peter Keary's eyes were like cold beach pebbles. His mouth was a thin line beneath the neat moustache and his face was ashen. He regarded her for a moment, holding her in his gaze as surely as a fly trapped in a spider web. 'Why didn't you tell me this before?' His voice was low, any emotion he might be feeling was tightly reined.

'There never seemed to be the right time,' she replied. 'I know I should have, but what with coaching and rehearsals and all the wedding preparations there just didn't seem to be a moment to ourselves.' She was babbling now, growing ever more nervous beneath his glare. She felt a chill of foreboding sweep over her and she reached out to touch him, in the hope she could somehow communicate her anguish and need for his understanding.

He moved his arm as if her hand might contaminate him and pushed away from the table. 'You lied to me, Catriona.'

'Not lied,' she replied swiftly. 'Just not told you before now.'

'It amounts to the same thing,' he replied with an icy reserve. 'You have deceived me, Catriona. You allowed me to believe you were innocent when we married. And yet you have the gall to sit there and tell me this disgusting tale and expect me to forgive you.'

Catriona blushed to the roots of her dark hair in shame. 'I'm not asking for forgiveness,' she said fiercely. 'Just for your understanding.'

He stood and leaned towards her. 'No, Catriona. What you're asking is for me to overlook your shady past and take in your bastard.'

Stung by this injustice she felt her temper rise. 'I was a kid,' she snapped. 'I didn't want Kane to do what he did, but I didn't have a choice. As for the baby, she's innocent and I won't have you call her a bastard.'

'Why not? It's what she is.' He picked up a cigar from the humidor and carefully snipped off the end.

Catriona knew she had to keep her temper. Things said in the heat of the moment could never be taken back. Yet his coldness frightened her. This Peter, who stood so calmly before her as he lit his cigar, was a stranger. He reminded her too much of Kane, and the thought made her feel sick.

She pushed her chair back from the table and stood to face him. 'Please,' she begged. 'If you love me, then please, please try and understand how hard it was for me to confide in you.' She grabbed his arm. 'But I had to, don't you see? She's out there somewhere and I have to get her back.'

He shook himself free of her grasp. 'You're in danger of losing your mind, Catriona,' he said flatly. 'For no sane woman would want to keep the progeny of such a perversion, let alone expect her husband to condone it.' He poured a large brandy into a crystal balloon glass, and tossed it down. 'There will be no more talk of this,' he said finally. 'I forbid you ever to mention it again.'

'You can't mean that,' she said, the tears welling in her eyes, a lump growing in her throat.

'I do,' he said filmly. 'I have a reputation to uphold, and I will not have my good name dragged in the mud.' His expression was grim as he looked at her. 'It won't do your career any good either,' he said. 'And after all the time and money I've put into getting you where you are today, I'm damned if I'll let you destroy it.'

Kitty stood there and looked at him. There wasn't a glimmer of compassion in his face. His stance was square, his demeanour impenetrable, his very presence a barrier to all her hopes and dreams. 'You don't love me at all, do you?' she breathed as the awful truth slowly dawned. 'You saw me as your protégée and to protect your investment you married me to keep me to yourself.'

'Very astute, my dear. But I hardly think there's any need to get hysterical over what, until now, has been a very pleasant business arrangement.'

Catriona threw down the table napkin and glared at him, her voice rising with each word. 'How dare you call our marriage a business arrangement. I married you because I loved you, not because I thought you'd make me famous.'

He remained silent, moving only to put the cigar to his lips and puff smoke into the hot evening stillness.

Catriona was trembling. The passion and the pain ripped through her as she saw behind the urbane mask of the man she'd married and realised he was concerned only for his business and his reputation. She counted for nothing. 'Why, Peter?' she asked. 'Why the pretence, the awful charade? You didn't have to make me fall in love with you – we could have worked together, remained friends.'

His gaze was still impersonal as he looked back at her. 'I saw a young, very beautiful girl with an amazing voice and realised this was my chance to really make a name for myself. Of course, I had to ensure you weren't poached by another agent and the only way I could do that was to marry you.'

'You bastard,' she hissed. 'You're as deceitful and manipulative as Kane.'

He slammed the glass on the sideboard and stood there for a moment, his back to her, his fists clenching and unclenching at his sides. 'You will never refer to me in that way again,' he said coldly. He swung round, his hands flexing at his sides, his face bleached of colour.

Catriona grabbed the back of a chair. She was trembling so much she could barely stand. Did he mean to hit her? Had she pushed him too far?

'You will never speak that man's name again in my house, and will certainly never compare me to him. I've spent a great deal of money on you, waited for three years until your mother gave me permission to marry you. You will show me respect and obedience, Catriona. I demand it.'

She shook her head. 'I'll do no such thing,' she retorted. 'How can I when you show no respect for me or my feelings? I told you about my baby because I thought you were a big enough man to understand how important she is to me.' She laughed, a harsh bark of sound that had the bite of scorn overriding a bitter humour. 'I can't believe how stupid I've been, and as for obeying you – forget it, Peter.'

'Then you leave me no alternative,' he said with a lack of any emotion. 'You may stay in this house, but you will sleep in another room and take all your meals there. You will keep out of my sight when I am at home, and I will not speak to you again until you have come to your senses and apologised.'

Catriona was almost vibrating with rage. She clenched her fists, willing herself to remain calm. 'Hell will freeze over before I ever share your bed again,' she snapped. 'As for apologising, forget it. I want a divorce.'

'Never,' he replied. 'Divorce is out of the question and will cause a scandal.'

'I don't care,' she stormed. 'I refuse to live under these conditions. If you won't give me a divorce, then I'll get one for myself.' She lifted the skirt of her evening gown and fled from the room.

159

Chapter Eleven

Catriona heard him slam the door and raced to the window. She watched him drive off, the car going too fast around the corner. Turning away, she hastily pulled the cases down from the wardrobe. The tiny knitted baby clothes were still lying in the bottom, wrapped in tissue and mothballs. She had been unable to leave them behind – unable to give them away – for it would have been like abandoning her child all over again.

She sniffed back the tears. They wouldn't help, and she didn't know how long she had before Peter returned. Stuffing her clothes into the cases, she gathered up the rest of her belongings and threw them in too. She would leave the jewellery he'd bought her, the silk negligées and gossamer wraps he'd liked to see her wear. The thought of him touching her made her go cold. How could she not have seen? How could she not have realised her marriage was a sham? He'd been so clever, so deceitful, she could never forgive him.

With her cases packed and the housekeeping money in her purse she tied the sheet music in a bundle with her books and photographs. She closed the front door behind her and shoved the key through the letter-box before hailing a passing taxi cab. At least living in the city meant that transport wouldn't be a problem.

The driver helped load her luggage, but his cheerful chatter began to grate and he eventually fell silent as he drove through the back streets of Sydney. It was as if her mood had been more eloquent than words. They arrived at their destination and she waited for him to unload her things, paid him off and turned to face the house.

Doris opened the door immediately. 'Hello, dearie. What's all this?' The pleasant face was wreathed in lines that no amount of make-up could hide.

160

'Where's Mam?' She heaved the cases inside and stacked the rest of her things on top before struggling out of her coat.

Doris eyed the suitcases, the expensive evening gown and Catriona's stormy expression. 'She's out the back making us a cuppa.' She hesitated and touched Catriona's arm. 'She ain't well at all, luv,' she whispered conspiratorially. 'Reckon it's 'er chest playing up again.'

Catriona nodded. Mam hadn't really been well since they'd left Atherton, and it wasn't just her chest that caused her worry, it was the state of her mind. She followed Doris down the hallway into the tiny kitchen at the back of the house.

Velda turned with the teapot in her hand and almost dropped it when she saw her daughter standing there in her evening gown. 'What are you doing here?' she demanded.

'I need somewhere to stay,' replied Catriona. 'I thought I could share with you for a while until I get my own place.'

Velda's mouth was a thin line of disapproval. 'Trouble already? I did warn you, Catriona. He's a much older, sophisticated man. He won't put up with tantrums.'

Catriona was all too aware of Doris standing in the doorway, face alight with curiosity. 'Can we go somewhere to talk, Mam?' she said quietly.

'You can say what you want in front of Doris,' she replied as she swiftly ran a cloth over the sink and the top of the great white cooker.

Catriona doubted very much if Velda wanted their dirty laundry washed in public, even if it was only Doris. 'I'll be up in your room, Mam,' she said between clenched teeth. 'We can talk there.'

Velda gave a great sigh, and handed the pot to Doris who was looking extremely put out at not being included in the conversation. She slowly followed Catriona up to her solitary bedroom and closed the door before collapsing, out of breath, on the bed. The house was quiet, the lodgers out as it was Saturday night. 'What happened?' she asked as she leaned against the pillows.

Catriona stood at the window where she'd stood so many times before. She gazed out at the lights of the city. 'I told him about the baby,' she said finally.

Velda gasped and sat up. 'You stupid, stupid girl,' she snapped. 'Have you not got the sense you've been born with?'

'It seems not,' she replied flatly. She went on to tell her the whole sordid little story and when she'd finished she was once again close to tears.

161

'You go back there and beg that man on your knees for forgiveness,' shouted Velda. 'He's done everything for you – everything.'

Catriona spun around to face her. She couldn't believe what she was hearing. 'How can you side with him after what he's done? He deliberately set out to marry me, to keep me for himself; he even had the brass neck to admit he'd never loved me. But he showed his true colours tonight and I'll never go back to him. Never.'

Velda was off the bed and standing before her. Her hand flashed out and hit Catriona's face, leaving the marks of her fingers against the pale skin. 'That's for your stupidity,' she snapped. She hit her again. 'And that's for letting Kane's bastard ruin your life and everything we've worked for over the years.'

Catriona touched the angry marks on her face. She was so shocked by her mother's reaction she could barely think straight, let alone speak.

'You're an ungrateful girl, Catriona,' she said, her breath coming in jagged gasps as she fought the tightness in her chest. 'Selfish. As if I'm not ill enough without all this.' Velda collapsed back onto the bed.

Catriona stared at her for a long moment and then left the room. Her high-heeled shoes clattered down the linoleum on the stairs and she almost knocked Doris over in her haste to leave.

'Whoa there, girl. You aren't going anywheres like that.' She put a plump arm around Catriona's waist and steered her into the sitting room. 'Come on, luv. Have a cuppa and calm down.'

'Can I stay here, Doris?'

The bright blonde hair remained perfectly in place as Doris shook her head. 'Sorry, luv. I'm full up.' She offered Catriona a cigarette which was refused and lit one for herself 'But I got a mate lives down near the 'arbour. She's got a lovely little unit for rent. You could go there.'

Catriona could barely breathe for the heavy cloud of smoke coming from Doris's cigarette. Fearful of what it might be doing to her lungs and vocal chords, she quickly wrote down the address. 'Could you phone your friend and tell her I'll be there tonight?' she asked. 'And then phone for a taxi?' She saw Doris hesitate. 'I'll pay for the calls,' she said quickly as she pulled a ten bob note out of her purse.

Within an hour Catriona was standing in the middle of a small, first-floor apartment that looked out over the harbour. The rent was reasonable and it was clean. The furniture and decor left a great deal to be desired, but she'd lived with worse. She felt strangely liberated, for this would be the first time she would live alone. Yet the events of the night still had a surreal reality about them and she was finding it hard even to think about the consequences.

She walked slowly through the bedroom, the tiny kitchen and bathroom and back into the lounge. There was a narrow balcony hanging outside the lounge windows and she stepped out and looked at the view. There were boats going back and forth and the Sydney ferry was just entering the harbour. The lights of the buildings were still shining out into the night sky, despite there being a war on. But of course they were so far away from Europe it probably wouldn't matter anyway. They would be quite safe here on the other side of the world.

She left the apartment early the next morning and went to see a solicitor. His advice had been delivered in a flat monotone. Women could not initiate divorce unless there was indisputable proof that their husbands had been unfaithful, and her reputation would indeed be ruined should he divorce her on the grounds of her heinous deceit.

Catriona picked up her handbag and left his office. Bugger her reputation, and bugger Peter. She would get the divorce and to hell with everyone. She marched down the street at such an angry pace she arrived at the theatre without remembering how she'd got there. Storming into her dressing room, she unlocked the small box in the bottom of the dressing-table and took out the contract. She held it for a moment, remembering how thrilled she'd been when she had first signed it, then tore it into tiny pieces. They fell on the floor like confetti – a reminder of her lovely wedding – and she burst into tears.

The dresser tapped on the door and came in. Brian Grisham was an effeminate man of indeterminate age, with a penchant for lurid waistcoats and tinted hair, who'd worked in theatres since he was a boy. He'd shortened his name to Brin, because he thought it sounded less butch. 'Oh, my Lord,' he exclaimed as he knelt in front of her. 'What's all this?' He put a hand on her arm. 'Come on, darling,' he soothed. 'Tell Aunty Brin all about it.'

'My marriage is over,' she sobbed. 'Peter Keary is a complete and utter bastard.'

163

'That's men for you,' he said with a flick of his head. 'Brutes – all of them.'

She smiled through her tears. Brin was as good and kind as any girlfriend and twice as understanding. 'I've torn up my contract,' she confessed.

He looked at the paper scattered across the floor and raised a fiercely plucked eyebrow. 'Oh, dear,' he sighed. 'That wasn't terribly clever, my darling. He'll sue the pants off you.'

'I don't care,' she said as she wiped away the tears.

'You can't work without an agent,' he reproached her softly. 'What are you going to do?'

'Find another one,' she retorted as she picked up the hairbrush and began to attack her long hair.

Brin took the brush from her and with soft, sweeping strokes began to soothe her. 'That won't be easy,' he said finally. 'Agents stick together; upset one, you upset them all.' He continued to brush her hair. 'I have a friend who might help,' he muttered after some thought. 'She's like you, independent, couldn't care less about gossip, and knows what brutes men can be.' He put down the brush and standing behind her, looked at their reflection in the mirror. 'Clemmie can be a bit butch, but she's got a heart of gold, and I'm sure she'll help.'

Catriona didn't know if she wanted anything to do with a lesbian agent. Her reputation was about to be damaged enough, and although she had worked with such women, she'd always felt uncomfortable in their company, and didn't relish the idea of being represented by one. She hesitated.

Brin seemed to read her thoughts, and he grinned. 'Clemmie's got three kids and a *very* handsome husband. She's tough because she works in a man's world – just as we all do,' he added with a sigh.

'Give me her number and I'll call her.' Catriona smiled up at him. 'Thanks, Brin. You're a sweetheart.'

Clementine Frost was tall and slim, with short brown hair, brown eyes and a determined air of efficiency. She was in her early thirties, and wore severely cut jackets and tailored trousers, softened by frilly shirts and large pieces of jewellery. Her make-up was flawless, her nails long and painted scarlet to match her lipstick. Catriona was pleasantly surprised to discover they struck up a rapport immediately.

164

The office was like no other. It was a large, sunlit room in the basement of her family home, comfortably furnished with deep chairs and couches, expensive rugs and vases of fresh flowers. The doors at the end of the room opened out into a lovely garden, and she could see children's swings and slides littering the grass.

The two women faced one another across the coffee table. 'You'll have to complete the rest of Peter's schedule,' Clemmie said in her clear, concise voice. 'But I don't see any reason why I shouldn't take you on once I've sent him a formal letter of explanation.' Her dark eyes were appraising. She'd asked few questions as to why Catriona no longer wanted her husband to represent her, and seemed unconcerned about the future. 'I've heard of you, of course.' She smiled. 'The reviews are wonderful. I'll be delighted to take you on.'

'Peter will sue me for breach of contract,' Catriona said. 'And then there's the question of the divorce. Are you sure?'

Clementine stood and smiled. 'I think we're both strong enough to deal with all that when the time comes,' she said. 'And should you need a good solicitor, I'm sure my husband can help you.' She reached out and they shook hands. 'Just remember you have a wonderful talent that will be your saviour in the end. I promise.'

Catriona took Brin a huge bouquet of flowers and a box of his favourite chocolates to say thank you.

A week later she took a phone call from Doris. 'You'd better come over,' she said tearfully. 'Your mum's not at all well.'

Catriona made her apologies to the music director and took a cab. The guilt was awful. She hadn't been to see her mother since the night she'd left Peter – she hadn't been well then – what if she was too late? Doris wouldn't have phoned unless it was an emergency.

She ran up the stairs of the boarding-house and into the room she had once shared with Velda. It was dark, the curtains drawn tightly against the bright sunlight. Velda looked very small in the narrow bed and the only sound was the terrible rattle and wheeze in her chest.

Velda opened her eyes and Catriona was shocked by the weariness in them, the almost blank appraisal. 'Kitty?' Her voice was just above a whisper.

'Yes, Mam. I'm here.' She turned to Doris who had puffed up the stairs behind her, Mr Woo draped like a fur wrap in her arms. 'Has the doctor been?'

Doris nodded. 'About an hour ago. He's making arrangements to take her into hospital.'

'What is it?' Catriona demanded.

'Pneumonia,' said Doris with a sniff. Her mascara was running and her lipstick was smeared. 'She never shook off that cold she had last winter, and her coughing has been something dreadful, but she refused to let me get the doctor sooner.' She hugged the dog. 'I did all I could, Catriona. She's my best friend.'

Catriona gave her a wan smile of understanding and then turned back to the ravaged figure in the bed. Despite all that had happened in her short life, Velda was still her mother and she loved her. As she sat there and filled the silence and the darkness talking about memories of the travelling troupe of players, she saw her mother's beautiful violet eyes clear and become focussed.

'Good days,' she murmured. 'We were so happy then.'

Catriona kissed the fevered cheek and stroked back the hair that had once been so lustrous. 'I love you, Mam,' she whispered.

'I love you too,' she gasped. Her eyes widened as she looked over Catriona's shoulder, and she lifted herself onto her elbow. 'Declan? Declan?' She fell back on the pillows, a smile on her face. 'Ahhh,' she sighed.

Catriona grasped the lifeless hand as the eyes closed again and the awful rasping, gurgle fell into profound silence.

Doris burst into tears and clattered downstairs. Catriona sat with Velda until the ambulance arrived. Her mother's pain and mental anguish was over, and if there truly was a heaven, then she would be with Da now.

Velda was laid to rest on a hot summer afternoon. The air was full of birdsong and the scent of newly mown grass and golden wattle. Catriona stood there after the ceremony was over and closed her eyes. The sounds and the scents were like the ones she remembered from her childhood. Velda was finally at peace.

The day after the funeral Peter Keary sued her for breach of contract. It took weeks and a great deal of manoeuvring by Clemmie's husband, John, to get the amount he was claiming brought down to a reasonable sum. Yet she would have to work hard for the next three years to pay him off.

The divorce took longer; but in the end he realised she didn't care one way or the other about her reputation, or his. He finally gave in when he met another woman, and the photographic proof of his infidelity pushed things through quickly.

Clemmie had proved to be a good friend, and when the news of the divorce was splashed all over the newspapers, she kept the reporters at bay and Catriona busy out of town. Yet, for all Peter's threats, the dreaded scandal was almost instantly suppressed by War news. The Japs had bombed Pearl Harbor – the Yanks were joining in at last to help poor, beleaguered England – and Singapore had fallen. The War in Europe had spread to the other side of the world and there was real fear that the Japanese would invade the great empty heart of Australia.

Catriona had never worked harder. With Brin and a small company of fellow singers and musicians, she travelled all over Australia to entertain the American troops who were in Australia for R&R, the Australian airmen of Broome and Darwin, and the ordinary people of the Outback who were struggling through a drought to survive without their men.

From Darwin down to Adelaide, from Brisbane to Perth and back to Sydney, she covered the breadth and depth of the country she'd travelled most of her life. She performed in village halls and hotel bars, next to aircraft hangars and Nissen huts. She travelled by train and by car, and even on horseback to reach the isolated towns of Australia's heartland – it was a powerful reminder of the years of the travelling troupe, and although she was exhausted, it gave her strength to carry on – for this was her heritage.

Her repertoire was eclectic, from opera to musical hall and the popular tunes of the day, and soon her popularity had spread and she earned the soubriquet of 'Outback Songbird'.

When Darwin and Broome were bombed and Japanese subs were spotted in Sydney Harbour she refused to give in to fear. The spirit of Australia was strong, and although she only had her singing to help the war effort, she knew it brought comfort and a few moments of pleasure into the lives of the men and women who defended her country with such bravery. It was a small sacrifice to make, even though she missed her apartment in Sydney and was exhausted by the long months of travelling.

As Britain and America won victory in Europe, the fighting intensified in the Pacific. It seemed it would never end. And yet the death of her mother, the divorce from Peter and the months of travelling had instilled in her a sense of freedom she had never

167

known. If it wasn't for the bureaucratic red tape, and the knowledge that her daughter remained firmly out of reach, Catriona would have enjoyed those War years.

She spent all her spare time searching in dusty offices through reams of paper, had bribed and begged and asked questions in every town. She had even charged Clemmie's husband to do what he could in his capacity of lawyer, but the heavy concert schedule meant she was rarely in one place for longer than a day, and with records and communications in chaos, it was impossible to make any headway.

Peace was declared and the men began to return home. Catriona was the star of the welcoming home concert, and after singing an aria from Purcell's *Dido,* she waited for the applause to finish and then introduced Bobby.

The boy she'd trained with at the Academy was now a man – a man who wept at night over the terrible things he'd witnessed in Burma. And yet his spirit refused to be broken, and his music had become his saviour. The first, quiet notes on the violin stilled the audience, and as the tune was recognised they broke into a rousing chorus of 'We'll Meet Again'.

It was a song made famous by Vera Lynn, and the most requested among the boys she'd entertained over those terrible years. As Catriona sang and the audience joined in with gusto, she was overwhelmed by the emotion that ran through the Sydney Town Hall. So many of the boys were injured, not only in their bodies, and yet, tonight, they had a chance to momentarily put all that behind them and rejoice in their home-coming.

A rousing chorus of 'Waltzing Matilda' followed and she was joined by her fellow performers on stage. Bobby grinned at her as he played his violin, the sweat running down his face, and Catriona grinned back. It was quite like old times when they used to jam in the refectory.

The audience seemed reluctant to leave and the concert finally broke up as the sky lightened. Catriona and Bobby stepped out of the stage door and spent almost an hour signing autograph books and posing for photographs. They eventually made their escape as the sun breached the horizon, and went their separate ways. Bobby to his wife and baby, Catriona to her lonely apartment.

Catriona was exhausted, and she asked Clemmie to give her a few months break so she could recuperate.

'Can't do that,' said Clemmie as she waved a contract at her. 'You're going to London.'

'I thought London was flattened?'

Clemmie shook her head. 'Battered, but never bowed. The bulldog spirit lives on despite Hitler.' She grinned. 'A bit like you and me, really,' she declared.

Catriona grinned back. She suddenly didn't feel at all tired. 'So, what's in London?'

'You'll be studying at the Opera School of the Royal College of Music for a few months, and then you'll join the Covent Garden Company and make your international debut at the Royal Opera House.' She looked down into Catriona's delighted face. 'You're on your way, Kitty,' she said proudly.

The following years passed in a blur. The Royal College of Music was far removed from the Sydney Academy, and she worked harder than ever to hone her skills to perfection. As the new year of 1949 began, Catriona celebrated her twenty-eighth birthday before her debut on the London stage.

She had found the sheer size and glamour of the enormous Royal Opera House overwhelming, for there had been nothing to match it back home. Despite the rationing and the hardships, the bombed-out sites and sheer devastation of the blitz, it seemed nothing could stop the British from pampering the arts. The scenery was magnificent, the orchestra huge, the lights and costumes bringing a magic to the whole experience that she would remember for ever. But the full power of the Opera House was seen from the stage. Tier upon tier of red velvet seats, and the rich gold decoration on the ceiling and around the walls were enhanced by the lights, the atmosphere and the music. It was breathtaking.

She was to sing the lead in Bizet's *Carmen*. The rehearsals had been going on for weeks and she was comfortable in the part, yet her legs were trembling so badly as she waited in the wings, she accepted a tot of whisky from one of the chorus to steady her nerves.

The orchestra had tuned up and the conductor had been applauded. A hush fell over the audience as the heavy velvet curtains drew slowly back as the prelude began. Catriona took a long drink of water and tried to use the nervous energy in a positive way. She had sung arias from this opera before – had been on stage before – but she knew how important this debut was, for if

169

it went well tonight her career would finally be set. She smoothed back her hair which had been left loose to fall to her waist and checked that the large gold hoops in her earlobes were fastened securely. Ruffling the scarlet and orange flamenco skirts she adjusted the red peasant blouse that drooped from her bare shoulders and then wriggled her toes. It had been her idea to play Carmen without shoes, but the damn floor was freezing.

The bell chimed out from the cigarette factory and the chorus girls pushed their way on stage. Catriona took a deep breath and steadied herself. As the shout 'Carmen' went up, she gathered her skirts and darted across the bridge and down the steps into the square, the crowd parting and making way for her. She flashed an insolent glare at the men pressing around her. 'Love you?' Her tone was scornful. 'Perhaps tomorrow. Anyhow, not today.'

She grinned at the men in the chorus and began to sway slowly to the rhythm of a habanera as she sang *L'amour est un oiseau rebelle*. She had become Carmen. Beautiful, wilful and dangerous, she moved around the stage as lithe as a panther, her violet gypsy eyes and flowing hair all part of the attempted seduction of Jose.

The performance finally reached its climax and the lights dimmed as the curtains closed on thunderous applause. Catriona was helped to her feet by the lead tenor who played Jose. He was a handsome man, but vain, and Catriona had been avoiding his advances for weeks. Yet tonight she let him kiss her. The adrenaline was flowing. She was still Carmen.

As she took curtain call after curtain call and the stage was smothered in the red roses the audience threw to her, she knew she had finally achieved her dream. How proud her parents would have been to see their daughter take her place on the world's stage and achieve the adulation of such an audience. If only they were still with her, she thought as they finally let her leave the stage. But their spirits would remain with her always – watching over her – giving her strength.

The next eleven years firmly placed Catriona Summers as an international diva. She sang the part of Floria Tosca at La Scala in Milan, Princess Turandot at the Metropolitan in New York, Mimi at the Grand Opera in Paris and Manon Lescaut at Covent Garden. She travelled to Spain and South America as well as the United States and now and again returned to sing in the smaller venues of Sydney, Melbourne and Adelaide.

It was 1960 and Catriona had returned to Sydney after a

triumphant debut at La Fenice in Venice where she'd sung the complex and exhausting title role in Handel's *Alcina*. She was thirty-nine.

Clemmie, John and Brin met her at the docks and drove her to the apartment by the river. She owned the whole building now, and after a complete overhaul, it was a luxurious hideaway from the bustle of her busy life. She loved being here, but her schedule rarely allowed it, so Brin had moved into the downstairs and kept an eye on it for her.

Brin, as flamboyant as ever, presented her with flowers. He was well past sixty, but still worked in the theatre. He adored Catriona, and the feeling was mutual. 'Welcome home, darling,' he cried as he kissed her hand. 'Now, I must rush – matinée performance – you know how it is.'

'He doesn't change,' murmured Catriona. 'Darling Brin. How he would have loved Europe.'

'You look well,' said Clemmie as John poured them all a drink. 'I wish I could keep my figure like that.' Clemmie had just turned fifty-four and had put on weight, and although it rather suited her, she felt it had made her look matronly.

'You shouldn't have retired,' replied Catriona as she slipped off the stiletto heels and wriggled her toes. 'You know you only get bored when you've no one to boss about but me.' Clemmie had closed the agency, but was still managing Catriona. Catriona grinned at her friend to take the sting out of the words and let her know she was only teasing. 'As for keeping my figure, I eat like a horse and sweat like one during rehearsals and performances. When I retire I'll probably get to be the size of a house – or at least a small barn.'

They all laughed and Catriona curled her legs beneath her on the couch and began to relax for the first time in an age. 'Of course sex has something to do with it,' she added quietly in the silence after the laughter. She giggled as John blushed. 'You've no idea what a rush it is to perform on stage in front of so many people. The music, the lights, the sheer passion of the opera is a wonderful aphrodisiac – you'd be surprised at the amount of times I've had to step around a couple doing it in the wings.'

'And you?' Clemmie glanced across at John who beat a hasty retreat into the other room. 'Have you found anyone special?'

Catriona pulled a face. 'There was a lovely artist in Paris. He painted that portrait over there.' She glanced at the painting and

171

could almost feel the sensual tension emanate from it. 'We made love in his studio – it was extremely satisfying – but then the French know all about sex. The only problem was, it was damn draughty in that attic and I nearly caught my death.'

They giggled like two schoolgirls.

'I also had a brief fling with an Englishman, but he lacked imagination when it came to the bedroom, and although he had a title and pots of money, I knew I couldn't keep up the pretence for the rest of my life. Far too exhausting.'

Clemmie looked at her with wide eyes. 'My God, Kitty, it's like the united bloody nations. I know it's the sixties, with free love and flower power, but I never thought you ...'

'Then there was Hank the Yank.' She giggled again. 'It's true what they say, one yank and they're off.' They fell about laughing and when John poked his head around the door and glared at them it only made it worse.

'So,' said Clemnmie once they'd calmed down. 'You haven't found Mr Right? You're leaving it a bit late, Kitty.'

Catriona shrugged. 'I've been married and that didn't work. I've been a mother and that didn't work either.' She smiled at her friend in whom she'd confided so many years ago and who never passed judgement. 'Don't worry about me, Clemmie. I'm having fun, and when I get too old and past it, I'll retire to the Outback and live out my days warm with the memory of the men I've loved.'

'That reminds me,' said Clemmie as she leaped off the couch. 'John has some really good news for you.' She hunted through the briefcase he'd been carrying and finally pulled out a sheaf of papers. 'Belvedere came on the market.' She waved the documents in the air with a flourish.

Catriona stared back at her. 'Belvedere?' she breathed. The excitement rushed through her and she was on her feet. 'How, when? Has John put in a bid?'

Clemmy grinned. 'As John and I have power of attorney over your business affairs while you're out of the country, we signed the deal three days ago. It's yours, Catriona.'

She took the documents and sat down with a thump. Belvedere had been a dream, an almost impossible dream that had been with her since childhood. Now she held the deeds in her hand. Her dream had become reality.

172

Chapter Twelve

There were still no theatres large enough in Sydney – or anywhere else in Australia – to stage a full opera or ballet. But in the 1950s, Goossens, the Director of the Conservatorium, began to pester the government to build a concert hall large enough to do so. The Sydney Opera House was an enormous project and caused discomfort to the government, stirring up scandal and rumours of shady dealings. It would take another thirteen years before Goossens' dream would come to fruition. Therefore, Catriona would be performing the role of Violetta in *La Traviata* in the Conservatorium.

She hurried out of the rehearsal hall and huddled beneath an umbrella. The rain was coming down so hard it bounced off the pavement and soaked her stockings. There wasn't a cab to be seen and she was beginning to wish she'd driven in that morning. As she stood sheltering from the rain, she was startled by a voice at her shoulder.

'Catriona?'

She turned and looked into the faded blue eyes of a stranger. The woman was, she guessed, in her sixties. She had no umbrella, was poorly dressed and her thin coat was soaked through, yet there was a certain pride in the set of her shoulders, a determination in the line of her mouth that seemed strangely familiar. 'Yes?' she replied, uncertain as to why this woman had approached her. She didn't look like an opera fan and Catriona suspected she was after money.

'You don't recognise me, do you?' she asked, her mouth turning down, the eyes sad.

Catriona looked at the lined and weary face, at the badly

bleached hair and smudged make-up. 'I'm sorry,' she muttered as she took a step forward to the edge of the pavement and quickly scanned the street for a sign of a cruising taxi. 'I think you're mistaken.'

'No,' said the woman forcibly as she reached out and grasped Catriona's arm. 'It's you what's got it wrong.'

'Let go of my arm,' said Catriona, now thoroughly disturbed by the intensity of this woman's expression. She'd heard of crazed fans, but that sort of thing happened to Elvis Presley, not opera divas. 'I don't know you, but if it's money you're after, here's a couple of dollars.' She scrabbled in her handbag and held out the coins.

The coins were ignored, but the intense gaze remained fixed on Catriona's face. 'Strike a light,' the woman breathed. 'I never thought I'd see the day when my little Kitty were too grand to speak to an old mate.'

Catriona froze. She recognised that voice, but it couldn't be. She ignored the taxi that had pulled up at the kerb – ignored the blast of his horn and the accompanying shout – for her attention was fixed to that pair of pale blue eyes. Recognition dawned as she finally saw beyond the bleached hair and the roughly applied make-up. 'Poppy?' she breathed. 'Poppy, is it really you?'

'Yeah,' she replied, digging her hands into her pockets. 'Not a pretty sight, I know, but it's me all right.'

Catriona flung her arms around her, ignoring the rain-sodden coat that was soaking her cashmere jacket, and the make-up that was probably marking the pale mink on her collar. This was Poppy, her friend, her surrogate mother, her partner in mischief and risqué stories. How awful she hadn't recognised her, but how wonderful to see her again.

They finally drew apart, the tears running down their faces, mingling with the rain. 'We must look a right sight,' sniffed Poppy as she dabbed her face with a none-too-clean handkerchief. 'And I've ruined yer lovely coat, an' all.'

Catriona could smell her cheap perfume in the mink, and could see the dampness spread through the expensive cashmere, but it didn't matter. 'A good dry-cleaner will sort it out,' she said swiftly as she sheltered them both under her umbrella. She linked arms with Poppy and drew her along the pavement. The taxi had gone screeching off to find another, more willing, passenger. 'Come on,

174

let's get out of the rain and have a cuppa.'

The milk bar was warm, the windows cloudy with condensation, and the smell of brewing coffee and hot meat pies made it all the more welcoming. There was a bustle about the place, with most of the tables occupied by office workers and women weighed down with shopping and children. Pop music blared from the juke box and a couple of teenagers were smooching in the corner.

They found a vacant table at the back of the room where it was a little quieter, and settled down. Divested of the ruined three-quarter length jacket and sodden umbrella, Catriona smoothed the fabric of the shantung suit she'd had made in Singapore, then checked her make-up in the small mirror from her handbag and re-applied lipstick.

'Blimey,' breathed Poppy as she struggled out of her dripping coat to reveal a cheap cotton dress that had faded from too many washes. 'You look just like yer mum. The dark hair and violet eyes are just the same, even down to the cleft in yer chin.'

Catriona put her things back in the crocodile handbag and snapped the clasp shut. 'Thanks, I'll take that as a compliment,' she said. She was feeling awkward suddenly, unsure of how to speak to this Poppy. Her delight in seeing her again was tempered by the knowledge their lives had taken very different directions. What on earth did they have in common any more?

'How is Velda? I ain't seen or eard of 'er since I left the troupe. I was 'oping she'd be with you today.'

Catriona leaned back on the slippery plastic bench. 'Mum passed away at the beginning of the War,' she said softly. 'She hadn't been well for some time, and when she got pneumonia, she wasn't strong enough to fight it off.' At the memory of her mother's last few hours she had to blink away the tears. 'She didn't live long enough to see all her ambitions for me fulfilled. She was the driving force behind my career, you see. I wouldn't have done all that I have without her.'

Poppy looked down at her swollen red hands which were tightly clasped on the table between them. The nails were bitten and the varnish was peeling. 'I'm sorry to 'ear that,' she murmured. 'I'd 'ave liked to 'ave seen 'er again.' She looked back at Catriona, her faded eyes bright with unshed tears. 'And yer dad?'

Catriona swiftly told her of the tragedy that had befallen her father and skimmed over the time she and her mother had lived

175

with Kane in Atherton. She had no intention of telling Poppy everything. The years as her confidante were long gone, and it would serve no purpose. 'Mam and I left Kane and eventually came down to Sydney. We lived in a boarding-house on the other side of town and worked in the dining room of one of the big hotels. She arranged for me to audition for an agent, and the rest, as they say, is history.'

'I never did trust that bloke, Kane,' said Poppy as she sat back in her seat and folded her arms across her skinny chest. 'Something funny about 'im. I remember telling Velda I thought 'e was a queer.'

Catriona didn't reply and there was an awkward silence between them after the waiter left their order on the table. As they sipped their tea and ate the toasted tea-cakes, Catriona took the opportunity to observe Poppy more closely.

She had aged badly, there was no doubt about it, and it was hardly surprising she hadn't recognised her. Poppy looked weary, lined with some unspoken troubles and had obviously not thrived since leaving the troupe. Yet there was still the same outrageous spark in her eyes which told Catriona that whatever had befallen Poppy, she hadn't given up on life entirely.

'You've changed,' said Poppy as if she'd been reading Catriona's thoughts. 'But then we both have.' She sighed. 'And you talk ever so posh.'

'Years of elocution lessons,' said Catriona with a grin. 'But the vocabulary I learned from you has come in handy on many occasions.'

Poppy grinned. 'Glad to know I done somethin' right. Ain't nothing like a good swear-up when yer pissed off.' She became solemn again. 'I've been following yer career in the papers. I was sorry to read about the divorce, but you've done well, Kitty. I'm proud of yer.'

Catriona pushed her plate aside. 'And what about you, Poppy? How did your life turn out?'

Poppy laughed, but there was little joy in it. 'You 'ave to ask?' she said. 'Look at me, Kitty. I ain't exactly an advert for success.' Her expression was sad as she fiddled with the spoon in the saucer. 'I'm sixty-one, Kitty. An old woman who's worn out with struggling. I work in the kitchens at the Sydney Hydro Hotel, and I live in a room right at the top that ain't big enough to swing a cat.' She grinned, her good mood fleetingly restored. 'If I 'ad one,' she added. 'But they don't allow pets.' She rapped the spoon on the saucer. 'The only good thing is I never 'ave to worry about feeding meself. The 'otel gives me bed and board as part of the wages.'

Catriona's heart went out to her as she remembered the pretty woman who'd been so excited about her adventure into the unknown. Poppy would have been in her mid-thirties then, she realised. 'What happened, Poppy?' Her voice was low as she reached out to still the busy hands.

'The usual,' she muttered with a shrug. 'I met a bloke and 'ad a bit of fun. We was working together in a factory in Brisbane, and I was still a bit of a looker meself back then. I fell hook, line and sinker. He was a good-looking bastard, with a charm about him I couldn't resist. I got pregnant, he shot through and I was left on me own again.'

She looked back at Catriona. 'I don't want you feeling sorry for me or nuffing,' she said sternly. 'I always was a sucker for a pair of brown eyes, and I knew what I was doing. I just hadn't planned on him shooting through like that and in nineteen thirty-two it was a real disgrace to get into that kind of trouble and have no man around.'

Catriona could imagine all too easily how Poppy would have found it a struggle. 'What did you do? Life couldn't have been easy, not with a baby to look after.'

'I got on with it. Well, you do, don't you?' she replied philosophically. 'I left Brisbane and come down 'ere, found another job in another factory and worked right up to the birth. Ellen was born on the Saturday, and I went back to work on the Monday.' She grinned. 'I was lucky it were over the weekend, 'cos I didn't lose any pay. My landlady was real nice and offered to baby-sit in exchange for me doing her washing and ironing.' She shrugged. 'I managed.'

'And then?' Catriona was finding it hard to imagine what life must have been for Poppy with no support, no family to help.

'I stayed at the factory right through the War and out the other side until Ellen was old enough to find work herself. Ellen's a good girl, hard-working and clever with 'er 'ands. She got a good place with a dress designer and was just beginning to do well when history repeated itself,' she said with a scowl.

Catriona sighed. The tale was all too familiar and her heart went out to her old friend.

'Ellen met Michael and got pregnant, but at least she got 'im to

177

marry 'er.' She grimaced. 'Not that it did her any good,' she said. 'He's a right bastard.'

'I'm sorry, Poppy,' sighed Catriona. 'It sounds as if you've had it really tough.'

'Yeah,' she said flatly. 'It 'as been tough, but you know me, never give up, that's my motto.'

Catriona heard the brave words, saw the brittleness in her determined smile and the tears in her eyes which betrayed the heartache inside. Poppy was obviously struggling to maintain her pride, and any offer of help would be seen as charity. And yet Catriona wanted to help, needed to help. Poppy had once been a good friend. 'Is Ellen here in Sydney?'

Poppy nodded. 'She's living in a unit down in Kings Cross with 'im and the baby. It's a rough place, Kitty – not somewhere to bring up a kid – but it's all they can afford on his wages as a potman in the pub.' Her smile wavered and didn't quite make it to her eyes. 'Reckon 'e drinks most of what's in them barrels, and when 'e's 'ad a few, 'e ain't good to be around.'

'You mean he's violent?' Catriona sat forward and clasped Poppy's fingers. 'Tell me what you want me to do to help.'

'Gawd,' she sighed. 'Am I that obvious?' When Catriona didn't reply, she gently withdrew her hands and reached once more for the empty cup. 'I need to get 'er outta there,' she muttered. 'He'll kill 'er one of these days, I knowl 'e will.'

Catriona's first instinct was to write a cheque and hand it over, but she knew Poppy's pride, however dented, wouldn't allow her to take it. She also knew it would bring her no satisfaction to do such a cold-blooded thing. Poppy needed more than money. She needed peace and her own home, needed reassurance that her little family were safe.

They sat in silence as the waiter brought them fresh tea. Catriona's mind was working fast. The germ of an idea began to grow. When the waiter had left and Poppy had revived from the hot, fragrant brew, she began to put the idea into words. 'Do you remember when we were going through Drum Creek, Poppy? I must have been about nine or ten, and I fell in love with a property down in the valley.'

'Yeah. Yer mum weren't too impressed, I remember, 'cos you kept on and on about leaving the life and settling down there. What about it?'

'I bought it six months ago,' she replied. She smiled as Poppy's eyes widened and began to sparkle again. 'I've not had the chance to go down there and see it again, but I can remember it as if it was yesterday.'

'A bit risky buying a big place like that without giving it the once-over,' said Poppy. 'If you ain't plannin' on living there, 'ow you gunna run it?'

'I've hired a manager,' she explained. 'He's experienced and came with excellent references. He'll run it until he retires and by then I'll have probably retired myself and settled down.' She stirred the tea and took a sip, thinking carefully of how to put her idea into words that Poppy wouldn't dismiss out of hand. 'There's a lot of land,' she began again. 'The homestead's probably in need of work if the agent's details were correct, but there's good outbuildings, a bunkhouse and cookhouse and all the usual barns and shacks. On the edge of the property, and nearest to the town, there's a small house and garden that used to be accommodation for the last owner's son. It's empty now.'

She let the words hang in the air between them, and watched the different fleeting expressions shadow Poppy's eyes. 'The house is basic, and not in very good order,' she finally went on. 'But it's close to the main track into Drum Creek, and there's a big area out the back which the owner's son used as a market garden. He evidently did very well selling his produce in the town.'

'Sounds nice,' said Poppy with studied indifference.

Catriona reached across the table and took her hand. 'Why don't we go there and explore, Poppy? I've been longing to see it all again, and it would be such fun if you came with me.'

'I got a job to go to,' she muttered. 'Can't be gadding about with you all over the bloody place, and anyways, what about them re'earsals? You ain't got time to bunk off.'

'The performance is a month away,' replied Catriona being rather liberal with the truth – it was in fact in three weeks' time. 'I can quite easily take a couple of days off,' she added adventurously. The conductor would be furious, not to mention the baritone who had a reputation for being pedantic about the timekeeping of any soprano who worked with him, but it would all be worth it if Poppy agreed to come with her.

She watched her face and saw the shadows in her eyes. Poppy was wavering, tempted by the chance to leave the city for a while,

179

but would her pride allow her to accept the offer Catriona was planning to make? She didn't know. She just hoped she hadn't pushed her too far too soon. All she could do now was wait.

'If I was to come,' said Poppy finally. 'I'd be paying me own way.' She looked squarely back at Catriona. 'How much is the fare from 'ere to there, anyways?'

'Nothing at all,' replied Catriona. She held up her hand to silence the protest. 'I have my own small plane,' she explained. 'It will take one telephone call to the pilot I use, and we can leave whenever we want to.'

'Blimey,' breathed Poppy, eyes wide in wonder. 'How the other 'alf live.'

Catriona smiled. 'It hasn't all been silk knickers and mink collars,' she said. 'I've had the bad times too, you know. So what do you say, Poppy? Want to risk it?'

'Too bloody right,' said Poppy as she gathered up her coat and cheap plastic handbag. 'I wouldn't miss this for the world.'

Catriona took Poppy to her apartment and after phoning Poppy's boss and telling him she was unwell and staying with her until she recovered, she made the necessary calls to her agent, her conductor and the pilot. She would leave the baritone to the conductor; they understood each other and had the same taste in flamboyant clothes and pink gins.

Poppy hung her coat in the hallway and kicked off her shoes. She rubbed her hair dry with a soft towel as she wandered barefoot around the apartment admiring the furniture, the fresh flowers, the deep carpets and enormous bed. She traced her fingers over the delicate ornaments and the crystal vases, and stood like a child at the window of a sweet shop when she opened the wardrobe doors that lined one entire wall of the bedroom and peeked inside at the rows of furs and silks. Catriona's gowns were sheathed in linen, her shoes neatly paired in racks beneath them. 'Bloody hell,' she breathed. 'You got more bleedin' clothes than 'arrods.'

Catriona laughed as she stripped off her suit and donned comfortable trousers and a silk shirt. 'Most of that lot are for when I'm on tour and have to do the dinners and interviews with the backers and the press,' she explained. 'This is what I prefer to wear when I'm not working.' She slipped on low pumps and draped a cardigan over her shoulders. 'Come on, Poppy, let's have a glass of champagne to celebrate our reunion. Then we can see

180

about getting you into something more comfortable for the flight.'

Poppy's protests were ignored and as the champagne began to take effect, she entered into the spirit of things. After a long soak in a deep bath, frothy with exotic bubbles, she changed into a neat pair of tailored trousers, a silk jumper and smart jacket. Their feet were different sizes, so there was nothing Catriona could do about shoes, but Poppy couldn't help but stand and admire herself in the pier-glass. 'Gawd,' she breathed. 'I ain't never seen nothing like it.'

Catriona left Poppy happily experimenting with her make-up and quickly packed an overnight bag for both of them. It was a two-hour flight to Belvedere, and they wouldn't be returning until the next day.

Poppy's initial excitement turned to fear as the little Cessna roared down the runway and took off into the night sky. ''ow can 'e 'see where's 'e's going?' she asked as she gripped the arm of her seat. 'It's as black as yer 'at out there.'

Catriona explained about charts and radar and flight-plans, making it sound as if she knew far more than she did, but it had the right effect and Poppy began to relax. Two hours later they circled over Belvedere. The broad strip that had been cleared from the bush was lit by flares, and as they came in to land, Catriona could see a utility truck and two people standing beside it. She felt a thrill of excitement. At last she was on Belvedere.

She led the way out of the little plane and was met by a man of average size and wiry build whose face was lined by the years of working in the sun. He wore moleskin trousers, a check shirt and scuffed boots, and there was a stained and battered bush-hat low over his brow. 'Pleased to meet you at last,' he drawled. 'The name's Fred Williams.' He turned slightly and introduced the tall, slender Aborigine standing at his side who was dressed in a similar manner. 'This here's Billy Birdsong, my right-hand man.'

She shook her manager's hand and smiled up at him. 'G'day Fred,' she replied before turning to greet the silent Aborigine. She introduced Poppy who was clutching her handbag as if her life depended upon it. 'We've come to have a look around,' she said.

Fred shoved back the sweat-stained Akubra and scratched his head. 'Reckon you won't see much tonight, Missus,' he drawled. 'What you think, Billy?'

'Reckon Missus see more at sun-up,' he replied. 'No good in dark.'

As Catriona hesitated, Fred made the decision for her. 'Better come up to the house and get a feed. We got plenty of room here, so your pilot can bunk in with the boys. But I don't knows about the homestead being suitable for city ladies,' he said shyly.

Catriona and Poppy exchanged grins and she assured him they were used to roughing it.

'Billy's missus has had a bit of a clean-up and changed the sheets. I'll be in the bunkhouse tonight if you need anything,' he said as he climbed into the ute and drove them out of the paddock and across the rough track to the homestead.

The homestead was nestled in a sheltering arc of trees. The clapboard needed painting, but the screens over the doors and windows were in good repair, as was the verandah. The inside was a revelation. Welcoming in the glow of oil-lamps, it was nevertheless decidedly shabby and obviously the domain of a single man. There were few decorations, no curtains or soft chairs, just the bare essentials, and the lingering odour of horse and cattle.

Fred poured them a cup of tea from the pot that was standing on the vast range, and then hurried off to get some food from the cookhouse. Billy had slunk off into the night, and they were alone.

'Blimey,' spluttered Poppy as she tasted the tea and added more sugar. 'This tea must've been stewing for hours.'

Catriona took a sip and grimaced. Setting the cup back on the table she took a long moment to look around her property. She felt at home here despite the clutter and neglect and she was imagining how it might look once she'd moved in.

The homestead was quite small, with only two bedrooms and this room which served as lounge, office and kitchen. There was no bathroom, only a shed out the back – the dreaded dunny – a dark and evil-smelling edifice which instilled fear in those not used to such a primitive arrangement. There was obviously no mains water or electricity, and the bath was a tin tub hanging on the wall outside the back door. 'I know I said we were used to roughing it,' she murmured. 'But I think this is going a bit far.'

Poppy grimaced. 'You make do with what you got,' she muttered. 'You've been spoiled, Kitty. Got outta the 'abit.'

Catriona knew she was right and was a little ashamed at how fussy she'd become. 'I reckon if I extended south and north and added a proper bathroom and lavatory, it would be a little gem,' she said as the ideas began to flow thick and fast. 'A good generator would provide electric light and hot water, and some decent furniture would make it cosy.'

'Not much point if you ain't gunna be livin' 'ere,' muttered Poppy.

'I will eventually,' she replied. 'But I'm sure Fred would appreciate a proper bathroom and decent lighting. I'll talk it over with him when he comes back.'

Fred returned with a hefty supper of cold mutton, pickles and potato. He seemed to like her ideas and promised to look into the cost and let her know. He left for the bunkhouse and the two women settled into the narrow single beds of the spare room.

After a long night of reminiscing, they were still groggy when they were woken at sun-up. Fred had arrived with an enormous breakfast of steak, fried potato and eggs. Catriona and Poppy looked at one another and tucked in. Never had breakfast tasted so good.

Fred lent them his utility and with a roughly drawn map of Belvedere, they set off. The Station was enormous and it would be impossible to see everything on this first visit, yet Catriona breathed a sigh of deep contentment as she steered the jolting, bouncing utility over the rough ground. This was her home now, and even though it could do with rather more than a coat of paint, she had the feeling that when she finally retired and came to live here, she would find the peace she'd been looking for ever since that terrible night back in 1934.

The little house on the edge of the property was really no more than a shack, she realised with disappointment as they drew up in front of the weed-filled garden. But it looked sturdy enough, and the roof was good. She led the way through the gate and up the steps. There was no key, for what was the sense of locking a house in such a remote spot?

'Pongs a bit,' said Poppy in her down-to-earth way. 'Let's open these shutters and get a bit of fresh air in 'ere.' She slammed back the shutters and the light streamed in. 'Blimey,' she breathed. 'I liked it better in the dark.'

Catriona nodded as her spirits plunged. The floor was rotten, the stone hearth was crumbling, and possums had made a nest up in the rafters. The single living room was littered with all sorts of junk and the previous owner had left behind his broken furniture. The kitchen area was off to one side of this main room and consisted of an old range that hadn't seen a rub of blacking in years, and a stone sink so stained with rust and filth it was good only for throwing out.

The second room wasn't any better. An old iron bed was leaning against one wall, and there was a filthy mattress on the floor which she suspected had become a very cosy home for countless generations of mice. The ubiquitous dunny was out the back, but at some point someone had set fire to it, and all that remained was a charred wall and a blackened pan.

'Looks like the swaggies have been using this place,' muttered Poppy as she picked her way over the rubbish in the backyard and kicked at a couple of empty beer bottles. 'Still, a bit of elbow grease should see it right.'

'You reckon it could be lived in then?' Catriona turned to face her.

'Yeah, why not? It's better than some I've seen.'

'If I get the builders in to do the repairs and add on another two rooms and a proper bathroom, do you think you and your Ellen could live here?'

Poppy's eyes were bright with tears and hope. 'Oh, Kitty,' she breathed. 'I never meant . . . Of course we could.' She looked back at the mean little shack as if she was being offered a palace. 'It could be a really nice little place,' she murmured. 'But what would we live on, Kitty? We're too far away from anywhere.' She shook her head, the sadness in her eyes tugging at Catriona's heart. 'It's kind of you, but we can't,' she finished.

'Yes you can,' said Catriona. 'The town's not that far away and I'll make sure there's a ute here for you so you can go back and forth whenever you like. And there's the vegetable garden; you could make something of that as well.' She hesitated. 'It will mean Ellen leaving her husband,' she murmured. 'Do you think she will?'

Poppy nodded. 'She lives in fear of 'im. We both do.'

Catriona took Poppy's hands and looked deeply into her eyes. 'Please let me do this for you, Poppy. Please say you'll bring Ellen and the baby here out of harm's way.'

'They'd be safer 'ere without that bastard around, that's a fact,' she murmured. 'But why would you want to do this for us, Kitty? We ain't charity cases, you know, and I never came to you asking for any of this, and . . .'

184

Catriona silenced her with a hug. 'This isn't charity,' she said firmly. 'This is taking care of my own.' She gently eased from the embrace and looked into Poppy's eyes. 'You were like a mother and a sister to me. You looked out for me and took care of me and loved me without reservation. Now it's my turn to take care of you and your family. Please let me do this for you, Poppy. I so very much want to.'

'Only if you let us pay rent,' said Poppy stubbornly. Her eyes were bright, her face alive with hope and excitement.

'Righto,' conceded Catriona. 'But not until you've found a job and got the garden going. Then we'll come to some arrangement.'

Poppy nodded and could barely contain her excitement as she linked arms with Catriona and they took a stroll around the property. They finally came to a halt at the bottom of the neglected vegetable garden and stood looking out at the magnificent view of hills and trees and endless pastures. Cattle grazed and horses stood beneath the wilga trees as white cockatoos screeched and brightly coloured rosella's darted back and forth to the water-trough.

'This is a good place to bring up a kid,' sighed Poppy. 'My grandson, Connor, will thrive here.'

Chapter Thirteen

Catriona returned to Sydney with Poppy, and six months later the little family moved into their new home. Catriona flew out with them and was astounded at the change in the place. The shack was clean and weatherproof, and twice the size, with a large generator to supply hot water and electricity. The garden had been dug over, the grass cut and the look on Poppy's face was a picture as she stood at the gate and stared.

Catriona glanced at Ellen and they exchanged an indulgent smile. Ellen was so like her mother at that age that Catriona found it difficult not to call her Poppy. But the girl seemed contented enough to live out here in the bush – even though Poppy had had to use a great deal of persuasion to make her leave her husband – and at two years old, Connor was a delight.

She took the little boy and held him on her hip. His hair was dark and brushed into a cockscomb, and his hazel eyes stared back at her so fixedly she wondered if he was trying to decide who she was. She felt a heart-swell of emotion as he gave her a cheeky grin and she thought of her own baby and the shock of dark hair that had peeked from the blankets, and handed Connor back to his mother. It was a bit late to get sentimental – she would have no more babies.

Harold Bradley had retired six years ago and was living with his wife in a small cottage in the rainforest which surrounded Kuranda. He spent his days working in the vegetable patch out the back, and his evenings on the verandah with his pipe. The war years had been fraught with worry for his son, but the boy had returned unharmed and was now the local policeman in Athertonshire. Harold was proud his son wanted to follow in his footsteps, and looked forward to the evenings when Charles joined him on the verandah and discussed the current cases.

He was enjoying retirement, and would have been content but for the nagging sense of having left certain things unresolved. The mystery of Kane's disappearance with the woman and child had never been explained. Neither had the whereabouts of Demetri, for the Russian had never returned to his hotel.

Harold had made a copy of the missing persons' report and brought it home on the day he retired. It was in a drawer in the bedroom, and every so often he would take it out and read it. Yet he knew it was a cold case, for Edith had passed away shortly after coming to see him, and the rest of the staff had seemed to be in ignorance. The hotel had never re-opened, and the military had taken it over during the war as a hospital. Now it was empty and crumbling, the rainforest slowly taking it over.

He sat on the verandah, the pipe smoke drifting in the humid air as he thought about that file. He'd discussed it with Charles, but his son was far too busy to open such an old case. The War had disrupted all their lives, records had been destroyed or gone missing, men had disappeared in the battlefields of Europe and Asia, and women married and changed their names. It would be like searching for a needle in a haystack.

'Grandpa?'

Harold was snapped from his thoughts and he looked down and smiled at the small boy who was tugging at his trouser leg. 'Tom,' he said as he picked him up and settled him on his knee. 'Shall I tell you a story about a Russian and an Englishman and the curious incident of the vanishing silver?'

Tom Bradley nodded. He loved it when Grandpa talked about the things he did when he was a policeman like Daddy. One day, he decided, he too would wear the same uniform and chase after robbers.

With the little family settled and thriving, and Fred and Billy Bird-song keeping an eye out for them, Catriona returned to her busy schedule. She left Australia and was soon immersed in the season of Verdi operas that were being held in Rome. This time she had kept her promise and taken Brin with her despite his advancing age and frailty.

Catriona's fortieth birthday was celebrated in Rome. She and Brin had been there for almost a year now, and the Verdi season was at an end. They would be leaving tomorrow for a year in Paris, before travelling to London for her brief appearance as Manon in a special gala for Queen Elizabeth. From London she would fly to New York to sing in *Tosca,* then return to Sydney to record an album of Puccini's most popular arias. Her reputation was firmly set as one of the finest sopranos of the age, and she knew her voice had never been richer or more pure.

Yet her success had been marred by Brin's increasing frailty. He'd loved their time in Rome, and she'd made sure he saw all the usual tourist haunts. But she soon realised he wasn't up to helping her any more in the dressing-room and she'd hired another dresser so he could rest. Brin maintained an almost nonchalant disregard for his state of health, and refused all medical help. But Catriona could see he'd lost a great deal of weight and she didn't like the look of the strange sores on his face and hands that no amount of salve could cure.

Catriona could stand it no longer. She went against his wishes and paid for the best medical advice in Rome. But none of the doctors could fathom what was wrong with him, and they offered varying diagnosis. There had been hints that his questionable lifestyle had probably contributed to his illness, and that he had simply lived too well and his body had worn out. There seemed nothing anyone could do.

The last performance was over and after briefly joining in the party, she left and caught a taxi back to the apartment she'd rented on the outskirts of the city. She didn't have the heart to celebrate when Brin was obviously so ill.

He was fast asleep on the couch when she let herself into the apartment. She stood and looked down at him for a long moment, remembering what a good friend he'd always been, and how he'd made her laugh at his outrageous stories, how he'd known better than she what clothes suited her and would spend long happy hours browsing in the shops for just the right dress. He'd always been there for her, and now it was her turn to look after him.

Perhaps, in Paris, she would find a doctor who would know what was wrong with him?

She gently drew the blanket over his shoulders, switched off the table-lamp and went into her bedroom. Taking off her clothes, she

188

showered and pulled on a silk wrap, then sat down to read the letters from home.

Clemmie was well and had become a grandmother for the first time, so her letter was full of the new baby. John had written separately with news of the changes in the adoption laws, and Catriona's hands trembled as she quickly scanned through the letter. The changes, he told her, meant she had access to some of the records. But she would not be permitted to gather enough information to contact her daughter. He had already written to the authorities and he hoped he would have some news very soon.

Catriona put down the letter with a frustrated sigh. The mail took so long to get here, and the telephone system in Rome was hopeless, even worse than at Belvedere. It could be weeks before she heard any more.

She swiftly read through the letter from Fred Williams. Belvedere was going from strength to strength, and the work on the homestead was almost finished. She sighed with longing. If only she could see it, she thought, but it would be at least another year before she could find the time to make the journey out there.

The last letter in the pile was from Poppy. She and Ellen had been working for almost a year in Drum Creek's one and only pub, and Connor was a sturdy three-years-old and thriving. They were busy with their vegetable garden and had already begun to sell their produce to the local store. Ellen had also begun a dressmaking business which was picking up nicely and all in all life was good and they were happy.

Catriona had been concerned over Brin's welfare during the short flight to Paris, but he seemed to have rallied a bit and was looking forward to seeing the Eiffel Tower and Montmartre. Paris was exciting as always, and as soon as they were settled into a hotel, Catriona took Brin shopping in the hope he would regain his old spark of enthusiasm.

It was not to last. The doctors were baffled and Brin was getting slowly worse, until even a short outing in a taxi up the Champs Elysee exhausted him. As time moved on, Catriona feared the worse, and when he asked to be taken to a hospital, she knew the end was near.

'I'm dying, darling,' he said as he lay in bed, propped up by pillows. 'But Paris is probably the best place for it.' His smile was wan. 'Thanks for letting me come with you, sweetie. I do adore you.'

Catriona took his hand. 'And I adore you too,' she breathed.

Brin asked her to brush his hair and help him into the richly hand-embroidered jacket they had bought at Chanel. Dressed for the occasion, Brin smiled sadly at his reflection in the mirror she held for him and then closed his eyes and left her. Catriona was numb with grief. It seemed as if life was intent upon taking away all those she loved, and as she sat there in the hushed French hospital room, she felt incredibly alone and very far from home.

Brin had the funeral he wanted. Black horses, a glass and ebony carriage, plumes, flowers and candles. He would remain always in Paris – the city of romance.

Eight months later she received a worrying letter from Fred Williams. He'd begun the long, carefully penned missive with news of Belvedere. The Station was doing well and the new herd was shaping up nicely. Billy Birdsong was a godsend – he had proved to be a man of infinite intelligence regarding the land and the elements they were constantly battling against. He suggested that Billy should be given a raise in wages, for he was now the proud father of three children.

Catriona smiled. She'd liked the Aborigine, and on her brief visits to Belvedere he'd taken her out into the bush and patiently explained the mysteries of the plants and animals to be found there. She turned the page.

Poppy and Ellen still worked in the pub and their market-garden was doing well. Unfortunately, Ellen had grown restless during the past month. She'd been heard complaining about how bored she was and how much she was missing the bright lights of Sydney. Without Poppy's knowledge, she'd written to Michael, her husband. It appeared she'd thought he'd changed, and – absence making the heart grow fonder – had told him where she was and had begged him to come and get her.

Catriona's lips tightened as she swiftly read the rest of the letter. Poppy had gone to Fred and told him Michael had turned up, taken one look at their nice little set-up there and immediately decided to stay. As a favour to Poppy, Fred had taken him on as a fence-poster. But he'd proved unreliable and too fond of the drink.

Michael Cleary then got work in the pub, but was soon caught with his hand in the till and sacked. He worked for a while at the feed-store before giving up all together and living off Poppy and

Ellen's meagre earnings. He was a no-good drunk in Fred's opinion, with a nasty temper, and he owed money to everyone.

Poor Poppy was too ashamed to tell him everything, but he'd read between the lines and things weren't at all as they should be. Poppy and Ellen had tried to disguise them, but he'd seen the bruises and the black eyes – and wanted to know what he should do about Michael Cleary.

Catriona was furious. Furious with Poppy for not confiding in her. Furious with Ellen for being so stupid as to let that awful man back into their lives, and furious she couldn't go there immediately and give the bastard a piece of her mind. She fired off a letter to Fred, telling him to take Michael to one side and warn him off – threaten him with violence if he had to – but to make sure he left the women alone. Then she fired off a letter to Michael himself, warning him that if he laid a finger on the women again she would personally see the police were informed. The last letter was more difficult. Poppy was proud, and when she realised Catriona was aware of her plight, she would do her best to deny it. But the little boy had to be protected before his father started beating him too, and Catriona needed to make it very plain that she intended to seek custody of Connor should the violence continue.

Connor had no recollection of the first time his father had hit him, and because it happened on a regular basis, he'd come to accept that was how life was. His father didn't need an excuse, and drunk or sober, in good mood or bad, Connor had become his whipping-boy.

By the time he was four years old, Connor had learned to keep out of his way, learned not to scream in terror and pain as he was knocked from one end of the wooden shack to the other. Learned to bury his face in his pillow at night and cry silent tears as the bruises throbbed and his head rang with his father's curses. His childhood had been swept away before he'd had a chance to know what it could be like.

He spent every day feeling confused and frightened. Each time he heard his father's footsteps on the verandah he experienced a shudder of terror. Were the steps light, was he sober and in a good mood? Or were they thudding, the very house shaking as he slammed through the screen door and roared for his dinner? It seemed to him that it was mostly the latter.

A terrible silence would fall in the kitchen as he strode in, the reek of drink on his breath, the gleam of malice in his eyes. Granny would cringe, her eyes downcast as Mum hastily put his food on the table and scuttled out of his reach and into the darkest corner. Connor would try to become invisible, hiding in the shadows, staying silent and watchful, poised to run. It was as if the house was holding its breath; waiting for the boot to fall, the fist to rise.

His mum tried to protect him. She had taken the beatings and kickings and shielded him with her bruised and battered body that was swollen with his baby brother or sister. Granny would scream and shout and be knocked flying by his fists until she didn't have the strength to get up off the floor again and continue her attack.

As he stood there that particular night in wide-eyed, terrified silence and watched his granny being kicked, he felt his own anger rising. He was going to fight back.

His fists looked so small as he beat against his father's sturdy thigh, and his bare feet seemed to make no impact at all on the thick ankles as he kicked and kicked and screamed for him to stop hurting his gran.

He was silenced by a vicious kick. The boot caught him on the chin, sending him crashing against the stone hearth. He lay there stunned, his sight blurred as Gran screamed and tried to pull his father away. He could make out the crumpled figure of his mother in the far corner and was slowly aware of something warm and sticky on his chin and down his neck. Then blackness closed in and the shouts and screams disappeared.

When he next opened his eyes he was in his gran's arms. She was singing to him in her funny voice as she washed his face with a cool cloth. He nestled into that bony frame and warm, loving arms and longed, simply, for the hurting to stop.

The year in Paris were almost at an end. Catriona had just come off stage when the dresser handed her the telephone. 'It's from Australia,' he said in whisper.

'Sounds urgent.'

Catriona took the handset. 'What's the matter?'

It was Fred. 'One of my men heard screams coming from the shack. He saw Cleary storm out and drive off and went in to have a look.'

192

There was a long pause and the atmospherics on the line hissed and clicked between Belvedere and Paris. Catriona gripped the receiver.

'Poppy's bruised and battered and Ellen isn't much better,' Fred said grimly. 'But poor little Connor got it this time.'

Catriona felt the chill of dread prickle on her skin. 'Is he all right?' she asked.

'He's shaken and terrified, and he'll always carry a scar on his chin where the bastard kicked him.'

Catriona's tears fell and she swiftly brushed them away. They wouldn't help Connor. 'Should he go to the hospital?' she said. 'I'll pay whatever it costs to make sure he gets proper medical care.'

'The local doc's already been in and patched them up,' he said, his voice rough with emotion. 'But the women refuse to leave the house. They're terrified of what Cleary will do if he comes back and finds them gone.'

Catriona gritted her teeth. Why did some women remain victims? Why the hell didn't they get out and find shelter at the homestead? If it had been up to her, she would have faced the bastard with a shotgun and not been afraid of pulling the bloody trigger.

Fred cleared his throat. 'The mongrel deserves a taste of his own medicine,' he growled. 'I want your permission to run him out of town.'

'You have it,' she replied.

He outlined his plan and Catriona admired his cold efficiency. 'Ring me and let me know when it's done,' she said flatly.

The men of Drum Creek gathered in the room behind the feed-store. There were ringers and drovers and jackaroos from Belvedere, the owners of the small stores in Drum Creek and the regulars of the pub. They had all come to dislike Cleary, and most of them were owed money by him; but it wasn't the money that had brought them to the feed-store that night, it was the disgust they all shared for the mongrel who'd beaten up an old woman, a pregnant girl and a little kid.

The landlord of the pub sent word that Cleary was drinking there, and if they didn't get there soon he'd have passed out. The men moved as one as they left the back room and walked across

the broad dirt road. Cleary was at the bar, shouting for the landlord to give him another drink.

'You've had your last drink here, mate,' said Fred as he stood
in the doorway.

Cleary turned and leaned against the bar. His eyes were bleary,
his face mottled with anger. 'Yeah?' he slurred. 'And how d'ya
figure that out?'

'We don't want you here, Cleary,' shouted one of the men
behind Fred. 'This was a nice little town before you arrived.'

Cleary swayed on his feet as he squared up to the men who were
pouring through the double doors. 'I'll fight every last one of you
bastards,' he shouted, spittle flying. He raised his fists and they
saw the bruising on them.

'About time you hit someone yer own size, yer bloody mongrel,'
shouted one of the drovers, who followed up this angry retort with
a shuddering right hook.

Cleary stumbled and would have fallen if he hadn't been pinned
to the bar by the landlord. The others moved forward and grabbed
him, dragging him out into the street. The blows rained down and
he fell to his knees, pleading with them to stop. A boot caught him
in his side, and another shoved him face down in the dirt.

The circle of men drew back as he screamed for them to stop.
They watched in silence as he crawled around in the dirt and
begged them not to hurt him. His face was bruised and one eye was
swollen shut. Snot and tears streaked his face and his mouth was
slack with fear.

Fred yanked him to his feet. 'Get out of town,' he said to the
befuddled Cleary. 'And if we see your face around here again,
we'll give you a beating you'll never forget.' He shoved Cleary in
the direction of his ute. 'Touch that kid again and I'll personally
take a stock whip to you.'

Ellen had gone into labour and Connor had been put to bed in the
other room and told to stay there. His gran had looked worried and
for the first time in his life she'd been short with him. He lay there
listening to the awful sounds of his mum crying out. Something
was hurting her, but how could that be, he wondered. Dad hadn't
come back.

He heard a strange cry – it sounded angry – but it wasn't his
mother. After what seemed an age, his gran came in and she was

194

smiling. 'Come on, me duck,' she said softly. 'Come and say hello to your new sister.'

Connor went to his mother's room and looked at the bundle in her arms. 'This is Rosa,' she said, her voice weary.

Rosa was a tiny little thing with a shock of black hair and a mighty yell. Her face was all screwed up and her fists were waving, her feet kicking as if she was furious at being born. Connor looked at her in awe and fell instantly in love. He'd no idea where she'd come from, or why she was here, but from that moment on he knew here was someone else he had to protect from Dad.

He watched as Gran put Rosa carefully into the wooden cot he used to sleep in, then he climbed into his mother's bed. Careful not to hurt her, he gave her a kiss on her bruised face. She looked very tired, but she smiled and stroked his hair, holding him for a while before she finally fell asleep.

The peace and silence was shattered by the slam of the door hitting the bedroom wall. Connor was jerked awake and scurried from force of habit under the bed. His mum started screaming and Rosa joined in. Michael Cleary was a terrifying sight, covered in blood, one eye swollen and turning black. He was drunk and in the darkest temper.

Connor cringed as his father's boots approached the bed. Mum had stopped screaming and was frantically trying to sooth Dad out of his temper. Gran was wrestling with him, trying to get him out of the room. And all the while, Rosa was screaming; a high-pitched, seemingly endless scream that hammered in Connor's head and made him yearn to silence her, for surely his father would hurt her if she didn't stop?

Michael Cleary swayed next to the bed, his voice rising above the awful din. 'Shut that brat up before I kill it,' he yelled.

Gran scuttled across the room and gathered up Rosa. Connor edged to the very depths of the shadows beneath the bed and Mum started to sob.

Connor held his breath, the tension in the room so strong he could feel it hammering in his head. He heard the creak of his father's boots as he stood by the bed and swayed back and forth. If only Mum would stop crying, he thought in despair. Dad hated it when she cried.

Without warning, came the awful sound of flesh punching flesh.

195

It was a single blow to the defenceless Ellen, delivered with all the strength and venom Michael Cleary could muster. Without another word he gathered up his few belongings and left the house.

His dad's departure brought an uneasy calm; a calm laced with the terror he might return. Despite all assurances from Fred and Billy Birdsong, they remained on their guard. At any moment they expected to hear the thud of his boots on the verandah and the crash of the screen door.

As the weeks passed and they heard no news of him, Connor and his mother and grandmother dared to believe they were really free. Yet it was to be years before Connor stopped cringing at any loud noise, years before he could sleep without a light on in his room.

Chapter Fourteen

After Michael's exile, Ellen grew more and more dissatisfied with life in the Outback. It was almost as if Michael's beatings had given her some excitement, had added the drama to her life she'd been missing. She began to neglect the children, leaving Poppy to look after them while she sat in the pub and drowned her sorrows.

It was there that she met a flashy travelling salesman by the name of Jack Ivory. He was a man who could talk his way into and out of any situation. He had a charm and a winning smile and never seemed short of money. Ellen, a woman who found life difficult without a man at her side, saw a chance to escape the drudgery of being a mother and breadwinner. Determined not to miss this promise of a new life, she returned to the cottage and began to pack her bags. After a furious row with Poppy and many tears and entreaties from her children, Ellen walked out and didn't look back. She and Jack drove away from Drum Creek and were never heard of again.

Catriona was saddened, but not surprised by Poppy's news. Ellen had always been flighty, her choice in men, questionable. But it was the children she really felt for – how could any mother turn her back on a small baby and a little boy who was bewildered and hurt enough already?

She fulfilled her engagements in London and New York and as soon as she returned to Australia, she made sure her busy life was organised so she could visit Belvedere on a more regular basis. Poppy was too old to be raising such young children, and although Billy Birdsong's wife went in each day to help, Catriona knew Poppy was at the end of her tether. Her offer to help financially had been gruffly turned down and it seemed Poppy was determined to raise the children as well as keep working.

Over the following eight years Catriona found she looked forward more and more to the short visits, and always took presents for the children, and make-up and perfume for Poppy. It was good to shed the formal suits and high heels for strides and flatties, and the chance to breathe the good clean air of Belvedere always meant she returned to Sydney refreshed and eager for work. Yet she despaired of Poppy ever being still, even though she admired her fierce pride – her strength – and realised her old friend would work until the day she dropped.

The little house smelled of freshly baked bread and furniture polish. The windows sparkled and the wooden floor had been swept. Through the back door, Catriona could see the neat lines of vegetables growing in the rich black soil, and the crisp white laundry flapping in the warm breeze. Poppy had returned from the pub, where she cooked good, plain food for the customers. Her lunchtime stint was over, but she would go back to cook the teas later that evening. The house was quiet; Connor and Rosa were at the local school.

Catriona sipped her tea and looked across at her friend. 'I can only stay for a couple of hours,' she said with regret. 'I have to be in the recording studio tomorrow morning.'

Poppy nodded. Her hair was grey, she'd given up dyeing it a long time ago, and it was cut into a severe bob. Yet, at seventy, she still wore bright clothes and make-up and there were gaudy earrings flashing in the sun that poured through the window. She called them her props and felt naked without them. Her face and hands were brown from the hours she spent in the garden, and although Catriona could see how tired she was, she seemed still to have the energy of a much younger woman. 'You'll wear yerself out, with all that rushing 'ere and there,' she said. 'Don't you ever get sick of it?'

Catriona thought Poppy was a fine one to talk considering what she did every day. 'I hate leaving here,' she admitted. 'But I can't imagine being in the same place for too long.' She smiled at Poppy. 'I was born to the life. It's in my blood.'

Poppy chewed her lip. 'It's a different kind of life to 'ow it was in the old days,' she said. 'The opera's ever so posh. How does a girl like you fit in?'

Catriona smiled. She would be forty-eight in a few weeks time – hardly a girl any more. 'I found it tough to begin with,' she said.

198

'Some of the other girls at the Academy used to laugh at the way I talked and poked fun at my clothes and the fact Mam worked as a waitress. I just had to remember why I was there and where it might lead. I stayed focussed on who I was and the sacrifices that had been made to get me that far. I worked hard at my elocution lessons and soaked up all the education they could give me.' She grinned. 'I learned very early on that no soprano could sing with the flat vowels of an Outback urchin.'

'But it ain't changed you,' Poppy muttered. 'You've still got that sweet way with you, almost innocent, if I didn't know any better.' Her faded blue eyes twinkled with humour. 'I bet them other girls are spitting tacks 'cos you done so well.'

Catriona studied her manicured nails and the rings that glittered on her fingers. 'Over the years I've worked with most of them in one production or another. Not all of them carried on their careers, they got married and had kids and couldn't do the travelling. But on the whole they were a fairly decent bunch once they were away from the influence of Emily Harris.'

'I remember you telling me about 'er,' Poppy said as she began to clear the table. 'Right little cow by all accounts. Whatever 'appened to her?'

Catriona smiled. 'She never did cure that break between her head and chest registers. Poor Emily. The last I heard, she'd become the leading light in an amateur Gilbert and Sullivan company her father set up and financed.'

'How are you coping, Poppy?' she asked after a brief silence. 'Do the children still ask after Ellen?'

Poppy pulled a face. 'I'm fine, the kids are fine. They don't ask after 'er no more, and why should they? She 'asn't written a letter or phoned in years, and Rosa was too young to even remember 'er.' She folded her arms and glowered. 'I reckon they're better off without 'er.'

Their conversation was interrupted by the sound of galloping hoofs. Catriona pushed back her chair and rushed to the door. Connor and Rosa had returned from the local school on their ponies. Rosa leaped from the shaggy little animal and almost knocked Catriona off her feet as she flung herself into her arms. Connor, as always, hung back shyly, his hazel eyes wary.

Catriona laughed as eight-year-old Rosa tugged her into the house in search of the presents she knew Catriona had brought with

199

her. The child was dark-haired and dark-eyed with an impish smile that was irresistible. Catriona looked back at Connor and smiled at him encouragingly. 'I've got something for you too,' she said.

Rosa was tearing off the paper with cries of excitement as the gangling youth quietly stood and watched from beneath the brim of his bush-hat. Catriona eyed him thoughtfully. He'd shot up over the past few months and looked very skinny – yet he seemed healthy enough, and she could already see the strength in his arms and hands. At twelve years old he was showing signs of the handsome man he would become. If only he wasn't so shy, she thought sadly as she handed him the large parcel. That bastard of a father had a great deal to answer for – as did Ellen.

Connor's face came alight when he saw the saddle. It had been hand-tooled in Spain, the pommel decorated with silver. It was an expensive gift, but Catriona had no idea what else to give him – boys were always difficult to buy presents for.

'Thanks ever so much,' he breathed, his eyes shining. 'Can I try it out now?'

Catriona nodded. 'Of course,' she said.

Rosa lifted out the dresses and the dolls and shrieked with delight. 'Look, Gran,' she yelled. 'She's got real hair and eyelashes, and has even got knickers!'

Catriona joined in the laughter, then went to stand on the verandah to watch Connor. He was getting a bit big for that pony, she realised, as he settled himself in the new saddle. So much so, he no longer used the stirrups, but let his long legs dangle past the fat little pony's belly. She would have to have a word with Fred and see if he could find another one.

Connor turned and smiled at her, a slow, sweet smile of deep affection that squeezed at her heart. How she loved these children; how she wished they had been hers. She pulled the cardigan around her and folded her arms. She was getting sentimental in her old age and would just have to accept they were Poppy's children and she shouldn't spoil them so much.

Poppy made a fresh pot of tea, and while the children were occupied with their presents, she told Catriona how well Rosa had been doing at school. 'She's a brain in 'er 'ead, that's for sure,' she said firmly. 'Though Gawd knows where she got it.' There was a pride in the gleam of her eyes and in the tone of her voice as she went on. 'She passed all her exams with flying colours. Her teacher

200

reckons she's one of the brightest students she's 'ad for a long time.'

'And Connor?'

Poppy shrugged. 'He ain't no brain-box, but that don't mean he ain't clever,' she said defensively. 'He's good with 'is 'ands, thinks things out until 'e's got it right.' She sipped her tea, her arthritic fingers gnarled as they clasped the cup. 'He's already talking about leaving school. Reckons 'e wants to be an 'orse-breaker.'

'But that's dangerous work and he's far too young,' protested Catriona. 'You must persuade him to stay on at school. It's important he gets a proper education.'

'You try telling 'im that,' said Poppy. 'The boy's only got one thought in 'is 'ead, and that's 'orses.' There was a long silence, then her quiet voice drifted like a sigh. 'You can't blame him, Kitty. Connor knows an 'orse will never let 'im down. They ain't like people.'

Catriona had a lot to think about on her flight back to Sydney.

Harold Bradley died in his sleep shortly after his seventy-fifth birthday. He was laid to rest in the little cemetery on the Atherton Tablelands beside his wife. Charles Bradley, his son, had to clear the house and divide up the few items of value between himself and his sisters. The house would have to be sold, for Charles had been given promotion and was due to relocate to Sydney where he would take over an investigative team as Chief Inspector.

He walked through the almost empty rooms, thinking of the hours he'd spent here with his father. The relationship had been a solid one, and he hoped his own son, Tom, felt the same way about theirs. The boy was shooting up like a weed, and in a few weeks time he would turn thirteen and start at his new high school.

He smiled as he sat down on the old rocking chair his father had placed long ago on the verandah. This was Dad's favourite place, and as the rockers complained against the floorboards, Charles could see why. He looked out over the tops of the trees and down into the valley, and although he was excited about the move to Sydney, he knew he would miss the peace and beauty of this trop-ical north. This was God's Own Country; the place he'd known all his life, the home he'd returned to after the War. He'd picked up the pieces of his life here, had married and had a son. Sydney's noise and bustle would seem alien.

201

Charles sat there until the sun began its final descent and the sky turned to fire. Then he picked up the box of papers and turned the key in the door for the last time. He walked down the path and through the gate and climbed into his car. Placing the box on the seat beside him, he wondered why he'd kept these particular bits of paper. They were mostly old diaries and account books, and out-of-date files relating to ancient cases his father had found interesting. They were probably only fit for burning.

Yet he was reluctant to destroy what was left of a way of life his father had stood for. He remembered well his stories about the old hotel and the missing Englishman, and had even been up to the old place to have a look around. It was a shell now, but Charles had long realised the unsolved mystery of the people who'd once lived there had niggled at his father right up to his death.

He sat in the car and stared out at the gathering darkness. The hotel might be crumbling, but the memory of it still possessed the power to make him shiver. Rumours had abounded, and like all rumours there was some kind of truth behind them. It was said the house was cursed, and on his last visit there, he could believe it was.

The house had originally been built by a rich farmer back in the 1800s. He was a Scotsman who'd made good and wanted to play the Laird. The work was almost finished and he was inspecting the building when the enormous chandelier he'd imported from Europe suddenly dropped from its moorings. Death was instant.

It was discovered later that the beam hadn't been strong enough to support it, and Charles suspected the builders of cutting corners for profit. Yet it did indeed seem as if the house was cursed. The Scotsman's son and wife moved in shortly afterwards. She'd been reluctant, and when her husband was found dead at the bottom of the stairs, she become convinced that the curse was real.

Charles thought it was probably just a tragic accident – some families attracted bad luck like a magnet. But the house was sold several times in quick succession and it seemed no one wanted to stay there for more than a few months. Then Demetri bought it, lavished money and time on the place and turned it into a hotel. Yet the Russian, his friend Kane and the woman and child had simply vanished. Was there really a curse on the place, or an even darker explanation?

Charles turned the key in the ignition and eased the car down the narrow street. He was a realist, not one to be swayed by rumour and speculation. Yet he hated loose ends as much as his father had done. With the advance in technology and communications over the last few decades, perhaps there was a chance, finally, of unravelling the truth. It would be a fine, last gift to his father's memory to solve the case once and for all.

By 1969 the laws on adoption had changed radically, and after long years of searching, Catriona was to finally learn what had happened to her daughter. Clemmie sat with her as she went through the sheaf of papers John had so carefully compiled. 'Take your time,' she said. 'There's a lot to go through, and, I warn you Kitty, not all of it pleasant.'

Catriona nodded. 'I'm in such a state I don't know how I feel about anything,' she said as she looked at the papers before her. 'I'm excited, nervous, apprehensive and dreading what I might find out.'

Clemmie patted her hand. 'Sounds like stage-fright to me,' she said softly. 'Remember what your voice coach always tells you before a performance. Use the energy in a positive way, it will give you strength'.

She smiled back at her friend and, after taking a deep breath, began to read.

The hospital records showed that her tiny baby had been kept in the hospital until she gained weight and began to thrive. Six weeks later she was placed in the orphanage next door. Catriona's heart ached with sadness as she realised how close she'd been to her and yet she'd had no way of knowing. Velda had lied to her when she'd told her the baby was already with her adoptive parents.

The child had been called Susan Smith, a plain, common-sense name that gave no hint of her character or personality, or any clue to her background. She was at the orphanage for eighteen months. The matron's reports said she was sickly and always crying. Prospective parents wanted plump, laughing babies, and she despaired of finding a home for her.

Catriona remembered how empty her arms had felt in those first few months, how the void in her life echoed and her dreams were filled with the presence of a child with laughing eyes and plump little hands. If only she'd been given the chance to hold her, to look after her and love her, surely then her little girl would have thrived?

Susan was eventually adopted by a middle-aged couple who ran a vast cattle station, south of Darwin, in the Northern Territories. She lived with them for ten years, and then tragedy struck. 'Oh, my God,' breathed Catriona as she picked up the newspaper cuttings. There had been a terrible bush-fire and Susan had been rescued by a drover who'd been awarded for his bravery. Her adoptive parents were both dead, and Susan was alone again. With no family to take her on, she was sent back to the orphanage.

'Poor little girl,' murmured Clemmie. 'She must have been so alone and bewildered.'

'It makes my heart ache to think about it,' whispered Catriona. 'We were both alone but kept apart by bureaucracy and red tape. If only things had been different.'

'John's done a lot of digging.' Clemmie smiled. 'He's getting a bit doddery now, but it's become a bit of a thing with him. He's appalled at how the institutions kept their files so secret. But at least it keeps his mind active, even if the rest of him is falling apart.'

Catriona smiled at her friend before returning to the records. Susan Smith had not been adopted again. No one wanted to take on a ten year old, especially in the middle of a war. So she was placed with a series of foster parents, who found her wilful and headstrong, even though she was exceptionally bright, and when the time came for her to take up the scholarship to a private school and leave the fostering system, she did so without a backward glance.

'That's the last of it,' sighed Catriona. 'I'll probably never know what happened to her.' She made a swift, mental calculation. 'She'll be thirty-five now. A woman in her own right, probably with children of her own.'

Clemmie nudged a thin stack of neatly typed pages towards her. 'I told you, Kitty. John's not the sort of man to be beaten by the authorities and the lack of information.'

Catriona read through the pages and when she'd finished she looked back at Clemmie, her smile wide, the tears running down her face. 'He's found her,' she breathed. 'At last I can talk to her.'

'No,' said Clemmie sharply. 'That wouldn't be wise. She has her own life now. The past must stay where it belongs. She probably thinks you gave her away because you didn't want her. Lord knows what they told her at the orphanage or when she was with the foster parents.' Clemmie put a consoling hand on her arm. 'She won't want to see you, Kitty, believe me. And I won't let you get hurt any more.'

'But I have to try,' insisted Catriona as she began to pace the room. 'Don't you see? I can't just let her think I abandoned her willingly.' She rammed her hands into the pockets of her trousers. 'I have to talk to her, have to make her understand I had no say in the matter, that I was just a kid myself.'

Clemmie looked back at her in horror. 'And how will you explain she's the product of a rape? Do really think telling her something like that will make her feel any better about herself? It's hardly something to boast about.'

Catriona was in a whirl of indecision. 'But to have come so far, to be so close to her after all this time – I can't stop now.' She poured a large whisky into a glass and took a sip. 'I don't have to tell her everything,' she said finally as Clemmie's silent disapproval began to get to her. 'I'll just say I was a precocious child and got pregnant after a fling.'

'She'll think you were a tart,' said Clemmie stiffly. 'You were thirteen, remember.'

'So, I'll lie. Make up a story.'

'Not the best way of starting a relationship,' said Clemmie gruffly.

'Why are you playing Devil's advocate?' she shouted in frustration.

Clemmie stood and put her arm around her, holding her tightly as the sobs tore Catriona apart. 'Because I love you,' she murmured. 'Because you're the best friend I have, and I don't want to see you hurt yourself, or your daughter.' She drew back from the embrace and tucked the long strands of dark hair back from Catriona's face. 'You might not be able to talk to her, Kitty. But there are other ways.'

Catriona blew her nose and wiped her eyes. She drained the whisky and set the glass on the low table next to the brightly coloured sheets of paper John had included in his folder. She picked up the series of photographs and drank in the sight of this young woman she'd known only at the moment of her birth. 'You're right, as always,' she murmured. 'What would I do without you?'

The two women hugged and Clemmie finally left the Sydney

apartment so Catriona could prepare for the evening. But Catriona had no intentions of performing tonight. She telephoned the Conservatorium, and for the first time in her career put on a gruff voice and said she was suffering from a bad throat. The producer wasn't happy about it, but he could get stuffed; she'd not missed a performance in thirty-odd years, and it was about time she took a night off. Besides, she reasoned, she had more important things to think about and her performance would have been marred.

As the darkness settled and the lights came on all over Sydney, she stared out at the magnificent building that was slowly emerging out of the rubble and decay of Circular Quay. The opera house was almost finished, and it would be a triumph of design and imagination – so very different from the old Town Hall and Conservatorium. How she envied the sopranos and contraltos who would make their debuts there.

She turned finally from the window and sat down at her antique desk. It was stuffed with programmes and fliers, letters from fans, conductors and fellow performers. Her life had been blessed, she realised. For although she had never known the happiness of rearing her own children, she had achieved almost everything she had wished for. She had Belvedere and Poppy's grandchildren, a flourishing, satisfying career, and enough money to ensure a comfortable retirement. Yet it all seemed empty without being able to share it with her only child.

After a long time of thinking, she began to write the letter which she hoped would see the final dream fulfilled.

Chapter Fifteen

After years of pestering, Connor had finally been allowed to join
in the brumby run. The experience surpassed anything he could
have imagined, and he spent every available hour by the corrals as
Billy Birdsong set about taming the wild and beautiful horses
they'd rounded up. His grandmother complained he was never at
home and his schoolwork was suffering. But he didn't care. This
was how he wanted to live; to be surrounded by the men and the
sounds of a breaking yard, to be free in the great expanse of this
wonderful country and a real part of the life on Belvedere.

When Billy brought the horse into the yard, Connor eyed him
with longing. He wasn't a particularly big animal, but he galloped
into the ring as if he owned it. With a flowing mane and tail, the
white blaze on his nose was startling against the chestnut coat. Yet
Connor noticed he was a gelding and saw the brand on the rump.
This wasn't a true brumby – at some point he'd escaped from
Belvedere's yards and had run free with the herd.

The animal was furious at being caught and sought escape from
the corral, kicking up the dust, pawing the air, screaming defiance.
Connor sat on the railings and watched Billy. Horse-breaking was
like a dance. A slow, almost sensuous interaction between determined man and reluctant horse, played out in the dust of the yard.
The horse was all fire and defiance, the man a watchful, soft-
voiced siren luring the animal into inevitable submission. Connor
was spell-bound, and more detennined than ever to be a breaker
like Billy.

Billy hadn't taken long to reacquaint the gelding with the feel of
a saddle on his back. He finally climbed on board and held the
reins tightly as the animal fought him. The gate was opened and

man and horse catapulted out of the yard. Connor watched the hectic gallop across the plains and waited. Sure enough, almost an hour later they returned, the horse trotting neatly over the rough ground, the Aborigine grinning widely.

Connor opened the gate and Billy slid from the gelding's back. 'Alonga you him,' he said in his pidgin English. He grinned. 'Reckon you and him alonga fine.'

'You mean he's mine?' breathed Connor. He slowly reached out his hand and the animal's soft nose nuzzled his palm. 'Beauty, mate,' he whispered. 'Bloody beauty.'

'Missus say you too big for pony,' said Billy as he handed over the reins.

Connor smiled as the animal nudged his shoulder and tried to nibble his hair. He stroked the blaze on the proud nose. 'I'm gunna call him Lightning,' he breathed.

Fred strolled over as Connor led the horse from the breaking yard and walked him around the clearing. He pushed back his sweat-stained hat and mopped his brow. 'Why aren't you at school?' he drawled.

'School's boring,' replied Connor. 'I'm nearly thirteen and I want to work with you and Billy.'

Fred smiled and the creases on his face wrinkled into deep crevasses. 'Reckon you'll be right,' he drawled. 'But it's up to the missus. She wants you to be properly educated.'

Connor knew when he was beaten. Catriona and Gran had been adamant. He could start work when he was thirteen and not a minute before. 'It's not fair,' he muttered, as he kicked the dirt.

'That's life, boy,' said Fred cheerfully. 'But there's only a few more weeks to go before your birthday, so stop whingeing. Now go and fetch your sister from school.'

Connor climbed into the saddle and took up the reins. Lightning pricked up his ears and stamped the ground as if impatient to be off. Sitting high above the men, Connor felt a glow of pride. This was his first real horse, and what a beaut he was. Rosa would be really jealous. He wheeled the horse in a circle, and with a whoop of excitement let Lightning have his head. Together they raced across the open land towards the little town of Drum Creek.

The school was a sprawling wooden building surrounded by trees. A wide verandah ran along the front beneath a bull-nosed tin roof, and at the back the large paddock had been turned into a play

208

area and sports field. The children didn't wear a uniform, just the clothes they wore every day, which usually consisted of dungarees, moleskins or jeans. The Aussie Rules posts stood tall in the pale grass, the pitch marked out with lime. Swings, climbing frames and a basketball hoop were placed off to one corner. There were four classrooms, each furnished with simple desks and chairs, a blackboard and a large map of the world. Ceiling fans stirred the hot air in summer and in the winter there was a log fire in the hearth.

The School of the Air was still in place for the children who lived too far out on their isolated stations, but Drum Creek School catered for those who lived closer in. The children were mostly the sons and daughters of the people who owned the vast sheep and cattle stations nearby. They would be educated here until it was time for high school, then they would either go as boarders to the city schools, or finish their education with the School of the Air. The running of the school was in the capable hands of Mr and Mrs Pike, their spinster daughter and a young, very attractive woman who'd recently moved here from Adelaide to teach the youngest pupils. The single men in the area were highly delighted, and Mr and Mrs Pike wondered how long it would be before they lost her.

Connor slowed the horse to a walk as he neared the school. He was aware of the admiring glances of those he'd passed along the road, and couldn't wait to show off to his sister. He came to the picket fence that surrounded the front yard and waited impatiently for the bell to ring. There was a mob of ponies hobbled under the trees – most of the children rode to school, making the long journey in the dark in both directions – but none could compare with Lightning.

As the first clang disturbed the stillness of that summer afternoon, the doors flew open and the children poured into the yard. The youngest ones raced out chattering like galahs as they ran around and restarted the games they'd been playing before lessons. The older children were quieter, but in no less of a rush to escape. The boys kicked a ball about and tussled with one another in the dirt before saddling up and riding towards home. The girls wound their arms around one another and gossiped and giggled as they cast admiring and envious glances at Connor and his new horse.

The yard was finally silent. Connor waited impatiently. As usual, there was no sign of Rosa. He was about to climb down and go and find her when she emerged from the schoolhouse, strolling arm in arm with her friend Belinda Sullivan. He gave a sigh of exasperation. 'Come on,' he yelled, making Lightning prick his ears and stamp his feet. 'You're late and Gran will be waiting.'

Rosa and Belinda giggled. The girls had become friends on their first day at school, and, although they were both dressed in over-sized dungarees, there the similarity ended. Rosa was small and slender with closely-cropped brown hair which glinted chestnut in the sun. Belinda was taller, broader, perhaps even a little plump, and her wiry, dark curls had been restrained into long plaits. Yet they shared an adoration of horses, dogs and anything which got them dirty or involved mischief. They both saw the horse and came running. 'Bloody hell, Con. Where'd you get him?' breathed Rosa. 'He's a beaut and no mistake.'

Belinda stood there gazing up at Connor in mute adoration and Connor blushed. He supposed it was flattering to be the object of such passion, but actually it was embarrassing and he was glad none of the other boys were around to witness it. 'Billy gave him to me,' he drawled with studied nonchalance.

'That's not fair,' snapped Rosa. 'Why should you have a horse like that, when I've got to ride poor old Dolly?'

'Because you're still a kid,' he said, firmly avoiding Belinda's worshipping gaze.

'I'm not,' she retorted, stamping her foot. Her dark eyes were blazing, her little face quite red with fury. 'I'm nearly nine.'

'Not for six months, you're not,' he drawled. 'Come on, Rosa. Get a move on. I want my tucker.'

'Can Belinda come too?'

He glanced at Belinda. The kid was always staying the night and he was getting a bit fed up with her following him about every-where. He shook his head. 'Maybe tomorrow,' he murmured.

'Why can't she come today?' Rosa was being very annoying. 'Gran won't mind.'

Belinda solved Connor's problem by leaving to fetch her fat little pony. When she returned she gave Connor a sweet smile and waved goodbye.

'Hurry up,' Connor muttered to his sister.

'All right, all right,' snapped Rosa before she stomped off, saddled Dolly and urged the shaggy little pony into a shambling trot in an effort to catch up with him.

210

It was only an hour's ride to the cottage, and within minutes Rosa was pestering him to let her ride Lightning. He resisted for a while, before giving in. He could never refuse his little sister anything, and although she was a pain in the rear, he loved her. With the pony trotting along behind them on a leading rein, and Rosa in the saddle in front of him, they rode home to the sound of Rosa's cheerful chattering.

He brought Lightning to a halt as they reached the house. The door was shut and he could smell burning. Swiftly climbing out of the saddle, he tied Lightning to the fence and hurried up the path. Rosa slid down to the ground and followed him.

Connor raced through the front door and skidded to a halt. The house was full of smoke. 'Stay there,' he ordered Rosa. He pulled the neckerchief up over his mouth and nose and fumbled his way into the kitchen. 'Gran? Gran, where are you?' he shouted through the coughing fit. The smoke was dense and tasted metallic. It was difficult to breathe and his eyes were stinging. He blindly found his way across the room and flung open the back door and the windows.

'Gran!' shouted Rosa from the front door. 'Where's Gran?'

Connor could see very little but as the smoke cleared he felt a great wave of relief when he realised Gran wasn't in the kitchen. But where had she gone? She was always here to give them tea after school. He looked wildly around the kitchen as the smoke poured out of the open door and window. The source of the fire was a saucepan which had been left on the range to burn dry. He grabbed a cloth and pulled it off the heat before dumping it in the sink and pouring water over it. The pan was ruined; there was a large hole in the bottom and the remains of a charred stew were glued on the inside.

'Where's Gran?' Rosa's eyes were huge in her little face as she appeared in the doorway.

'I don't know,' he muttered. 'Come on, let's get out of here.' He took her hand and led her onto the back verandah. Rosa was coughing fit to bust and he could hardly breathe, let alone get rid of the horrible taste of that burning pan.

As they stepped down into the garden, something caught his eye through the drift of smoke. He looked again, the feeling of something not being right growing stronger. 'Better stay here,' he told Rosa as he hurried down the steps and ran to the washing line at the far end of the garden.

The freshly laundered sheets flapped and snapped over the tiny, still figure like great beating wings, the wooden pegs strewn around her, the basket upended.

'Gran?' He rushed to her, but even before he'd touched her, he knew she was gone.

Rosa screamed and he swiftly turned and pulled her into his arms, shielding her from the awful sight of their grandmother's open mouth and staring eyes. 'What's wrong with her, Con?' sobbed Rosa. 'Why's she lying in the garden?'

Connor tried to soothe her, but her screams and her sobs brought back the horror of his childhood and he had to fight his own tears. 'She's in Heaven, Rosa,' he murmured finally. 'She's gone to sleep with the angels.' He looked up at the flapping sheets. They reminded him more of the great wings of an unnamed predatory bird, but he would keep that thought to himself. Rosa was frightened enough.

Rosa clung to him fiercely. 'You won't go to Heaven, will you?' she begged. 'You promise you won't disappear?'

'Of course I promise,' he said, his voice unsteady as he struggled to stem the tears and be strong for her. Yet his heart was breaking, and as he picked his little sister up and carried her away he realised he was all she had. It was time for him to be strong – to be a man – to look after her and keep his promise never to leave her.

Catriona was in Brisbane preparing for *Tosca*. It would be a full opera, staged in the open on the South Bank to celebrate Australia Day. The rehearsals had been going on for three months, and there were another two weeks to go until the final full dress rehearsal.

Catriona picked up her handbag and smoothed the creases from her shift dress. Linen was always a mistake. Brin had warned her often enough, but she'd seen the dress in the shop window and hadn't been able to resist. She eased her feet in the high-heeled shoes – they were pinching, and she couldn't wait to get back to the apartment and soak in a hot bath.

She left the rehearsal rooms and climbed into her car. The drive to the rented apartment wasn't long, but she was tired and for the first time in her life, felt her age. At least she would have a break for a couple of days, she thought as she weaved through the afternoon traffic and headed north into the suburbs. And when the final dress rehearsal was over she would have two more days off before the first performance.

She swung the car through the automatic gates and parked outside her apartment. It was a low-rise block of apartments with a patio area overlooking a swimming pool and pleasant gardens. She stepped into the cool hallway and closed the door behind her. Kicking off her shoes she picked up the mail, padded into the lounge and collapsed on the couch.

The sound of children playing in the pool drifted into the apartment and she closed her eyes. *Tosca* was the most challenging of the operas, very dramatic, dark and full of passion; and although she'd sung the part to great acclaim and was considered to be the greatest Floria of her generation, the hectic schedule was proving too much, and after so many years in the business, she'd lost her hunger.

She opened her eyes at this startling realisation. Was that why she felt tired all the time? Why her voice was beginning to lose some of its tessitura– its texture and clarity? She stood and walked over to the window and drew back the heavy curtains to let the sun stream in and give her a view over the pool. The changes in her voice were subtle, so subtle that, so far, only she had noticed them, but she knew. She could hear it every time she struggled for the perfection that had once been so effortless. 'How long have I got?' she breathed.

She left the window and padded into the kitchen and made a cup of tea, but her mind refused to be still. A life on the stage was precarious at the best of times – she'd been lucky – but just how long could she maintain her status? There were other divas taking centre-stage now: the electrifying Callas in America, the regal Joan Sutherland from Australia, as well as the stunning New Zealander, Kiri te Kanawa, who'd just made her first recording after being at the London Opera Centre.

She sipped the tea and stared into space. She was still a diva; still respected, loved and sought after. But how long would that last? She was almost fifty, and because she'd started so young, her voice would soon fail her. Then what? The idea of retiring scared her rigid. What would she do? How would she spend her time? Belvedere was her home, the place she yearned to be when she was away from it. But she was realistic enough to realise Belvedere was far removed from the bright lights of the city, another world from the drama of the opera and the excitement of travelling the world. How long would it be before she tired of the endless space, the small population and the day-to-day grind of life on a cattle station?

Perhaps she could commute? Her money had built a new academy in Melbourne, and supplied scholarships for the poorer students, and she could teach and nurture their talents. But then again she would miss the cut and thrust of performing, the adrenaline of standing on a huge stage in front of an appreciative audience. She could record or make guest appearances, of course, but that wouldn't satisfy her at all. Catriona had always believed in all or nothing. If she retired, then it would be the end – it had to be – for she was damned if she would turn into a deluded diva who carried on into old age accepting the charitable offer of any part available because she couldn't bear the thought of not performing.

Catriona blinked and snapped out of her gloomy thoughts. She wasn't past it quite yet. She was about to star in *Tosca*, her most famous role and they wouldn't have offered it to her out of pity. She was just tired and needed a rest. Tomorrow was another day, and as it was a break in rehearsals, she wondered if she might fly over and visit Poppy. It would be good to see her again; the last trip had been fleeting.

The letters lay on the table where she'd thrown them, and she sifted through until she came to something that looked interesting. The large envelope was addressed in an unfamiliar hand, and had been re-directed from the Sydney apartment. She tore it open.

Her own letter fell out. It was still in its envelope, but it had at least been opened. Catriona's hand began to shake. There was no accompanying note. Catriona stared at the handwriting, wondering if her letter had been read right through, or whether it had been glanced at and ignored. But the very act of returning it was a powerful message. Her daughter wanted nothing to do with her.

'I've waited too long and searched too hard to be knocked back now,' she murmured. 'I'll write another letter, and then another and another until she gets sick of sending them back. Then, perhaps her curiosity will make her read one.'

The telephone interrupted her thoughts and she reached for the receiver. She listened in horror as Fred told her about Poppy. 'Keep the children with you. I'm on my way.'

*

214

The funeral was to be held early the following day. Catriona arrived late at night, but the lights in the homestead were spilling out into the darkness. 'Where are the children?' was her first question.

Fred was pale beneath the suntan, his eyes sad. 'We put Rosa to bed in the spare room. Billy's wife, Maggie, gave her a hot drink with one of her potions in it to calm her and help her to sleep. She's in with her now, just keeping an eye.'

'And Connor? How's he holding up?'

Fred ran his hand over his grizzled chin. 'He's out with Billy,' he said. 'The boy's taken it hard. But he'll be right, tougher than you give him credit for, and already talking about working here to keep him and his sister.'

Catriona said nothing, but deep down she raged at the unfairness of Connor having to act tough and manly when he was still only a boy. It seemed Poppy's determination and strength had been handed down to her grandson, and although she wished it otherwise, she knew Connor would do as he saw fit regardless of any advice from her.

She walked into the homestead and shed her fur coat. It was too quiet and there was already the smell of death in the house. She wished the children were here so she could put her arms around them and reassure them they weren't alone. She needed to hold them for her own sake as well as theirs, for losing Poppy was her last tie to the past, the final thread of the woven cloth that was her childhood.

Catriona peeked in at Rosa and resisted scooping her up in her arms. The little girl was wearing her favourite Snoopy pyjamas, and was curled up asleep, one small hand cupping her rosy cheek. Maggie was sitting in a chair by the bed, her head drooping in weariness, her dark hand resting protectively on the child's arm. Not wanting to disturb either of them, she quietly closed the door and crossed the narrow hall. Taking a deep breath, she glanced at Fred before she opened the door.

Poppy had been laid out in the parlour which was lit by the light from dozens of candles. She looked as if she was sleeping, and her face was calm, the lines of care somehow smoothed away. Her hair had been brushed and her hands were folded on her chest, a string of rosary beads clasped in her lifeless fingers. The dress she wore was one Catriona had given her years ago – it had been her

215

favourite – bright yellow with big red flowers all over it.

Catriona stood and looked down at her, the tears caught in her eyelashes. The carpenter had made a coffin from local timber and had varnished and polished it until it gleamed. There were brass handles, she noticed, and the lining was pale lilac silk. 'How did you do all this in such a short time?' she asked through the tears.

Fred cleared his throat. 'The chippy always has a store of coffins,' he said gruffly. 'It would take too long to get one made and flown in, and we only ever have twenty-four hours at the most before the funeral.' He shuffled his feet. 'Maggie and the other lubras saw to Poppy. I hope everything's all right?'

Catriona didn't reply, just looked at Poppy and tried not to give in to the terrible need to howl with grief. The dress clashed with the earrings and bracelets, and everything jarred against the lilac lining – but that was Poppy. Brightly coloured and chatty like the rosellas, as mischievous as the possums she could hear scampering over the roof. 'I hope she didn't suffer,' she murmured.

'The doc said it was a heart-attack. She wouldn't have felt a thing.'

Catriona nodded. 'I'll sit with her tonight,' she whispered.

Fred left the room, and she pulled up a chair and covered Poppy's hands with her own. They were cold to the touch, unresponsive, so unlike the Poppy she had known. And as she sat there in the flickering shadows, she remembered the jolt and creak of wagons trundling through the Outback. Remembered the chorus girl with the paste jewellery and long legs who'd had such a zest for life, and who could tell such entertaining and naughty stories. She refused to remember the dark days – the days of poverty and prejudice – the days when life had been a struggle and they had all thought they couldn't go on. For Poppy had overcome it all, her strength of character and lust for life giving her the will to survive long enough to see her grandchildren safe and thriving. It was a powerful legacy, already apparent in young Connor.

Connor was glad it was dark, for the night hid his tears as he followed Billy Birdsong into the bush. The ache for his grandmother was a weight in his chest, and he wondered how he and Rosa would manage without her. She had always been there, always protective and loving, even in the darkest times.

'Alonga me,' said Billy in his sing-song voice. 'Follow footsteps of ancestors into land of Never-Never.'

216

Connor was drawn by the soft voice, for he had known the Aborigine Elder since early childhood and had loved to hear his stories and go bush with him when Gran allowed him to. Billy was his hero, his mentor, and one day he hoped he would be as knowledgeable about the land and the animals and plants which flourished here in this great open country.

They had come a long way from the homestead. The horses had been left behind and the two figures moved like shadows through the long grass and into the stands of trees. The wind was soft, like another voice, whispering in the darkness as it sighed in the leaves and ruffled the grass. Connor followed the sure-footed Aborigine through the trees and out onto the plains. He could hear only the siren song of the man he followed, could see only the darker shadow against the night sky as they came to a clearing.

Billy stopped walking finally and stood waiting. He was a tall, thin silhouette against the starlit sky, his hair like a halo around his head. He held out his arm. 'Alonga me, Connor,' he sang. 'Sit under stars and I tell you of Dreamtime, and how death is not for tears.' He crossed his legs and sank in one graceful, flowing movement to the ground.

Connor sat beside him, wondering what words Billy could say that would ease the pain.

Billy began to speak, his voice hypnotic and compelling as he told Connor about the final journey into the heavens. 'Poppy have strong spirit,' he said. 'She make good journey into land of the sky.' He threw a handful of grass in the air and they watched as it was caught by the wind and carried away. 'Like the blades of grass we are blown here by the Sun Goddess to protect Mother Earth. As we plant seed for new generations we grow old, and the Sun Goddess call us home. She sing and we cannot close our ears, it is time to rest.'

Connor sniffed and rubbed his nose on his sleeve.

The Aborigine smiled, his teeth gleaming in the moonlight. 'Your tears will nourish the seeds she has sown,' he said. 'They will bring life to the spirits who wait in the earth to be born.' His voice softened to a murmur. 'Her time is over, but her spirit always with you.'

Connor looked at him, his eyes blurred with tears, his heart breaking.

'Do not be sad,' said the Elder. 'She is lifted up in Spirit Canoe, and if you look very carefully you will see she sails on Great White Way.' He raised a bony arm and pointed.

Connor blinked back the tears and looked up. The sky was enormous, reaching over and around him in such magnificence it was almost as if he could see the curve of the world. And there, among the millions of stars was the Milky Way, a broad swathe of pinpoints of light that were too numerous to count. It stretched from horizon to horizon in a great, glittering arc, and as he watched he thought he could see a solitary star travel along that celestial highway.

'Spirit Canoe carry her to land of Moon God,' said Billy softly. 'There, she will lose earthly shape, shed it like bark of gum tree and fly high and high across sky until she is a star. A star that will always shine alonga you and those she loved.'

Connor's tears were warm on his cheeks as he watched the tiny pinprick of light traverse the Milky Way. Then, without warning, there was a flash and something streaked across the sky.

'It is done,' sighed Billy.

Connor blinked and looked again. There was a new star in the sky, he was certain of it, and although he was sure Billy had made the story up, he wanted to believe it more than anything. 'Will the star always be there?' he asked.

'Always,' said Billy. 'Her spirit live in sky now. She is happy.'

Connor sat beside the Aboriginal Elder for a long time. They said little, just watched the sky and the stars until they faded to a pearl grey which heralded a new day. Then, in silent unison, they rose and walked back to the homestead.

The neighbours had begun arriving the night before, and as the sun rose and bathed Belvedere in a glow of gold, the makeshift camp of tents in home paddock came to life. Water was fetched and food was cooked on camp-fires. Utilities were parked out by the bunkhouse, horses were let loose in the corrals, and small aircraft landed and taxied to the clearing on the far side of the strip. There was even a collection of wagons and buggies under the trees, some of them probably antiques that wouldn't have looked out of place in a museum.

Catriona had worried about how to feed all these people. Five loaves and two fishes would be stretching it and she wasn't up to miracles. Yet, to her relief and grateful astonishment it seemed a tradition amongst these big-hearted Outback people to bring food for such an occasion. It was carried on plates and in hampers and boxes into the cookhouse where it was laid ready beneath cloths for after the service. It was the product of many hours of baking in stifling kitchens where the temperatures often rose beyond one hundred degrees and would be enough to feed a veritable army.

Clemmie arrived with the director of *Tosca* in his plane, and the locals of Drum Creek came on horseback or in a long convoy of utilities. The Sullivans drove in with Belinda and their three strapping sons.

Catriona stood on the verandah, Rosa clinging to her skirts, Connor silent and watchful at her side. She hadn't slept, keeping vigil over Poppy through the lonely night, talking to her, crying, raging at the unfairness of it all until the priest arrived and calmed her. It was too soon to be holding a funeral, she thought in despair, she hadn't come to terms with the shock of Poppy's death, let alone prepared herself or the children for today. Yet the heat demanded the funeral be held as swiftly as possible. It was part of life and death in the Outback, a part she must accept if she was planning on living here eventually.

She welcomed Pat and Jeff Sullivan. She had met them many times before and was pleased to see them again even though it was such a terrible reason for their visit. Belinda went straight to Rosa's side and, hand-in-hand the two little girls wandered off to the back verandah. Connor tipped his hat and strode off across the yard in the company of the Sullivan boys. He'd hardly said a word since returning at dawn this morning, but everyone had their way of handling grief and Catriona realised that whatever Billy had said or done the previous night, it had given the boy some comfort and prepared him for today.

'I can't believe so many people have taken the trouble to come all this way,' she said to Pat as they stood on the verandah. 'And they're so kind. We've enough food to feed twice as many.'

'Poppy was unique,' said Pat as she slipped off her cardigan and mopped her hot face with a handkerchief. The temperature had soared into the nineties and the flies were already a nuisance. 'She was such good company, used to make me laugh with her stories. I reckon Drum Creek won't be the same now she's gone.' Pat blew her nose. 'She was always the first to offer help, you know. She baked cakes for fêtes, organised costumes for the school plays and

219

baby-sat for some of the younger parents so they could have a night out at the pub. We're all going to miss her.'

Catriona stared as even more people arrived. Poppy had certainly made her mark on this small corner of Australia, and was obviously held in high regard. She watched the ebb and flow of the crowd, noting how the men wore bush-hats, long-sleeved shirts and moleskins or jeans, and how the women were almost uniformly dressed in faded print dresses and white sandals. She looked down at her manicured nails, at the gold bracelet and diamond rings. She was wearing a black dress by Chanel, black patent high-heeled shoes and silk stockings – the height of fashion in the city – but she felt overdressed beside this comfortably proportioned country-woman in her faded cotton frock and sensible shoes.

The priest had flown in the night before and had already performed the last rites. Now he emerged from the gloom of the house, his black robes sombre in the bright sunlight that streamed onto the verandah.

Clemmie rounded up Connor, and Pat found Rosa and Belinda. When they were all gathered a great silence fell on the crowd as the procession began. Poppy's coffin was carried by Connor, Billy, Fred, the landlord of the pub, the owner of the general store and the eldest of the Sullivan boys. It was draped in her favourite black shawl, the one with the red roses painted on it. The floral tributes were carried by those who'd brought them and the lilies and carnations and roses sweetened the air with their perfume.

The procession slowly wound across the yard and into the eastern paddock. Belvedere's little graveyard had stood there behind a picket fence since the homestead had first been settled. It served as a poignant history lesson, for the gravestones and wooden markers told the story of the people who'd lived and died here: from accidents to still-birth, from fire and flood to illness and old age.

As Catriona stood by the graveside she couldn't help but remember all those who'd left her. Mam and Da, Max and his little dog – and now Poppy. Summers' Music Hall had finally come to the end of the road. She blinked back the tears, and just for a moment she thought she could hear the trundle of the wagon wheels and the soft, reassuring plod of Jupiter and Mars. Perhaps they had returned for Poppy – it would be nice to think they were all together again – making tracks across the skies.

She put her arm around Rosa and held her tightly as the coffin was lowered into the earth. Glancing across at Connor she saw how pale he was, how tightly he was holding in his emotions and she yearned to reach out and hold him too. But he was trying so hard to be a man; a man in a child's body, a boy on the threshold of adulthood who wouldn't thank her for making him appear weak.

The service was over and the crowd melted away as the men began to cover the coffin with the dark red earth of Belvedere. Catriona had sent Rosa back to the homestead with the Sullivans, but Connor was standing alone, watching the men finish their task. She went to stand beside him, not really knowing what to do or say.

Then his hand reached out for her fingers and he grasped them tightly. He turned to look at her, his hazel eyes swimming with unshed tears. 'She wasn't just a gran,' he said, his voice uneven. 'She was a mum and a friend. I loved her very much, you know.'

Catriona had to struggle to keep her voice steady and her emotions under control. She squeezed his hand. 'We all did, darling,' she murmured. 'Poppy was a wonderful, courageous woman and I'm proud to have known her.'

He fell silent for a long moment, staring at the ground, and Catriona wondered what he was thinking. Then he cleared his throat and lifted his chin and told her what Billy had said the night before. 'Do you really think it's possible?' he asked finally.

Catriona's heart went out to him. 'Why not?' she replied softly. 'Poppy always wanted to be a star.'

Chapter Sixteen

The food had been demolished, and as the sun dipped low, the people began to leave in their wagons and buggies, the utilities and horses wending their way down the long driveway, the small planes roaring down the airstrip and lifting into the sky. The clouds of dust lingered long after they had gone, and when they had cleared, it was almost sundown.

The men of Belvedere sat outside the bunkhouse smoking their cigarettes and talking, their voices a muted hum in the stillness. Pat Sullivan had taken Rosa with her to Derwent Hills Station for a few days, in the hopes Belinda's company and different surroundings would help her to heal. Connor was nowhere to be seen, and Catriona guessed he was with Billy.

'It's been quite a day,' sighed Clemmie as she handed Catriona a glass of gin and tonic. 'How are you holding up?'

Catriona sipped the drink and tried to ease the ache in her neck and back. It felt as if every muscle had been stretched beyond endurance. 'I'll be right,' she murmured. 'A good night's sleep wouldn't go amiss, though.' She put her hand on Clemmie's arm. 'Thanks for staying,' she said. 'I didn't want to spend the night alone.'

Clemmie patted her hand. 'I'll stay as long as you want,' she said. 'John's quite capable of looking after himself for a while, and as you're my only client now, I have nothing more important to do.' She smiled. 'Franz said to tell you to take a week off.'

Catriona stared in amazement. The director never let anyone off rehearsals, they were too important. 'Has he been smoking pot, or something? It's most unlike him.'

'Don't worry, Kitty. He's not all heart. He expects you to be word perfect and fully aware of the stage directions when you get back for the final dress rehearsal.' She grinned. 'You know Franz. Takes no prisoners, just has his soprano shot if he thinks you've been slacking.'

'At least it'll give me something else to think about,' she replied with a wry smile. 'I thought it was too good to be true.'

They sat in the cane chairs and looked out into the night. The yard was quiet, the sky dark and twinkling with stars. The Southern Cross hung high above them, so clear it was as if you could reach up and pluck it from the sky.

'There's nothing like an Outback night,' said Clemmie dreamily. 'I never knew there were so many stars, and look at the Milky Way, it's fantastic.'

Catriona smiled. 'You should get out of Sydney more often,' she chided softly.

'Mmm.' Clemmie stirred the slice of lemon in her drink. 'I don't think I'd last very long out here,' she said finally. 'It's so . . .'

'Isolated?' Catriona smiled as her friend nodded. 'But that's the beauty of the place, don't you see? No hustle or bustle, no light pollution or loud pop music, no directors yelling and singers screeching at one another; just the wind in the trees, the click of crickets and the scent of eucalyptus and dust.'

Clemmie brushed her black skirt and grimaced. 'There's certainly enough dust,' she muttered. 'This skirt is filthy and I just know my hair is full of it. Lord knows what it's doing to my complexion.'

Catriona's smile was wan as she looked back at her friend. Clemmie was sixty-three and looked at least fifteen years younger after having been on a strict diet. Her complexion was flawless, as was her make-up. Her hair had been tinted light brown and was swept back in a chignon which showed off her long, elegant neck. Her dress was a simple black sheath that had cost a fortune and her snakeskin shoes were handmade. 'I don't think you need worry,' she said.

'I can't imagine living out here,' said Clemmie, obviously determined to keep this conversation going. 'You only have to look at the women to see what the place does to them.' She fell silent for a moment. 'Even the young ones are weather-beaten and lined from the sun, and none of them seem to care what they look like. I mean,' she said in exasperation. 'Those ghastly cotton frocks, and those awful shoes – any normal woman would rather die than wear such horrors.'

Catriona laughed. 'Don't be so disparaging,' she said. 'People here work in the kind of heat that would have you flat on your back for weeks. It doesn't matter what they wear or what they look like, as long as they're cool and the clothes are practical. They are hard-working, honest people who would give you their last dollar.' She toned down the defensive quality in her voice as she realised she was letting the stress of the last twenty-four hours get the better of her. 'Life isn't a fashion parade here,' she said quietly. 'No one cares a hoot.'

Clemmie's expression was enigmatic as she looked back at her. 'That's why you wore a Chanel dress and high-heels, is it?'

'They were a mistake,' she admitted. 'But I left in such a hurry, I didn't think.'

'Mmmm.'

Despite their long years of friendship, she was beginning to get on Catriona's nerves. 'Something's obviously niggling you, Clemmie, so for goodness sake spit it out.'

Clemmie's narrow eyebrows lifted momentarily, then she sighed and began to fiddle with her charm bracelet. 'I was trying to imagine you living here,' she said finally. 'And, frankly, Kitty, I can't.'

'Why?'

'Because you've become a city woman,' replied her friend. 'Because your adult life has been spent travelling the world, living in the best hotels and apartments, fêted and adored every time you step on stage. You shop at Chanel and Givenchy, you attend functions at embassies and palaces, and are escorted by some of the most eligible men in the world.' She turned, her gaze direct. 'In short, Kitty,' she said, 'you are a star, with a lifestyle to match. Can you really imagine settling here amongst these rough country types?'

Catriona was silent. She couldn't be cross with Clemmie, she was, after all, only voicing some of the doubts that had gone through her own mind the day before. She decided to change the subject. 'I wrote to my daughter,' she said in the silence.

'Oh, no.' Clemmie stared back at her.

'You were right,' she admitted, her voice soft. 'She didn't want to know. She sent back my letter without even a note of explanation.'

'I did warn you, darling,' said Clemmie. 'Perhaps it's best to

224

leave things as they are. At least she knows who and where you are, and if she changes her mind, she can always write.'

'I doubt she ever will,' she murmured. She fell silent. Clemmie didn't need to know she would carry on writing to her daughter until all hope was lost. As they sat there and watched the stars she thought of her daughter and wondered what had gone through her mind when she'd read the letter.

Clemmie interrupted her thoughts. 'What will you do now, Kitty?'

Catriona frowned. 'I'll spend a few days here, then fly back to Brisbane. I've got an opera to sing, remember?'

'Don't be clever with me,' muttered Clemmie. 'You know perfectly well I meant the children.'

'Rosa's with the Sullivans. She'll be safe there. Connor seems determined to work, so, as his birthday is only a few weeks away, I've given him permission to work as stand-off for Billy.' She paused. 'But only on the proviso he tunes into the School of the Air every morning and finishes his education.' She smiled. 'He didn't like it, but it's a compromise.'

'Rosa can't stay with the Sullivans indefinitely. This is her home; her brother's here, and he's all she's got. It would be cruel to keep them apart. You'll have to find someone to look after them.'

Catriona sat deep in thought. Her mind was whirling with the complexities of the situation. Then, as if a light had been switched on, the whole thing became perfectly clear. Fate had made the decision for her. 'You're right,' she said as she stood and leaned against the railing. 'This is Rosa's home, and Connor and I are the only family she has left. It's time for me to retire.'

Clemmie was out of her chair in an instant. 'I wasn't suggesting you give up your career,' she said hastily. 'Only that you consider what's best for the children.'

Catriona grinned for the first time in two days. 'That's exactly what I am doing,' she said firmly. She grasped Clemmie's hands. 'Don't you see, Clemmie? It's fate.'

'Fate my eye,' snorted Clemmie. 'You're tired and out of sorts, still grieving for Poppy. Of course you can't chuck it all in for the sake of a couple of kids that aren't even your own.'

'Then what exactly do you expect me to do?' retorted Catriona. 'Dump Rosa into boarding school and leave Connor here to fend for himself? He's not thirteen, and Rosa's eight. They're still babies and I'd be letting Poppy down if I deserted them now.'

'My children came to no harm in boarding school,' snapped Clemmie.

'Your children weren't brought up in the wide open spaces of this place. Your children had parents to go home to at weekends and in the holidays.'

'You can provide a home for Rosa in Sydney. Connor's better off here. He's got Billy and Fred to look after him, he doesn't need pampering by you.' Clemmie's usually placid nature had been swept away, and her eyes were sparking dangerously as her voice rose. 'As for chucking it all in because you think fate demands it ...' She took a deep breath and let it out in a hiss. 'It's a load of bloody nonsense,' she snapped.

Catriona realised tempers were rising. Sooner or later one of them would say something that couldn't be taken back. This was their first serious row in over thirty years, and the last thing she wanted to do was alienate her best and most loyal friend. She grasped Clemmie's arm. 'I don't want to fight with you,' she said softly.

'And I don't want to fight with you either,' she replied, still not mollified. 'But you've worked so long and hard, I can't bear the thought of you just walking away from it.'

Catriona folded her arms around her waist and shivered. The breeze was cooler now, sifting over the yard, rustling the leaves in the nearby trees. The moon sailed regally across the skies, untouched by the frailty of the humans below, its pale yellow face casting light and shadow over Belvedere. 'I've achieved everything I ever set out to do,' she began, her voice quieter now. 'I have fame and fortune and a lifestyle most other people could only dream about. I've been lucky.'

'Luck has had very little to do with it,' protested Clemmie. 'You worked bloody hard, and made some terrible sacrifices.'

Catriona nodded. 'Yes,' she admitted. 'It hasn't all been wine and roses.' She sighed and looked at her friend. 'But what was it all for, Clemmie?'

'A comfortable bank balance, and a portfolio of investments which would be the envy of most of us. Then there's the satisfaction of knowing you'll go down in history as one of the great divas of your era.'

Catriona waved all that away with the flick of her hand. 'Money

226

and fame are transient things; they mean very little when you are alone,' she said softly. 'And I am alone, Clemmie. I have no husband, no children – but for a daughter who wants nothing to do with me.'

'That wasn't your fault,' declared Clemmie.

Catriona shrugged and carried on. 'I was never given the chance to raise my own child. She grew up without me and I had no part in her life, in her sorrows or in her triumphs. Fate is giving me a second chance to be a mother and I intend to grasp that opportunity and do the best I can with Rosa and Connor.'

'And your career?' Clenmmie's face was pale beneath the careful make-up, the tension evident in her stance.

'I've reached the pinnacle, Clem. My voice isn't what it was.' She held up her hand to silence her friend's denial. 'I can hear it, and soon others will too. My time in the spotlight is almost over.'

Clemmie stood in silence for a long moment. Then her voice became business-like as she pulled the diary out of her handbag. 'You'll have to do *Tosca*,' she said. 'It's too late to pull out now.' She turned the pages. 'And what about New York? Then there's London and the Royal Opera House in August.'

'They will be my farewell performances,' she said firmly.

Clemmie winced. 'In that case I'd better get on the phone, speak to the press and make arrangements. It's lucky you're singing *Tosca* in New York as well, because it will be the most fitting finale to your career.' She spoke rapidly as she blinked back the tears. 'The Royal Opera House has already fixed their programme of ballets and operas. I doubt they'll change the programme at such a late date. You'll have to end your career with Columbine/Nedda in *I Pagliacci*.'

Catriona laughed and clapped her hands. 'That's perfect,' she said. 'My first appearance on the stage was with a troupe of players when I was only a few minutes old. I'm the quintessential child of the theatre.'

Clemmie stared at her.

'My father made me learn Shakespeare until I could recite it without any mistakes. But the Bard got it so right,' she said with a smile. '"All the world's a stage, and all the men and women merely players. They have their exits and their entrances; and one man in his time plays many parts." I will finish as I began,' she murmured. 'As one of a troupe of players, making my exit so I can play another part in the next chapter of my life.'

'Oh, Kitty,' she sobbed. 'I can't bear to think of you stuck all the way out here.'

'Don't be sad,' said Catriona softly. 'I'm starting out on a new adventure. Just be happy for me, Clem. I'm finally going to get the chance to be a real mother.'

'Motherhood isn't easy,' she sniffed. 'They can be little buggers at times.'

Catriona smiled. 'I know. And I'm really looking forward to the challenge.'

'I need to make some calls,' she said as she blew her nose. 'Where's the phone?'

'There isn't one.' She laughed out loud at Clemmie's expression of horror. 'We use the two-way radio, and that links us to the telephone exchange.'

'How on earth do people survive without a phone?' gasped Clemmie.

'I don't know,' Catriona replied. 'But I'm looking forward to finding out.'

Fred had taken his things to the bunkhouse, but Catriona and Clemmie went to bed in the spare room. The metal springs of the old iron bedsteads squeaked every time one of them moved, but Clemmie eventually stopped complaining and settled down and Catriona soon heard her deep, steady breathing and knew she was asleep.

As she lay there in the sparsely furnished room and watched the moon-shadows drift across the ceiling, Catriona felt the silence close in on her. Beyond the timber walls of the house lay thousands of miles of empty land. Her nearest neighbours were in Drum Creek, but surrounding that little settlement was the vast and achingly lonely sweep of the Outback which stretched from horizon to horizon.

She experienced a moment of panic. What if Clemmie was right and she couldn't cope with the isolation? It would be very different from the short visits she'd made so far. What if the children didn't want her to mother them? What if it proved she was a lousy mother and failed miserably? She turned over and buried her face in the pillow. She was desperate for sleep, but her mind seemed determined to keep her awake.

Her decision to retire would mean a great deal of organisation.

There was *Tosca* for a start, and the tour to London and New York that would take up much of the next eighteen months. Clemmie would no doubt organise press interviews, television appearances and more recordings. Fred would have to move out, and one of the other shacks made habitable. If she planned to live here, then changes had to be made: rooms added to accommodate the children, the kitchen updated and the whole place renovated. It might have been all right for Fred, but she was used to a bit of comfort and didn't see why living out here should change that.

She rolled over on to her back and stared at the ceiling. The apartment block in Sydney was probably the best investment she'd ever made. With the opening of the Opera House in the next couple of years and the regeneration of the whole quay area, it would be stupid to sell it. After Brin's death, she'd leased the downstairs apartment to a middle-aged couple who paid their rent on time and took care of the place when she was away. The arrangement suited them all, and she decided to keep things as they were. There would no doubt come a time when she needed an escape from Belvedere, and what better place to go than Sydney? She could take Rosa to watch plays and ballets and even the opera. They could shop and go on ferry rides as well as visit the art gallery and museum.

Catriona closed her eyes as the doubts swarmed. Rosa was still a little girl. What if she didn't like the opera or the ballet? And what of Connor? She'd had few dealings with boys his age, and she had no idea of how to handle him. Her dream of owning Belvedere had begun when she herself was a child. Now she wondered if perhaps the reality of living here, of taking on Poppy's grandchildren, would prove to be a mistake. Clemmie was right. Her life in the city was far removed from life in the Outback. She would have to adapt, have to compromise at every turn. She had set herself an enormous task – and she wasn't at all certain she was up to it.

She must have fallen asleep, for when she opened her eyes again, it was dawn and the rosellas and parakeets were making enough noise in the trees to waken the dead. She looked across at Clemmie and grinned. Her friend was sitting in bed, a cup of tea in her hand, a disgusted expression on her face.

'At last,' she grumbled. 'What with your snoring and those damn birds, I hardly got a wink of sleep.' She looked at the delicate gold watch on her wrist. 'Do you realise it's five in the bloody morning?'

'I don't snore,' Catriona protested as she reached for the tea pot and poured out a cup for herself. She took a sip, added sugar and relaxed back into the pillows. 'And you were asleep the minute your head hit the pillow; you've had at least eight hours, so don't come the old soldier with me.'

Clemmie was about to protest when they were both startled by the roar of a fast-moving utility outside. 'Now what?' she said crossly. 'Doesn't anyone sleep around here?'

Catriona frowned and pulled on a silk dressing gown over the matching pyjamas. The utility had screeched to a halt outside, and she could hear voices. She hurried out of the room, down the narrow hall to the front door.

Rosa tumbled out of the utility and flung herself into Catriona's arms. 'Don't go,' she sobbed. 'Please don't leave me, Aunty Cat.'

Catriona tried to calm the little girl's fears as she held her. 'I'm not going to leave you,' she said firmly. 'Shh, there's a good girl, don't cry.' She looked over the child's tousled head at Pat Sullivan.

Pat's face was pale. She'd been up most of the night and had then had to drive across country to Belvedere. 'Rosa was OK on the journey to Derwent Hills,' she explained as she came up the steps. 'But she woke up screaming and was absolutely convinced she would never see you or Connor again.' She sighed and stroked the child's hair. 'Poor little kid,' she said. 'I tried to tell her she was only with me for a holiday, but she didn't believe me. I suppose she's convinced that sooner or later everyone leaves – you can hardly blame her under the circumstances.'

Catriona picked up Rosa and, sitting on the verandah chair, settled her on her knee. 'I'm not leaving you,' she said again. 'I'm going to live here with you and Connor and take care of you.'

The dark brown eyes were filled with tears, the little face pinched with fear and weariness. 'You promise?' she hiccupped.

'I promise,' said Catriona firmly. 'Now, let's dry those tears and go and find some breakfast. I bet you're starving. I know I am.'

'Where's Connor?' she demanded, the fear returning. 'I want to see Connor.'

'I'm here,' said a soft voice from the steps.

Rosa scrambled off Catriona's lap and raced into his arms. 'I thought I'd never see you again,' she sobbed as she flung her arms around his neck. 'I didn't want to go away. Please don't send me away again.'

His hat fell off as he picked her up and she clung to him like a limpet. His hazel eyes met Catriona's; they held the wisdom and care of a much older boy. 'Are you really staying on?' he asked quietly.

Catriona nodded. 'Of course.'

'What about your singing?'

'I have commitments, but you and Rosa will come first from now on,' she said firmly.

The boy regarded her for a long moment then nodded. 'Thanks,' he said gruffly. 'Rosa needs us both but I think she needs you more.' He hesitated and a spot of colour tinged his cheeks. 'Reckon we both do,' he added.

Catriona felt the tears fill her eyes and the lump grow in her throat. She couldn't speak, so she put her arms around the boy and his sister and held them close. She had made the right decision.

Over the following days Rosa clung to her side, and at night she cried herself to sleep. She was frightened and confused and missing Poppy. Catriona realised immediately that things would have to change in the homestead. With Clemmie in the spare room, she moved the other bed into Fred's, so that when the child woke in the night, all Rosa had to do was clamber across and get in with her. Connor slept on the couch, it wasn't the perfect solution, but Catriona didn't want him returning to the old house on his own, and the bunkhouse was no place for a boy of such tender years. The men who worked on Belvedere might be gruff and good-hearted, but their language left a lot to be desired, as did their cleanliness.

As the week drew to a close, Catriona left Rosa with Clemmie, and headed off to Poppy's cottage. There hadn't been time to sort through things since the funeral and frankly she hadn't had the heart for it until now. But she would be flying to Brisbane with Rosa and Clemmie tomorrow, and she didn't want to leave it any longer.

She drew the utility to a halt and sighed. The house already had an abandoned air about it, and as she let herself in, there was the musty smell and the lingering reminder of the burning pot in the air. Catriona threw open doors and windows. She would get Maggie and the other lubras to clean the place up, but for now she just wanted to be alone.

231

Wandering through the rooms she remembered Poppy's delight at coming here. Her excitement at the thought of finally having her own place – and her determination and energy she'd put in to making it a home – was all here in the poignant reminders of the scrubbed kitchen table, the homemade curtains and rag rugs. She stared out of the window to the back garden. Mercifully, someone had brought in the laundry, and there was no sign of the tragedy that had happened there. With a sigh she began to gather up the children's things and pack them in boxes. There wasn't very much, just jeans and shirts and underwear, and a single dress Rosa wore on special occasions. Books and toys, and boxed games went in one box, Rosa's dolls and her teddy in another.

With the boxes in the utility, she returned to the house. Poppy's bed was covered in a handcrafted homemade patchwork quilt of many colours. The wardrobe held a collection of dated cotton dresses, worn-down shoes and a couple of knitted cardigans. At the back of the cupboard she found a shoe box, and as she opened it, she realised it held Poppy's mementos.

There were some old fliers, printed during the days of the travelling musical hall troupe. A sequined tiara, a feather fan and boa, and a pair of elbow length gloves were all she had left of those days. Catriona sifted through the black and white photographs. There was one of a very young Poppy standing between a man and woman, the dome of St Paul's rising behind them. Another of Poppy dressed in her stage finery, posing with the chorus girls in a cramped and chaotic dressing-room. That had to have been taken when she was at the Windmill, she thought. There were a few more of people she didn't know, but who had obviously been important in Poppy's life, and a couple of her with Ellen as a baby. Closing the box she set it to one side. She would keep it for Rosa and Connor.

The battered leather box on the top of the chest of drawers held Poppy's treasured jewellery collection. It consisted of cheap, colourful beads, paste brooches and earrings. There were bracelets of varying colours, hair slides and a gold locket that was badly tarnished. Catriona fiddled with the catch and eased it open. Inside was a photograph of a handsome, smiling man; she guessed it was probably Ellen's father.

Sorting through the clothes, she put them to one side. Someone would get use out of them, and she couldn't bear the thought of burning them. The quilts would be a reminder of home for Rosa and Connor, so she put them in the utility with the other things. The sheets and blankets were worn, as were the towels. They joined the pile of clothes to be given away.

Catriona packed up the utility and then stood in the silence of the house. She could hear the echo of Poppy's laugh, and the tramp of her feet on the floor. She closed the door and turned the key. The ghosts of the past would always remain here.

Connor had come in from the paddocks where he'd been helping Billy separate the calves from the cows. After a hot bath in the tub on the back verandah, he joined his sister and the two women at the table.

Catriona handed out the plates. Cookie had sent over a stew, and the smell was mouth-watering. The boy had a healthy appetite, she realised, and even Rosa was tucking in. It was early days yet, but it seemed the children were tougher than she'd thought. Maybe they were beginning to let go and look to the future. With that thought in mind, she cleared her throat. 'We'll have to leave very early tomorrow,' she said. 'I must be in Brisbane by nine.'

'Are we really going in a plane?' Rosa's eyes were wide with excitement.

Catriona laughed. 'Don't speak with your mouth full, Rosa. And yes, we are, it will drop us off in Brisbane, then take Aunt Clemmie down to Sydney.'

'How long will you be away?' Connor finished his dinner and pushed the plate aside. 'It's just that Billy said I could go on round-up with him and the others.'

'I'll be back for a couple of days in about a week's time,' she said. 'Then over the next two months I'll be popping back whenever I can.' She grinned at Connor. 'You can go on the round-up as long as you promise to keep up with your school-work.' She saw him pull a face. 'And I'll be checking your work when I come back, so don't think you can get away with anything.'

'Fair go, Aunt Cat,' he drawled, giving her a shy smile.

Catriona smiled back at him. She had asked him if he wanted to join her and his sister in Brisbane for the Australia Day celebrations and he'd said he preferred to stay here. They had grown closer during the last few days, and she had come to realise Connor wanted only to work on the land and be like so many of the other men who lived out here – quiet, shy men, who loved the land and their way of life – men who spoke slowly, and who preferred the company of horses and cattle to humans.

'Will I have to do lessons in Brisbane?' chirped up Rosa. 'I don't want to miss anything and we've got exams next term.'

Catriona laughed. How could two children be so different? 'I don't think you'll miss much for the first few days, but after that I'll get you a tutor to give you lessons and look after you while I'm working. How does that sound?'

Rosa screwed up her face as she thought about it. 'Will it mean I have a teacher all to myself?' she asked.

Catriona nodded.

'Wow! Wait 'til I tell Belinda.' Her excitement was momentary, and her expression became crestfallen. 'But what about my friends?' she wailed. 'I won't see Belinda at all, and Mary Carpenter will be her best friend instead of me.'

Catriona stroked her cheek. 'You'll see them when we come back to Belvedere,' she reassured her. 'You'll only have a tutor when I'm travelling, and once I've finished all my commitments, I'll make sure I only go away during school holidays so you can come with me.' She kissed her. 'Belinda can come and stay whenever she likes, and perhaps her mother will let her come to the city sometimes, too.'

Rosa seemed content with this, and as the meal was finished and the plates cleared away, Catriona realised the pattern had been set until it was time for Rosa to attend high school.

Rosa had been so excited at attending the Gala performance in Brisbane, that she'd hardly taken it all in. The flight to Brisbane had been thrilling enough, and the fireworks after the show were amazing, but it was seeing a full opera for the first time that really overwhelmed her. *Tosca* had come as a shock to Rosa, who hadn't realised how dramatic and powerful it would be, or how wonderful Aunt Cat was. Her voice made her skin tingle and sometimes, when it was soft and sad and achingly pure, it made her want to cry for the sheer beauty of it.

New York was a revelation. The streets were packed, the buildings reached almost to the sky and the constant noise and bustle was far removed from the leisurely pace of Brisbane. They had stayed in a luxury hotel suite overlooking Fifth Avenue, and she'd agreed with Miss Frobisher, her nanny and tutor, that she didn't like being up so high.

Rosa fell in love with London. It was so old, and although the streets were busy, there didn't seem to be the same thrusting energy of New York. She enjoyed riding on the big red buses, and shopping in Carnaby Street and Harrods. Miss Frobisher took her to see the Houses of Parliament, the changing of the guard at Buckingham Palace and the Beefeaters at the Tower of London, and Aunt Cat had taken her to tea at Browns, where the sandwiches were tiny, the cakes delicious and the cups of tea tasted very different from those at home.

But Rosa's favourite place in London was the Royal Opera House where they were staging *I Pagliacci*, *Swan Lake* and a series of orchestral concerts which ran in strict rotation. Backstage, it was a vast warren of tiny dressing-rooms, stairways and narrow corridors, and underneath the stage it was like a giant's tool-shed with huge machinery that growled and murmured as it operated pulleys and trap doors.

Miss Frobisher didn't seem to approve of the men and women strolling around half naked, and clucked like an irate hen at some of the language used during heated arguments, and the free and easy way the singers and dancers hugged and kissed one another. Rosa loved it all: for the colour, the costumes, the lights and the very people themselves reminded her of Grandma Poppy. She could still remember her tales of when she'd been in the theatre, and being among the dancers, musicians and singers brought those stories to life.

They had been in London for almost three months now, and it was the night of Catriona's last performance on stage. Rosa sat in the audience with Miss Frobisher. She had celebrated her tenth birthday only a week ago and was wearing the new dress and shoes that had been her presents. She couldn't help but grin in delighted anticipation, for although she'd attended some of the rehearsals, seen the ballet, and been told the story of *I Pagliacci,* she had yet to see the full opera.

Catriona was dressed in her Columbine dress of black and white, and sat in the back of the gaudily painted cart which would be pulled on stage by a high-stepping horse. The tenor playing Beppe, the Harlequin, was standing at the horse's head, waiting to lead him on. Tension was high as they waited for Tonio to finish the prologue.

The great red velvet curtains began to swoop up and back, the golden tassels swayed back and forth as the auditorium was finally revealed to the players. It was a breathtaking sight, and one that Catriona knew she would never forget. For, in the lights, the theatre came alive, the gilded balconies and cherubs glimmered against rich red velvet and the sheer size and splendour of the wonderful old building was a powerful force.

Catriona lounged back, her costume spread out around her as Harlequin lead the horse on stage to the thundering beat of Canio's big bass drum. Her pulse was steady, but she was transported back to those long ago days when this was no scene from an opera, but the reality of her life. This was her swan-song, her final performance. How very fitting it was.

Rosa sat forward not wanting to miss a moment of the tragic final scene. Aunt Cat's screams had been so real, her terror so powerful she'd wanted to rush on stage and protect her. Now she lay still on the stage, pale and beautiful as the curtain closed in front of her.

The audience erupted and the cries of 'bravo' lifed to the ornate roof as the applause thundered all around her. Rosa slowly got to her feet, then began to clap and cheer and jump up and down as the cast took their curtain call.

Catriona was led by Canio and Silvio to centre-stage, where she sank into a graceful curtsy. Flowers rained down from the balconies and circles, bouquets were brought on stage and laid at her feet.

Rosa's hands stung from clapping so furiously, but her overwhelming pride in Catriona brought a lump to her throat, and she could barely see for the tears. This Catriona was vibrantly alive – more real than at any other time – how could she bear to give it all up?

Catriona curtsied low as the audience applauded and stamped their feet. The flowers lay all around her as the spotlight beamed down. The sweat was cold on her skin and her emotions were almost out of control. She wanted to cry, to sing, to take this audience and their applause and hug them to her. This was her final appearance

236

on stage – her final part to play in this episode of her life – if only she could keep this atmosphere in a bottle so she could take it out in later years and relive it.

She blew kisses to the audience, garnering their approbation, dreading the moment when the curtain would fall for the last time. How could she have thought this would be easy? How long would it be before she was tempted back on the stage? This was her life, what she had been born to do. Was she really being wise to throw it all away? Then her gaze fell on Rosa. Her little face was radiant as she clapped her hands, and as their eyes met, Catriona realised there was nothing more precious, or sustaining, than the love of a child.

Catriona took a deep breath and swept down into a final curtsy and with a signal to the stage-hand, waited for the curtain to drop for the final time.

Chapter Seventeen

To the outsider, life on Belvedere appeared dull, with little to mark the change of seasons. But, as Catriona settled in, she discovered there was always something going on, and the Outback life began to attract her far more than the cities. Her city trips were dealt with swiftly, for she'd become impatient with the noise and bustle and just longed to return to this peaceful oasis. Yet those trips were necessary, for Catriona had a particular reason for visiting Sydney, a reason known only to herself. And although they caused her heartache, she knew it was her only chance to see her daughter.

Catriona sighed and closed her eyes, lifting her face to the sun. They had never spoken, never even met – and Catriona suspected they never would – but to see her, to know she was well and successful had to be enough. Rosa, although a child, was good company on those seemingly innocent forays to Sydney. They would shop and have lunch or supper in the little bistros that were strung along the waterfront, then round off their stay with a visit to the theatre or the ballet. Rosa had discovered a passion for Gilbert and Sullivan, and although Catriona thought of them as pantomime for adults, she was happy to take her when a show was on.

Catriona leaned on the fence, waiting for the mail plane. It came once a month, unless the weather dictated otherwise. She looked out over the pastures and saw how the wind blew in the long grass, turning it into a pale green ocean that dipped and swayed across the great valley beneath the ironstone hills. She had been here for a year now, and felt very much at home.

The improvements to the homestead had been finished while she was in London; now the little house boasted four bedrooms, a proper bathroom and a very modern kitchen with an Aga imported from England for cooking. Ceiling fans cooled in the summer, and during the long, cold nights of winter there was a fire in the sitting room.

Fred had been wonderfully patient in those early months. He came each morning with the account books, stock sheets and rosters for the day, and explained everything in great detail until she was familiar with how Belvedere was run. Connor and Billy had taken her around the yards and paddocks and after getting re-acquainted with riding horses again, she'd joined in on her first brumby run – an exhilarating race amongst the wild horses of the Outback – which proved more energising and thrilling than any operatic performance.

Then there were the parties and dances, the picnics–races and school functions to attend, as well as the committees for the Country Wives Association, the Musical Appreciation Society, the School Board and the Outback Conservationists. The people of the Outback might live far from each other, but the community was tightly knit and they enjoyed their moments of relaxation. It was also the time to exchange gossip, to discuss farming and the price of beef and lamb, and for the youngsters to meet and forge close friendships, which often led to marriage and the joining of vast properties.

She turned and looked at the homestead and smiled. It was very different to the little shack she'd first stayed in. The roof was shin-gled, the screens painted green, and the verandah had been rebuilt. There was bougainvillea trailing up the verandah posts and the fronds of a pepper tree drifted over the roof. Inside, she'd made it cosy with soft chairs and comfortable beds, fresh curtains and table-lamps.

The distant drone of the heavy plane made her turn back. She watched it descend and finally land, and waited for the pilot to taxi down the dirt runway and stop. Billy and two of the jackaroos took the heavy mail-bag and the boxes of supplies and stacked them by the railings. Within minutes the plane had turned and was lifting off again. The pilot was on a tight schedule and his round encom-passed several thousand miles – he couldn't hang around and yarn.

Catriona climbed over the fence and hurried over. 'I'll take the mail,' she said.

'Alonga me,' said Billy gruffly. 'Too heavy for missus.'

She had to agree. The damn thing weighed a ton. But her impatience was all-consuming and she shuffled her feet and sighed as the men sorted through the various boxes and bundles and distributed them to the cookhouse, the bunkhouse and the blacksmith.

'Cookie in betta mood now,' said Billy as he swung the mail-bag over his shoulder. 'Tinned peaches and custard for tucker tonight.'

Catriona smiled as she tried to keep up with his loping stride. Cookie knew Rosa loved tinned peaches. He spoiled her. 'Did Fred get those tools he was waiting for?'

The Aborigine nodded. 'Plenty tools. Fred fix ute now. Bluddy thing crook.' He dumped the mail-bag on the kitchen table and studied her for a long moment. 'Reckon you wait for somethin' special, missus. Fair remind me of a chook on a hot tin roof.' He laughed and shook his head as she tried to deny it. 'Reckon you got fella. Wait him write.'

'I should be so lucky,' she breathed as he left the house and sauntered over to the barn. All the men she knew had faded away once she'd retired – talk about fame attracting the wrong sort of suitor. But, she reasoned, she couldn't blame them. It took a special kind of man to live out here, and they were thin on the ground.

She turned swiftly and tipped the mail out onto the table. It was a great stack, and working with swift familiarity, she began to sort them into piles. Fred's were mostly store catalogues and animal auction brochures. There were letters for the men and several parcels. Cookie was obviously popular; he had a stack of letters, each of them written in the same hand in red ink. She raised an eyebrow as she caught the scent of perfumed paper. It would seem he had an admirer.

There were comics for Rosa and catalogues for Connor and she set them aside. Connor was riding the fences and wouldn't be home for a while. Rosa was due back from school at any moment, and was bringing Belinda with her as usual. The child seemed to spend more time here than at Derwent Hills, and she hoped Pat Sullivan didn't mind. She grinned. Poor Connor. Belinda's adoration hadn't faltered, and he was so embarrassed by it he often took himself off and wouldn't return to the homestead until she was gone. Perhaps that was why he'd been so keen to do the one job on the place every man hated?

Her hand hovered over the two letters and her spirits plummeted. They were her latest attempts to reach her daughter, and like all the others had not been opened, merely returned to sender.

Determined not to let this further rejection get to her, she scooped up the rest of her mail and put it aside to read later. Sorting out the other piles, she put them in the large shopping bags she kept specifically for the purpose, carried them across the yard and distributed them at the bunkhouse, the kitchen and Fred's cottage. When she returned to the homestead Rosa and Belinda had already rubbed down their ponies and set them loose in the paddock, and were now tucking in to bread and jam.

Catriona hugged Rosa and kissed her grimy cheek. 'What on earth have you been up to?' she asked as she made a fresh pot of tea. 'You're covered in dirt.'

Rosa grinned and rubbed her hands through her short hair. 'Me and Belinda made a camp in the bush, and some of the boys tried to take it over.' She and Belinda exchanged glances. 'But we showed 'em what for, eh?'

Belinda nodded, her dark curls bouncing around her plump shoulders. 'Reckon they won't try it again,' she said through a mouthful of bread and jam. 'Rosa gave Timmy Brooks a black eye.'

'Good on you,' said Catriona cheerfully. 'We girls have got to stick up for ourselves. As for getting dirty – it won't kill you.'

'See,' said Rosa with an air of triumph to Belinda. 'I said she wouldn't make a fuss.'

Catriona smiled and sipped her tea. Getting dirty and having tussles with boys was what childhood was all about. Rosa was a tough little larrikin – she would need to be in this modern world – so what harm was there in a dirty face? 'Are you both looking forward to high school?' she asked after they'd finished eating.

'Yeah,' they said in unison. 'We can't wait,' babbled Rosa. 'Only three more weeks and it's the end of term. Are we going to Sydney for our uniforms?' She didn't wait for a reply. 'Can Belinda come too?'

'I'll ask Pat,' Catriona replied, trying not to laugh at the earnest expression on the little face. She saw the excitement and felt a tug of longing. It would be strange not to have them at her tea table during the long school terms away, but every mother in the Outback had to make this sacrifice if their children were to realise their full potential.

She watched them run down the hall. Heard the slam of the screen door and the thunder of their feet on the verandah. They were growing up. Time was moving too swiftly, and before she knew it, they would be young women.

It was late and she'd finally got the girls to turn out their light and stop talking. Walking into the lounge, she saw the stack of letters and poured herself a gin and tonic. With the stereo turned low, the sweet voice of Callas soothed away the cares of the day. She set aside the two letters that had been returned unopened and began to read through the rest.

Clemmie and John were on a cruise – they were always away now Clemmie had no clients to manage. There were letters from fans which had been forwarded from her recording company, and news bulletins from the Academy she'd set up in Melbourne. They wanted her to present the prizes at the end-of-year concert, and she made a note in her diary. There were postcards and letters from friends still working in the theatre, another appeal from the charity she patronised, and a reminder she was due at the dentist at the end of the month.

Two very important looking letters remained. One turned out to be an invitation to attend the opening of the Sydney Opera House where she would be presented to Her Majesty Queen Elizabeth. The other was a formal declaration from Her Majesty's Government. Catriona Summers was to be honoured with the title of Dame in recognition of her work in the field of opera. The ceremony would take place privately before the opening ceremony.

'Bloody hell,' she breathed. She flopped back in the chair, and read it again. It had to be a joke. A Dame! How preposterous! Dames were men dressed in drag for pantonime, not skinny little women who just happened to have enough balls to get onto a stage and sing their hearts out. How Poppy would have laughed.

She drank deeply from the glass and read the letter several times more. The seal at the bottom looked genuine enough and the letter-heading seemed right. Perhaps this wasn't a joke after all? It was a sobering thought – and a tremendous surprise. Yet, as she sat there in the soft lamplight and listened to Callas singing one of the beautiful arias from *Tosca*, she seemed to remember Clemmie wittering on about something months ago. Catriona hadn't really been listening, she'd been engrossed in final rehearsals for her London finale, and thought Clemmie was merely talking about *seeing* Buckingham Palace – not receiving an honour from there.

'Strewth,' she breathed. 'It's really happening. I'm going to be a Dame of the British Empire.' She giggled and put on a plummy accent. 'How frightfully spiffing. One will have to watch one's ps and qs now, my gel.' Giggling even more, she poured another drink. 'Cheers,' she said as she lifted it in salute to her portrait above the fireplace. 'Legs up and laughing, girl. I bet you never thought this would happen when you were having your fling with Rupert Smythe-Billings.'

Catriona wanted to tell someone. But, as always at times like these, there was no one around. The telephone was linked to the two-way radio, and within seconds the whole of the Outback community would know, but this was too precious a gift to squander. She wanted to tell someone special. Rosa was asleep and Connor was camping out overnight somewhere on Belvedere's hundreds of thousands of square acres. Poppy was long gone and Clemmie was abroad. That left Pat Sullivan who would be asleep, and it wouldn't be fair to wake her after the long, tiring day she'd probably had.

Her gaze fell on the returned letters and her spirits tumbled. If only she could tell her daughter. She sank back into the chair, the stark reality of her situation quenching her joy. Did those in charge of such honours know about her past? Did it matter to them, would it make a difference? Perhaps she should write back and decline the offer? But that would merely cause gossip and speculation. What to do, what to do? If only Clemmie was around, she would know.

Catriona walked over to the two-way radio and made the connection. There was a slim chance Clemmie and John's holiday was over. The post was erratic out here, and the letter was dated weeks ago. As she waited for the operator to put her through, she drummed her long nails on the polished pine. Her impatience was making her edgy. 'Please let her be there,' she whispered. 'Please, Clemmie. Pick up the bloody phone.'

'Hello?' The voice was distant, almost lost in the white noise of the telegraph wires.

'Clemmie?' Catriona gripped the phone.

'What's the matter?' The voice was sharper now.

'I got a letter from England,' she said. She had to be careful, there were no doubt many ears listening in. 'It's terrific news, but I need your advice.'

243

'Oh, good,' replied Clemmy. 'I was expecting to hear from you sooner than this. Did you also get the invitation to the opening?'

'Yes. But I can't accept either.'

'Why ever not?'

'I can't say much, the line's too open. But you know why not, Clem.' She paused and listened to the hum and buzz of the static. 'Susan Smith,' she said finally.

Clemmy laughed. 'Don't be daft,' she said. 'They don't care about all that. They just want to reward you for the sterling work you've done over the years. And for the money and time you've given to your Academy and all the other charities you've set up and supported.'

Catriona felt light-headed. 'You're sure?' she persisted. 'I would hate to have it snatched away again.'

'It won't happen, darling. You've earned it.' She chuckled. 'Dame Catriona Summers certainly has a ring to it. Congratulations. Now will you let me get some sleep? I'll ring again in the morning.'

Catriona cut the connection and turned back into the room. She was excited and nervous, thrilled at the news – yet beneath that joy was the deepest sorrow. Her daughter would never share this moment. Would never know how much she was loved and missed. Catriona picked up the letters, and cradling them to her chest, burst into tears.

Rosa stared into the shadows cast by the moon. She didn't know what had woken her, but something had. She lay alert and listening. It was probably just a possum on the roof, she decided after a while. But it was a nuisance, because now she was wide awake and needed to go to the bathroom. Throwing back the covers, she climbed out of bed.

As she pulled open the door she heard a sound that at first she didn't recognise. She glanced over her shoulder at Belinda. Her friend was buried beneath the covers, her breath deep and even in sleep. Rosa tiptoed out of the room and crept down the short hallway. There was light pouring from the open door of the lounge. This was where the sound had come from.

Easing along the wall, she took a peek. What she saw made her want to cry out – to rush into the room and offer comfort – but something in the way Catriona was crying stilled her. Her tears

244

were streaming down her face, but there was little sound from her as she huddled over some letters, rocking back and forth as if they were something to be protected. Whatever could it mean? Rosa bit her lip. She shouldn't be here. Shouldn't be prying. Yet she couldn't move, for she was fascinated by what Catriona did next.

The old tin trunk had stood beside the desk ever since they had moved into the house. It was a treasure trove of clothes and gloves and shoes which Catriona had allowed her and Belinda to try on. There were programmes and sheet music and letters from fans as well as photographs of Catriona in the roles she'd sung, but Rosa had never been left alone with the trunk, and now she understood why. It was Catriona's hiding place for the most private of things.

As Rosa stood in the shadows beyond the door, she watched her unlock the trunk and carefully place the letters in the bottom. She held her breath as the key was hidden behind the large clock on the mantel. Then had to race back to her bedroom as Catriona turned and headed for the doorway. Her pulse was racing and she was having trouble trying to keep her breathing muffled as she dived beneath the covers and feigned sleep. She heard Catriona's footsteps in the hallway. Heard them stop outside the door she hadn't had time to close. After a long moment of silence in which she was certain Catriona would find her out, the door was closed and the footsteps moved on towards the kitchen.

Rosa was far too excited to sleep, but time seemed to drag as she waited for Catriona to go to bed. Belinda was still asleep, and she was tempted to wake her. They shared everything, and this was a real mystery. Yet, as she was about to give her a poke, she drew back. This was private, she decided. Catriona's secret must be kept.

She crept out of bed again and opened the door. The light had been switched off in Catriona's bedroom, but it would be best to wait a bit longer just to make sure she was really asleep. She was a little fearful, for if Catriona caught her messing about with her trunk she'd really cop it. Yet, laced with the fear was the sense of adventure. Rosa swiftly went to the bathroom and climbed back into bed to wait.

The time ticked away and as the clock in the hall struck eleven, Rosa finally decided Catriona had to be asleep by now. She tiptoed down the hall and listened at her bedroom door. She could hear steady breathing. With her own heart banging, and her breath ragged in her throat, she crept into the sitting room and climbed on a chair to reach beneath the clock. The key was small and glimmered coldly in the moonlight as she turned to face the trunk.

It was a mysterious presence, lying in wait for her, its very silence a magnet for her curiosity. Rosa's legs were trembling, and she plumped down on the couch, her gaze fixed to the rusting metal and the weathered leather straps. Time was passing, the chance of getting caught more likely by the minute. Yet, in a way this only sharpened the anticipation, for she might never have the opportunity again.

The silence of the house surrounded her and the images conjured up by Catriona's storytelling began to parade before her. They were silent, fleeting images, recalling a time and a place that Rosa could have no knowledge of, yet they seemed so familiar, so welcoming, she couldn't resist them. She knelt and undid the buckles. The straps fell away and she wrestled with the key in the padlock. It turned finally and the lid creaked open.

She stilled, tense and listening for any sign that would mean she'd been discovered. But all she heard were the familiar creaks and sighs of the house. She rested on her heels and looked at the trunk. Her mouth was dry, her throat so tight she could scarcely breathe.

Sheets of music, old programmes and publicity photographs lay inches deep over a sheet of muslin. The pungent smell of mothballs made her eyes water as she sifted through the music sheets and set them to one side. The photographs were professionally done, some in black and white, some in colour, showing Catriona from her early twenties and on through to the end of her career. The programmes mirrored those Catriona had stored in her desk, and were printed in many different languages. From La Scala in Rome, to Paris, Madrid, London, Sydney and Moscow. Rosa had seen them before and hastily set them aside.

Beneath the programmes and assorted clutter lay the newspapers. They had been rolled firmly and secured with rubber bands that had perished over the years. Rosa glanced at the headlines, and as the abdication of the King, the declarations of war and the Coronation of the Queen didn't interest her, she put them on the floor. With trembling hands she slowly drew back the sheet of muslin.

The dresses were old friends, and as she took each one out, she remembered the stories behind them. The dark red, velvet ballgown was the one Catriona had worn for her portrait. Rosa drew

246

it out of the trunk and held it against her. She could still catch the memory of Catriona's perfume and the dusting of talc in the cloth. Draping it over the arm of the chair, she pulled out the next. It was purple silk, shot with blue and green with a full skirt and glittering crystals stitched around the neck. An elegant black dress followed. Catriona had said it was made by Dior, but that didn't interest Rosa. She was impatient to find the letter.

There was another Dior dress, a Chanel suit, and a cocktail dress by Balmain. Long, white kid gloves had been carefully wrapped in draw-string bags, and frothy, laced lingerie had been folded away between sheets of tissue paper. As Rosa carefully laid them on the couch, she felt her pulse begin to race. For there, shimmering in the lamplight was the wedding dress that Catriona had refused to allow them to try on. She hardly dared touch it now, for it was the most delicate, beautiful thing she had ever seen. The lace was old, and it swept in layers from the shoulders to the floor in a slender waterfall of seed-pearls and diamante.

As she held it close, she thought she could hear the music of a church, could almost smell the flowers and feel the trembling excitement of the young bride as she walked up the aisle. Catriona must have felt like a queen that day, she thought. I know I would have. I wonder if she'll lend it to me when I'm a bride?

She realised she was wasting time. With the wedding dress carefully draped over the back of the couch, Rosa reached into the trunk and found dainty satin shoes and white gloves. As she lifted out the gossamer veil she discovered the single yellow rose. The petals were dry now and brittle, the scent faded. Something about that fragile rose reached out to her and she experienced a pang of sadness. Why, she wondered, had Catriona kept it?

Her hand stilled over the letters. Some had been tied in ribbon, others stuffed into large brown envelopes and marked FAN MAIL. She set them aside, glanced towards the door and after a momentary hesitation, drew out the final packet of letters. Her fingers trembled as she plucked the pink ribbon which tied them together. She could feel Catriona's vibrancy fill the room, could almost hear her voice warning her not to pry.

She threw the letters back into the trunk, as if by this swift action she could silence the voice in her head. Catriona trusted her. She would be furious if she discovered what Rosa was doing. Rosa ran her fingers through her hair. Catriona's presence seemed to be

247

at her shoulder. She glanced around, fearful she'd been caught out and although she was alone, Catriona's spirit seemed to be in everything around her. Her life before she came to live on Belvedere was scattered across the floor and in the trunk. Her life now in the very fabric of the walls in this room, and as Rosa eyed the oil painting above the fire-place, she could have sworn those violet eyes were watching her. Catriona's enigmatic smile unfaltering, the gaze steady and accusing.

Unable to resist any longer, and despite the feeling she was being watched, Rosa again lifted out the letters. It was a small collection, and clearly addressed. Rosa's fingers were clumsy as she plucked out the sheets of paper from the only envelope that had been opened. It was dated several years ago, and when she'd finished reading it she understood why Catriona had been crying.

Blinking back her own tears, she quickly replaced everything and locked them away. She put the key back under the clock, checked the room for signs she might have left of her midnight search, and hurried on tiptoe back to her bedroom.

As the moon sailed past her window, Rosa stared into the night and wrestled with the knowledge of what she'd discovered.

Chapter Eighteen

St Helen's High School for Girls was a private establishment, favoured by wealthy landowners and city elite. It had once been a grand house, but after the Depression it had been bought cheaply by two enterprising spinsters and turned into a school. The spinsters were long dead, but their legacy lived on in the new buildings, the stables and paddocks and in the well-stocked library and neat classrooms. An enormous gymnasium had been paid for by a grateful parent, and the dormitories were comfortable and homely thanks to generous donations from others. Off to one side was a large swimming pool, sheltered from the sun with canvas sails.

The main building was square, with white columns holding a portico above the stone steps. The red brick was almost smothered in ivy, which turned a glorious red in the winter. There was a tree-lined, gravel driveway which swept up to the steps and encircled a large fountain, and as Catriona sat in the taxi she was forcibly reminded of the hotel in Atherton.

'What's the matter?' asked Pat. 'You look as if you've seen a ghost.'

Catriona shook off the memories and concentrated on other things. 'I hope I've packed everything,' she murmured. 'The list was endless.'

Pat laughed. 'If we have forgotten anything, then it's too late.'

They climbed out of the taxi and a man appeared from the side of the house, checked his list and loaded everything on to a trolley before taking it away. Belinda and Rosa were subdued which was unusual, but Catriona was remembering her first day at the Academy, and understood exactly how they were feeling. She wanted to hug Rosa and take her home again. It was such a big place, and there were so many other people here. What if she wasn't happy?

'She'll be right,' murmured Pat. 'Look, they've already seen someone they know. They won't be homesick for long.'

Catriona watched as the girls greeted their friends, and were joined by more. 'Looks like half the Outback is here,' she said, recognising most of the girls.

'There's certainly some money about,' muttered Pat as they prepared to go up the steps and into the house. She nodded towards a chauffeur-driven car.

Catriona watched the little girl step out of the car and wait obediently while the chauffeur unloaded her trunk and passed it to the school porter. She was a pretty little thing, with lustrous fair hair and big blue eyes. Like Belinda and Rosa she wore the uniform gingham dress, white socks and dark blue blazer with the school badge emblazoned on the pocket. The panama hat sat jauntily on the lovely hair, but Catriona noticed how tightly she was clutching her expensive leather satchel. 'Poor little mite,' she said softly. 'I wonder where her parents are?'

Pat sniffed. 'Too busy making money probably. People like that shouldn't have children if they can't even be bothered to bring her to school on the first day.'

'She looks very lost. Do you think we ought to encourage our girls to talk to her?'

Pat eyed the girl for a moment, then shook her head. 'Better to let nature take its course,' she said, as the child shook hands with several of the staff and stood talking quietly with them. 'But it's unsettling to see such composure in one so young.'

Catriona sighed. Pat was right. She was just feeling like a mother hen with an empty coop. She pulled the fur collar more closely around her neck. It was cold in Sydney, with winter still making itself felt in the wind that came off the sea.

They went up the steps into the echoing hall and were introduced to the headmistress who turned out to be very jolly and a great fan of the opera. After a cup of tea in her drawing room, they were escorted around the school by one of the older girls and shown where Belinda and Rosa would sleep during their first year here. Catriona eyed the two rows of beds in the enormous dormitory. How she envied Rosa, for this was a proper boarding school, just

250

like the ones she'd read about as a child. What fun the girls would have, she thought wistfully as they turned to leave. There would be midnight feasts and whispering through the night, proper lessons during the day, and the chance to ride the sleek horses she'd noticed in the stables.

The girls came flying into the hall just as they were beginning to wonder where they were. 'It's fab, Mum,' yelled Rosa, as she threw herself into Catriona's arms. 'There's loads of horses, a huge pool and me and Belinda already know most of the girls in our year.'

Catriona held her tightly. She could barely breathe. 'What did you say, darling?'

Rosa pulled back and looked up at her. 'I said there's a pool and horses ...'

'No,' interrupted Catriona, her heart beating a rapid tattoo. 'Not all that. The first bit.'

Rosa blushed to the roots of her untidy hair. 'Mum,' she said with uncharacteristic hesitancy.

Catriona's tears streamed down her face and the girl rushed back into her embrace and held her tightly. 'I know it's silly,' Catriona sobbed. 'But you've never called me that before and I've waited so long to hear it.'

Rosa drew back and looked into her face. 'Mum,' she said firmly. 'You're the very best Mum I could ever have, and I'm sorry you've had to wait so long. But I wasn't sure if you'd mind.'

Catriona hugged her again and kissed her forehead. 'Oh, darling,' she sighed. 'I think it's the most beautiful name in the world. Of course I don't mind.'

Rosa grinned as she emerged from the embrace, and Catriona wiped the lipstick from her forehead and tried to bring some order to her hair. 'What on earth have you been doing?' she chided softly. 'Why can't you keep tidy for more than five minutes?'

'We've been to see the horses,' she explained. 'They're beaut, Mum.' She took a breath. 'And they've got a real science block here. Belinda and I are going to make stink-bombs and let them off at the boys' grammar school up the road.'

Catriona looked over Rosa's head to Pat. They exchanged a smile of relief. Their girls were going to be just fine.

Pat had left an hour before and Catriona sat on the back verandah and stared out over the pastures. It was too quiet. The house echoed, and she felt very alone. Yet she realised there was no point in sitting here feeling sorry for herself. She'd known this moment would come, had prepared for it by making plans to become more active in her charity work and in the organisation of the Melbourne Academy. Life would go on, and the thrill of seeing Rosa and Connor mature into adults would compensate for these moments of sadness. For this was their home, and she, their mainstay. They would always keep in touch no matter what life's adventures held for them.

A movement in the shadows made her tense. Then she smiled as a kitten stalked towards her. For such a tiny, bedraggled little thing, it had a very demanding mewl and a determined strut. She reached down and picked it up. Beneath the dirt, she could see he was a ginger tom, with white bib and socks and a skinny, striped tail. 'Where have you come from?'

The scrap of fur sat in her hand and stared back at her with disconcerting yellow eyes. He looked half-starved and didn't weigh more than a few ounces, and Catriona guessed he was only a few weeks old. She stroked the dirty fur and he began to purr, his eyes rolling back, his tongue sticking out between his needle-sharp baby teeth. She laughed. 'Well,' she murmured. 'It looks like you enjoy that, but I suspect you're really looking for food.'

She carried him into the house, knowing she was breaking all the rules. The kitten was no doubt the runt of the litter and had been abandoned by his mother. Like everything else on Belvedere, the cats had to earn their keep, by hunting the vermin that got into the barns and occasionally attacked the livestock. This little chap didn't look capable of hunting anything, and had been left to survive or die.

She put some milk in a saucer and watched him lap it up. When he'd finished, he looked up at her and demanded more. She gave in and sliced up some of the chicken she'd kept for her supper. He ate with a voracious appetite, and when he'd finished, he spent a long time cleaning his whiskers and grooming his fur. Sated and sleepy, he clawed at her leg and demanded to be picked up. Content, he curled up in her lap.

She stroked the fur and felt the bones of his skinny frame as he purred. The house suddenly didn't feel so empty now. It was strange and rather wonderful how fate had intervened, for now she

252

had someone else to care for and mother. 'What am I going to call you?' she murmured.

He flicked his ears and opened his eyes to regard her with arch composure. He seemed to be telling her he'd come here for food, warmth and kindness, and that Catriona should understand he was in charge from now on, that he was doing her a favour by adopting her.

She grinned and gave him a hug. 'I'll call you Archie,' she said as she carried him into the lounge and settled them both on the couch. 'I reckon you and I will get along just fine.'

Rosa had been away at school for almost five weeks, and although Catriona realised Connor missed her, she knew he was relieved to see the back of Belinda. He was already beginning to dread the school holidays.

Rosa flew home for the half-term break and spent the entire weekend telling them about her new friend Harriet Wilson. Catriona listened as this paragon of virtue and beauty was extolled at length to anyone who would listen. It seemed Harriet, or Hattie, as Rosa called her, was a wonderful dancer, rider and gymnast. She was also very clever, and often helped Rosa with her home-work when the teachers weren't watching.

Connor seemed less than impressed and appeared more inter-ested in the horses the school provided, and the rides the girls took at the weekends and evenings. He thought it very odd there should be stables and paddocks in a city, and Rosa promised he could come and visit, so he could see for himself

The mid-term break was soon over and Catriona watched from the paddock as the Cessna lifted into the sky. She would be seeing Rosa again the next week, for it was almost 20 October, the date of the official opening of the Opera House. She was sad Connor had decided not to witness her moment of glory, but the boy hadn't really understood what it meant to her, and had seemed less than enthusiastic about a trip into Sydney anyway.

She smiled as she returned to the homestead and made the final preparations for her trip. He certainly wouldn't enjoy sitting through the arias and music recitals, the speeches and the endless round of polite conversation at the reception afterwards and, although he would have done his best to appear interested for her sake, she knew he would have been bored rigid and desperate to get out of the formal suit and back onto a horse.

Rosa, on the other hand was bubbling with excitement. She had a new dress and shoes and Catriona was going to lend her the single strand of pearls Velda had left her so many years before. It was to be Rosa's first formal occasion, and Catriona was keeping everything crossed that the child would behave herself.

That special day dawned with warm sunshine. There was bunting and strings of lights all around Circular Quay. All manner of craft were out on the river, the fire boats sending great arcs of water from their jets in salute as the bigger ships sounded their horns and sirens. The Sydney ferries and tourist pleasure boats had been dressed in flags and the excited crowd was already pressing several hundred deep behind the barriers as the Royal Australian Air Force band struck up a rousing tune.

With roars of delight and the enthusiastic waving of flags, the people of Sydney welcomed the Royal cavalcade which slowly drove up to Bennelong Point and stopped at the bottom of the graceful flight of steps. A red carpet flowed up the steps to the main door which was sheltered by one of the magnificent sails of the Opera House roof.

Catriona stood calmly in the reception line, Rosa next to her. The child was pale, but her eyes shone as she smoothed the frills of her dress and shuffled her feet. As Queen Elizabeth was escorted into the red-carpeted foyer by the British Ambassador, the child's eyes widened. 'She's got a real crown with diamonds in it,' she breathed. 'Look how they sparkle.'

Catriona told her to hush, but she could see why the child was impressed. Her Majesty's tiara, necklace, earrings and brooch shot fire in the sun, the diamonds sparkling against the dark blue of her dress. 'Get ready to curtsy,' she muttered as the Queen approached. 'And don't talk unless she asks you a question.'

Her Majesty paused as she moved down the line and was introduced to the great and the good of the cultural world. There were dancers and singers and musicians, divas by the dozen, as well as the Mayor of Sydney and the ministers of the Australian Parliament.

Catriona held her breath as the Queen drew close to Rosa. The child dipped into the slow and quite elegant curtsy she'd been practising all month. The Queen smiled and said 'Well done,' and moved on to Catriona.

Catriona dipped low and lifted her head only when the Queen asked how she was enjoying her retirement. 'Very much, Your Majesty,' she replied. The Queen smiled and nodded, glanced once more at Rosa and then moved down the line.

The line gradually disintegrated as the Queen was escorted into the Exhibition Hall where she would be presenting the honours. 'Go with Clemmie,' she whispered to Rosa as her friend moved forward from the crush behind the reception line. 'I have to wait here until I'm called.'

Rosa nodded, then stood on tiptoe and kissed Catriona's cheek. 'Good luck, Mum,' she said, her eyes shining with pride.

Catriona watched her walk away with Clemmie to take their seats in the hall. She took a deep breath to still the flutter of nervous excitement in her midriff. The volume of the chatter around her was growing and she was delighted to see so many old friends again. There were baritones, contraltos and sopranos she'd worked with, conductors she'd fallen out with, managers and directors with whom she'd clashed, and members of the chorus she'd shared dressing-rooms with. It was fun to catch up on the gossip, but there was little time, for the first names were already being called. The babble died to a whisper as the line edged into the exhibition hall.

A gilt and red velvet chair had been set at the end of a long strip of red carpet. The Queen stood beside the Governor who was handing her the appropriate medals and advising on the name of the recipient.

Catriona glanced swiftly at Rosa and Clemmie as she waited her turn. Then she was walking along the carpet, bowing to her Sovereign and receiving her honour. With a few words, the Queen congratulated her on the work she had done to help fund the building of the Opera House, and thanked her for the years of pleasure Catriona had given her with her singing. The Queen stepped back, Catriona curtsied again and moved away.

The rest of the day disappeared in a haze of happiness and disbelief. As she was congratulated by the Mayor, the Ambassador and the Minister of Culture, she could barely hold back the giggles. Dame Catriona: it made her sound terribly important, but she just felt bemused by it all. What an extraordinary honour for one who'd started life in the back of a painted wagon.

Chapter Nineteen

Christmas came and went and Catriona was once more saying goodbye to Rosa. 'Can Hattie come and stay the whole of next holiday?' Rosa asked as they loaded the trunk into the Cessna.

Catriona thought for a moment. 'Won't her parents want her at home?'

Rosa shook her head. 'Her dad's dead and her mum's always away on tour.'

Catriona's interest was piqued. 'On tour? Is she in the theatre then?'

Rosa shrugged. 'Yeah. She's a dancer or something.' She looked up at Catriona. 'So can she?'

Catriona had to force herself to concentrate. 'What's her mother like?'

'She's all right, I suppose. But she's not like you.' Rosa hesitated as if trying to find the right words. 'She's not warm and smiling like you, and she's really thin. Always complaining about the cold and fussing about crumbs in the car.'

'When did you go in their car?' Rosa hadn't mentioned outings during the term.

'We went out for tea when Hat's mum came back from London. Belinda and three of the other girls came too, but I don't think she liked any of us very much.'

'Why?' Catriona tried not to laugh, the child was looking so serious.

Rosa shrugged. 'How should I know?' she said baldly. 'She just doesn't like girls, I suppose. We were a bit noisy.' She grinned. 'But we had a bonzer tea, much better than we'd have had at school.'

'Oh, dear,' sighed Catriona as she tried not to smile. 'Perhaps Harriet'd better not come and stay if her mother's a bit ...' She let the sentence hang in the air.

'She won't care,' retorted Rosa with the carelessness and inhibition of a twelve-year-old. 'She'll be in Paris anyway.'

'So the child will be on her own all through the holiday?'

Rosa nodded. 'Yeah, she'll have to stay at school with Miss Hollobone. She says she doesn't mind, and that she's used to it, but I think she'd much prefer staying with us.'

Catriona couldn't bear the thought of that lonely little girl spending her holiday in an empty school. 'Then you'd better ask her,' she said as the pilot started the engine. 'I'll ring Miss Hollobone later today.'

'That's some view, isn't it?' sighed Rosa as the Cessna banked in a slow arc in preparation for landing.

Harriet nodded. No words seemed adequate to describe what she was feeling, for the sight before her was like something out of a picture book. A track wound its leisurely way down the hill and into a peaceful valley that was golden in the afternoon sun. Outbuildings were dotted about the flattest part of this valley like so many bales of straw carelessly cast from some passing wagon. The homestead nestled within the broad clearing of dark red earth, shaded by the citrus bright fronds of pepper trees. The sheltering mountains were blue on the shimmering horizons, giving an edge to the broad swathes of grass that rippled and swayed in the warm wind like a great yellow ocean. The sky was almost bleached of colour and cloudless, its very breadth and width enough to make her feel small and insignificant in the scheme of things.

'There's Mum, and Connor waiting for us,' shrieked Rosa. Belinda shoved her out of the way and leaned to look out of the window. 'Where?' she demanded. Rosa giggled and looked archly at Harriet. 'Belinda fancies my brother,' she said in a loud whisper. 'Though God knows why, he's a real pain at times.'

Belinda blushed and jabbed Rosa in the ribs with her elbow which led to a rough and tumble. Harriet smiled, unsure of what to say. She was still getting used to the easy way these girls had with one another, for being an only child with a mother who was rarely at home, she'd never experienced such a close relationship with anyone before. She turned back to the window and felt a tug of longing as a mob of kangaroos bounced across the plains. How could Rosa and Belinda bear to leave this wonderful place? There was just so much space, so many places to explore, so much sky and clean air.

Rosa giggled as the low-flying Cessna disturbed a pair of grazing emus into a curious knock-kneed lope which ruffled and waggled their tail feathers. 'They look like disgruntled can-can dancers,' she spluttered. 'All feathers and flounce.'

Harriet grinned as she watched the ridiculous birds, but her attention was soon drawn back to the fence by the landing-strip and the people waiting there. She'd heard a lot about Rosa's family, but this would be the first time she had met Catriona Summers, and she was nervous. Rosa had told her so much about the woman who'd taken them both in and given them a home, and Harriet couldn't help but be impressed that the great Catriona Summers was to be her hostess for the entire autumn holiday.

Rosa was the first out of the plane, running across the clearing and into the arms of a teenage boy with a wide smile. 'How ya going?' she shouted in delight as he swung her off her feet and gave her a great hug. 'Geez, bruv, no need to break the ribs, mate.'

He set her down with a frown. 'Sorry, Rosa. I didn't hurt you, did I?'

Rosa giggled. 'Na. But just remember I'm a girl,' she scolded. 'Not a bullock.' She turned swiftly to Catriona and gave her a kiss and a hug. 'Hello, Mum,' she said warmly.

Catriona's cheeks flushed and her eyes sparkled with pleasure. 'I see boarding school hasn't changed you, Rosa,' she said with brusque affection. 'Still a larrikin.'

Rosa kissed the soft cheek again. 'It's bonzer to be back, Mum,' she retorted with an infectious giggle.

Whilst Belinda and Rosa were being greeted by their mothers, Harriet took the chance to watch the scene being played out before her. She was used to being an observer – used to being on the outside of close family units – and she'd realised quite some time ago that she had a talent for seeing things unobserved by others. Belinda certainly had eyes only for Connor, and although the sixteen-year-old boy was obviously aware of her adoration, he was studiously ignoring her. Rosa's affection for her brother was certainly reciprocated, and their closeness was clear in the easy

258

way they had with one another. But it was Catriona Summers who really fascinated her.

Catriona was small and slender and didn't look very different from the old publicity photographs Rosa had brought to school. Yet there was a hidden core of steel within that slim frame, evident in the violet eyes and in her bearing. Her hair was short and thick and beautifully styled, and her clothes might have been casual, but Harriet recognised the cut of expensive trousers and the rich fabric of the deceptively simple shirt. She wore little jewellery apart from the rings on her fingers, just gold studs in her ears and a pendant and chain around her neck.

As if she realised she was being scrutinised, Catriona turned, the violet eyes curious and bright with intelligence. 'This must be Harriet,' she said pleasantly. 'Welcome to Belvedere.'

Harriet felt the softness of the hand as it took her own in greeting. The slender, fragile bones of the fingers belied the strong grip as the diamonds sparkled in the sun and the violet eyes continued their close scrutiny.

'I'm glad you could come,' she said. 'Rosa has told me a lot about you.' She grinned, the violet eyes lighting up. 'I'm sure we're all going to have great fun this holiday. But for now, I expect you'd all like some tea before Belinda leaves? Come on into the house.'

Rosa's face was flushed with pleasure, her eyes glittering with laughter as she helped Connor up the steps. He'd been kicked on the knee by a bull several weeks before and still walked with a stick, and he grimaced as he swung his stiff leg up each tread. 'Harriet, this is Connor,' she said rather unnecessarily.

Harriet looked up into eyes that could have been brown, or perhaps the autumnal hues of a winter forest. The irises were ringed with black, the sleepy eyelids thickly lashed. Her hand was swamped in his and she felt the warmth and the roughened skin of a person who'd never worked behind a desk. The sleeves of his checked shirt had been rolled to the elbow, exposing tanned, muscled arms lightly sprinkled with dark hair. Dressed in narrow moleskins, he stood, dark haired and tall in the flat-heeled leather boots that carried the dust of many long hours in the open.

Connor smiled, the cobweb of lines radiating from the corners of his eyes, making his tanned face even more appealing as they shook hands. 'G'day,' he said in his slow, Queensland drawl. 'Sis

259

has told me a lot about you in her letters. Good to meet you at last.'

'G'day,' murmured Harriet, all too aware of his amused scrutiny and the effect his smile was having on her. Connor Cleary was not really handsome – the features were too irregular. But she could see why Belinda had such a crush on him. He was gorgeous.

Catriona's laughter rang out. 'Oh, dear, Connor. Looks like your fan club is growing.'

Connor blushed and Harriet dipped her chin, avoiding Belinda's glare of animosity by letting her hair fall around her face like a curtain. The last thing she wanted to do was alienate her friends, and Catriona's gentle teasing wasn't helping.

They all followed Catriona into the kitchen, and Harriet hovered, unsure of what to do as the others dumped their bags and made themselves at home. Belvedere was very small, she realised as she looked around at the room. The whole place would fit in just a fraction of their city penthouse, yet the kitchen was cosy and welcoming, and obviously the favourite room in the house.

Catriona soon began to organise everyone. 'Rosa, you get the milk and the cake. 'Harriet,' she said as she turned and smiled. 'Why don't you lay the tray and take it into the lounge?'

Harriet nodded, pleased to be given something to do, but it took a while to find the plates and the cutlery, and her task wasn't helped by Belinda glaring at her at every turn. A dig in the ribs from Rosa's sharp elbow made her start. 'Don't take any notice of her,' she whispered as they carried the plates from the cupboard to the table. 'She's always like this when Connor's around.'

'But why?'

'Frightened of the competition,' muttered Rosa through the slice of cake she'd filched from the plate.

Harriet shot a startled look at Belinda. 'That's silly,' she hissed.

'I know,' said Rosa. 'I mean, who on earth but Belinda could find my brother attractive?' They shared a conspiratorial grin, and Harriet followed Rosa with the loaded tea-tray into the lounge.

The room was cool in the late afternoon, the sun sinking rapidly behind the surrounding mountain ranges. The furniture had definitely seen better days, but the roll-top desk and stool were antiques, and the vast collection of china and glass in the cabinets was exquisite. Harriet set down the tray on a small side-table, noting the thick layer of dust that veiled everything. How very

260

different this little house was to her mother's luxury penthouse, she thought. Not a speck of dust was allowed there, and yet this was a comfortable, homely place, and she felt strangely at ease amongst the clutter.

Rosa went back to the kitchen, and Harriet took the opportunity to look around the room. There were three paintings over the brick hearth, and she wandered over to study them. They were portraits, and although they looked very old, and needed cleaning, the characters of the sitters shone through.

'My parents,' said Catriona as she entered the room, trailing Rosa behind her. 'Those were done just after they arrived here in Australia. They had money for such things then.' She must have noticed Harriet's gaze flit between the portraits, for she gave a wry smile as she came to stand beside her. 'That's me,' she said, pointing to the one in the middle. 'I was a looker then, wasn't I?' She didn't seem to want a reply, for she laughed and turned her back on the painting and sat down. 'Age is a bit of a leveller,' she said lightly. 'Having that damn thing up there reminds me of every passing year, and the onset of age and decrepitude.' She grinned. 'But the alternative is far worse, so I suppose I'll just have to put up with it.'

Harriet, having been raised by a mother who took umbrage at the slightest hint of her ageing, and who despised and resented every birthday, kept silent. Catriona had certainly been a beauty, but that beauty still radiated from her in the flawless skin, the violet eyes and the proud bearing, the kind of beauty that went far deeper than her skin.

Rosa poured the tea and the others joined them. The talk was lively and Harriet was content to sit and listen. Yet beyond the room, she could hear the enticing sounds out in the yards – the calling of calves, the whinny of horses and barking of dogs – each sound interlaced with the jangle of harness and the laughter and chatter of the men. How different it all was to the world in which she lived, she thought, as she sipped the milky tea and began to relax.

Over the next four weeks, Catriona regaled the two girls with stories of her childhood. Harriet had never experienced storytelling before outside a classroom, and she looked forward each night to snuggling down with Rosa on the sofa in her pyjamas to listen to Catriona's tales of the travelling players. They had become so real, that she often imagined she could hear the trundle of the wagons and the laughter of the chorus girls.

During the days, when Catriona hadn't organised a picnic, or an outing to one of the many Outback events or parties, Harriet got the chance to explore Belvedere on horseback. Rosa had taken her to see all her favourite places, but she'd left the most special until the last day of the holidays.

The barn stood in isolation at the far corner of home paddock. It was a tumbledown affair, the roof much patched, the walls leaning inwards. Rosa dismounted and tugged at the door. It creaked and complained and bits fell off as it caught in the long grass and the weeds that had grown beneath it. Harriet climbed off the gelding and stepped into the gloomy barn. Rays of sunlight drifted down laden with dust motes and the scent of hay and oats still lingered, but Harriet's attention was held only by the incongruous sight of the solitary presence hidden in there.

'Mum's pride and joy,' breathed Rosa as she walked around it, her fingers brushing over it with love.

Harriet stepped forward and touched the pristine paintwork. The red and green and yellow glimmered in the dusty sunlight, the legend printed on the sides was as clear as if it had been put there yesterday. 'It's the wagon,' she breathed. 'Catriona's wagon. But how did she find it after all these years?'

'It was in a station auction. The owner had been using it to house his chickens,' replied Rosa. 'Mum had it trucked over and she and Connor worked on it after she retired from the theatre. Beauty, eh?'

Harriet experienced an overwhelming sense of déjà vu. After Catriona's storytelling, it felt strange to actually be faced with something she would have recognised anywhere. It was as if she'd returned to a past she'd never known, but was as familiar with as her own. 'Must have taken years,' she murmured as she noted the delicate fretwork running along the bottom of the wagon, and the carefully painted wheels.

Rosa dug her hands in her pockets and nodded. 'Me and Belinda used to play in it. Pretend we were gypsies. But I know how precious it is, and that there probably isn't another one like it. The Historical Society begged Mum to let them have it, but it means too much to her to let it go again.'

'I wonder what happened to the others,' said Harriet as she

262

craned her neck to look inside. It was disappointingly empty, but she could imagine the costume baskets, the bedding, pots and pans and general clutter that would have been carried in their travels.

'Who knows?' replied Rosa sadly. 'Probably left to rot somewhere. Mum said people aren't interested in history until it's too late, or if they think there's a profit in it.' She grinned and ran her hand over the wheel. 'At least this one's safe.'

Harriet nodded, touched the paintwork one last time and turned away. As she stood in the doorway of the decrepit barn she thought she could hear the trundle of wagon wheels, the steady plod of heavy hoofs and the jingle of harness, and as she gazed towards the horizon she could almost see the cavalcade in the heat-haze of the skyline, the dust rising beneath the wheels, the laughter echoing in the silent hills.

'Hat? Harriet, what's the matter?'

She blinked away the images and looked at Rosa, her head still full of the sounds of a long-forgotten era. 'Catriona made it all so real,' she began. 'And seeing this, it's as if it's all come to life again.'

Rosa grinned. 'You want to watch that imagination of yours, Hat. You'll let it run away with you one day and you'll end up in the loony bin.'

Harriet laughed. The images had faded and reality returned. She ran out into the sunlight and untied the reins from the hook on the wall. 'Let's go for a ride,' she said eagerly. 'We've only got today, and then it's boring old school.'

Once they reached the endless plains they gave the horses their heads and with whoops of pleasure raced across the open land. Time suddenly had no meaning, and the sheer pleasure of being young and carefree in the great heart of Australia was all they needed. It was as if they were in flight and free, as free as the birds that flew above them, as free as the single little cloud that hovered so stubbornly over a distant mountain.

They finally brought the horses to a standstill and slid from the saddles. 'Whew,' breathed Rosa as she patted her horse's neck and loosened his girth. 'It's been a while since I rode like that.'

'Too right,' gasped Harriet, who was out of breath from the hectic chase. 'I don't know about you, but I'm starving, and could do with a drink.' She took off her hat and wiped away the perspiration. Her hair was soaking, and her shirt was sticking to her back. Rosa was a tough act to follow, and despite her years of riding, Harriet had had to fight to keep the chestnut under control in the headlong race across the open plains. She would ache tomorrow, she realised, but it was worth it. The ride had chased away the ghosts and had invigorated her with a sense of well-being she hadn't known since she'd ridden with her father through the bush surrounding the Glasshouse Mountains.

The chestnut tossed his head and showed his enormous teeth as she patted the patrician nose. His ears were pricked and there was an impish gleam in his eyes that told her he'd enjoyed the run as well.

'There's a stream running along that curve,' said Rosa. 'We'll have our lunch there before we head back.'

They led the horses over to the natural fold in the land, and with their reins dangling, the animals drank deeply from the thin trickle of water that snaked its way over a shingle bed. Kneeling beside them, Rosa and Harriet scooped up the water in their hats and tipped it over their heads, laughing and splashing until they were refreshed. Then they flopped down beneath a tree and looked up through the leaves to the bleached sky.

'Bit different to school, I reckon,' said Rosa with a contented sigh. 'I remember doing this when I was real little with Mum. We'd often come out here after school, and just lie under this tree and talk. She never minded me getting dirty, in fact, she encouraged it.'

She turned over onto her stomach and picked up the pack of sandwiches. With her mouth full of chicken and salad, she continued. 'Mum's brilliant. She understands kids, and knows we need to experiment and get dirty and into scrapes. Me and Con are very lucky.'

'I only did things like this when I was with Dad,' replied Harriet as she poured cordial from the bottle into tin mugs and handed one to Rosa. The chicken sandwich had tasted better than anything in the city. It was probably the fresh air and the exhilaration of the ride that made it so good. She swallowed the last of it, and wiped her hands down her trousers, an action which would have horrified her mother. 'Mum's always going on about staying clean, and being on best behaviour. When she's at home, she makes me wear horrible frilly dresses that show every mark.' She giggled. 'When I was really little, she used to enter me into pageants, dressed up like a doll, with make-up and everything. That didn't last for long though. I hated going in front of the judges, and used to pull terrible faces at them, and misbehave. She was furious, but there was nothing she could do about it.'

'Poor old Hat,' murmured Rosa in sympathy. 'Must have been hell.'

'It was OK all the time Dad was alive, 'cos he always took my side against Mum, but after ...' Harriet swallowed and blinked away the tears. 'Things changed,' she went on. 'But it's really hard without him, and once Mum realised I was never going to be a dancer like her, she's sort of given up on me.'

'Then I'm glad we're friends,' said Rosa with a warm smile. 'You can always come here for the holidays. Mum said so this morning.'

Harriet returned the smile, warmed by the generosity and friendship she'd received during her stay. 'Thanks,' she said, unable to put into words the emotions that were rushing through her.

Rosa shrugged. 'No worries, Hat. If it hadn't have been for Mum, then I don't know what would have happened to me and Connor. I'm glad I can share this with you.'

Harriet was still on the brink of tears; she had never known such kindness, such an open-handed giving of friendship. It was an emotional moment. When she'd finally got her feelings under control, she rolled onto her back and breathed in the warm air that was scented with wattle, pine and eucalyptus. Lying there in the grass, she gazed through the leaves and up to the sky. She felt sleepy and at peace. The sky was clear, and she could hear the crickets sawing in the trees, and the laughter of a kookaburra nearby. It was so remote here, that Sydney, school and her mother could be a million miles away. If only it could stay that way, she thought wistfully. But of course it couldn't.

Harriet sighed as she closed her eyes. She'd been shown a different way of life on Belvedere. Catriona had spent hours with her and Rosa, organising picnics and swimming in the billabong, telling stories and encouraging the girls to explore and have fun. It was all so distant from the ordered, but restricted existence in Sydney where she was expected to be polite and well behaved. Rosa was luckier than she could ever have imagined, yet she felt no jealousy, how could she when Rosa had so openly offered to share it all with her?

Harriet's mother's insistence that children should be seen and

265

never heard was a lesson she'd learned very early on. Most of her childhood had been spent in boarding schools, and during her mother's brief appearances in the holidays she'd been expected to comply with her relentless social climbing. The parties and weekends away with people she hardly knew and didn't like, had been made just to keep the peace, for Jeanette Wilson's ambition was not something to be crossed.

School was an escape from the strictures of the very neat apartment in the city, and the stifling rules and regulations she'd had to adhere to since she could remember. It had been a little easier when her father was around, and she missed him terribly. Dad had always found time in his busy schedule to come to open days and take an interest in her triumphs and offer consolation in her failures. He'd been her best friend, her rock, encouraging her to be ambitious for herself – to take pride in what she could achieve – always boosting her confidence and showing his pride in her bright intelligence.

Her mother, Jeanette, had different ideas, and as Harriet grew older, she'd come to realise that the private education was merely another tool in her mother's quest for her to meet what she called the 'right people'. She was already talking of finishing school in Switzerland, and the possibilities of snaring a wealthy and connected husband so she wouldn't have to work for a living. Harriet was confused by the mixed messages she was receiving from her mother. Jeanette had worked all her adult life – she was a prima ballerina in the Sydney Ballet Company – and had worked long, exhausting hours to reach the peak of her career. Why should it be different for her?

'What's the matter, Hat?' Rosa's voice snapped her from her thoughts.

'Nothing,' she said with a contented sigh. 'I'm just happy to be here.'

Over the next six years, Harriet's friendship with Rosa and Belinda was firmly established. Belvedere had become a second home, Catriona a warm and welcoming presence during the school holidays. Belinda's unrequited love for Connor never dimmed despite his numerous conquests in Drum Creek, and Catriona became convinced the piratical swagger his injured knee had left him with went a long way towards his success with women.

As she stood in the yard with Pat Sullivan and watched the three girls saddle up their horses and ride off, she realised with a start that Rosa, Belinda and Harriet were no longer children. At seventeen, Rosa was still small and slender, but she'd filled out in all the right places, which was startling in such a little thing. Her hair was short and spiky, tipped with bright red dye. She liked wearing dark eye make-up and lipstick, and her clothes were unorthodox to say the least – usually black, skimpy and totally out of kilter with the lifestyle of the Outback station. Her fondness for jewellery, short skirts and miniscule tops had become the talk of the neighbourhood. She was getting more like Poppy by the day.

Belinda was taller, broader and of stocky build like her brothers. She still preferred to wear jeans and T-shirts, and was more at home on a horse than in the classroom. Despite her age, Belinda would always be a tomboy. Her hair was a halo of dark curls which tumbled over her shoulders and almost to her waist, and her eyes were the brightest blue. When she smiled she could melt an iceberg and her personality defied criticism.

Harriet was of average height, slim and elegant, her deportment like that of a dancer. Her thick blonde hair swung to her shoulders, her complexion was creamy and her eyes were sometimes blue, and sometimes green. She was still the calmest of the three, but her sense of fun and her confidence had blossomed during the years at Belvedere, and she was a different girl to the one who had arrived, shy and alone at school on that first day.

'Time seems to have flown,' Catriona murmured. 'I can't believe those three larrikins are almost eighteen.'

Pat smiled. 'Eighteen going on ten, more like,' she said. 'Horse mad, and as mischievous as a wagon-load of monkeys. Just look at them going hell-for-leather, not a thought in their heads.' She turned to Catriona. 'It seems like only yesterday since you came to live here,' she murmured. 'No regrets?'

Catriona laughed and ran her fingers through her short-cropped hair. It was much more practical – cooler too – and at fifty-seven it suited her. 'None,' she said firmly. 'But I couldn't have settled in so quickly if it hadn't been for you.'

Pat shrugged. 'I didn't do very much,' she demurred. 'Your personality and the way you've brought up Rosa and Connor were enough to earn respect from everyone.'

Catriona dug her hands in her trouser pockets. 'I knew I'd have my work cut out trying to raise someone else's children, and I was worried about fitting in after the years of travelling,' she said quietly. 'You helped more than you realise, Pat. I was terrified of saying or doing the wrong thing, of turning up in some designer dress when jeans and a shirt would have been more suitable.' She squinted in the sun. 'I didn't want to be different, you see,' she confessed.

Pat gave her a swift hug. 'You'll always be different,' she said with a smile. 'But it's a nice difference, and we all love hearing your outrageous stories. It's as if Poppy's come back.'

Catriona watched the three distant figures that were almost drowning in the heat haze. 'I think that's the greatest compliment you could have paid me,' she said finally.

They strolled back to the house. Archie demanded feeding as usual and was most disgruntled when he was served the remains of some dried food. He was a big, fat, ginger tom now, with a voracious appetite and a penchant for sleeping all day. Catriona was in no doubt as to who was in charge in this relationship, but he was pleasant company when the girls were away and she enjoyed his warm, purring weight in her lap during the long, cold winter evenings.

After making a cuppa, Pat and Catriona sat in the shade of the verandah and watched the men go back and forth from corral to paddock, from barn to shed. The calves had been separated from their mothers and were complaining loudly as they kicked up the dirt in the corral. The road-train would be coming later today to load them up and take them to the stock market. It was the one time on Belvedere she hated, but she was wise enough not to say anything. There was no place for sentimentality out here: just good business and common sense.

'Poor Connor,' sighed Pat as he peered out of the blacksmith's shed before crossing the yard. 'He's still terrified of Belinda.'

The two women giggled. 'She follows him about like a shadow, all eyes and trembling lip,' spluttered Catriona. 'He spends half his time avoiding her.'

'Unrequited love,' sighed Pat. 'Poor Belinda. I was hoping she'd grow out of it and find a nice boy at college.'

'Perhaps she'll meet someone at university?' said Catriona.

Pat chewed her lip and began to fidget with a button on her cardigan. 'She's decided not to go,' she murmured.

Catriona's eyes widened in surprise. 'But I thought she was as set as Rosa and Harriet on a career in the law? They've talked of nothing else for years.'

Pat tucked her short, greying hair behind her ears. 'Belinda's tired of school,' she said flatly. 'She can't wait to get out into the great big world and start earning money.' She sighed. 'I've tried talking to her, but she's made her mind up, and you know how stubborn she can be. Once she's set her heart on something, nothing will sway her.'

Catriona thought of the girl's passion for Connor – it didn't bode well for the poor boy, but then he was almost twenty-two; some girl would catch him sooner or later. And she rather liked the idea of Belinda for a daughter-in-law. She gathered her wayward thoughts and returned to the subject in hand. 'I suppose she'll work on Derwent Hills? I'm not surprised. She's a country girl through and through.'

Pat shook her head. 'Her brothers are already taking over. There really isn't a job for her there any more. She's decided to stick with the law, but on the enforcement side of things. She's been accepted at Police College in Sydney.'

Catriona looked at her friend and saw the disappointment in her expression. Pat had wanted so much more for her only daughter. 'I'm sorry, Pat,' she said. 'But Belinda always was happier doing something physical rather than poring over books.'

'Yeah, you're right. But I was quite looking forward to having a lawyer in the family.' She grinned. 'Something to boast about. Still, if I know my daughter, she'll do well at whatever job she chooses.' She laughed. 'I pity any poor bloke who tries to get the better of her though. With three brothers and a life on a station behind her, Belinda's more than capable of handling herself.'

The two women finished their tea and went down to the utility. 'I'd better get back, there's a ton of things to do before it gets dark.'

Catriona gave her a hug. 'I'll bring Belinda back on Sunday night,' she said. 'Then we can all fly over to Sydney on Monday and settle the girls in for their last semester.'

'It's hard to believe they're finishing college,' sighed Pat as she turned the key in the ignition. 'Feels like only yesterday they were in junior school.'

Catriona stood on the step and waved as Pat drove through the first gate. She watched the trail of dust billow and ebb before turning back to the house. Closing the door behind her, she went into the lounge and sat down at the piano. After a moment's thought, she began to play, her fingers sweeping over the keys.

The tune was called 'Summertime', from Gershwin's *Porgy and Bess*, and it seemed to encapsulate the very essence of this moment. As she began to sing the haunting melody she realised that change was coming into her life again and, although it was sad to think the childhood days were gone, she was looking forward to the next stage in life's adventure.

The three girls came slamming through the screen door just after sunset. They were filthy, out of breath and starving – as usual. Catriona sent them off to the bathroom, and closed the piano lid. The day had disappeared as she'd become lost in the music.

Rosa came rushing into the kitchen just as she was carving the roast beef. 'Mum,' she shouted. 'Billy says he'll take us out tonight. You can come too,' she added hastily. 'Please say we can go.'

Catriona smiled at the concession. 'Maybe,' she said as she carried on carving. 'Where exactly is Billy planning to take you?'

'Isn't Connor coming in for his tea?' asked Belinda as she and Harriet entered the room and sat at the table.

'He's eating with the men,' said Catriona as she swiftly finished carving the joint. She saw the crestfallen face and relented. 'But I expect we'll see him later,' she added.

'Can we go out with Billy, then?' asked Rosa impatiently.

Catriona looked down at her and smiled. 'Hadn't you better explain exactly what Billy plans to do out there in the middle of the night?'

Rosa shook her head. Her eyes were shining and she positively glowed with excitement. 'I promised not to say. It's a surprise.'

Probably one of his mysterious walkabouts, Catriona thought. But why not? It could be fun. 'As it's your last weekend at home, I think we should all go,' she said. She looked across at Belinda. 'Why don't I see if Connor wants to come too? I'll go and ask him after tea, shall I?'

Belinda blushed and dipped her chin. 'If you like,' she muttered with a studied lack of enthusiasm.

Rosa and Harriet nudged one another and giggled, and Catriona glared at them to behave. Rosa teased her brother unmercifully about Belinda, and it was all getting past a joke. Perhaps being at

270

Police College would cure Belinda of this passion and set her mind to other things.

There was something about the stillness of the night which made conversation unnecessary. Catriona sat easily in the narrow stockman's saddle, one hand on the reins, the other on her thigh as they followed Billy Birdsong and his two strapping sons out into the country. Her senses were sharpened by the crisp, cool air, and the scents of the night drifted up to her as the horses trotted at a leisurely pace through the long grass. Eucalyptus, pine, crushed grass and wildflowers mingled into a delicious potpourri as the moon gilded the tops of the trees and threw deep shadows beneath them. The rustle of a gentle breeze sifted through the clumps of brittle spinnifex and chattered in the drooping eucalyptus leaves like whispers from ancient spirits. The effect was spellbinding.

Catriona glanced across at the three girls and saw they too were affected by the grandeur of their surroundings, although how much of Belinda's was due to Connor's moody presence she had no idea. The girl was positively radiant.

The land opened up and the stands of trees were now behind them, the hills a distant line of dark shadows on the far horizon. Billy Birdsong slowed his horse to a walk and pointed to a series of low swells in the land. 'Eggs of Rainbow Serpent,' he muttered.

'Good Dreaming Place. Plenty Ancestor Spirits.'

Catriona's lips twitched into a smile. Billy was being a little dramatic as usual. He was a wonderful storyteller, but inclined to over-egg the pudding when it came to performing for an audience. Yet, as she glanced at the others she could see they had become enchanted by their surroundings and the mystery behind this strange journey into the night, and were staring ahead, their expressions rapt as the Aborigine talked in his sing-song voice of ancestors and spirits and totems from the Dreamtime.

The fleeting urge to treat this outing as bit of a lark was swept away in the realisation that Billy fully believed the Dreamtime story of the Rainbow Serpent, and was leading them into territory uncharted by any white man, into the myths and legends of creation. And how could she doubt them? This place, this sense of timelessness, was overwhelming. The very essence of all she believed lost in the sheer grandeur of this ancient and mystical land, and in the soothing, lyrical voice of the Aborigine who led them further into its silent heart.

271

The sense of being in a sacred place grew stronger as they turned their horses' heads towards the voluptuous curves of those low hills, and Catriona became aware of how she was being drawn to them. It was as if she was dreaming, as if she had been willingly overtaken by an unseen power that was too strong to resist. Yet she didn't feel afraid, and had no wish to turn back for there was a profound conviction that she was about to experience something extraordinary.

The gentle undulations rose against the night sky like the humped backs of benign whales that had been frozen in time as they plunged through the ocean of grass. The Aborigines led the way, the older man's voice drifting with the soft wind as each of them was slowly engulfed in the deep shadows cast from the hills across the grassland. The gentle swish of horses' hoofs through the grass accompanied the music of his voice and the sigh of the wind. They were being drawn into the Dreaming, back into the time when the first Spirit Ancestors left their footprints upon the newly created earth.

The riders were strung out in a line behind the Aborigines, and Catriona wondered if they too were experiencing this deep sense of aloneness, of being small and insignificant against the ancient hills and the all-encompassing sky. Were they sensing the presence of long-dead spirits, or was she just imagining things? She shifted in the saddle and looked around at the others, but they were like awed children as they followed the sweet, tantalising song of their Pied Piper into the Never-Never.

They finally came to a halt and slid from their saddles. With the horses hobbled, they silently followed the barefooted black men along a narrow, twisting track that spiralled up the highest of the hills. Billy Birdsong was muttering, his words unintelligible, but somehow soothing as he drew to a halt beside a long flat mesa and sat down.

Catriona and the others followed suit, each of them utterly enchanted by the sound of his voice and the view spread before them. Gilded pastures stretched to the horizon and silver snakes of water meandered in and out of deep shadows as the land curved and folded against itself beneath the moon. But it was the sky that drew them, and Catriona found it was the most natural thing in the world to lie back against the brittle grass and to stare up and become lost in the magnificence of it all as she traced each glittering path of the heavenly constellations.

The Milky Way splashed a broad sweep across the darkness, Orion and the Southern Cross seemed so close it was almost as if she could reach up and pluck them from the sky, almost as if she could hold the golden orb of the moon in her palm and feel its power. As Catriona followed the draw of the moon and the stars she heard the siren song of the Aborigine and felt the earth melt from beneath her. She was weightless, drifting, being rocked in the cradle of creation by unseen hands that were slowly taking her towards infinity. There was no fear, just a profound sense of peace, of being where she was meant to be.

The stars were nearer now, closing around her, carrying her along the Great White Way where every star was the spirit of a long-dead ancestor. She could see their faces, hear their voices and although they were strangers she felt the warmth of their welcome and was not afraid.

Drifting, forever drifting, rocking in the arms of a benign and loving Creator high above the earth it was easy to cast aside mortal thoughts and fears. For here was eternity, here was the mystery of death and life, and she embraced and welcomed it. The lullaby of Billy's voice was in her head and she was once again an innocent child – naked of ambition and guile and earthly cares – fearless of the power that carried her so gently among the endless stars. She was sleeping in the arms of eternity and was content to remain there.

Time lost all meaning as she explored the great darkness which lay beyond the stars. She saw the birth and death of un-named planets. Saw the flight of comets streaking through the endless darkness and the heads of the craggy mountains of the moon which reared up in the cold blue halo of light that encircled it. She felt the warmth of velvet infinity, the chill of the ring around the moon and the breath of creation against her cheek.

With infinite sadness she began to drift away from this celestial celebration of life. Slowly and inexorably the earth was calling to her, drawing her back, settling her once more on the dewed grass of that sacred hill. She felt the chill of the night seep through her clothes, heard the cry of a lone bird and the great silence that cloaked the land around her. Yet the stars were still there and she yearned to be among them again. Yearned to feel the timeless peace, the comforting rock of those great, spirit arms that had held her so lovingly throughout the journey.

The rustle of movement beside her broke the spell and she emerged from the magic and blinked owlishly at the others. She'd forgotten she wasn't alone and in that moment of awakening, she felt a stab of longing to retreat once again into the endless solitude the stars had offered. For this night had revealed the dreamscapes of her youth, the dreamscapes that were now indelibly etched into her very soul – and from which she never wanted to escape.

Chapter Twenty

The past ten years had flown, and Catriona was startled when she realised she was soon to celebrate her sixty-seventh, birthday. How could she have suddenly reached such an age? Where had the years disappeared to? She ran her fingers through the short-cropped hair that was now more silver than ebony, and wandered back to the homestead with the mail. She didn't feel that old, in fact, she thought with a smile, most of the time she felt several decades younger. Her figure was still good, and she always made sure she was well groomed and smartly dressed, even if it was only in trousers and a shirt. Old habits died hard. She was too used to being in the public eye to change now.

She dumped the mail on the table and resisted opening it – the anticipation was all part of the pleasure. The newspapers arrived sporadically out here, as did the letters, but it was rather nice to have them all in one big delivery, almost like Christmas. As she waited for the kettle to boil, she stared out of the window and looked back over the past decade.

It had been a busy time, with triumphs and sadness for them all. Her work for the various charities meant she travelled back and forth to Brisbane and Sydney, and her involvement in the Academy had grown. She had gone to London to visit friends and take part in master classes and workshops in the Royal Opera School of Music. It had been a rewarding time, one that kept her young in mind as well as spirit, for how could one work with such young talent without their vigour and enthusiasm rubbing off?

Her visit to Paris had been bittersweet, for as she'd placed the flowers on Brin's grave, she'd thought of the illness that had taken him from her. It was no longer a mystery, for medical science had moved on and identified the Aids virus. Now it was almost commonplace. Yet there was still no cure, and others, like Brin had fallen victim to it.

Clemmie had passed away a few months after her husband. Catriona still missed her longest, closest friend and when she was in Sydney she always put fresh flowers on their memorials. Fred Williams had surprised everyone by marrying a widow from Bundaberg, and once Connor was old enough and experienced enough, he'd handed over the management of Belvedere and retired to the coast.

Rosa's swift and unexpected marriage to Kyle Chapman had barely staggered through their first anniversary. They had married in lust while still at college, despite all Catriona's warnings that they were too young. Sadly, she was to be proved right, for Kyle soon came to resent Rosa's driving ambition, and got his revenge by sleeping with as many other women as he could. Thankfully there had been no children. The divorce had been acrimonious on both sides and everyone was relieved when it was all over.

Now, at twenty-eight, Rosa was a fully fledged lawyer, having graduated with top honours. Instead of taking up the offers from more prestigious city firms, she'd chosen to work for a small firm which handled legal aid cases. She was tireless in her pursuit of justice for those who had no voice, and Catriona wondered if perhaps it was her family history that spurred her on.

Belinda had graduated from Police College and was now a Detective Constable in the Brisbane Drug Squad. Pat Sullivan worried about her, as did Catriona. It was a tough, ugly job, but at least she had a stalwart protector in Max, a large German Shepherd who'd been trained to sniff out trouble. Belinda was popular and led a hectic social life, but she still lived alone in a unit overlooking the Brisbane River. She rarely came home, and although Rosa and Harriet stayed in touch with her, and Pat told her all her news from her letters, Catriona hadn't seen her for years.

Harriet still came to Belvedere whenever her busy schedule permitted. She worked for a firm of solicitors in Sydney as a corporate lawyer, and was swiftly being recognised as an excellent candidate for a partnership. She had confided in Catriona that her mother was not entirely happy about this career in the law, but was determined she should marry one of the junior partners who came from a good family and was due to inherit a fortune when his father died.

276

Catriona smiled as she thought of the young woman who had become such a part of her family. Hattie was a determined young woman with a mind of her own. She would carry on defying her mother and make her own decisions, and for that Catriona admired her. And soon the house would be ringing with the sound of their laughter, for Harriet and Rosa were coming to Belvedere for a couple of weeks to celebrate her birthday. She shrugged off the thought that she was far too old to be celebrating anything – birthdays still held a touch of magic, despite her age – and she was actually looking forward to the party she'd arranged.

Sifting through the letters, and finding only one or two of interest, she swiftly read through them and carried the bundle of newspapers out onto the verandah. She would sit out there in the sun with Archie and catch up with the news.

Catriona's eyesight wasn't what it was, but even without her reading glasses, she had no difficulty in seeing the newspaper's headline. The words, printed over two weeks ago, leaped out at her in screaming, thick black letters above the photograph. The hotel in Atherton had finally given up its terrible secret.

Her hands trembled and she experienced a disturbing flutter in her chest as she reached behind her and grabbed the arm of the verandah chair. Fear struck deep, shifting the layers of her life, making their hues and textures suddenly too bright and sharp-edged. Sinking into the soft cushions, she closed her eyes. Yet the images remained with her, clearer now than they had been for decades. It was as if the newspaper article had somehow ripped away the shroud she'd deliberately erected over the memories, and exposed them in the cruel black and white of truth.

Catriona opened her eyes and stared through the glare of a summer afternoon at her surroundings. Her gaze was drawn inevitably to the Poinsianna trees. They were still in bloom, the scarlet flowers weighing down the branches, the petals drifting like bloody confetti onto the grass. A sob rose deep in her throat and she fought the overwhelming need to cry out, to shatter and disperse the memories of what had happened all those years ago.

She took a deep breath, blinked away the tears and glared out from the shaded verandah into the dazzling shimmer of heat. Her experiences in life had taught her to control her tears, to stifle the emotions and stiffen her resolve. Kane's abuse had been firmly relegated to the depths of her memory – his subsequent murder

277

lingering only in the occasional nightmare. She had realised very quickly that if she was to survive and succeed, then the past had to be firmly left where it belonged. Yet the shock of seeing the news report had brought back the almost debilitating fear that had been her companion through those terrible times. Her secret was about to be exposed. Did she have the strength to deal with it, to tell her family, and admit to what she and her mother had done?

She stared out, unseeing, her mind in turmoil. There was no way to avoid it, but how to relate such a tale? How on earth could she possibly reveal the catalogue of abuse and murder without shattering the trust she'd built up with Rosa and Connor? Suddenly, her age seemed to weigh on her as she faced the daunting prospect of what must come. Life had always proved a challenge, but now her armour was no longer bright, her defences weakened by the passing years. Things were about to change, just as they always did when you least expected them to; that was how the world was, and now the challenge of that change brought a dread she'd never experienced before.

With a deep sigh she made a conscious effort to dispel the fear and relax. Her pulse eventually steadied, but as she looked down at her hands, still elegant, the nails painted, the rings glittering, she realised they were trembling. The diamonds sparked fire in the sunlight, and the plain gold band accompanying them was loose, and worn with age. It had been so many years since Peter had put it on her finger and there had been a time when she'd contemplated throwing it away. Yet, despite the sad memories of what it had once stood for, she knew why she'd never discarded that gold band. It was constant reminder of her mistakes, a warning never to trust a man again. She touched it, turning it round and around her finger, remembering her short marriage and the betrayal that had ended it.

The raucous squabbling of the rosellas drew her back to the present, and with an impatient flick of her hand she swept the newspaper from her lap. In awful fascination she watched how the pages detached themselves and floated to the verandah floor. She gave a wry smile. Fate seemed determined to mock her, for the front page settled at her feet, the stark image of the hotel looking sinister in the bright sunlight.

She placed her foot firmly in the centre of it and scooted the page beneath her chair. It was out of sight, but could never be far from her thoughts. Soon she would have to face the past and the demons which she'd fought against all her life. The shadows had always been there, now they were emerging from the darkest recesses of her mind, demanding to be faced.

Catriona shook her head in an attempt to be rid of them, and with a cluck of impatience got to her feet. She had lived with the inevitability of this day most of her life – until now she'd managed to ignore it – and would carry on doing so for as long as possible. As she stood at the verandah railings and looked out, she realised her emotions were getting the better of her. Despite the lurid headlines, the police would hardly be interested in a murder that had taken place over fifty years before. They had their work cut out with current cases, and no doubt, by the time they got their fingers out and started working on this one, she'd be long gone. Besides, she reasoned, she had been a child back then, and anyone who might have remembered her would be long dead. There probably wasn't any clue to link her to the place either, so why on earth was she getting into a panic? Stepping down from the verandah, she dug her hands into her pockets and lifted her face to the sun before striding off to check on the new fences and corrals.

Belvedere Cattle Station sprawled over two hundred square miles of grazing land, mallee scrub, mountain and bush, its furthest pastures edging the tiny settlement of Drum Creek, a small community still clinging to the old ways despite the exodus by the youngsters who preferred the bright lights and opportunities offered in the cities. Nestled within the triangle of the Great Dividing Range and the Chesterton Range, the creeks and billabongs rarely ran dry, and although this latest drought had lasted five years, there was still a glimmer of water running over the polished shingle and sleek black boulders of Drum Creek.

Yet the grass had no goodness in it, and Connor had advised taking the herd of cattle up to the mountain pastures for the summer, or at least until the rains came, for it was an expensive business hand-feeding the mob. With most of the men and the cattle gone from Belvedere, there was a strange lifelessness about the place, an emptiness that seemed to reinforce her sense of being alone. Yet, as Catriona walked through the long, pale grass, her senses were piqued by the scent of dry, warm earth, sweet wattle and eucalyptus. The sky seemed closer here, all-encompassing and endless. No city lights masked the magic of a starry night, or polluted the Wedgwood blue of the day, and Catriona often felt she was at one with the primal men who must have trodden these paths before her, for they were untouched and unsullied by modern life and still held the magic of a land undiscovered.

The peace surrounded her, the whisper of her trousers against the grass a reminder of the times when she'd ridden across these pastures, the wind in her hair, the sun on her back as the horse galloped full-stretch towards the empty horizon. A reminder of carefree walks, of picnics with the children and long, lazy days by the billabong, drying off in the sun after a swim and as she walked she felt the dread drift away and the calm return.

She came to the creek and settled on the bench she'd had erected many years before around the base of the ancient Coolabah tree. It was a sturdy piece of work, she acknowledged as she sat down on the sun-bleached wooden bench and leaned back against the rough bark. This was her favourite place – an arbour for contemplation – a shady corner of the vast property which had become her private hideaway over the years.

The water in Drum Creek was clear, reflecting the diamond specks of sunlight that dappled through the overhanging eucalyptus branches. It eddied around the black boulders and chuckled its way downstream to the billabong. She could hear the birds calling to one another, an orchestra of sound far more beautiful than any manmade music. The bellbird chimed, the magpies crooned and the galahs and parakeets squabbled. A kookaburra laughed in the distance and she smiled, for above all, that was the sound which reinforced her love for her Outback home and warmed her soul.

Despite the tenuous shade of the Coolabah tree, she could feel the reassuring warmth of the sun on her shoulders. She flicked her hand at the swarming flies, but it was ritual, a habit honed over the many years she'd spent in the Outback, and she knew it would have little effect for the flies were persistent and wouldn't leave until the sun went down.

Leaning against the solid, warm bark of the old tree, she watched the water and the bright blue flit of the tiny wrens as they swooped down from the trees to drink. It was too hot and bright for the wallabies and kangaroos, but once the sun went down, they would come here to drink. It was a sight which always gladdened her and made her feel at one with her surroundings. 'Getting too bloody soppy in your old age,' she muttered crossly as she stood and brushed the dust from her trousers. 'Time you pulled yourself together, woman.' She glared at the river as if defying it to reply, then turned away and looked back at the homestead.

The little wooden house had been repainted many times over the years, and it bore little resemblance to the tiny shack she'd first seen as a child. The new extensions had doubled its size, and although the verandah needed some work doing to it – the steps were constantly being chewed by termites, the posts were a favourite scratching pole for Archie, and there were a couple of tiles missing on the roof – it looked sturdy and was the home of many happy memories. With faded shutters and fly-screens, the house reflected the earthen colours of its surroundings and seemed settled and comfortable amongst the tall pale grass and stands of drooping eucalyptus. She could have spent more money on the place – after all, she had enough – but, actually she preferred it the way it was. 'We can moulder into old age together,' she muttered. 'And to hell with everything.'

She took a deep breath of the good clean air and drank in the sight of her beloved home. Belvedere was somnolent in the afternoon heat, the surrounding bush alive with the call of birds and the sawing of crickets. Horses dozed in the shade of the pepper trees in the far paddock, and the cows complained as they waited to be milked. The great barns and the cookhouse stood off to one side of the main clearing, and behind the bunkhouse and horse corrals there were the chicken coops, dog pens and dairy parlour. Belvedere was almost self-sufficient, but was beginning to look its age.

Catriona shielded her eyes against the glare and looked over at the manager's cottage. Connor was expected to return tonight, and she was looking forward to hearing how the summer drove had gone. She sighed and began to walk back to the homestead. It was quiet without the majority of the men around, and she missed Connor's cheerful smile. He had turned out to be a man she could be proud of; a man who, strangely, often reminded her of her father for he loved the isolation of this great Dreaming Place, and understood its delights and its dangerous beauty.

Archie carefully jumped down from his customary cushion and stretched his neck so she could scratch under his chin. He was over fifteen now, arthritic and overweight, very different to the scrap of fur she'd found all those years ago. Catriona stroked his sleek

281

ginger fur and ran his plumed tail through her fingers. 'Reckon you want your tucker,' she muttered. 'You only talk to me when you're hungry.'

The screen door squealed as she opened it and Archie stalked into the narrow hallway, turning to check she was following. She snatched up the discarded newspapers and let the screen slam behind her as she entered the cool, dark interior and made her way to the kitchen at the back of the house. Built squarely, and despite the additions she'd made, the timber homestead retained much of its character from when it was first built almost a century before. Only now there was a proper bathroom and a new generator. This generator gave her electricity, but her hot water came straight from the bore and she still cooked on the Aga she'd had sent out from England all those years before.

She stuffed the newspaper into the furnace and watched the flames devour the print; how easy it was, how quickly it turned to ashes. The heat from this Aga chased away the draughts which whistled through the gaps in the wooden walls during the winter, but in the summer, as now, it turned the little kitchen into a furnace.

Catriona wrestled with the can-opener and fed Archie who set about his dinner with alacrity. Leaning against the rail in front of the range, she watched him gobble down the food, and not for the first time wished he'd show the same enthusiasm for catching the rats and mice that plagued Belvedere. As station cat he had a duty to keep it free from vermin – but unlike the feral moggies which roamed the barns and outbuildings, Archie was fat and smug and far too lazy to do more than sleep his days away, and for that, Catriona could only blame herself. Archie had been spoilt.

She shrugged and made a cup of tea, struggling somewhat with the heavy black kettle that always stood on the range before taking a seat at the table. Making a space for her cup and saucer, she eyed the clutter. She had always despised housework – preferring to be out with the children, or being involved in her work or her music – and for most of her adult life she'd lived in hotels or apartments where someone else did the cleaning. Now the children had grown up and fled the nest, there was no one to judge her housekeeping skills, and she saw little point in keeping the place tidy. The dust always came back, anyway, so what was the point?

Sipping her tea, she looked around the room and felt comforted by the clutter. Newspapers and catalogues were piled on every flat

282

surface. Boots, shoes and coats were heaped in corners and the table was covered with books and sheet music and letters which had to be answered. Fly papers hung from the ceiling, black with their victims, and cobwebs drifted in the corners and from the ceiling fan which creaked with age as it stirred the stifling air with little effect on the temperature.

She pulled a face and decided perhaps she'd let things get out of hand. The girls would be coming soon and they would be shocked at how she'd let the place go. She found some rubber gloves and an apron and set to work, finding a strange sort of release in the physical effort it took to scrub and wash and clear away the accumulated mess, for it didn't allow her to think. The cobwebs proved difficult to deal with, but she finally managed to clear them away, sweep the floor and bundle most of the boots and jackets into a cupboard.

Once the kitchen had taken on some semblance of order, she changed the bed linen and loaded the washing machine before making a sandwich of cold mutton and damper bread, which had come from the oven that morning, and took her early supper into the sitting room. There was still a great deal to be done, she realised, but it could wait for a while. There was only so much housework she could do in a day, and by the looks of it, the place needed a complete spring clean. Making a mental note to get hold of Billy Birdsong's wife in the morning, she closed the door behind her and set down her supper on a low table.

She liked this room, she decided. It wasn't very big, but the windows were shaded from the sun by the vast pepper tree at the side of the house, and through the fronds she could just make out the corrals and the bunkhouse. The couch was comfortable and settled around her with a sort of reassurance that nothing bad would happen here. Cabinets of china and glass took up most of one wall, and the roll-top desk still spewed diaries, correspondence, programmes and play-bills. Two shelves of books sagged beneath the front window, and the baby grand, covered in silver-framed photographs and a fringed shawl, needed tuning. The man was due to call in a few days, and she hoped he'd keep the appointment and not let her down again. She missed not being able to play, and wanted it tuned and ready for her party.

She walked over to the stone fireplace and stared at the portraits on the wall above it. Her parents made a handsome couple, with their dark Irish hair and she could see her likeness to them in her own portrait. Staring at the painting, she was made even more aware of the passing years. She had been in her prime then, beautiful, talented and much sought after. There was no hint of the darkness that shadowed her, no clue as to what had gone before in those clear violet eyes. She'd proved to be a consummate actress.

The evening gown was red velvet, draped becomingly from slender shoulders to reveal a creamy décolletage. Ruby earrings and a diamond necklace reflected the fire of youth in her eyes. Her black hair was artfully pinned behind one ear by a corsage of perfect orchids, and the slender neck was arched seductively, giving a hint to the passions that lurked so close to the surface of this elegant young woman. The artist had been handsome, she remembered, his love-making exciting, and for a fleeting moment she wondered if he was still alive, if he remembered that passionate month in Paris when they'd barely left the chaise-longue in his studio. 'I doubt it,' she muttered, turning her back on the painting. 'Lovers come and lovers go. I should know, I had enough of them in my time.'

She grinned as she sat down and picked up her sandwich. How Clemmie had loved to hear about the men she'd met on her tours. How they'd laughed about Hank the Yank, and Jean Paul with his handlebar moustache that had tickled more than her fancy. She giggled. Those were the days.

Having eaten her sandwich, she poured a large gin and tonic, turned on the stereo and relaxed into the soft cushions as the Puccini aria drifted into the room. She closed her eyes, but the thought of what the future might hold made her restless. It wouldn't be pleasant, she was sure of that, but then she'd been no stranger to the darker side of life, and would deal with it when it could no longer be ignored.

The gin and the soft music began to take effect as she thought of her long-lost daughter. She no longer wrote to her; there was no point, for there had been no reply, no acknowledgement. But, oh, how she wished things could have been different. Her thoughts drifted effortlessly to Rosa, Connor and Harriet and she smiled. There had been wonderful compensations, though, invaluable gifts with which she had been blessed.

It was way past dawn by the time Connor and the others arrived back at Belvedere. They had been gone for three weeks, and were ready for a proper wash and some decent tucker. Connor swung from the saddle and stretched. His back was aching, the old injury in his knee reminding him that sixteen hours a day in the saddle, in temperatures way over a hundred, was not good for a man of thirty-two.

The grit and dust from over a thousand head of cattle clung to his skin, and the dried sweat on his clothes made him itch. Yet, despite the heat, the flies and the dust, Connor knew he would have it no other way. As he saw to his horse and set it free in the corral, he silently acknowledged that the three weeks drove was a necessary part of living out here, and if he was totally honest with himself, he loved the freedom it offered. There was nothing like riding behind a mob of cattle across the vast, empty plains of Queensland to give a man an appetite for life and the traditions of his heritage.

'Tucker's up, mate,' said the drover. 'Reckon I could eat a horse.'

Connor grinned and wiped away the sweat from his face before settling the Akubra back on his head. 'I'd stick to beef, mate,' he said. 'Tastes better.'

The drover cupped his hands around the match as he lit a roll-up. 'Reckon the missus is up and about,' he muttered. 'Lights are on.'

Connor looked over at the homestead and nodded. 'Better go and report in,' he said wearily. 'Catch ya later.' He hitched up the moleskins and tucked in his shirt as he walked across the yard. He would have preferred to wash first, and his belly was rumbling at the thought of bacon and eggs and a heap of mashed potato, but knowing Ma, she would be waiting for him.

He tapped on the screen door, and getting no reply, stepped into the hall. Maybe she'd fallen asleep before turning out the lights, in which case, he'd come back later. Yet there was always the fear that one day he would come home to find her dead, just as he had with his grandmother. Ma was getting on a bit, though she wouldn't admit it, and despite her keen mind and her vigour, Connor dreaded leaving her on her own for too long. He accepted that his fear stemmed from his own insecurities, and that Ma would have been horrified if she could read his thoughts. But he couldn't help the way he was.

He stepped into the sitting room, guided by the sound of music.

285

It was one of Ma's favourite songs, and she'd obviously nodded off. He took off his hat and looked down at her, the affection for this feisty, loving woman, soft in his face. She'd hit the gin by the looks of it. Good on her. Yet, in sleep she appeared so vulnerable, so very tiny in the depths of those great cushions, and he felt a wave of protectiveness come over him.

Connor glanced around the room. It was glowing with the yellow of a new day, the dust motes dancing, the shadows deep in the corners. He stepped away from the couch and headed on tiptoe for the door. He'd come back after breakfast. Ma wouldn't appreciate being caught asleep.

'Who's there?' The greying head lifted from the pillow, the eyes blinking owlishly with the remnants of sleep.

'Only me, Ma,' replied Connor from the doorway. 'Sorry. Didn't mean to wake you.'

'What's the time?'

Connor looked at the clock on the mantel, remembered it had stood at half-past three for ten years and squinted out of the window. 'Sun-up,' he said. 'About five.'

She wrestled with the cushions and dug herself out of the sofa. Running her hands through her hair, she tried to bring some order to her appearance. 'You shouldn't sneak up on people like that, Connor,' she said chided softly. 'Fair gave me a fright.'

He was used to her ways after all these years and the mild rebuke washed over him. 'Saw your light on,' he said. 'Thought you was up.'

She glared at him for a moment, but couldn't remain stern for long. 'I am now,' she retorted with a grin. 'So, come on then. How did the drove go?'

Connor nodded. 'Good. Reckon the mob could smell the good grass, no worries getting them up there.' He rammed his hands into his pockets and eased from one foot to the other. His knee was still playing up. 'The paddocks up there are good, and there's still plenty of water in the creeks. Some of the fences need seeing to, so I'll send a couple of blokes up later to sort them out.'

'And Billy's grandson? How'd he go?'

Connor thought of the young Aborigine and smiled. Johnny Two Toes had been riding since he could sit on a horse. He'd lived on Belvedere all his life and his family were so much a part of the place it would seem very odd indeed if they weren't around. 'No worries,' he replied. 'Born to it, just like Billy Birdsong.'

She smiled back at him. 'Ridiculous name for the poor kid,' she muttered. 'He can't help having two small toes on one foot.' She pulled a face. 'Doesn't seem to stop him getting into mischief though. Cookie told me he's short of a tin of biscuits.' She looked at him quizzically. 'Any ideas on that, Connor?'

Connor grinned and looked down at his boots. 'Reckon we all enjoyed the biscuits, Ma. No worries.'

Catriona raised an eyebrow, but she couldn't quite hold the stern expression and broke into a smile. 'Good. Makes a change from bush tucker anyways,' she murmured.

'If there's nothing else, I'll get some breakfast,' he said. 'Why don't you come over? Been a while since you ate with us.'

'Not bloody likely,' she said flatly. 'Sweaty men, a bad-tempered cook and over-done steak are not my idea of a pleasant breakfast. I'll eat here as usual.'

Connor eyed her with affection. Ma had often eaten in the cookhouse during his first years on Belvedere, but she was aware of how awkward it made the men feel, and was astute enough to realise she was better off out of it. 'No worries,' he murmured.

'Wait.' Catriona tugged at his sleeve. 'I need you to do something for me first.'

He looked down at her and grinned. 'What's so urgent it can't wait for me to wash and eat?'

'Mind your own damn business,' she retorted with a soft nudge in his ribs. 'Come on.'

Connor towered over her as he followed her out of the room and into the hall. She pointed up to the hatch in the ceiling. 'I need you to get the big tin trunk down,' she said. 'And mind how you handle it. It's full of precious things.'

Connor fetched the ladder from the back porch and climbed up into the narrow roof space which smelled of dust and animal droppings. The heat was stifling despite the fact it was barely past sun-up, and the trunk was perched across the rafters in a far corner. He wriggled across the rafters and dragged it towards him, pulling it through the hatch and depositing it on the floor. It was battered and heavy and covered in cobwebs and possum shit.

'Can you bring it into the lounge-room?' Catriona was hovering beside the ladder.

Connor's knee was a ball of fire, and his belly was squirming with hunger, but he did as he was ordered. He cleaned the mess off the tin trunk, re-acquainting himself with the fascinating labels that were stuck all over it and which had intrigued him as a boy. He'd heard the stories about her life before Belvedere, and although he'd seen the trunk many times before, he'd never really explored the contents as thoroughly as his sister. He lugged it into the lounge and left it against the wall out of the way. 'What do you want this old thing for, Ma?' he asked. The bloody thing weighed a ton, God only knew what she kept in there.

'There are things I want to look at,' she said, a far-off expression on her face. 'Go and have your tucker, son. And thanks.'

He eyed her thoughtfully for a moment. There was something strange in her expression, and there were shadows in her eyes he'd never seen before. 'You right, Ma?' he asked with concern.

'Of course,' she replied, her chin high, eyes defiant, daring him to question her motives.

'Fair enough,' he muttered before squashing his hat back on and limping into the hall. Ma was up to something, but no doubt she would tell him what it was in her own good time.

DI Tom Bradley stepped out of the shower and wrapped a towel around his waist. Smearing the condensation from the bathroom mirror, he stared short-sightedly at his reflection and began to lather his face. At thirty-three, he was getting too old for the job, he decided as the fresh blade rasped through the stubble. The late nights, the heavy work-load and the sickening violence that was so much a part of his work were beginning to tell, and after almost sixteen years in the force he'd had enough. He could see the shadows below his eyes, the stress in the lines on his face and in the first grey hairs that glinted in the brown, shaggy mop he'd never been able to tame.

The force had changed since his father's day, even more so since his grandfather had been the local copper up in Atherton. There was more violence, more drugs and corruption – less time to deal with it all – more paperwork clogging up the system and fewer coppers to do the leg-work. Perhaps it was time to jack it in and find something else to do? He was sick of murder, of the darker side of humanity he had to deal with day after day. It had cost him his marriage, his home and his kids – surely nothing was worth that?

288

Splashing cold water over his face, he dried off and wrestled with the contact lenses. The damn things were necessary, but he still couldn't quite come to terms with deliberately poking something in his eyes every morning. He blinked, wiped away the tears and padded naked into his bedroom. The suit would do for another few days and the shirt was one of a batch that had just been returned from the cleaners, pristine in a polythene wrapping. He tied his tie, shoved on his shoes and gathered up the loose change on the bedside table.

The photograph stood there by the phone. It reminded him he hadn't spoken to his sons for a couple of weeks – hastily scribbled letters and cards just didn't give him the satisfaction of a one-to-one conversation – even if that did involve the usual teenage grunts and monosyllabic replies to any questions. He checked the time – they would be in school by now, he realised. Western Australia was in a different time zone. With a sigh he shoved his wallet into his jacket pocket, picked up the faded folder and left the apartment. Perhaps he could find time later in the day to ring them?

Brisbane shimmered in the early morning heat, the glass towers reflecting the river and the passing traffic that streamed along the fly-overs and bridges that ran beside the river and over to the southern side of the city. As he waited in yet another queue at traffic-lights, he switched on the tape recorder and let the hauntingly beautiful aria wash over him. Puccini was his favourite composer and Catriona Summers' voice had captured the very essence of the tragedy of *Madame Butterfly*.

Relaxing back in the icy air-conditioning he stared out of the window at the passing cavalcade of tourists, shoppers and business people who poured over the crossing. He liked living in the city – he enjoyed the buzz it gave him, yet he was all too familiar with the evil that lay so close beneath that veneer of modernity and success – but sometimes, like this morning, he wished he didn't.

As Catriona's voice filled the car, he looked down at the folder on the seat beside him. His father had kept it, and Tom remembered sitting on his grandfather's knee as the old man told him about the Russian, the Englishman and the missing silver. When the body had been found, his father had contacted him immediately. A quick visit to collect the file at the weekend, and the advances in modern technology meant that Tom had finally managed to trace Velda and her daughter; of Yvchenkov there was nothing; it was as if he'd simply disappeared into thin air.

289

It had come as a shock to realise that one of the greatest Australian divas had had such humble beginnings, and that she could have been implicated in the murder all those years before, even though she could only have been a child at the time. Nevertheless, children often knew more than adults gave them credit for, they saw and overheard things because they were almost invisible in the grown-up world as he'd discovered time and again during his years in the force.

Yet he was not naïve enough to believe the police would do much about such an old murder. There was more than enough work to do sorting out the modern crimes without digging back over fifty-odd years. It was a cold case, and would be shoved to the bottom of the pile until it could be ignored no longer. Which meant it would give him time to do something about it and clear it up before the press got to hear about Dame Catriona's involvement and turned the whole thing into a media circus.

The loud blare of a horn roused him from his thoughts and he stepped on the accelerator. His office was just around the corner, and minutes later he was parked in his slot and heading for the stairs.

DS Wolff was waiting for him. 'The boss wants this sorted,' he said as Tom walked in and hung his jacket by the door. 'Today, if possible.'

Tom took the bulging case-file, looked at it and dropped it on his desk. It was an on-going case that was getting them nowhere. 'He'll be lucky,' he muttered as he locked the Atherton folder away in his desk and helped himself to stewed coffee. 'The witnesses aren't talking, especially the girlfriend. Everyone's got a heavy dose of amnesia and so far we've got nothing to link the victim to any of our suspects.'

'I'll get the witnesses to talk,' Wolff muttered as he shifted his narrow shoulders in what he obviously thought was a menacing way. 'You're too bloody soft on 'em.'

Tom grimaced as the sour coffee hit his throat and he left the mug on the windowsill beside his desk. This latest murder was just one of many unsolved crimes they had to tackle, and Wolff's belligerent attitude was getting on his tits. He didn't like the man, but he'd been seconded here for three months from Sydney and was designated to his team. There was nothing he could do about it, but he'd be glad when Wolff's time was up and he was on his way back down south. The man was too quick to adopt bully-boy

290

tactics, too ready for a scrap when one could easily be avoided. 'Violence just provokes more violence,' Tom said as he sifted through the files in his in-tray. 'Sometimes it's better to have a quiet word, and try to show a bit of understanding. I'd rather have them think of me as someone they can trust rather than an enemy, and you'd be amazed at how mulish people get when they think they're being bullied.'

'She's a rich tart who thought it might be fun to mess with the big boys. She's got her fingers burned and rushed home to daddy,' sneered Wolff.

Tom leaned back in his chair. He regarded Wolff for a long moment, taking in the hawkish nose, the thin face and bad-tempered mouth – at twenty-nine, Wolff looked more like a villain than one of the good guys. 'You'll leave the witnesses alone,' he said firmly. 'That girl is scared enough without you bullying her. She'll talk once she realises it's for her own good.'

Wolff snatched up the folder Tom had discarded. 'I didn't realise there was one law for the rich and another for the rest,' he snapped. 'Just because the silly bitch's got a rich daddy, doesn't mean she's above the bloody law.' His eyes glittered. 'She knows things about Robbo Nilson that will get him off the streets for good. She's obstructing the law, and if I was her daddy, I'd give her a sharp slap.'

Tom gritted his teeth. He'd like to give Wolff a slap, but that wouldn't solve anything. 'Watch your mouth, Wolff. Or I'll shut it for you,' he drawled.

Wolff glared at him and brushed down his lapels and shifted his shoulders, his stance bullish. 'Thought you were against violence?' he sneered. 'I could have you up on a harassment charge.'

'Try that and I'll have a word in the Super's ear about your scams on the side,' shot back Tom. 'Now get out of here and do something useful.'

Wolff's glare was one of pure malice. He turned on his heel and slammed through the door, muttering about getting his own back.

The draught of his leaving scattered the papers from Tom's desk. He picked them up and stood in deep thought before coming to a decision. Before he could change his mind, or think of the consequences, he dumped everything back on the desk, snatched up his jacket and strode down the corridor to his Superintendent's office. The keys to the desk drawer winked in the sunlight that streamed through the window – in his haste, Tom had forgotten them.

291

Chapter Twenty-One

'I don't want to marry him,' Harriet said firmly. 'In fact,' she added. 'I don't want to marry anyone at the moment, so give it a rest.' She faced her mother and wondered how on earth they'd got on to this topic when her visit had been planned for an entirely different reason. Yet she suspected Jeanette Wilson had deliberately sidetracked the issue, and Harriet knew exactly where this argument was leading. It was always the same when they got on to this particular hot potato, and although Harriet was experienced in the art of logical debate and argument in the Law Courts, she'd never quite managed to circumnavigate her mother's tortuous logic, or even understand it.

Jeanette was not the sort of woman who could take a hint, however blatant. She was a well-preserved fifty-three, with a one-track mind, and at the moment it was centred on her daughter's spinsterhood. She folded her arms, her lips drawn into a thin line of disapproval as her scathing glare took in the smart black suit, the white blouse and sensible shoes. 'You're getting too old to be fussy, dear,' she said mildly. 'And you don't exactly make the best of yourself. Black can be so draining, especially with your colouring.'

'I can hardly turn up at the office in a mini-skirt and fish-net stockings.' Harriet took a series of deep breaths in an attempt to quash the rising fury. 'I'm twenty-eight,' she said flatly. 'Hardly in my dotage.' She ran her hands down the narrow skirt and was furious to discover they were trembling. How, after all these years, could Mum still stir up such strong emotions?

'Twenty-eight and unmarried,' replied her mother with what looked suspiciously like smug satisfaction. 'The time clock is ticking, Harriet. You'll soon be too old to even think about having children.'

Harriet ignored the jibe. She had years yet, and she was damned if she was going to marry Jeremy Prentiss just so she could breed. 'Jeremy's the last man I'd have father my children,' she retorted. 'They'd all end up with a Pommy accent and no damn chin.' She took a breath and tried to calm down. That was unfair on Jeremy, who was actually a very handsome, nice man, but her mother's goading had made her bitchy.

'I don't understand you, Hattie,' replied her mother, using the childhood endearment in a belated and rather obvious attempt to take the heat out of the argument. 'Jeremy's the junior partner and an eligible bachelor with an enviable pedigree. He's rich and obviously besotted. Surely you can see this would be advantageous to both your career and your lifestyle?' She clasped her hands in her lap, the pale pink cashmere sweater enhancing her still-perfect skin. 'What with the waterside apartment and the boat, you'd want for nothing.'

'I don't feel the need to marry for money.' Harriet yanked the clip out of her fair hair and let it swing around her shoulders. She had inherited her father's colouring as well as his impatience, and Mum's less than delicate admiration for Jeremy's stud qualifications was just about the last straw.

'Is that meant as some kind of dig?' Jeanette's voice sharpened. She snatched a cigarette from the silver box on the glass coffee-table, and after tapping it furiously on the lid, lit it with the gold lighter.

Harriet silently admitted it was a cheap shot and, although her mother probably deserved a taste of her own medicine, she knew it wasn't fair, or clever. But she was sick of this badgering. Sick of her mother constantly shoving Jeremy bloody Prentiss in her face. 'Just leave it, Mum,' she said wearily as she ran her fingers through her hair. 'We'll never agree, so why keep on?'

'I'm your mother,' Jeanette said through the cigarette smoke. 'It's my duty to care.'

'I know,' admitted Harriet. 'But if you really cared you wouldn't want me tied to Jeremy just for the sake of a house and a boat and money in the bank. I don't love him.'

'Hmph. What's love got to do with anything?' Jeanette eyed her through the smoke, her blue eyes narrowed. 'Marriage is all about security, and you'd have that with Jeremy.'

Harriet could have said a whole lot in her defence, but she'd lost the will to fight and besides, this wasn't the first time this argument had been aired and she was sick of it. Mum probably did care what happened to her, but Harriet suspected Jeanette was only really interested in having grandchildren. All her friends had them, and Jeanette was obviously feeling left out of the coterie of doting grannies.

Harriet sighed and busied herself by pouring coffee. Mum had married Dad on the eve of her twenty-fifth birthday. Harriet had been born exactly nine months later, and having considered she'd done her bit, Jeanette had proceeded to carry on with her dancing career, and do the most damage she could to her wealthy husband's wallet.

Brian Wilson had made his fortune supplying the oil fields with plant and machinery, and Jeanette had blatantly admitted she'd deliberately set out to snare him. He'd been a loving father when time and business allowed it, but he hadn't been happy in his marriage, and the rows between him and Jeanette had been blazing. Harriet was ten when, during one such titanic fight, he'd collapsed with a fatal heart attack. 'I'd rather be happy,' Harriet muttered. 'Security isn't all it's cracked up to be.'

Jeanette smoked her cigarette, her silence far more eloquent than words.

Harriet turned her back and stood before the wall of glass that overlooked Circular Quay. It was only early morning and already it was turning into a long day. She wished she hadn't decided to visit on the way to her office, but force of habit had brought her here to tell her mother her news, and check she was all right. Yet she still had to approach another particularly thorny subject and had no idea how to do it.

Jeanette had taken an instant dislike to Rosa and Belinda, and had refused to acknowledge Harriet's friendship with them. She'd considered the two girls unsuitable companions and had done her best to discourage the strong bond between them. Harriet was leaving Sydney tomorrow to visit Belvedere for two weeks, and her absence would have to be explained.

She stared out of the window, seeking inspiration. The penthouse apartment had a panoramic view of the refurbished Circular Quay. She could see the city of elegant glass towers, delicate Victorian church spires and the graceful sweep of the sails of

Sydney Opera House. The Harbour was already busy with the tourist boats and paddle steamers which cruised back and forth among the water-taxis. Luxury yachts bobbed at their moorings beyond the Botanic Gardens, and white ibis, with their black necks and heads and long, curved bills picked their way among the flotsam at the water's edge and in the grassed parkway.

Since the opening of the Opera House, the 80s had brought regeneration to this part of Sydney. Gone were the old docks, the warehouses and accumulated clutter of the old Harbour, and in their place had come sculptured glass and cool chrome. Café society had arrived. Little tables were set beneath colourful umbrellas all the way around the horseshoe of the Harbour, and expensive boutiques and luxury hotels did a roaring trade. Buskers worked the crowds at the weekends, and even the tiny houses in The Rocks had been painted and refurbished to entice the visitors to the markets.

To her left was the Harbour Bridge which arced across the water from the north shores of Sydney to the forest of blue and green glass office towers and architecturally innovative apartment blocks that reflected the scenes around them. Known as the Coathanger to most Sydney-siders, its two railway lines and eight traffic lanes were the main arterial routes into the city.

Harriet sighed. She knew the view was even more magical at night. Twinkling lights reflected on the water, and in the fountains, and all along the busy walkways the pubs and bars and restaurants brought vibrant life to this once derelict side of the city. The paddle steamers were festooned in coloured lights as they departed for their dinner cruises, and the neon signs above some of the business towers blinked and shimmered against the night sky.

She turned back to her mother. Jeanette had stubbed out the cigarette and was repairing her make-up in the gilt-edged mirror above the inset gasfire. She didn't look bad, Harriet admitted. Her shock of dark hair had been artfully tinted and streaked to cover the grey, and the cut was becoming. Her figure was still trim, honed by the years of dancing with the Sydney Ballet Company and an almost regimental fitness routine in her retirement. She was a small woman, but with a forceful personality, one that Harriet suspected she herself had inherited. Perhaps, she thought wearily, it's why we fight so much. We're too alike.

Their eyes met in the mirror and Jeanette was the first to look away. 'I know why you came today,' she said as she scrutinised her appearance. 'But I will not discuss it.'

'It's time you stopped burying your head in the sand, and took a reality check,' Harriet said firmly. 'Rosa's my friend, and like it or not, you're going to have to accept it.'

Jeanette turned to face her. 'No I don't,' she said with cool detachment.

Harriet's exasperation made her sharp. 'It's important to me. Can't you see that?'

Jeanette's eyes were dull with determination. 'To you, maybe. Not to me.' She picked up her handbag from the table and snatched up the lilac pashmina from the back of the leather couch. 'I'm late for a charity coffee morning, Harriet. You should have warned me you were coming. I would have changed my arrangements.'

Harriet picked up her briefcase. Jeanette had never been known to change a social engagement in her life – unless it was to her advantage – and she doubted she'd start doing so to rake up old arguments. 'My trip out to Belvedere is far more important than a bloody coffee morning,' she snapped.

'Don't be vulgar,' retorted Jeanette as she turned in the doorway. 'I didn't raise you to speak to me that way. No doubt it's that slut Rosa's influence.'

'How dare you talk about her like that?' Harriet hissed as she stepped into the hall. 'You've spoken to her once, you know nothing about her. And I'm bloody well sick of you putting her down.'

They glared at one another in silence until Jeanette slammed the door and began to walk down the deserted corridor towards the elevator.

'Don't walk away from me, Mum.' Harriet caught her arm and stilled her. 'This argument won't go away by ignoring it. What is it with you? Why do you hate her so?'

Jeanette's fury was incandescent, the electricity emanating from that neat little body in waves. 'She's a tart,' she snapped. 'Divorced before she's twenty-one, working in that down-and-out office in Paddington, mixing with the lowest of the low. Mud sticks, Harriet. You'll find her reputation rubbing off on you before long if you persist in this ridiculous friendship.' Her narrow chest rose and fell as she attempted to control her rapid breath. 'Reap what you sow, Harriet. But don't expect me to give a damn when your career goes down the drain.'

Harriet backed away. This was a side to her mother she hadn't witnessed since Dad's death. 'Rosa is not a tart,' she breathed. 'I came to tell you I'd be out at Belvedere for a couple of weeks and all I get is venom.'

Jeanette stepped into the elevator and stabbed the button. 'You're a big girl, now, Harriet. You don't need to tell me your plans. Especially when they involve that place.'

'Fair enough,' she muttered as she stood beside her mother.

Jeanette's dark eyes regarded her coldly and Harriet flinched. She'd known her mother would react but this was beyond reason. She reached for her mother's hand. It was cold and unresponsive. 'I just want you to accept my friendship with Rosa and Catriona and be glad for me. They gave me a home when you were away, offered me love and kindness even though you made it very plain you didn't appreciate it. Please, Mum. Be reasonable.' Her voice was soft, the need for approbation making it falter.

Jeanette snatched away her hand. 'You make your own decisions. Just don't expect me to front the cheerleading section.'

They stood side by side in the elevator, both staring in silence at nothing, their emotions firmly under control. Harriet breathed in the familiar scent of Rive Gauche. It was so much a part of her mother that, had she worn anything different, it would have seemed strange. Yet, in such close and hostile circumstances it was overwhelming.

The polished steel door finally slid back in a whisper and they stepped out of the icy air-conditioning into the heat of the basement car park. Harriet took a deep breath. 'I'm sorry you don't approve, Mum, but don't you think your jealousy is getting out of hand?'

Jeanette eyed her for a long moment then unlocked the BMW. 'Jealousy is not an emotion I am acquainted with,' she said firmly. 'God forbid I envy those dreadful people.'

'Oh, for God's sake,' snapped Harriet.

Jeanette turned to glare up at her, her eyes very blue and sparking with anger. 'They might have given you bed and board during the school holidays, but that doesn't mean I have to be grateful. *I'm* your mother, Harriet, not Dame Catriona Summers. It wouldn't hurt to remember that.'

'Of course you're my mother,' she said in exasperation. 'What on earth are you on about now?'

'Just don't come crying to me when it all gets shot to hell,' snapped Jeanette as she slid into the car and slammed the door.

Harriet frowned. Her mother's jealousy of the affection shown by Rosa's family had always been a contentious issue but this was more than envy, it was spiteful and it made no sense. She unlocked her MG and climbed in. With the roof down and her foot hard on the accelerator, she drove out of the underground car park and into the sun. There was little point in saying any more, not even goodbye.

Tom found Belinda Sullivan in the canteen. Max was lying under the table, his muzzle on his paws, brown eyes following each mouthful of egg and bacon his young mistress was devouring. 'G'day, Tom,' she said cheerfully as she fed the last piece of bacon to the drooling German Shepherd. 'What can I do you for?'

Tom pulled out a chair and sat down. Belinda was what the other blokes called 'A Lovely Big Girl', a description she loathed, but nevertheless took on board with varying degrees of good humour. Her hair was thick and curly and was the same dark brown as her eyes. She was tall, her figure generous like her character but she was superbly fit, and he suspected it was all those years of riding and hauling hay bales around her parents' sheep station that had made her so. 'I need a favour,' he began.

'Thought you might,' she murmured, her gaze steady on his face. 'Go on, then. What is it?'

He decided to come straight to the point. 'You know Dame Catriona Summers, don't you?'

She nodded and grinned. 'What's this, Tom? Autograph hunting at your age?'

He shook his head. 'It's a bit more serious than that,' he replied. He glanced around to ensure they weren't being overheard. 'I need to go out to Belvedere and talk to her, and I thought that since you've known her most of your life, you could come with me.' He paused. 'It's a bit delicate, and it would be better if a woman officer was there,' he finished.

Her dark eyes were steady, her expression serious. 'Catriona's been like a second mother to me,' she said quietly. 'I think you'd better explain exactly what you're talking about.'

Harriet was taking her turn at the wheel. She and Rosa had decided to drive to Belvedere for a change. It was a chance to catch their breath and enjoy the countryside after their long months in the city. They had flown up to Rockhampton the previous morning, and having hired a car, they were now driving down the main street of Emerald and heading for Drum Creek and Belvedere Station.

Despite a good night's sleep, she was still haunted by the argument with her mother, yet it was important she concentrated. These Outback roads were deceptively quiet, and road trains could appear from nowhere, hurtling down the road, making it necessary to get off the tarmac and out of the way.

Rosa ran her fingers through the spiky black hair she'd had liberally streaked bright pink for the holiday – the law courts frowned on such outlandish behaviour and she was determined to have a bit of fun while she was out of the office. 'It's good to be on the open roads,' she said. 'Even though Connor said he'd fly over to pick us up.' She squinted over at Harriet who was concentrating on the road ahead. 'He's still single, you know,' she said with a giggle. 'You sure you don't fancy him, Hat?'

Harriet pulled a face. 'Don't you start,' she growled with mock severity. 'I get enough of that from Mum.'

'Oh, Hat,' sighed Rosa. 'You know he's lovely, even Belinda's still got the hots for him even after all these years.'

'He's handsome,' she admitted. 'But that's as far as it goes. Strong, silent and masculine is all right if that's what turns you on, but he's your brother, and it would feel like incest.' She giggled. 'Apart from the fact my mother would have a purple fit if I was to hook up with him.'

Rosa laughed. 'You don't fool me, Harriet Wilson,' she said. 'I just know you won't be able to resist much longer.' Then she sighed. 'There are definitely times I'm glad I've got Catriona,' she said. 'It saves a lot of energy not having to explain my every move like you do with your mother.' She finger-combed her hair again, bringing further chaos to the tousled style as she stared out of the window.

The long boardwalks and shaded hotel verandahs had given way to enormous pastures and tiny wooden houses. 'Gee, it's been a while since I've been out this way,' she sighed. 'Everything looks so small, even though the town hasn't changed since I was a kid.' Her giggle was a deep sexy gurgle in the back of her throat that men found irresistible. 'Strewth, Hat,' she breathed. 'The highlight of the week is an evening in the hotel. Even the blokes are still talking sheep and cattle and utility trucks; it's all they think about. Thank God I escaped.'

Harriet grinned as she glanced over at her friend. Rosa, divorced and unencumbered with children, led a riotous social life when work allowed. She was determined to see out her twenties with a flourish. The eye make-up was striking, the black and pink hair gelled into spikes, the clothes a riot of colour. No one would guess she was the driving force of a small firm of solicitors who worked long hours defending the rights of those who couldn't afford legal representation. Yet the lack of money, and the seemingly endless workload never appeared to dull her zest for life. Harriet was delighted they had remained close, despite her mother's disapproval. 'Reckon you could be in with Dwayne,' she teased. 'I saw the way he looked at you in the hotel last night.'

Rosa laughed and adjusted the seat-belt over the generous bosom that was in danger of spilling over the scarlet wraparound top. 'Dwayne's an old mate, but he's part of the reason I couldn't stay in the Outback. He's not going anywhere, and like his dad and his grandad, he'll stay put in Emerald until he turns up his toes.'

'Fair go, Rosa. He's a decent enough bloke, and although your get-up brought the male population of Emerald to a drooling standstill, he still shouted us dinner last night.'

Rosa giggled. 'Perhaps the little black number was a bit daring,' she said. 'But to hell with it. If you've got it, flaunt it, and if that scares them rigid, at least it'll give them something other than sheep to talk about for a while.'

Harriet grinned. The little black dress had barely covered the essentials and, as Rosa's figure was lusciously top-heavy, the men of Emerald could barely keep their eyes off her every move in anticipation of seeing more. Rosa had no doubt chosen the wrong profession. She should have been an actress but then she was good at taking centre-stage in court, so maybe that was enough for her. 'It's lovely having the chance of two weeks together,' she said as they picked up speed and headed down the highway. 'But it's a shame Belinda couldn't make it. It would have been great for us all to be together again.'

Rosa pulled a face. 'She's up to her eyes in paperwork and drug-dealers. I don't envy her one bit.'

'I had to grovel to get time off; luckily I had some vacation owing. But I'm surprised you could escape.'

'I haven't had a break for months,' Rosa sighed. 'The work will still be piling up, but Mum's birthday is more important.' She grinned, her urchin face lighting up with mischief. 'A girl can get bogged down and stale if she's not careful, and it's time I cut loose and shook a bit of life into the old place again.'

Harriet raised an eyebrow as she concentrated on the road. Rosa could never be stale, she had too much energy. As for cutting loose? Her appearance might give the impression she was still a larrikin, but beneath that veneer was a young woman who took her work very seriously. Yet, in the mood she was in today, God help the men of Belvedere.

Rosa adjusted the gaping top and leaned back in the seat, her eyes closed. Her slim legs were encased in tight, multi-coloured patchwork jeans, which were cinched at the waist by a broad belt of purple leather. Her feet were bare and the toe rings and silver and turquoise anklet glinted in the sun. 'Give me the open road,' she sighed. 'The wind in my hair, the sun on my face.' She opened one eye and grinned at Harriet. 'But only for a while, all this emptiness can get claustrophobic.'

Hattie understood how life in any small town had to be difficult, but with the added restriction of hundreds of miles surrounding each tiny settlement, the phrase, 'neighbourhood watch' took on a whole new meaning. But as they drove through the endless ochre land with its termite mounds, green pastures and graceful eucalyptus trees, she couldn't help but feel drawn once more to the great openness of Australia's Outback. There was a primitive splendour here, the sky so high and wide above the starkly beautiful land that she could almost sense the ancient ones who'd come before. As Billy Birdsong had often told her, they were truly in the heart of the Great Dreaming. 'Dreamscapes,' she murmured. 'We're driving through dreamscapes.'

Rosa squinted in the sun as she turned to look at her. 'You're not going all poetic on me, are you Hat?'

Harriet smiled. 'Probably,' she admitted. 'But it's what Catriona once called it, and I have to agree with her. The majesty of this place brings out the romantic in me. Can't help it.'

Rosa nodded. 'Majestic it might be,' she said. 'But you just try living out here for more than a couple of months at a time. It's hot, dry and fly-bound or freezing, flooded and impossible to escape. The men are mostly the strong silent type – very boring if you want a bit of a laugh – and would probably run a mile if a girl so much as looked as if she might pounce. Give me Sydney any day.'

Harriet wasn't sure she agreed with this sentiment. The wide open spaces were alluring after the bustle and noise of The Rocks where she had a small Victorian terraced house. The road was empty of cars, the air so pure, it made her quite dizzy. She didn't miss the chaos of the morning traffic in the city, or the crowds on the pavements, and had realised long ago that this was another world, one in which she felt very at ease. 'You must be looking forward to seeing Connor again,' she said as she steered around a dead kangaroo and its accompanying flock of scavenging crows.

'Yeah, it'll be good. Been too long, really, but our worlds are so different, and it's a long way for either of us to travel. I doubt we'll have much to say to one another after all this time. Sad really, but that's life.' She scooted back in the seat and closed her eyes. 'He never was one for long conversations, and will no doubt bore us with the price of cattle and the state of the beef markets. But it'll be good to see Mum again. It's over a year since my last visit, and talking on the phone isn't really the same.' She yawned expansively. 'Wake me up when it's my turn to drive,' she muttered.

The hours drifted by and the view from the front mirrored that behind them – endless miles of narrow bitumen disappearing beyond both horizons. The Great Dividing Range stretched away to her right, the smaller ranges lying in a purple haze beyond the Outback bush. The scenery was magnificent, and as the miles brought her nearer to Belvedere she eagerly began to look for the first signs of her second home.

Despite all her good intentions, Catriona had spent two restless nights, and rose well before dawn that day. Her mind was too active, the memories too demanding for sleep, and she realised she couldn't ignore the past any longer. Having seen to Archie, she took her cup of tea into the lounge and sat looking at the trunk. Her past life was in there – the very essence of who she was – yet she couldn't quite find the courage to open it.

The shadows were drawing ever closer despite the brightness of the electric light and she thought she could hear the ghostly voices calling to her from beyond this fragile life. She closed her eyes and tried to will them to silence. They refused to be ignored – and with them came the sights and sounds she thought had long gone with another age, another world. Yet these whispering voices brought not only the scents and music of those memories, but a sharp reminder of when her youthful innocence had been no protector from life's harsher lessons.

Harriet leaned back in the passenger seat and eased the waistband of her jeans. Her mother would have been delighted with her outfit, she thought with a wry smile, for the blue denim was stone-washed and clung to her figure, and the sleeveless turquoise blouse was layered chiffon with a pale yellow lining and anything but sombre and sensible. She ran her hands through her heavy hair, lifting it from her neck so the air could circulate. Her turquoise earrings matched the nugget which was suspended from a delicate silver chain around her neck. Rosa had given it to her as a birth-day present long ago, stating that turquoise held magic properties. Harriet was sceptical, but she always felt calm and at peace when she wore it, so accepted the fantasy.

'Nearly there,' muttered Rosa as she lit another cigarette and pointed to the dirt track which meandered off the road and disappeared into the bush. They had been on Belvedere land since leaving Drum Creek.

Harriet snapped her thoughts back to the present, and with excited anticipation, looked out at her surroundings.

Rosa slowed the car, turned off the road and drove beneath the broad-beamed archway that had BELVEDERE STATION burned into the wood. The track's bitumen had long since been washed away, and the salmon-coloured earth meandered through the overhanging trees and around the great clumps of spinnifex grass which waved plumed heads in the breeze created by the passing car.

Bush wallabies stood alert, ears turning like tiny radar dishes as they watched the intruders with curious brown eyes. Birds rose complaining from the trees, and a herd of feral goats bounded out of the way as Rosa navigated a path around the potholes and deep tyre tracks. A timid echidna swiftly buried itself in the road-side dirt as sun-basking goannas scuttled away, their deadly claws digging into the bark as they raced up the nearest tree.

Harriet gripped the door handle and tried to maintain some kind of balance as the rental car dipped and jolted and swayed over the ruts. 'Just remember the fifteen hundred dollars waiver we'll lose if we damage it,' she grunted as Rosa crunched the gears and one of the rear wheels caught a deep rift in the track, making the exhaust scrape on the scree.

'Can't be helped,' muttered Rosa. 'Connor said he was going to get this fixed years ago.'

The track was obviously little used, and would probably have cost a fortune to tarmac, so Harriet could understand Connor's reluctance to repair it. She stared out at the scenery, her breath catching as they came out of the shade of the trees and crested the low hill. Belvedere lay sprawled in the valley beneath them. Mellow in the afternoon sun, as familiar and welcoming as it had always been. She breathed a sigh of contentment. She'd come home.

Catriona sat at the dressing-table and eyed her reflection. Sleepless nights and dark thoughts were playing havoc with her complexion she realised, as she plastered on make-up and brushed her hair. Drawing the strand of pearls from her jewellery box, she fastened it around her neck and put the matching studs in her ears.

Her diamond rings glittered as she stood and smoothed the dress over her hips. It was the colour of butter, narrow and straight, falling to just below the knee. A chiffon scarf and low-heeled pumps were her only accessories. It would have to do. She took a deep breath and forced a smile: the girls were coming home and she was damned if she was going to let them see she was worried about anything.

The sound of a car approaching turned her to the window. It was them. Hurrying out of the room she crashed through the screen door and arrived at the bottom of the verandah steps at the same time as the car.

'Mum!' Rosa flung her arms around her, almost knocking her off her feet.

'Catriona,' shouted Harriet as she too embraced her.

She held on to them tightly, reluctant to let them go. Her girls were home again.

Everything would be all right.

Chapter Twenty-Two

Harriet left Rosa and Catriona to catch up on their news, and walked down the narrow hallway and out through the screen door to the verandah. The murmur of voices came from the lounge, and although the words were indistinct, she could tell by the laughter that Rosa was regaling her mother with her city exploits.

Harriet leaned against the verandah railings and took a deep breath of the warm, scented air, and experienced the familiar contentment that always came when she visited Belvedere. She looked out over the vast clearing, at the Station buildings, the pens and corrals and compared them with her usual surroundings, drinking in the scenery, remembering her childhood days here. It was far removed from her city life.

In Sydney she would be at her desk, or battling traffic on the way to court. Her view from the window was of a different kind of majesty, with glass towers overlooking the rippling water which flowed past the elegant sails of the Opera House. She spent her working day in the studious hush of the Law, and the ritual of the Court System – the constrictions of her chosen profession. But here? Here was freedom.

She sighed with pleasure. The sun was high in the cloudless sky, the heat a shimmering haze over the surrounding land and outbuildings. A road-train had pulled in, a vast, articulated lorry with three live-stock trailers bringing a cloud of dust in its wake. This dust eddied and swirled and finally settled in a rusty veil over everything as the mob of bellowing bullocks was herded up the ramps and into the double-tiered pens.

Connor had yet to come to the homestead to welcome them, but he turned now and grinned, tipping his hat in acknowledgement.

Harriet watched him and the other men for a while until she realised that she too was under covert scrutiny. It was there in the glances beneath sweat-stained bush-hats, there in the studied nonchalance as they strolled back and forth and tried to look as if they were gainfully occupied rather than checking her out.

She dipped her head and bit back on a smile. There were no cat-calls and wolf-whistles, but it reminded her of the terrors of walking past city building sites – and that was something she'd not worried about for years – so, in a way it was flattering to be such a focus of attention.

She moved back into the shadows and wandered along the veran-dah until she was on the other side of the homestead and out of sight of the men. The view from here was magnificent, with thousands of acres of tough yellow grass rippling in the hot breeze, the meagre shadows of drooping eucalyptus barely visible. Stands of pine shot green spires skyward, the almost impenetrable darkness beneath them looking welcoming after the glare.

Harriet gathered up her mop of hair and anchored it firmly on the top of her head with a clip. The thought of a long cool shower was tempting, but she would wait until bedtime, when it might actually do some good. She wiped the beads of perspiration from her face with a handkerchief and sat down. It was hot, even in the shade and she could feel the sweat running down her back, soaking her thin blouse. The jeans had been a mistake, they were too tight, and she wished she'd worn shorts.

As she sat in the battered cane chair, her thoughts drifted back over the years she'd come here. Catriona had been a kind and generous host, the sort of woman she wished her own mother could be. It was surprising how little the years had affected her, she realised. Catriona's hair had gone the lovely grey which only very black hair managed. Her eyes were still amethyst, and her skin was flawless. It was hard to realise she was almost sixty-eight.

'Thought you'd gone walkabout. Here, you probably need this.' Rosa appeared around the corner, her bare feet making little noise on the floorboards. She handed Harriet a glass that tinkled with ice, plumped down in the chair beside her and gave a sigh of pleasure. 'Gin, tonic, ice and a slice. Just what the lawyer ordered.'

'It's a bit early, isn't it?' Harriet protested.

Rosa squinted into the sun. 'Sun's over the barn. Late enough.'

Harriet took a long drink. 'Hits the spot,' she agreed. 'Where's Catriona? She doesn't usually miss out on a spot of gin.'

'She'll be here in a minute,' muttered Rosa. 'Someone's just phoned, so I left her to it.' She took another sip before placing the glass on the floor and lighting a cigarette. Blowing smoke, she leaned back in the chair and closed her eyes. 'I'm a bit worried about her, actually,' she said finally. 'She looks tired, and I have the feeling she's worried about something.'

Harriet eyed her friend. 'What on earth could Catriona be worrying about?'

'I don't know,' Rosa shrugged. 'I did ask, but she just said she wasn't sleeping well.' She opened her eyes and leaned her elbows on her knees. 'But Mum sleeps like a log, always has done. Something's not right, I just know it.'

'Perhaps we ought to get the doctor out here to give her a thorough check-over?'

'I already suggested that, and she won't have it,' said Rosa.

'I'm not having any doctor prodding and poking me about.' Catriona came into view, her heels rapping on the wooden floor. 'And I'll thank you not to discuss me behind my back.'

Harriet and Rosa started like two guilty children. 'If you won't tell us what's worrying you, then what else can we do but speculate?' said Rosa firmly.

Catriona glared at them both before she sat down in another chair and stared out over her land. 'I've already told you,' she retorted. 'I'm having trouble sleeping. Probably indigestion.' Her tone brooked any more argument, and she changed the subject. 'Did I tell you girls how I first saw this place?' She didn't wait for an answer. 'I used to dream about it when I was a kid, you know. Saw it from up there,' she pointed to the western hills. 'I just didn't realise how long it would take before the dream became reality, and now I've been here thirty years.' She grinned, her face coming alight again as she raised her glass of gin and tonic. 'Here's to another thirty.'

Catriona studiously kept the smile on her face; it was easier now they were at home, easier to put the dark thoughts behind her. 'How's work?' she asked Rosa.

'Troubled kids, divorce, abuse, violent marriages. The usual, but it's rewarding,' replied Rosa as she smoked her cigarette.

Catriona turned to Harriet. 'I imagine corporate law is a lot less stressful?'

Harriet laughed. 'You've got to be kidding. There's more blood spilt on boardroom floors than in any city alleyway. Big money means big egos and even bigger crooks. But I enjoy it.' She smiled, the extraordinarily blue eyes sparkling with humour.

Catriona realised Harriet's youthful promise of beauty had been fulfilled, and with her slender figure and graceful ways, she could have been a wonderful dancer. The law was such a dry, dusty profession, but the girls seemed to thrive on it. She sighed, suddenly envious of their youth and enthusiasm. How different it had been in her day when women were denied access to such professions and expected to give up their careers the minute they married.

Catriona stared out at the shimmering land, deep in thought. The newspaper article meant there were many things to come to terms with, many facets of her story that would perhaps change these young women's opinion of her, and that made her reluctant to share the burden. Yet share she must, for one day it could become public knowledge, and it wouldn't be fair for them to hear it in the press.

Harriet touched her hand, bringing her back to the present. 'Penny for 'em, Catriona.' Her expression was concerned.

She forced a smile. 'I've had a bit of bad news,' she began. She paused as they sat forward, tense and expectant.

'What is it, Mum?' Rosa's eyes were wide with dread. 'You aren't ill are you?'

Catriona realised she was going about this all the wrong way. 'No,' she said firmly. 'I'm perfectly fine.' She took a sip of her drink, her thoughts in a whirl as she watched a eucalyptus leaf float along the verandah floor. Realising she didn't have the heart, or the courage to reveal the truth, she decided a white lie could do little harm. She was jumping the gun, letting her heightened imagination and the lack of sleep turn her into a neurotic. The police were hardly likely to come rushing out of the shrubbery to arrest her, and as for the press, she'd been out of the news for so long, they'd probably forgotten who she was.

'Mum?' Rosa's voice quavered.

She pulled her thoughts together, straightened her back and smiled. 'It's some old scandal I thought was long buried,' she said, the irony of her words making her grimace. 'I had a lover once, and he's threatening to reveal all if I don't pay him off.'

'Then you should tell him to print and be damned,' retorted Rosa. 'Bastard. What's his name? I'll send him a stiff letter, warning him that blackmail is a serious crime.'

Catriona laughed. 'You're like a Jack Russell when you get defensive.' She put her arm around Rosa and gave her a hug. 'I'll deal with him, no worries, darling. And I promise, he won't get a penny out of me.'

'I'm surprised you've let such a little thing worry you,' said Harriet. 'After all, the press would hardly be interested in an old bit of scandal.'

Catriona stood and folded her arms around her waist. 'You're right, Hattie,' she said firmly. 'I've just let the whole thing blow up out of all proportion. I should be flattered to know he even remembers me. It was years ago.' She flashed them a grin. 'I obviously made a lasting impression.'

Rosa laughed and went to top up their drinks. But Catriona noticed Harriet's steady gaze, and realised the girl had not really been fooled. Determined to bring an end to the subject, she turned away and stared out at the stand of pine trees and breathed in the glorious scent of eucalyptus and pine and dry, hot earth. A glimmer of movement made her look up and she smiled with delight and pleasure. This was a sight she'd seen so rarely of late, for this particular bird never came too close to civilisation.

The golden-brown wedge-tailed eagle soared high above home pasture, its wings fanned to catch the warm thermals, its predatory eye fixed on something hidden in the grass. She watched the slow, almost lazy glide of this magnificent young bird of prey as it circled lower and lower. His wings made little sound. Death would be silent and immediate.

Her breath caught as it swooped, plunging to earth like an arrow to rise up almost immediately with its prey clutched in cruel talons. The rabbit had been snared – and Catriona wondered if perhaps this was an omen of things to come.

Harriet held her breath as she watched the aerial display. She gasped as it struck the rabbit and flew away, and watched in awe until it was a mere speck in the fiery sunset.

'It's a bonzer sight, isn't it?' asked Catriona as she settled back in her chair. 'Not one we see every day.'

'Then I feel doubly privileged,' breathed Harriet. 'I was right about dreamscapes. This place has a magic all of its own.'

Catriona smiled. 'Dreamscapes,' she muttered. 'An apt description, which I seem to remember using years ago. But not all dreams are happy ones, and life out here can be cruel and harsh and downright bloody, so don't get too carried away.'

Harriet felt the heat rise in her face at the gentle admonition. 'Sorry,' she stammered.

Catriona smiled. 'No need to apologise, Harriet. I like your imagination. This, after all is the land of the Dreaming, the place where the Dreamtime legends were born.' She cupped Harriet's chin and gently tilted it until they were facing one another. 'I expect Billy's stories and legends have influenced your thoughts on this place, I know they have for me. He's quite a storyteller, but he'll remain faithful to the Dreaming, it's his heritage and what makes him the man he is.'

Harriet nodded, mesmerised by the violet eyes and the keen scrutiny. She was very aware of the older woman's touch, of the gentleness in her that was so at odds with the sophisticated, worldly persona she projected. Catriona had given her so much over the years and her affection for this woman made her determined to find out what was really troubling her.

Catriona must have seen the questions in her eyes, for she pulled abruptly away. 'Righto,' she said as she became business-like. 'Enough chatter. It's time for showers and tucker. I expect you're tired and we start early out here, remember, so you'll need to get to bed soon. I've put you in together; saves all that creeping about in the night because you want to gossip.'

Harriet couldn't resist looking at her watch. It was barely past seven, the sun only just dipping behind the hills. She'd forgotten about the early nights and even earlier mornings.

'I know it's early compared to the hours you probably keep in the city, but the rules are different here. We need to use up all the daylight – can't work cattle at night.' She began to walk back towards the front door. 'I've got plenty of food in. The men no doubt already know you've arrived and will only go all unnecessary if you two go into the hallowed hall of the cookhouse. Poor old Connor is already having trouble.'

'Bloody hell,' muttered Rosa as she followed Catriona along the verandah. 'Anyone would think they hadn't seen a woman before. It's not as if they don't know us.'

'Neither of you are children any more,' she retorted. She came to a sudden halt and eyed Rosa's outfit. 'Do try and cover up a bit more, Rosa,' she said wearily. 'It took weeks to calm the men down after your last visit and this is our busiest time of the year. Can't afford to have 'em off their feed.'

Rosa pecked her on the cheek and grinned. 'I'll dress like a nun if you promise we can borrow the best horses and go out with the men to run with the brumbies.'

'Hmph.' Catriona glowered, but she obviously couldn't stay cross for long. 'It might almost be worth it,' she said, her eyes gleaming with humour. 'But I reckon you won't have packed a wimple and habit, so all bets are off young lady.'

Rosa giggled, ran down the steps and grabbed her overnight bag from the car. She pulled a wisp of black layered chiffon from the bag and held it up. 'This should do for tonight. Reckon it will go down a treat when I go and say g'day to my old friend Cookie.'

Harriet stifled the giggles as Catriona eyed this miniscule garment with horror. It was the dress Rosa had worn to such effect in Emerald the night before. 'You win,' said Catriona barely suppressing her own laughter. 'If Connor says it's okay then you can go at the end of the week. But you're to promise me you'll never wear that here and especially not anywhere near the cook-house. There are too many sharp knives and I can't afford to loose my entire crew when the fighting breaks out.'

'Strewth,' muttered Rosa as she stuffed the scrap of material back in the bag. 'They should get a life.'

Harriet was inclined to agree, but the look on Catriona's face kept her silent. She reached into the car and took out her own bag, and they all went inside.

'Home sweet home,' sang Rosa as she crashed through the screen door. 'Bags I first in the shower.'

Harriet followed Rosa down the narrow hall. It was all so familiar, so unlike her neat terrace in Sydney and her mother's penthouse suite and, as usual, she felt immediately at home. The bunch of wildflowers had been crammed into a jam jar and placed on the bedside chest of drawers. There was a piece of paper leaning against it, welcoming them home.

'You must have made a good impression,' muttered Rosa as she eyed the flowers, dumped the bag and snatched up two towels and her wash-bag. 'Connor's never done that before.'

Harriet put her bag on the floor and tried to rescue the wilting flowers. She divided them up, found another jam jar in the kitchen and put it on the dressing table. It was a nice touch, she thought. Connor was obviously pleased to have his sister back. 'I reckon he just wanted to cheer us up,' she murmured.

Rosa raised an ebony eyebrow. 'Con's not into interior design, Hat. He's either feeling guilty about something, or trying to impress you.' She giggled. 'I bet he did that on the quiet. Can you imagine the joshing he'd have got if any of the others saw him?'

Harriet could imagine this all too well and had a fleeting moment of sympathy for Rosa's brother. It must be very difficult having to keep up the macho image all the time. 'There are times when I'm really glad I'm a woman.' She went into the kitchen and accepted the cup of tea. 'Though I have to admit I didn't exactly choose the right profession. Lawyers are incredibly attached to their old school ties and what with that and male bonding, it's not the easiest way to make a living.'

'Too right. Mateship gone mad if you ask me, but what's a girl to do? If you can't beat 'em, join 'em. Girl power is growing, Hat. Watch this space.' She stomped off to the bathroom and in minutes could be heard singing enthusiastically off-key.

Harriet and Catriona shared a smile of contentment – they were all together again.

The bedroom they always shared during Harriet's visits hadn't changed a bit. It was as if the clock had been turned back. The room held childhood memories and was still cluttered with Rosa's dolls and books and decorated with the rosettes they'd both won at the local gymkhanas. The divans were covered in patchwork quilts, and there were soft, fluffy rugs on the polished wooden floor. It also reminded Harriet of their student days when she and Rosa had shared a tiny unit in King's Cross. The small rooms had been more basic than this, but they'd brightened them up with cushions and curtains and big posters to cover over the damp patches on the walls. Paper flowers, scented candles and joss sticks had added touches of the exotic and made them cosy.

Her mother had been horrified and had tried her best to persuade Harriet to move into an expensive condominium in the city, but Harriet didn't want to feel different to the other students and had held out, knowing she would appreciate her student years far more by being in the same environment as her friends.

As they jostled for space between the two narrow beds, Rosa seemed to have had the same thoughts. 'Quite like old times,' she said as she squeezed past Harriet and began to towel-dry her hair. 'But it's a bit cramped and could do with a real sort out.'

Harriet smiled. 'We've been spoiled,' she said as Rosa pulled on jeans and a shirt. 'I remember you taking me to see that cottage you lived in with your grandmother. It wasn't as luxurious as this by any means.'

Rosa ruffled her damp hair until it fell like chrysanthemum petals around her face making her look about eighteen. 'You're right,' she admitted. 'In fact it was a dump. Probably the reason it's been empty for so many years.'

Because his cottage didn't have a bathroom, Connor had to wait his turn at the communal showers. He couldn't help but grin at the conversations going on around him, and the effort the men were putting in to their ablutions. He hadn't seen anything like this since the last country fair at Drum Creek. It was amazing what the sight of a couple of women could do, even though the majority of the men had known Rosa and Hattie since they were kids.

He finally managed a quick shower and shave, and changed into clean jeans and a freshly laundered shirt before following the others over to the cookhouse where he was to fetch the supper for those at the homestead. Like Belvedere, the cookhouse had been standing for almost a hundred years. It was dilapidated in places, and needed a coat of paint and new window-frames, but on the whole it was sturdy enough and would probably stand for another century as long as the termites and bush fires didn't get to it first.

As broad and long as a church, the roof soared above heavy rafters. An immense hand-crafted table ran down the middle of the dusty wooden floor, with benches on either side. There was no tablecloth, just a line of sauce bottles and condiments and baskets of freshly baked bread.

Connor walked through the door and was assailed by a wall of sound, impressed by how much noise thirty men could make. The voices echoed up into the rafters as the men swapped tales and laughed and joked, at ease at the end of another long day. The scrape of cutlery on china was accompanied by the scrape and scratch of chairs and boots on the floor. And presiding over all this was a monolith of a man: Cookie.

313

No one knew what his real name was, and if they had ever known, it had been long forgotten, for he'd been here for ever. Cookie was of indeterminate age, with a fat red face which gleamed with sweat as he served steaming vegetables and freshly grilled steaks. His arms were the size of hams, the large stomach a testament to his fondness for his own cooking. His temper was legendary and the only person who could get away with any cheek was Rosa, whom he'd adored the minute she'd arrived on Belvedere as a skinny eight-year-old. 'G'day, Connor, mate,' he shouted above the noise. 'How's my girl? She ain't been to see me yet. Tell her to get her arse in gear and come and visit her old uncle Cookie.' He leaned forward. 'Hear she brought Hattie with her this time?'

'So what?' he shouted back.

The silence was instant. Connor was aware of every eye turned to him, every ear flapping for a scrap of gossip. 'Stick the tucker on this tray,' he muttered. 'We're all eating over at the house tonight.'

'Keepin' 'em both to your bloody self, then, mate?' shouted one of the drovers.

'Yeah,' drawled Connor. 'Wouldn't let you bunch of mongrels anywhere near my flamin' sister.'

'What about the other one? Fair looker. Reckon you should share, Connor, me old mate. I'd show her a real good time.'

'Not bloody likely,' he retorted above the roar of laughter this statement elicited. He grinned as he realised the speaker was a little skinny bloke who had to be past fifty-five and lacked most of his teeth as well as any social graces. 'Don't reckon she'd go for an old bludger like you, mate. But I'll get her gran's phone number if you like.'

This caused another shout of laughter and Connor hurriedly loaded up the tray and made his escape. Striding across the clearing to the homestead, he saw that Rosa and Harriet were waiting for him on the verandah. At least they were properly dressed, he thought thankfully.

Rosa gave him a hug and a kiss. 'What was all the laughter about?' she asked as she held open the screen door and followed him into the kitchen.

'What do you think?' he muttered as he helped her put the food on the table. 'It's going to be flamin' murder trying to keep that lot in order with you two here,' he added, shooting a glance at Harriet.

'Nah,' said Rosa dismissively. 'You know what they're like, Con. All mouth and trousers. I bet if Harriet and I went over there right now they wouldn't have a word to say. They'd shovel down their food and get out, quiet as lambs.'

He grinned, for he knew this was true. The men of the Outback were unused to such exotic women as Rosa and Harriet; they were shy enough with the girls at Drum Creek pub, and more used to the masculine surroundings of the Station where they understood cattle and grass and the vagaries of the elements far better than the needs of any woman. They would see the educated Rosa and Harriet as a threat, as alien females from the city, and therefore unapproachable. Not that he was much better, he admitted silently as he tucked into his steak. Rosa he could understand, even though their lives were so distanced by her education and the life she'd made for herself in Sydney. But Harriet was a different matter.

He'd kept up with her news through Rosa's letters and although he'd known her since she was a kid, she had grown up into a very attractive young woman. It was unnerving, and made him feel uncomfortably aware of her sitting opposite him at the table. She looked so cool and sophisticated, and yet was obviously still totally at ease here on Belvedere.

He glanced up from his plate and found he was looking into eyes the colour of a deep-water pool. He held her gaze for a long moment, before he grinned and looked away. Harriet was a cool customer, there was no doubt about that, but what did she really think of Belvedere, of him? It might be interesting to find out.

Harriet climbed out of bed and stretched. She'd dreamed deeply and now felt refreshed and ready for the day. Shivering a little from the chill, she pulled a sweater over the T-shirt she used as a nightdress, grabbed a thick pair of socks and looked across at the other bed. Rosa was buried in the blankets, only the tip of her spiky hair visible as the muffled snores came from within the pillows. It would be unfair to wake her.

Harriet padded out of the bedroom and into the kitchen. The light was pouring through the window and she was amazed to find it was barely five-thirty, a time of the morning when she was usually dead to the world. She shivered again and garnered some welcome heat from the Aga. It was surprisingly cold, even though the summer was well into its stride, but she'd remembered her

315

other visits over the years and had come prepared with the thick ski-socks which she pulled on as slippers.

Moving quietly around the kitchen, she made a cup of strong tea and settled down to read an old magazine Catriona had left on the dresser. It was lovely to have the time in the morning, to sit in the silence without the urgent ring of telephones or the clatter of typewriters spoiling the peace.

'I hope there's more tea in the pot?' Rosa shuffled into the room, her hair on end, eyelids puffy with sleep. She pulled a face. 'My, you do look attractive, Hat. Love the socks!'

'It's bloody cold,' Harriet said firmly. 'And I didn't want to wake you by trying to find my clothes.' She eyed Rosa's pyjamas, which swamped her and made her look like a little kid. 'You're not exactly dressed in the height of fashion yourself,' she countered. 'Are those Connor's?'

'Yeah, found them in the bottom of a drawer. Left in such a rush I forgot to pack anything to sleep in.' Rosa poured out a cup of tea and slumped into a chair by the Aga, the sleeves of the oversize garment dangling over her hands as she fumbled with her pack of cigarettes.

Early mornings weren't her thing, unless she was coming home from a club or a party, and Harriet knew it was best to let her wake slowly and leave her to her morning tea and cigarette. She left the room, washed and dressed in loose cotton trousers and a thin T-shirt, with a sweater slung over her shoulders to chase away the chill. Dragging a brush through her hair, she twisted it into a rough chignon and anchored it with a series of brightly coloured clips. She eyed her reflection in the tiny mirror over the basin and decided she couldn't be bothered to put on any make-up – she had to wear it every day in the city, and going without it would make a pleasant change.

When she returned to the kitchen some twenty minutes later, she found Rosa hadn't moved, but was now awake enough to read the magazine. 'Go and shower. I'll do breakfast,' said Harriet. 'Have you seen Catriona yet?'

Rosa ran her fingers through her hair. 'She's not in her room,' she replied through a vast yawn. 'Probably out for her usual morning ride.' She hitched up the pyjama legs and shuffled off to the bathroom.

Harriet made the tea and toast and listened to Rosa's appalling singing coming from the bathroom. At least she was awake, she thought with a grin, but she shouldn't ever contemplate giving up the day job. With a voice like that she'd never make a career out of it.

She took her breakfast out onto the verandah and with her cup of tea balanced on the railings, stood and watched Belvedere come to life. There was smoke coming from the cookhouse chimney, and men were emerging through the doors, hands in pockets, strides slow and easy as they made their way across the clearing. The sound of a hammer on metal broke the early morning silence, and a thin veil of dust began to swirl and eddy in the corrals as the horses shifted and stamped in expectation of the day ahead.

Connor came out of the cookhouse and waved before disappearing around the corner. Harriet finished her toast and sipped her tea. He was a nice man, she admitted silently. He obviously adored Rosa and Catriona, and although he gave the impression of being tough, she had been touched by the thought behind his jam jar of wild flowers. Connor obviously had hidden depths.

'I'm going over to see Cookie,' said Rosa through a mouthful of toast as she emerged through the screen door. 'He won't speak to me again if we leave it any longer.' She finished her breakfast and looked across at Harriet. 'Coming?'

Harriet eyed the demure trousers, and the crisp cotton blouse. Rosa's hair was brushed to a shining cap of pink and black and there was only a smudge of mascara and lipstick. The jewellery had been left in the bedroom but for the silver watch on her slender wrist. Rosa looked almost respectable. 'Strewth,' she breathed. 'You look good, girl. I hardly recognised you.'

Rosa sniffed. 'Can't hide behind the make-up and clothes out here, they all know me too well,' she said. 'Come on.'

Harriet shoved her feet into comfortable loafers and they stepped down from the verandah and crossed the yard in the full glare of thirty pairs of eyes.

Connor came around the corner, his arms loaded with saddles and bridles. He didn't seem too pleased to see them. 'The homestead's that way,' he said sternly to Rosa.

'Lighten up, Con. We're just going to say g'day to Cookie.'

Connor glowered, eyed Harriet and glanced across at the men who were now standing about doing nothing. 'Make it quick,' he muttered. 'We've got a lot to do today.'

317

Rosa pecked him on the cheek. 'You know, Con, you're getting to be a real old bludger. No wonder no woman will have you.' She ducked away before he could retort and Harriet could only shrug and grin as she was left to trail after her.

Catriona hadn't slept well again, and she'd left the homestead before sun-up for her morning ride. Billy Birdsong had been down by the corrals and she'd invited him along. They had forgotten the time as they cantered across the great sweep of land, and as they talked together and discussed their plans for the place, Catriona found her cares diminishing.

She returned to see the girls disappearing into the cookhouse. The men were standing about, staring after them and she smiled as they realised she was watching them and hurriedly got on with their chores. It was amazing how the presence of two attractive girls could bring life to a grinding halt.

'Reckon them girls betta watch out,' said Billy with a broad grin. 'Fella's watch 'im good.'

Catriona grinned back. 'I think those two are perfectly capable of handling themselves, Billy. Don't you worry.' She waved goodbye to him as he strolled off to see what his wife and family were up to.

Billy's family had had an encampment here since before her time, but they still refused to live in the shacks she wanted to build for them, preferring the humpies and tents that were gathered on the western side of the clearing. This encampment was unhygienic, cluttered with rubbish and the remains of their fires. Dogs and kids played in the dirt and the women sat most of the day under the trees, suckling their babies and swapping gossip.

Catriona turned her back and began to rub down her horse. She'd tried to teach them the rudiments of cleanliness, and had eventually coaxed them into seeing the doctor when he came out, and to inoculate their babies, but that was as far as she'd got. Billy had come to her finally and had told her his people didn't need the white man's medicine and that they preferred to stick to their tribal ways.

She set the horse free in the paddock. Billy's extended family were surprisingly healthy, most of them well behaved and useful about the place; the only problem was with alcohol. She and Billy had discussed this, and he'd brought in the other Elders and made

318

it a rule no one was to touch the stuff. But every now and then one of the young jackaroos spent his wages in the pub and would return to the Station ready for a fight.

She sighed. With ownership came responsibility, but she wouldn't swop any of it for a life in the city. She turned her back on the corrals and headed for the homestead and breakfast. She was starving.

Archie complained long and loud that it was way past his breakfast time, and as he wound himself around her legs and got in the way, Catriona trod on his paw and almost fell over him as he shot through her feet. Grasping the rail in front of the Aga to steady herself, she burned her hand. 'Damn and blast the bloody thing,' she hissed as she ran her hand under the cold tap. 'As for you, Archie. You'll be the bloody death of me.'

Archie's yowls were louder now and more demanding. He was being kept waiting and he didn't like it.

'There,' she said as she slammed the bowl on the floor. 'Eat that and for God's sake shut up.' Her head swam as she stood upright too quickly, and she grasped a chair to steady herself until the blackness cleared.

'Mum? Are you all right?'

She looked up at Rosa and Harriet through the swirl of darkness. 'I'll be right,' she breathed. 'Just need to sit down for a minute.' She allowed Rosa to help her into a chair and accepted the cup of strong tea. 'I'm all right, really,' she insisted. 'Just done too much on an empty stomach, that's all.' She sipped the tea and grimaced. Rosa had put a lot of sugar in it.

'You need sugar to boost your energy,' said Rosa firmly. 'So don't pull faces at me. Go on, drink it all up.'

Catriona raised an eyebrow at Harriet. 'Bossy little thing. Never could take orders herself, mind. Now she's making me feel as if I'm her naughty child and have completely lost my marbles.' She glared at Rosa over the lip of the mug, grimaced again and drank her tea. It was foul, but she had to admit it went a long way towards reviving her.

'I'll get you some breakfast,' said Harriet. 'What would you like?'

'A bit of toast and some bacon and eggs, please.' The darkness had been banished and she felt much better.

Rosa started banging the flying pan about as Harriet searched the fridge for the bacon. 'Sugar deficiency,' she stated. 'You really should eat before you go out, Mum. Cookie would be only too pleased to feed you. He told me so this morning.'

Catriona closed her eyes and took a deep breath. Rosa sounded like a bossy schoolmistress. 'When I want his help I'll ask for it,' she said firmly. 'My appetite is fine, always has been, and I'll thank you to mind your own business, Rosa.' She opened her eyes. 'I know you mean well, but I don't need Cookie running after me just yet.' She smiled at them to take the sting out of her mild rebuke. 'Archie and I are both getting older and less agile, we're too set in our ways for change, and we like cooking our own meals.'

'That damn Archie's a spoilt brat,' muttered Rosa as she eyed the fat ginger tom preening in front of the Aga. 'He does nothing but sleep and eat and get under your feet.'

'He's my mate,' said Catriona. 'And if I don't mind him sleeping on my bed and getting under my feet, then neither should you. Leave him alone.' She ignored Rosa's muttering, finished the tea and stood. 'If you want to help, you can make me another cup of tea with less sugar, and bring my breakfast into the lounge.' She waved away Rosa's protest. 'Harriet, you come with me. I've got something to show you.'

Harriet followed her into the lounge, wondering what on earth Catriona was planning now. She had more colour in her face, and seemed quite herself again, but it had been a shock to come into the kitchen and find her so obviously out of sorts.

Catriona pointed at the roll-top desk as she sat down on the couch. 'My will's in there,' she said. 'And all the papers Rosa will need when I'm gone.' She must have seen the denial on Harriet's face, for she shook her head impatiently. 'Don't look like that Hattie. I've always been a realist, and one day you'll need to know these things.'

Harriet hovered and bit her lip. 'Don't you think it would be better if Rosa . . .?' She didn't get a chance to finish the sentence.

'If I'd wanted Rosa to sort them out, I would have asked her,' she said firmly.

Harriet bit her lip. 'Those documents should be lodged with a solicitor, not left lying about where they could get lost or destroyed.'

'I know. That's why I wanted to talk to you. Will you fetch them, dear?'

320

Harriet walked over to the desk and opened the lid. A waterfall of papers and old theatre programmes slid out and floated to the floor. She bent to retrieve them, her attention caught by the brightly coloured programmes from London, Paris and New York, play bills from theatres renowned the world over and a collection of letters from admirers.

'That's only a part of my life,' said Catriona from the other side of the room. 'The rest is in that damn trunk, but then you know that, you and Rosa have tried on the dresses often enough.' She laughed. 'I suppose I ought to go through it myself and sort it out once and for all. Most of it is junk.'

Harriet swept everything together and put the pile to one side. Sifting through the collection of memorabilia in the desk, she finally found what she was looking for. She handed them to Catriona who swiftly looked through them and handed them back. 'Read them and make sure everything is in order.'

Harriet read through the deeds. Catriona had signed Belvedere over to Rosa and her brother ten years before, thereby avoiding inheritance tax. 'Do they know they already own this place?' she asked.

Catriona shook her head. 'My accountant advised me to do it, and they don't need to know until I'm dead.'

Harriet sifted through the rest of the papers. Her eyes widened as she read down the long list of properties and stocks and shares Catriona had in her portfolio. Widened further as she noted the amount of valuable jewellery she had amassed. 'I hope this jewellery is somewhere safe,' she breathed. 'It must be worth a fortune.'

'Most of it's in a safety deposit box in Sydney. There should be a letter there from the bank confirming it's in trust for Rosa and Connor's children – if they ever get around to having any,' she added. 'The paintings are on permanent loan to the Victorian Art Gallery in Melbourne.'

Harriet looked at her in admiration. Catriona was a clever, resourceful woman. She had put her affairs in perfect order and the tax man would find very little to get his sticky hands on. The will was the last document, and Harriet read through it swiftly. It had been drawn up twenty years ago, signed and witnessed by two board members of a well-known bank. There was only one codicil, added five years later. She read the words, read them again and

321

for a third time. She looked over at Catriona. 'This codicil,' she began, her voice husky, hands trembling. 'Are you sure . . .?'

Catriona waved away her doubts. 'You've been like a daughter to me, Harriet. And if I want to leave you a little something, then I will.'

'Three apartment blocks is rather more than a little something,' she protested. 'Just one of those properties has to be worth over a million dollars.'

Chapter Twenty-Three

Catriona tucked into the breakfast and cleared the plate. When she'd finished she drank the tea and carried the dirty dishes into the kitchen. 'I'm off to see Billy's wife. I need her and the other girls to help spring clean this place before the hordes descend.' She waved away their offers of help. 'You're here on holiday, and as I'm not going to be doing my own housework, I don't see why you should.'

'But we don't mind,' protested Harriet.

'Well, I do,' retorted Catriona. 'Go and find something nice to occupy yourselves for the rest of the day. Youth shouldn't be spent doing chores.'

Harriet and Rosa looked at each other as Catriona slammed through the screen door. They listened to the rapid tattoo of her boot-heels on the verandah floor and heard her calling to one of the men to get on with his work and stop hanging about the homestead.

'They broke the mould when she was made,' murmured Harriet. 'She's definitely unique.'

'She's a pain in the rear end,' snorted Rosa. 'She won't let anyone help her, and is as stubborn as a bloody mule.' She lit a cigarette and shot a plume of smoke up to the ceiling. 'You realise, of course, she was lying about that lover and the blackmail?'

'Yes,' Harriet replied. 'She's avoided the issue entirely, and it will be like pulling hens' teeth to get to the bottom of what is really worrying her.'

'What was all that about in there? Why did she want to see you?'

Harriet bit her lip – it was confidential. 'She just wanted me to go through some of her papers,' she said finally.

'What were they?'

'Just her will, and some deeds and things.' Harriet hesitated. 'I shouldn't worry, Rosa. Everything's in order.'

Rosa stubbed out her cigarette. 'Let's hope it's a very long time before they have to see the light of day again,' she said firmly. She shook her head as if to dismiss the dismal thoughts. 'How about a cut lunch, and a ride out to our favourite picnic spot?'

They worked in companionable silence until Rosa burst out laughing. 'No wonder Mum was so good on the stage,' she said as she packed the sandwiches in greaseproof paper. 'She's a born actress.'

'Yeah, she nearly had me fooled as well,' muttered Harriet.

Rosa grinned as she grabbed some wine from the gas fridge and began to pack the saddle-bag. 'I never told you this, but when I was really little I wanted to be an actress.' She giggled at Harriet's startled expression. 'I even contemplated following Catriona into the opera.'

Harriet laughed. 'You've got to be kidding,' she spluttered. 'With that voice?'

Rosa's giggle was deep in her throat. 'I didn't know it was that bad, not then, anyway. I was twelve when an extremely honest singing coach told me he'd rather listen to a chorus of cane toads, and that I should set my sights on something else. Ever the realist, I accepted his judgement, and I think Mum was quite relieved.' She shook her head. 'It must have been hell having to listen to me practising, and I suspect she only got the coach out here to shut me up.'

Rosa's giggle was infectious and Harriet joined in as they gathered up cheese and salad and finished packing the saddle-bag. She could just imagine Catriona's torment at having to listen to Rosa's singing. It certainly hadn't improved if this morning's effort was anything to go by. 'The law has gained a diva of a different kind,' she said finally. 'You might not get the curtain calls and the bouquets, but at least you've found what you do best. I should stick to it, if I were you.'

Connor had spent the morning going through the accounts and making telephone calls to various suppliers. He'd been constantly interrupted by men coming and asking damn fool questions which they could have sorted out for themselves if only they'd given them a bit of thought. With an exasperated sigh he slammed the account books shut and dumped them on the desk.

His office was a square room which had been added to the side of the cookhouse, and although the ceiling-fan did its best to stir some life into the air, the reminder of thousands of meals still clung to the walls. He shoved back his chair and went outside to check on the men and the tasks he'd set them for the day.

Billy Birdsong was squatting in the shade of the machine shed, his deft fingers neatly rolling a smoke. 'G'day, boss,' he drawled, his bloodshot eyes peering at Connor through the tangle of greying ochre hair.

Connor looked down at the Aborigine. No one knew how old he was, and he suspected even Billy had no idea. Billy Birdsong was a mainstay of Belvedere. He had taught him all he knew, and was Connor's mentor and best friend. 'G'day, mate. You finished with the ute?'

'Yeah, boss.' The Aborigine lit his smoke. 'Reckon she'll be right. But the gearbox is crook – soon have to change it.'

Connor nodded. It was what he'd suspected. The ute was old with so many kilometres on the clock it was a miracle it still went at all. If it hadn't been for Billy's wizardry in mechanics it would have died years ago. He was about to move away when Billy's voice stopped him. 'What's with the missus, boss? She crook?'

Connor shook his head. 'Not that I've noticed,' he muttered. Nothing much went on out here without everyone knowing about it, but he was surprised to hear Catriona might not be well. She'd seemed okay last night, a bit tired, maybe, but that was to be expected with all the plans she'd been making for her party. 'Why, Bill? What've you noticed?'

'Nutting,' he said through the cigarette smoke. 'Bit tired, alonga me this sun-up, is all.'

'Everyone's tired at that time of the morning, mate.'

Billy nodded, then he grinned. 'Good see Rosa again,' he said. 'Fair grown up, now. Like my boys.' He sighed. 'Time goes fast, boss. Reckon soon be right for Billy Birdsong go last walkabout, make peace with totem spirits.'

Connor was startled by this pronouncement from the man he'd admired since boyhood. Surely Billy wasn't that old? 'Plenty of life in you yet, you old bludger,' he said fondly. 'What the hell would the boss lady do without you around to mend all the machinery and tell tall tales? If it's a few days off you're wanting, then take them. But I need you here for a while yet, so don't go getting any ideas of disappearing.'

The Aborigine slowly shook his head, his eyes thoughtful as the cigarette smoke drifted over his face. 'If spirits sing Billy then he have to go,' he said softly. 'Reckon boss lady know what I mean.'

Connor eyed him carefully. He'd learned the stories of the Dreamtime from this man. Had sat for hours listening to his sing-song voice as he'd explained about the importance of walkabout, and the traditions of the corroboree, but there were other, stronger, more mysterious forces at work in the tribal culture of the Aborigines that no white man, even Connor, could logically explain. 'What are you trying to tell me, Billy?' he asked.

Billy stared into the distance. 'Spirits sing,' he said. 'We have to follow.' The amber eyes held centuries of ancient knowledge as they looked back at him. 'Same for missus. Only she hear different song to black-fella.'

Connor rammed his hands into the pockets of his jeans. 'Don't let her hear you talk like that, mate,' he said gruffly. 'She'll fair have your guts for garters.'

Billy grinned, exposing yellow tombstone teeth. 'Reckon she put up a fight, boss. No worries. She ain't ready yet, still work to be done here.'

Connor frowned and would have questioned Billy more closely, but the Aborigine stood and ambled away, bringing the conversation to an end. Connor turned and headed for the homestead. All this talk of singing spirits and death was unsettling, and he wanted to know just what the hell was going on.

He'd reached the bottom step when Rosa opened the screen door and stepped out onto the verandah. She was closely followed by Harriet, both of them laughing and looking cheerful. 'How ya goin'?' he asked.

Rosa grinned and gave him a hug. 'Good,' she replied as she ran her fingers through her hair. 'We're off for a picnic.'

Connor realised he was probably over-reacting to one of Billy's dark, mysterious flights of fancy. If there was anything wrong with Ma, Rosa would know about it, and by the look of things, he had nothing to worry about. He grinned down at her, still trying to equate this sophisticated young woman with the larrikin his sister had always been.

326

She squinted up at him. 'Got any decent horses on this place?' she asked. 'I feel the need for speed.'

Connor scratched the scar on his chin and tried to look doubtful. His sister was a demon rider, perhaps a little too enthusiastic and daring for his liking, but he could trust her with any horse on the place. He eyed Harriet. 'I suppose that's an order for two of the fastest, and most belligerent horses we've got, then?'

Harriet smiled, her face lighting up with pleasure. 'Of course,' she replied. 'You know me, Con. Can't let Rosa get away with showing off on her own.'

'Why don't you come too, Con?' asked Rosa, shielding her eyes from the sun. 'Loosen your stays a bit, and relax.'

Connor shook his head. 'Too much to do here,' he said with regret. Then he had a flash of inspiration. 'But what about tonight? Remember how it used to be with Billy Birdsong?'

Rosa's smile was soft with memory, her gaze distant as she stared out towards the horizon. 'Oh, yes,' she breathed. 'How could I ever forget?'

'Might even manage to persuade Ma to come with us,' muttered Connor. 'Be quite like old times.'

Rosa turned to Harriet. 'Remember you're first time, Hat? Bonzer, wasn't it?'

Harriet would never forget it, and the thought of going out into the night, of letting go of all earthly cares and floating up with the stars was enticing. 'Reckon so,' she sighed.

Connor linked arms with them as they strolled across the yard to the tack-room. Having found boots and bush-hats for them, he stood by the weathered railings and watched them tack up before trotting their mounts out of the yard. His sister had chosen the stroppy roan, just as he'd known she would, but Harriet had gone for the chestnut, a flashy gelding that stood sixteen hands and had an ego the size of Queensland.

'Now that's what I call a sight for sore eyes,' murmured one of the drovers.

Connor realised he wasn't the only one smiling in admiration at Harriet's neat rear end which rose from the saddle as she nudged the chestnut into a gallop. She was a fair looking Sheila and no mistake. And she certainly knew how to ride. That fancy school she and his sister had attended had been good for something.

*

327

Tom Bradley glanced at Belinda and grinned. She wasn't enjoying the trip. He could tell by the slight green tinge to her tanned skin, and the way her fingers were clawed around the armrest.

As if reading his thoughts, Belinda grimaced, her eyes firmly shut. 'I don't know why I agreed to come with you,' she said through gritted teeth. 'I hate flying at the best of times, but this damn thing's likely to drop out of the sky any minute.'

'This helicopter is perfectly safe,' he shouted through the mouth-piece that was attached to the headphones. 'It's been checked over and the pilot's an old hand at flying her. Isn't that right, mate?'

'Too right,' replied the Vietnam Veteran over his shoulder, his voice almost drowned by the clatter and rattle of the aircraft. 'This old crate and me go way back. She wouldn't dare drop out of the sky after all the years we've been together.' As if to prove it, he swung the thing back and forth, and executed a series of tight turns. He'd flown over a hundred missions in 'Nam, and still piloted his craft as if he was under enemy fire; as far as he was concerned, it was the only way to fly.

Tom grinned and patted Belinda's hand. 'See? No worries, mate. She'll be right.'

'*She* might,' Belinda snapped. 'But that's typical of you blokes. One word from you and Biggles there, and I'm supposed to relax and believe we won't go plummeting to our deaths. What if we're hit by a flock of birds? What if the wind gets up? Or ... Or ...' She seemed to run out of words and out of breath.

'Trust me,' he said.

Belinda opened a scornful eye, her expression telling him he'd said the wrong thing, again. There was just no helping some people. He left her to her fears and looked out of the window. Far beneath them the Outback of Australia was laid out like a green and red patchwork quilt, stitched together by stands of trees, salt pans and mountain ranges. The glinting waters of billabongs and lakes and the endless pastures gave way to mountains and water-falls, and on to dusty miles of ochre interspersed with thousands of acres of wheat that rippled like a great yellow sea in the down-draught of the 'copter's blades. Tom experienced the overwhelming sense of pride that always came when he travelled across his country. For this was his land, his heritage, and there was nothing like it the world over.

He turned back to Belinda, wanting to share the scenery with her, but she was still rigid in her seat, eyes tightly shut, hands clawed around the armrest. She wouldn't appreciate anything in that state, he thought. He watched her for a moment, admiring the battle she was putting up against her fear of flying. Belinda was a good officer, fun to work with and as honest as the day. He hadn't had to persuade her to accompany him, not once he'd explained why he needed to speak to Catriona. He sighed. At least he'd distanced himself from Wolff, and that had to be a bonus.

Belinda groaned as the helicopter tilted in a long, sweeping turn west and then dipped so low it almost touched the tree-tops. 'How much longer is this torture going to take?'

Tom eyed her. The green tinge had definitely deepened. 'I hope you're not about to throw a rainbow yawn?' he asked uneasily.

'If I do,' she retorted through gritted teeth. 'I'll make sure it's all over you.'

Tom bit his lip and tried not to laugh. 'We should be there in about two hours,' he said, his voice unsteady. 'Try to concentrate on something else. It might make you feel better.'

'I doubt it,' she muttered. 'And don't you dare laugh at me, or, I swear, I'll kill you.'

He blew his nose, hiding his smile in the handkerchief until he was sure he had the laughter under control. Poor Belinda. For all her swagger and verve, she had an Achilles heel. Life on an Outback sheep station obviously hadn't prepared her for helicopter rides with Sam Richmond.

Tom turned away and looked once again out of the window as Sam manoeuvred the little machine through the Great Dividing Range. They were getting closer to Belvedere, and he hoped that by having Belinda with him, he could persuade Catriona Summers to talk. If she didn't, then there would be complications. For his boss had made it plain he wanted some kind of result from this visit.

Harriet and Rosa had been out for hours. They slowed their horses to a walk as they neared Belvedere, almost reluctant to leave the wide open spaces they had ridden across and knew so well. The heat was intense, shimmering in a watery mirage that submerged the homestead and outbuildings and made the trees look as if they were growing in a great, restless sea. A mob of kangaroos drowsed in languid disarray in the long grass beneath a stand of eucalypt,

329

their ears twitching at the noisome clouds of flies that hovered over them, their curiosity fleeting as they eyed the riders and returned to their sleep. The bush was alive with the sibilant chatter of a million insects, the birds' calls muted as though they didn't have the energy to chirp and chatter in such heat.

'What the hell is that?' Rosa pulled up her horse and shielded her eyes as she looked towards the sun.

'Sounds like a helicopter,' muttered Harriet as she searched the endless sky. 'Yes. Look. Over there.'

'Bloody hell,' muttered Rosa, kicking her horse into a startled trot. 'It's heading this way. God knows what chaos it'll cause in the pens.'

They galloped into the yard and were met by Connor and the other men who'd stopped work and come out to see what the noise was. Harriet and Rosa swung down from their saddles as the helicopter clattered above home paddock. Dust swirled in a blinding cloud as the trees bent and thrashed and the grass was flattened. The horses pulled and propped and danced on their toes, ears tight to their heads, eyes wide in terror. The breeding cows bellowed and stamped and skittered back and forth in the pens, while the native dogs barked alongside the blue-heelers. The stock horses whinnied and pawed the air before racing away to the far end of the paddocks. It was chaos.

Harriet and Rosa struggled to calm their mounts, and in the blinding fury of the dust-storm were bumped and jostled and in danger of being trampled. Harriet could see nothing, could hear nothing but the awful machine-gun rattle of the helicopter blades and the terrified screams of her horse. She had no idea where she was going in that thick red blanket of stinging dirt and blinding grit, and the gelding was pulling so hard on the reins it was only a matter of time before he broke free. Yet she had to hold on, had to find shelter however poor, for if the gelding broke loose he'd probably do himself some serious harm.

A strong arm encircled her waist and a competent hand covered hers and took the reins. She found she was being led through the fury and into the lee of the stables where she blinked the grit from her eyes and tried to catch her breath enough to thank her saviour.

'Reckon you'll be right now, miss,' said Billy Birdsong as he gentled the gelding. His dark face split into a wide grin, but the amber eyes held little humour as he looked over his shoulder at the

330

helicopter that had come to rest in the paddock. 'Bluddy fools,' he muttered. 'Alonga here, make trouble.'

'Thank you, Billy,' she gasped as she mopped her face with a handkerchief and tried to get the worst of the dust out of her eyes. 'I don't know what I would have done without your help.'

'No worries,' he drawled. 'You alonga missus. She need you, I reckon.'

'Come on, Hat,' yelled Rosa. 'I'm going to give those dickheads a piece of my mind.'

'I'll catch you up when I've seen to the horses,' shouted Connor to their retreating backs. 'And be nice, Rosa,' he added. 'Remember you're supposed to be a lady,' he muttered to himself.

'Like hell I will,' Rosa retorted.

Harriet was in no mood for polite conversation either. She hadn't appreciated the noise and the potential danger all of them had been in because of the idiots in that helicopter, and with every stride through the long grass, her temper grew.

The blades were still turning, the clattering down-draught battering them as they were forced to come to a halt on the edge of the paddock. The door opened and two figures emerged. They were bent double as they ran from beneath the blades to safety, their backpacks bumping them as they moved. 'Looks like they're planning on staying,' Rosa snapped. 'What do they think this is, a bloody camp-site?'

Harriet's reply was lost in the roar of the helicopter engine as the machine rose once again and headed back over the hills. She and Rosa turned their backs, their hair whipping their faces in the thrusting wind that threatened to knock them down.

'Sorry about that. I hope no one was hurt?'

Harriet and Rosa turned as one and glared at the dark-haired man. 'More by luck than sodding judgement,' yelled Rosa above the noise.

'What the hell did you think you were doing, bringing that thing so close to the homestead and stables? Of all the stupid, thoughtless, ignorant, idiotic ...' Harriet found she'd run out of words as she became aware of the amusement in the brown eyes that looked so steadily down at her.

His companion finally turned round. 'I did tell that idiot pilot it wasn't a good idea,' she said. 'But like all men, he thought he knew better.'

'Belinda!' They both rushed forward and enveloped her in a

331

group hug. 'What the bloody hell are you doing here?' asked Rosa as she pulled away. 'You said you couldn't come.'

Belinda grinned and tried to bring some order to her hair. 'I know,' she said ruefully. 'But something came up.'

'What's with the chopper?' demanded Harriet, glaring once more at the man by her side. 'And who's this?'

A hand was thrust forward. 'Detective Inspector Tom Bradley,' he said. 'Sorry about that, but Sam gets a bit carried away.' He grinned. 'Still thinks he's in 'Nam.'

Tom was lost in a pair of blue eyes. He could see flecks of green and violet and was reminded of a stormy sea. He noticed how the sun glinted gold in the thick eyelashes, and how the sprinkling of freckles enhanced the delicate skin of that beautiful, dusty face. Her hair was long, tumbling about her shoulders in a blonde mass, tendrils of which snaked to caress her cheek and kiss the very corners of her delicately formed mouth. He wanted more than anything to be that golden tendril. Wanted to watch those eyes and see them change with her mood. The sharp dig in his ribs jolted him back to reality. He hadn't heard a thing that had been said. He glanced at Belinda, saw the amusement in her eyes and reddened as he realised he was still holding the blonde woman's hand. He cleared his throat. 'G'day,' he said. 'Call me Tom.'

Her grasp was firm, the handshake almost brusque, yet it had been enough to send a shock wave through him. 'Harriet,' she said without a smile. 'This is Rosa.'

Tom dragged his attention from Harriet and looked down into an elfin face and intelligent eyes. 'Good to meet you,' he drawled. 'I'm sorry about that.' It was interesting at last to put a face to the person he'd heard about from Belinda, but as attractive as she was she was no match for Harriet, and he found he couldn't help but glance over to her, hoping for one more chance to look into her eyes.

'I didn't realise you had a boyfriend, Belinda,' said Rosa, digging her friend in the ribs with a sharp elbow. 'You kept him quiet. What's wrong with him?'

Belinda picked up her backpack and slung it over her shoulder. 'He's not my boyfriend,' she hissed. 'He's my boss.'

'Your boss?' Rosa and Harriet turned to look at him. 'Why did you bring your boss to Mum's party?' There was a moment of awkward silence before Rosa spoke again. 'This isn't a social call, is it, Belinda.'

'No,' butted in Tom hastily. 'Look, it's nothing dramatic, so there's no need to get your knickers into a twist. We just need to talk to Dame Catriona.'

'Why?' Harriet faced him, her expression fixed, her magnificent eyes regarding him fiercely.

'That's something I can only discuss with Dame Catriona,' he replied, his eyes pleading with her to try and understand his predicament. 'My boss thought it was a good idea for us to come out here and talk to her. Belinda's here because I asked her to come.'

'How could you, Belinda?' Rosa's arms were folded, her stance defensive. 'Why didn't you at least phone and give us a bit of a warning?'

'I did,' she replied. 'I spoke to Catriona yesterday afternoon.'

'She never said anything,' muttered Harriet, the golden lashes sparking in the sun.

Tom was drowning again and had to make a concerted effort to remain fully in control of his thoughts, and the situation. 'I have the greatest respect for Catriona Summers,' he said firmly. 'And have absolutely no intention of being underhand about this. I would really like you to understand that neither I or Belinda will do anything to upset her. But I have a job to do.'

Harriet noticed the way the sun struck gold in the brown eyes, and how stray threads of silver sparked in the tousled hair at his temples. The touch of his hand had been fleeting as they were introduced, but she'd had the impression of strength, of honesty and earnestness in that firm grip. Now she recognised the tight control over his emotions as he pleaded his case. There was something about Tom Bradley she found infinitely appealing, and even though their acquaintance was fleeting, she felt a strangely deep conviction that she could trust him.

'It's up to Catriona,' she said as the brown eyes held her. 'But as her lawyers, we are entitled to be there at all times if she decides to co-operate with you.'

He smiled, his face lighting up, the dark eyes lively with relief. 'Thank you.'

'Don't thank me,' said Harriet with a returning smile. 'Catriona

333

hasn't agreed to anything yet and none of us has the slightest idea of what is going on.' It was a broad hint, one that was studiously ignored by both officers.

Connor's knee was on fire. In his fear, the horse had kicked him, and had caught the old scar with one hell of a wallop. He limped over from the corrals, determined to sort out the fools who'd caused such chaos in his yard. He could see the man clearly, but his companion, a woman, was standing in his shadow. No matter, he thought crossly. He'd give them both a large piece of his mind and send them packing.

He was within yards of the small group on the edge of the paddock when the woman emerged from the shadows. There was something familiar about her he couldn't place but he knew that if he'd seen her before, he would have remembered her. She was gorgeous. Nevertheless, he was not going to let that deter him. 'I'm the manager here,' he yelled. 'And next time you mongrels land a 'copter in one of my fields, I'll sue the pants off you.'

'Promises, promises. G'day, Connor. How y'goin'?'

He came to an abrupt halt. There was no mistaking that voice. 'Belinda?' He gaped at the luscious figure in the tight jeans, the beautiful face and halo of dark curls.

'Got it in one. Long time, no see, Con.' She grinned. 'Careful, mate, you'll catch flies.'

He snapped his mouth shut, and blushed furiously. That had certainly taken the wind out of his argument and no mistake. Yet he couldn't stop looking at her. Surely this couldn't really be that awful little fat pest who used to follow him around and make his life a misery?

'You don't look so bad yourself,' she teased as if she could read his thoughts.

'Let the dog see the rabbit,' shouted Catriona as she ran through them and hugged Belinda. 'It's so lovely to see you again after so long,' she breathed into the thick hair. She drew back and studied her. 'Whew,' she said. 'No wonder you've knocked Connor sideways. The last time I saw you, you had plaits and were charging about in dungarees.'

Belinda hugged her swiftly and then stood back again and studied her with disconcerting honesty. 'Look, Catriona,' she began. 'I didn't want any of this, but I thought it best if I came to make sure you were OK.'

She glanced across at Tom. 'Me and Tom have taken a few days out of our holiday entitlement to be here, so it's unofficial, official business, if you see what I mean. And I'm sorry it's come at the wrong time. I'd forgotten about your birthday party.'

Catriona shook her head. 'No worries, darling. I know this is none of your doing.'

Connor realised there was little point in trying to make sense of exactly what was going on. Belinda was obviously here on police business, but what on earth it had to do with Ma, he had no idea. No doubt someone would tell him sooner or later. He looked at Belinda and her expressive eyes glinted. Connor found he was grinning back. This grown-up, gorgeous Belinda was easy to like, and he admired her style. He eyed the heavy rucksack at her feet and reached to pick it up.

Belinda got there first. 'Nah. You're right. I can manage,' she said cheerfully as she swung it easily onto her back. 'But I could do with the bathroom.' She grimaced. 'Hate flying. Hate helicopters even more. Feeling a bit crook, if you know what I mean.'

He looked at her more closely and noticed the green tinge around the expressive mouth. 'Better come up to the homestead. You can use your old room.'

'Thanks,' she muttered. With the heavy bag bouncing on her back, she matched him stride for stride as they led the way to the homestead.

Rosa slowly followed her brother and Belinda across the yard. What the hell was going on? Mum obviously knew what it was all about, and would no doubt enlighten them when she felt the need, but it was frustrating not to be in charge of all the facts, especially since Harriet had told Bradley they were Catriona's solicitors. She snapped out of her thoughts when she realised the policeman was walking beside her. She eyed the bulky haversack he carried on his back. 'You'd better dump that over at the bunkhouse. We don't have guest accommodation here.'

Tom didn't seem at all put out by her sharpness. 'I brought a tent,' he replied.

'Well, aren't you the boy scout?' she said with scorn.

'Nothing wrong with being prepared for every eventuality,' he countered.

Harriet stepped between them. 'Time out, guys.' She smiled and

335

shook her head. 'You sound like a couple of kids. How about a cup of tea, Rosa? I'm sure we could all do with one.'

'That sounds an excellent idea,' said Catriona. 'And how very thoughtful of you to make your own sleeping arrangements, Tom,' she said with a smile. 'But there's plenty of spare beds around the place, you don't have to be uncomfortable.'

'No worries,' he drawled. 'I like camping, especially out here.'

'In that case, Harriet, show him where to pitch his tent. Under the old Coolibah is probably the best place.'

Harriet glared, her mouth open ready to protest. Catriona glared back and Harriet stomped off towards the Coolibah, not waiting to see if Tom was following.

Catriona smiled at Rosa. 'Come on, let's get the tea brewed.'

'What's going on?' asked Rosa as she lengthened her stride to keep up with her. 'Why didn't you tell us Belinda was coming, and why are the police interested in talking to you?'

Catriona ran up the steps and slammed through the screen door. Archie, was, as usual, shouting to be fed. She scooped the mess from the can and put it in Archie's bowl. 'Perhaps I have been somewhat liberal with the truth,' she began. 'But it's really nothing for you girls to worry about.'

'If it's not important,' she retorted, hands on hips. 'Then there's no harm in telling us about it.'

Catriona sat down at the table, her fingers plucking at the pages of an old newspaper that was lying there. 'I know you mean well, darling,' she said with a sigh. 'But I don't need protecting.'

Rosa folded her arms and glowered. The exasperation was overwhelming and she was about to lose her temper for the second time that day. 'So, tell me what this is all about,' she snapped.

Catriona straightened her back, the determination clear on her face. 'I'll tell everyone everything in my own time, Rosa. For now, you'll just have to humour me.'

'Rosa doesn't mean to be so prickly,' said Harriet as she walked across the yard beside Tom. 'But Catriona's been like a mother to all of us, and we're just trying to make some sense of what is going on.'

Tom could see only her profile as she stared ahead. The soft curve of her cheek and the sweep of her delicate brow above the slightly turned-up nose were so appealing he almost forgot why he

336

was here. With enormous effort, he willed himself to concentrate. 'I can understand that,' he replied. 'I feel kind of protective about her too.'

Harriet came to a standstill, hands in the pockets of her trousers, eyes quizzical as she looked up at him. 'Why?'

He hitched the bag to a more comfortable spot on his shoulder. 'Because I love her music,' he replied with simple sincerity. 'Her voice was so pure, the passion so deep, it gives me goose bumps every time I hear her sing.'

Harriet raised an eyebrow, a glimmer of humour in her eyes. 'You surprise me,' she said. 'I wouldn't have you down as an opera buff.'

'Not all policemen are philistines,' he muttered.

She reddened and looked away. 'Sorry. I didn't mean to be rude.'

He tried to make light of it, for he didn't want her to find fault in him. 'No worries. It's a common assumption that all coppers are meat-heads.' They began to walk again and he explained his reasons for admiring Catriona. 'My dad was a huge fan. He had all her records, and I grew up in a house that fairly rang with opera. Rock and roll and heavy metal are for parties, opera touches all the senses and allows the imagination to fly.' He reddened as he realised he was beginning to sound like a train-spotter, and changed the subject. 'Do you live out here?'

Harriet shook her head. 'I live in Sydney. But this my second home,' she replied. 'Although there are some who would rather I didn't.'

Her reply intrigued him, and he thought he saw a fleeting shadow of something in those lovely eyes which belied the almost careless tone of her voice. It would be interesting to find out more, but not yet. She had to trust him first.

Catriona had chosen the site well, he realised as he finished pegging in the tent. It was within a short walk to the cookhouse and the wash-block, and across home yard from the main house. Set on a level strip above the river-bank, sheltered by trees and clear of any clumps of spinnifex that might be hiding a nest of snakes, it was the perfect place to while away the hours with a fishing rod. If he'd thought to bring one, he thought ruefully.

'This isn't a bloody holiday,' he muttered. 'Won't be time for fishing.'

337

Despite his reasons for being here, he realised how at peace he was. It had been many years since he'd camped. The last time had been up in the Blue Mountains with his sons, but they now deemed themselves too adult and sophisticated for such things, and preferred surfing. He grinned as he thought about the only time he'd tried riding the waves at Surfers. Nearly drowned his bloody self, and ended up so stiff and sore he could hardly walk for a week. The boys had thought it hilarious, with jokes about age and decrepitude, some of which had hit the spot, he admitted. But it had been fun nevertheless.

He rolled out the sleeping bag, sorted through the few clothes he'd brought with him, and collected all the paperwork he would need for later. Zipping up the one-man tent against any creepy-crawlies that might think it was a good hiding place, he sat down on the old wooden bench that ran around the bole of the spreading Coolibah and thought about Harriet and the startling effect she'd had on him.

His job meant he had to be a realist, some would even say a cynic. And he supposed he was. A man couldn't work for so many years amongst degradation and violence without being affected by it. The sights and sounds and the stories he had to listen to day after day had been like water dripping on stone, wearing away the softness, leaving only hard, brittle edges to the man he'd once been. His wife hadn't liked this different Tom, and had left. His kids had become strangers, and now preferred the company of their stepfather. So how on earth had he allowed himself to fall so hard, so swiftly, and why was he feeling so happy about it, so confident that Harriet found him attractive even though she'd given no sign? After all, he reasoned, what on earth could such a beautiful and obviously intelligent woman see in him?

Tom picked up a pebble and tossed it into the clear rivulet of water that chuckled over the gravel bed of the stream. Love at first sight was a myth, something written about in women's magazines and not to be taken seriously. It was ridiculous to feel so strongly on such fleeting acquaintance, especially when the recipient probably saw him as a threat.

He tried to dismiss the whole idea. He was too long in the tooth for all this nonsense, he told himself sternly. And yet he couldn't deny the thunderbolt that had struck him when he'd first looked into her eyes. Couldn't ignore the frisson of pleasure he'd experi-

338

enced as he'd walked and talked with her or the compelling need he had to just look at her. If that wasn't love then he didn't know what else to call it.

He tossed another pebble and watched the diamonds of water sparkle in the sunlight. The whole situation was ridiculous. Harriet was the sort of woman who, in different circumstances, wouldn't have given him the time of day. She was beautiful as well as being a lawyer, and had obviously benefited from an exclusive education and wealthy background. The signs were there, if only he hadn't been so blinded. Her voice, the way she moved, even the casual clothes she wore with such panache were the tell-tale signs of a woman at total ease with who she was and where she'd come from.

'Bugger,' he muttered as he got to his feet and rammed his hands into his pockets. For, despite all the evidence to the contrary, he still felt there could be something between them. He needed to find out more about her. She had brought something inside him back to life, made him feel good about himself, and he knew, without a trace of doubt that she was worth pursuing.

'That copper fancies you,' giggled Rosa as she and Harriet prepared tea.

'Don't be daft,' retorted Harriet. 'He thinks that by flirting with me, it'll make it easier for him to get to Catriona.' She found some cake and put it on a plate in the centre of the kitchen table.

'Fair go, Hat. Have you ever considered he might be flirting because he genuinely likes you?' Her dark eyes were glittering with fun as she looked Harriet up and down. 'You aren't bad looking, you know.'

Harriet flicked at her with a tea-towel. 'Jealousy will get you nowhere,' she giggled. 'We can't all have skin that never tans and peels at the first sight of the sun. As for the hair. Just remember, Rosa, natural blondes never go grey, they just fade gracefully.'

'Bugger gracefully,' retorted Rosa. 'Grey is not a colour I intend ever getting familiar with. Give me hair-dye any day.' She took a breath. 'Anyway, you've dodged the issue, Hattie. The man fancies you, and I get the feeling you quite like the look of him too. So what are you going to do about it?'

'Absolutely nothing,' retorted Harriet.

'What are you two girls whispering about?' Catriona came back into the room and started clattering dishes about. 'Anyone would think you were a pair of teenagers the way you're carrying on.'

'We were just discussing the lengths to which some people will go to get their own way,' said Harriet.

Rosa explained as she finished setting out the tea things on the table. 'Romance has flown in on a helicopter,' she said with relish. 'And Harriet has an admirer. Can't wait to find out what happens.' She rolled her eyes and waved her hands dramatically. 'Will she succumb, fainting into his strong arms? Or will she shun him, leaving him to traipse back to Brizzy with his tail between his legs?' She gave an impish grin. 'Watch this space.'

'Hmph,' snorted Catriona. 'I'm glad you can both find something funny to giggle about in the circumstances. This isn't a bloody game, Rosa.'

Chastened, both girls rushed to her and gave her a hug. 'We didn't mean to make fun of the situation,' babbled Harriet. 'But our nerves are on end because you won't tell us what it's all about. And I think Belinda's got a real cheek turning up here like this.'

Catriona shook her head. 'Belinda and I had a long talk over the phone,' she said. 'The girl's only doing her job, so don't blame her for all this.' She smiled, but it was weary and didn't quite reach her eyes. 'It's my mess, and I'll clear it up, no worries.'

Catriona kept busy by moving around the kitchen and preparing supper. It would probably have been easier to have Cookie send something over, but she didn't want any more complications. The men had seen the police officers arrive and no doubt gossip was rife. It would take one careless word to fuel that gossip and she had enough to deal with without a riot on her hands.

'How y'going?' Belinda emerged from one of the spare bedrooms and strode across the room to give Catriona a hug. 'Jeez, it's good to be back. I'm just so sorry it had to be under such circumstances.'

Catriona's smile was warm as she emerged from the embrace and took stock of the young woman in front of her. The dark hair was a halo around her pretty face, tumbling down her back in a riot of ebony curls. Her eyes were the deepest brown, and her figure, although generous, was perfectly in proportion. 'Have you told your Mum and Dad you're here? I know Pat would love to see you.'

Belinda dug her hands into the pockets of her tight jeans. 'I'm

340

going to try and get to see them before I go back,' she replied. 'Might even stay on for a while and catch up with my brothers.'

Catriona turned as Connor came into the kitchen, glowered at Tom and sat down at the table. She noticed he couldn't quite help glancing across at Belinda; at least he noticed her now, she thought with a smile. It would be hard not to.

'Would someone please tell me what this is all about,' snapped Connor.

'All in good time,' replied Catriona. 'Let's just enjoy our supper first.' She ignored his protests, settled into a chair at the head of the table, and turned to Tom. 'Belinda's the daughter of friends of mine who run a station a bit further down the track. The first time we met she was a plump little schoolgirl with pigtails. She was a real tomboy, forever racing about the place and getting into mischief with Rosa.' She smiled at Belinda. 'You've certainly changed since those days. In fact,' she added as she looked around the table, 'you all have.'

Belinda shook the tumble of hair from her eyes and laughed. 'Thank goodness,' she said. 'I'd hardly look the part with pigtails and acne.'

Catriona's pleasure in seeing her again was dowsed in the reality of why she was here. 'I never did understand why you chose to go into the police force,' she said.

'It's a challenge, and one that I'm enjoying for the most part,' replied Belinda. 'But I do miss home and the wide open spaces out here.' She looked across at Tom, who so far, hadn't said a word, but was sitting at the table making sheep's eyes at Harriet. 'But it's a man's world, no doubt about it, and it's lucky I grew up surrounded by older brothers and stockmen. It made me tough, and being thick-skinned from the start helped me stand my ground against the chauvinistic attitudes of my male colleagues.'

'I'm not a chauvinist,' Tom blustered. 'That's not fair, Belinda, and you know it.'

She smiled back at him, her dark eyes bright with mirth. 'Did I accuse you personally?' She looked across at Rosa who'd come to sit at the table. 'Aren't they all the same?' she asked. 'Egos as fragile as an egg. The slightest hint of criticism and they throw all their toys out of the pram.'

'Too right,' murmured Rosa. 'But if you think cops are bad, you should try working with us. Solicitors are the worst.' She dug

341

Connor in the ribs with her elbow. 'Brothers aren't much better,' she teased.

Connor reddened and he and Tom shared a glance of sympathy. 'Reckon sisters can be a pain in the backside,' he drawled. 'And if you put a woman in charge of anything, she breaks a nail and has to lie down for a week to get over the trauma.'

A chorus of voices rose in disagreement, and Rosa slapped his arm hard enough to make him wince.

Catriona was enjoying herself despite the reason behind this gathering. It had been years since she'd had a group of young people around her table, and it reminded her of the old days when Rosa and Connor would bring their school-friends home. She sat and watched them, delighted that such exuberant life had been brought into the old house again.

As the noise rose above the clatter of knives and forks, she realised how lonely she had become despite all her involvements in the outside world. Her life had stagnated, and for the first time in many years she yearned for the old days when she had travelled the world, met new people and experienced the excitement of a different city, a different opera. They had been heady days, she remembered, but had never brought her the deep satisfaction of life on Belvedere.

The voices rose and faces reddened as the debate flew back and forth across the table. She decided reluctantly that things were getting out of hand, and to bring some order to the proceedings she rattled the spoon against the china. 'Shut up,' she shouted. She shook her head in mock disapproval. 'I don't know. You young people think you're the first generation to strike out on your own.'

'The glass ceiling is disappearing,' said Harriet as she passed around the pudding. 'And we have equal pay and equal rights. No generation of women has had that before.'

Catriona looked at the three of them, so young and naïve despite all their education, and decided she would break her own rules and further the argument. 'My mother's generation was liberated, probably far more than you ever will be.' She held up her hand to silence the chorus of disagreement this statement elicited. 'She left home at seventeen, was married and sailing to the other side of the world before her eighteenth birthday. She had a sense of adventure, a thirst to see things that very few men had seen. She was a mainstay of our travelling troupe, taking on any task that needed doing. She drove the wagon, chopped wood, went fishing and laid traps. Her home was a wagon, her bed a pile of blankets in the back, but that didn't stop her from raising me, it didn't stop her pursuing her ambitions as a singer. If that's not liberated, then I don't know what you'd call it.'

Catriona caught her breath and eyed them triumphantly. They would find no argument to that.

'It was a different kind of freedom, Mum,' said Rosa. 'If she'd tried to get work, proper work, she'd have soon found her pay was less than a man's and that she wouldn't have been given the chance for advancement. Women couldn't be lawyers and doctors, the professions were closed to them. You're talking about the dark ages, when women were very definitely supposed to stay at home and breed. Your mother was unique.'

Catriona had to bite the inside of her lip to stop herself from laughing. Trust Rosa to find a plausible argument.

'Tell us about those days, Catriona,' said Belinda in the ensuing silence.

'Why?' Catriona was immediately on guard. This was neither the time, nor the place to talk about Kane's murder.

Belinda grinned. 'Because I'm interested, and because it's been years since you told us one of your stories.'

Catriona looked at the faces around the table. Rosa and Harriet were leaning forward, their expressions wary. Poor Connor just looked bemused. Tom Bradley had managed to tear his gaze from Harriet and was sitting back in his chair, arms folded. Despite the relaxed pose, Catriona could see the alertness in him and realised that Detective Inspector Tom Bradley would never be off duty.

She looked back at Belinda and saw no guile in that sweet face. 'Why not, but it's a tale I've told many times, so I hope you won't be bored.'

Chapter Twenty-Four

Connor was as enthralled as the others, but he could see Ma was getting tired. He glanced out of the window and checked his watch. 'You've been talking for over an hour, Ma,' he said. 'It's dark outside and you need to rest,' he said purposefully.

'Oh, dear,' she said with a smile. 'Must I?' Her question was plaintive – she was clearly reluctant for the storytelling to come to an end.

'It's late, Ma,' he said firmly, glaring at Tom. 'And I'm sure our visitors won't want to keep you up any longer. Whatever they've come for will have to wait until morning.'

The tension in the room was almost palpable, the pleasant atmosphere swept away with the reminder of why they were here. 'Belinda knows where her room is,' said Catriona in an effort to alleviate the tension. 'But as the girls probably have a lot of catching up to do, I suspect she'd prefer to be in with them.'

Harriet bestowed a frosty smile on Belinda. 'Maybe Belinda would prefer not to talk over old times, considering the circumstances?'

Connor wondered what she was up to. He considered whether or not to try and diffuse the situation, then thought better of it. Belinda was more than capable of coping with anything Harriet might throw at her; they'd been sparring for years.

'Too right I would,' said Belinda cheerfully. 'It's been years since we had the chance of a girly chat. I'm looking forward to it,' she said sweetly, a clear challenge in her eyes to Harriet. 'So I'm game if you are.'

Harriet's jaw tightened as she began to clear the remains of the tea things. 'This isn't a contest,' she muttered. 'I was simply

344

giving you the chance to redeem yourself'

'For which I'm very grateful,' Belinda replied with a tight smile.

Connor frowned. Women were a mystery, their thought processes inexplicable. Why all the frostiness, when it would have been so much easier to just say what they meant, and clear the air?

Catriona gave a chuckle. 'I do love putting cats and pigeons together,' she spluttered. 'Makes life so much more interesting.'

'Depends on which one's the cat,' muttered Harriet as she clattered the plates together and dumped them on the drainer.

Connor tried not to laugh. Belinda had always been able to wind up Harriet, and she, as usual, had risen swiftly to the bait. Yet the friction between the two girls worried him. They should have grown out of their childish animosity.

'Leave all that,' Catriona ordered with a dismissive wave of her hand. 'A few dirty plates won't hurt, and I'm sure you'd rather find some clean linen for Belinda, and help her settle in.' She gave Harriet a beguiling smile before she turned to Tom. 'Please don't go building camp-fires down by the Coolibah,' she said. 'It's my favourite spot and I don't want it spoiled.' She sighed. 'I used to love sleeping out under the stars. I envy you.'

'That reminds me,' said Connor. 'I had a word with Billy Birdsong and he's willing to take us all out tonight.'

'Sounds mysterious,' muttered Tom.

'It is,' said Harriet, her surly mood swept away in a wide, genuine smile. 'It's one of the most amazing experiences you'll ever have. Trust me.'

Connor grinned and looked back at Tom. 'Up for an adventure?' he challenged.

He nodded warily.

'We'll be going quite a way from the homestead, and our stock horses are tough to handle.' He turned to Belinda. 'I presume you still ride?'

'Is a duck's arse waterproof?' scoffed Belinda as she threw back the challenge. 'Bet I could out-ride you any day.'

Connor looked her straight in the eye. 'I have no doubt of it,' he said quietly, the admiration for this young woman growing despite her reasons for being here. 'What about you, Bradley?'

Tom reddened and looked at his boots. 'Never found the need, mate. The city's not really the place for horses.' He looked up and found five pairs of eyes looking at him in horrified amazement.

'What?' he blustered. 'Anyone would think I'd committed a terrible crime. I can't ride, so what?'

'So you won't be coming with us. Sorry mate.'

Tom's jaw clenched and he could feel the tiny muscle jump in his cheek. 'I could borrow a ute and follow you,' he said.

Connor shook his head. 'We'll be on sacred land, mate. No machinery allowed.'

Tom knew when he was beaten. He swiftly glanced at Harriet, who at least had the decency to look embarrassed by the short exchange, and was cheered by the thought she didn't find him completely worthless. He decided to make plans of his own. 'How's the night fishing here?' he asked. 'Any chance of borrowing a rod or is that forbidden as well?'

Connor had the grace to look away. 'Not at all,' he muttered. 'Cookie's got enough fishing gear to kit out a store. I'm sure he won't mind lending you some.'

'Right, that's all sorted then,' said Catriona as she shoved the cat off her lap and stood up. 'I won't be coming this time. It's been a long day and I need to be fresh and ready for tomorrow's interrogation,' she said cheerfully.

Tom noticed how tenderly Harriet, Rosa and Connor said goodnight to her, and felt a keen sense of being an outsider, despite Belinda's presence. It had been a long time since he'd had anyone to kiss goodnight and after spending the evening with Catriona, he'd been reminded of how he'd loved his own mother, and how much he still missed her.

They walked out into the moonlight, and he slowed his pace until he and Belinda were left behind as the others headed for the corrals. 'What exactly is everyone going to be doing out there tonight?' he asked.

Belinda told him about Billy's magical journey up into the Milky Way. 'I've done it loads of times,' she said finally. 'It really is a wonderful experience. Such a shame you can't ride, Tom. You're missing a treat.'

'Watch yourself out there,' he muttered. 'Harriet's claws are out, and even Connor is on the defensive.'

Belinda grinned and swatted her hair out of her eyes. 'I'm going because Harriet doesn't want me there,' she replied cheerfully. 'And because it's a chance to be with the man I've adored since I was a kid. Enjoy your fishing.'

346

Catriona was weary, but her mind was too active to allow her to sleep. She slipped the old fur coat over her nightdress, and padded, barefoot out to the verandah. Standing in the drift of moonlight that pooled on the floor, she looked up at the sky. The moon floated against a cloudless backdrop which was encrusted with millions of jewelled stars, and as she studied them, she was able to determine those which shone blue, rather than red, and those that glittered coldly white. It was something she'd learned to do as a child, and at one time, she'd known the reason why they shone in different colours but over the years the lesson had been forgotten and now it didn't seem to matter.

She sighed. The Aborigines had their own folklore about creation and the stars, and she envied the experience the youngsters would be having right now, and wished she'd joined them. It had been quite a while since she'd accompanied Billy Birdsong out to the sacred hills and drifted along the Milky Way to touch the moon.

Catriona pulled the fur coat around her shoulders and shivered. It was cold tonight, but that had little to do with the chill of foreboding that swept over her, for Billy knew things far beyond the understanding of modern white men. He could see signs in the wind, could hear the voices that called from the other side and feel the draw of the singing that would eventually call them all to rest. Now, as she stood in the silence of the night she thought she too could hear that insidious whispering, thought she could feel the spirits draw closer, their fleeting shadows playing hide and seek across the pastures and beneath the trees.

She smiled at her own foolishness. The voices she heard were coming from the two men down by the river. Cookie was no doubt boring the pants off Tom as he boasted of his fishing prowess, and she hoped Tom would be patient with him. 'Poor old Cookie,' she muttered. 'Doesn't often get the chance to share his passion for fishing.'

Catriona watched the dancing light from the lantern as the two men moved around the camp by the river, and was sharply reminded of her childhood years. How long ago it seemed, how distant and strangely impersonal those memories had become – as if they had happened to another child, another Catriona.

Her thoughts were interrupted by the sharp ring of the telephone.

'Who the hell's ringing at this hour?' she muttered as she ran back into the house. The screen door clattered behind her. 'What do you want?' she snapped into the receiver.

'Is that Dame Catriona Summers?' The voice was male and purposeful and didn't sound familiar.

Catriona was immediately on guard. 'Who is this?' she demanded.

'My name is Martin French and I have some very important information for Dame Catriona.'

'Never heard of you,' she retorted. 'And I don't appreciate being disturbed at this time of night.' She was about to replace the receiver when his next words stopped her.

'I'm ringing to ask you to comment on the article that will be appearing in tomorrow's edition of the *Australian*.'

The chill of foreboding returned, and she gripped the receiver. 'Go on,' she ordered, her tone resolute.

'We have received information regarding the murder enquiry being led by Detective Inspector Tom Bradley.' He paused, whether for effect, or because he was searching for the right words, Catriona wasn't sure, but it was certainly hitting the spot. Her pulse was racing and her legs were trembling so badly she had to draw out a chair and sit down. He carried on. 'We understand you used to live in Atherton where the body was found, and are now helping DI Bradley with his enquiries. I wonder if you'd care to make a statement?'

Catriona's jaw clenched and she took a series of deep breaths to calm her rising temper. 'Where did you get this spurious information?' she demanded.

'We cannot reveal our sources, Dame Catriona,' was his glib reply. 'But I'm giving you this chance to clarify matters and give us your side of the story.'

Catriona slammed down the receiver and glared when it immediately rang again. She pulled out the jack, tempted to throw the infernal thing against the wall. 'How *dare* they?' she breathed.

She sat there for a while, her thoughts in a whirl. She instantly dismissed the idea that one of her family had done this, for none of them knew why Tom was here. But the police did and that had to be where the leak had come from. She was heartsick to think it could have been Belinda, tried very hard not to accept she could betray her like this after all the years they had known one another.

Then there was Bradley. She'd been prepared to trust Bradley, had even begun to like him. Now it seemed the lure of big money from the newspapers had corrupted him, or someone close to him, just as it always did.

She shoved back the chair and wrapped the old fur coat more firmly over her night-clothes. Shoving her feet into well-worn boots, she stomped outside. The lantern still glowed down by the river, and Tom Bradley was about to experience the other side to Dame Catriona Summers.

Cookie had left half an hour before and Tom was enjoying a few minutes of silence before he turned in for the night. The beefy cook had been good company, and the two men had shared several cans of beer as they swopped fishing tales and made tentative plans to spend some time at a large lake nearby where Cookie kept his boat and the water ran deep.

The fishing tonight hadn't yielded much, just a few tiddlers which they'd thrown back. But the very act of sitting by a river with a rod and line had been enough to relax him, and Tom was pleasantly sleepy and looking forward to his night in the tent when he was startled by the sound of someone's approach. 'Who's there?' he asked sharply, peering into the darkness beyond the lantern.

'Me,' snapped Catriona as she stomped into the light and stood over him, arms tightly crossed over the bulk of her fur coat.

Tom looked at her. The agitation fairly radiated from her. 'What's got you all riled up, Dame Catriona?'

She glared down at him, her face a mask of fury. 'You,' she said shortly.

He was startled by her vehemence. 'How? Why?' he blustered.

'I don't like two-faced liars,' she retorted.

Her words shocked him, and he bristled as he got to his feet and towered over her. No one, not even Dames could get away with calling him a liar. 'You'd better have a good reason for calling me that,' he said quietly.

She glared up at him, her eyes hard in their contempt. 'You promised to be discreet,' she snapped. 'Promised me anything I told you would remain confidential. It was the only reason I agreed to you coming out here.'

'Yes,' he said firmly. 'And I stand by that promise.'

'Liar,' she said again, her voice acid with loathing.

349

Tom stuffed his hands in his pocket to stop them from shaking. He would not let her see how her accusations were affecting him. His thoughts were in turmoil as he searched for some clue that might shed light on this extraordinary attack. 'What's all this about?' he asked finally.

She told him about the telephone call from the reporter. 'So much for keeping my name out of the press,' she snapped. 'So much for your promises.' She glared up at him, her eyes challenging. 'The information was too detailed for it to have come from anywhere else but through you, or someone close to you. What have you got to say about that, Mr Detective Inspector?'

Although he was relieved to know the reason for her anger, Tom was tense with rage at the insidious betrayal of this woman he'd admired for so long. 'It wasn't me,' he said firmly. 'I give you my word.'

'Prove it,' she countered. 'Otherwise you can get the hell out of here.'

Tom clenched his fists. He just didn't need this right now. Catriona had begun to trust him, had even opened up enough to tell him something of her childhood. Who the hell had gone to the press, and why? What would it achieve? He ran his fingers through his hair in agitation. God, it was a mess.

He looked down at the woman who glared back at him, the loathing in her eyes making him uneasy. Strewth, he thought. If looks could kill, she'd have him as dead as a doornail. The whole scene was farcical, but to try and make light of it would ring the death-knell of any hope he might have of getting to the truth with Catriona. He had to prove somehow that he was not involved. As they squared up to each other his mind was racing.

Having dismissed the members of the family he was left with Wolff, the most likely candidate. His mouth hardened into a grim line. Wolff liked living on the edge, enjoyed the backhanders and perks of turning a blind-eye. He also had an expensive lifestyle and a fondness for the casinos; it was likely the paper was paying a huge sum of money for such a story. Then, with icy clarity he remembered the keys. He'd left them on his desk, had lost them beneath the paperwork, and had eventually found them in a drawer. He'd been puzzled at the time, now it was obvious. Wolff had used those keys to unlock the drawer and read through the file; he was making good his threat to get his own back and cause trouble.

'I have to make some calls,' he said tersely. 'Why don't you go back to bed? I'll let you know how I get on tomorrow.'

'You don't get away with it that easily,' she said firmly. 'I'm staying right by your side until this is sorted.'

Tom eyed her with frustrated affection. She was a tough cookie, and quite magnificent in her rage. Yet he could see the fear beneath that anger and it made him want to protect her. They walked back to the homestead and he picked up the phone. He had a mate who worked on the sports pages at the *Australian*, and who owed him a couple of favours. It took four calls to track him down, and after half an hour of conversation, he hung up. 'He's got a few calls to make,' he explained to Catriona who was still glowering at him. 'He's promised to get back to me as soon as he can, but it could be a while.'

Catriona dipped her chin, the anger leaving her in a long, drawn-out sigh.

He eyed her thoughtfully. 'I really think you should go back to bed,' he said kindly. 'This won't be resolved tonight.'

'I don't care what you think,' she retorted. 'If I want to stay up all night in my fur coat and wellingtons, then I will.'

There was no answer to that, and Tom looked across at her in frustration. What was it about women of a certain age that made them think they could be rude, acerbic and downright awkward? He grinned. Because they could get away with it, he realised.

'What are you grinning at?' she said, a smile tweaking at the corners of her mouth.

'The thought that when I reach your age, I too can be as rude as I like and speak as I find, and get away with it,' he said softly. 'Come on, Catriona. It's late, it's cold, and we both need to get some sleep.'

She smiled at him and looked at him thoughtfully. 'You're a good man, Tom Bradley,' she said. 'But I won't apologise for my accusations. This Wolff you mentioned on the phone. One of yours, is he?'

Tom nodded. 'If it was him, then he'll lose his job,' he muttered. 'I'll make sure of that.'

The telephone call from the reporter had unsettled Catriona more than she'd thought. Once Tom had left, she'd made a cup of tea to ward off the chill, and with Archie close behind her, went into her

351

bedroom. She sat in the old wicker chair, the cat curling on her lap, his purr vibrating like a well-oiled engine. She wrapped the moth-eaten old fur coat around her, the teacup cradled in her cold hands as she thought about the consequences of that call.

She might have been living like a hermit for the last few years, but her career and reputation had surprisingly lived on in the great outside world through the records and tapes that were still being sold. Because of her charity work and the foundation of the Music Academy, she was obviously still newsworthy. No doubt the gossip-mongers would have a field day, and the Pandora's box of secrets would finally be spilled for all to see.

With an angry sigh, she realised she'd lost control of the situation, and although Tom seemed a decent enough young man, there wasn't much he could do to stem the tide of speculation now the dam had been breached.

She closed her eyes and silently acknowledged that the truth must now be told. She had held the secrets for too long, had spent her life pushing away the dark memories until they were faded snapshots of a ghostly past that could no longer hurt her. Now she must find the courage to speak out, something she should have done many years before. There had always been a price to pay – a penance owed for the terrible things that had happened – now it was time to acknowledge it, and free herself of the shackles of the past.

Yet her concern was not really for herself, but for her daughter. How to protect her, to keep her name out of this? Catriona's eyes misted with tears of regret, and her sigh came from deep within; it carried the weight of regrets for things undone, and the lost chances of making them right. She'd spent her life running away and in denial – yet no matter how fast or how far she ran, the past had always been two steps behind – now it had caught up with her and she would have to face it.

Fragrant steam rose as she put the cup to her lips and sipped the brew of tea and eucalyptus. There was no milk, and only a few grains of sugar to sweeten it, but it was an old habit to add a eucalyptus leaf to the pot, one she'd learned from a very early age when the tea had come in a smoke-blackened billy from a camp fire. The moon was glowing through the window, the overhanging branches of the tree dappling the light on the counterpane. Yet her thoughts were far away from this little room. Like the moving-picture shows that had destroyed her parents' way of life, the memories of yesteryear flickered in her mind's eye, each scene a tiny cameo of who she was and how those days had moulded her into the woman she had become.

Harriet nudged Rosa and nodded towards the figure emerging from the homestead. 'I thought he was supposed to be going fishing?' she muttered, as she gathered up the tack and closed the corral gate.

'He was,' replied Rosa, her eyes dark with suspicion. 'But I reckon he was angling for more than a few fish. I wonder how long he's been up there with Mum?'

'If Tom said he was fishing, then that's what he was doing,' said Belinda defensively.

Harriet and Rosa eyed her in silence and Connor snorted in derision before loping away to see to the horses. Rosa had filled him in on the situation during the ride home, and his suspicion of Tom had been justified.

'Why don't you ask him, if you don't believe me?' Belinda challenged. 'He's coming over.'

Harriet moved the saddle from one arm to the other and waited as Tom strode across the cleared yard to the corrals. He was a handsome man, with the moon sparking in the grey hair at his temples, and his masculinity radiated from him in every stride. He hadn't struck her as being devious, just rather uneasy with the situation in which he'd found himself, and she was surprised how disappointed she felt at the thought that he'd been questioning Catriona while they were all occupied elsewhere.

Rosa spoke before he had a chance to greet them. 'How was the fishing?' Her voice dripped with sarcasm.

His welcoming smile faltered and he looked in puzzlement at the three women. 'Good,' he muttered. 'Nothing for the pot, though, all too small.'

Rosa glared up at him. 'I wasn't talking about fish,' she snapped. 'I was alluding to your angling for information from Mum.'

His jaw dropped and he stared at Rosa. 'I didn't,' he gasped.

'Then explain what you were doing coming out of the homestead,' she challenged, arms folded. 'And don't deny it, because we saw you.'

His jaw firmed and his eyes hardened. 'I don't have to explain

353

anything to you,' he said coldly. 'But if you're so concerned about my honesty, why don't you ask Catriona?' He turned from Rosa and looked at Belinda. 'A word,' he said. 'Now.'

Harriet saw the anger in him, and the way Belinda shot Rosa a confused glance before following him into the deeper shadows of the farm buildings. She turned to Rosa. 'That was a bit strong,' she said. 'What's got into you, Rosa?'

Rosa looked into the darkness as the two figures stood close together deep in conversation. 'I don't trust him,' she said. 'And I bet he said he couldn't ride just so he could get to Mum while we were out.'

'Fair go,' she replied. 'You don't know that for certain, and there could be an innocent explanation for his being in the homestead.' Harriet shifted the tack in her arms and began walking to the barn to put it away. 'I've never seen you like this before, and it worries me, Rosa. Perhaps you're too close to be objective – it's not like you to be so ... so catty.'

Rosa dumped the saddle and hung up the bridle. She turned and eyed Harriet for a moment, then grinned. 'And I reckon you're feeling sorry for him,' she declared. 'The cow-eyes he's been making at you have started to have an effect.' Her smile faded and her gaze was thoughtful. 'But I wouldn't trust him as far as I could throw him.' She turned to Connor who had just come into the barn. 'What do you think?'

He stowed the tack and leaned against one of the sturdy roof-bearing posts. 'I reckon Harriet's right,' he said. 'You've lost it, sis. The man's a copper, what did you expect?' He dug in his pockets for the roll of tobacco. 'If you want the truth, why don't you do as he suggested and ask Ma why he was in the house? The light's still on over there, so you won't be disturbing her.'

Harriet decided it would probably be best to let Rosa work off some of the head of steam she'd raised by going alone. 'I'm going to raid Cookie's store and fix us some tucker.'

'I'll come with you,' muttered Connor. 'I'm starving after that ride.'

'I'll be back,' muttered Rosa crossly before she headed out across the yard.

'God,' sighed Harriet. 'She sounds like a pint-sized Arnold Schwarzenegger.'

*

354

Tom looked at Belinda and his relief was immense, for if there had been even the slightest possibility Belinda was behind the leak, then their work here would be at an end. 'I had to ask,' he said by way of an apology.

'I thought you trusted me,' she replied. 'I wouldn't even have suspected you, let alone grilled you the way you did me just now.'

He took a deep breath and slowly let it out. The night was still relatively young but it felt as if he'd been arguing with one woman or another ever since he'd put a foot on the place. At this very moment he would have preferred to be facing a line-up of hardened villains. At least a man knew where he stood with them, whereas women were a whole different ball game. 'I'm dealing with a complicated issue here,' he explained. 'I may have the only living witness to a murder that happened over half a century ago, and all the time she mistrusts me, I'll get nothing from her. On top of that she sees this leak as my fault, and I promised to deal with it, and keep it secret. You are not to tell the others about this, OK?'

'If you say so,' muttered Belinda. 'But they only need to read a paper or listen to the news to find out. Don't you think this whole situation is difficult enough without keeping secrets?'

His smile was jaded as he rammed his hands in his pockets and kicked the toe of his boot against a clod of grass. 'It's what Catriona wants, Belinda. We'll deal with the flak when it happens.' He sighed. 'I'm sorry I doubted you, but I needed reassurance that at least you were on my side.'

'Of course I am, you idiot,' she said fondly. 'But it would have made things much easier if you'd only explained why you were with Catriona tonight.' She eyed him quizzically. 'Don't you think you also ought to explain the lengths you had to go to, so you could take time out and come here in the first place? Shouldn't you tell them about the strings you had to pull to get me to come with you?' She smiled. 'You know, Tom,' she said softly. 'Sometimes, you are your own worst enemy.'

He ran his fingers through his hair, making it stand on end in his frustration. 'I just wanted to clear up my grandfather's mystery,' he said crossly. 'I never meant for things to get so out of hand. Catriona's a national treasure, a woman whose life and talent I've admired for years, and I'm determined not to let anything muck up this chance to bring an end to it all.'

355

'Then tell them that,' she said with a hint of impatience. 'Be open and above-board with them, instead of mooning over Harriet and biting back every time Rosa winds you up. She's defensive, and the best form of defence is attack, you should know that, Tom. Give her a break, and you might find she's not so bad.'

'I'm not mooning over Harriet,' he denied hotly, the colour rising up his neck and into his face.

Belinda grinned. 'Oh, yes you are,' she said sweetly. 'But then there's no accounting for taste.'

He was startled by her tone. 'You don't like her, do you? But I thought you and she went back years, thought you were all very close?' He was curious about the relationship between her and the other two, and deeply intrigued as to how Harriet was viewed by another woman.

Belinda chewed her bottom lip, deep in thought. 'I used to get on with her all right when we were kids, and for a while I even felt sorry for her. Her mother's a grade A bitch.'

Tom raised an eyebrow, but knew better than to interrupt Belinda's flow of thought.

'I suppose its silly really,' she went on. 'But Rosa was my friend, and when Harriet came along, I felt left out. When I decided to opt out of Uni and go to Police Academy, we began to drift apart.' She stared out into the darkness. 'We've stayed in touch, but it's mostly been through Rosa.'

'What do you think of her now?'

She grinned. 'She's not as prickly as Rosa, that's for sure, but she's always been cool and a bit too distant for my liking. She's also attractive, and very intelligent, which is probably why she's ignoring your rather pathetic attempts at wooing her.' He was about to deny the accusation, when she grinned and carried on. 'Reckon it's my country upbringing,' she said. 'But I've never been a fan of these slick city women who appear to have it all, and believe me, Tom, that one has it all.'

'What do you mean?' Tom was intrigued.

She looked at him, her expression solemn. 'Her father was Brian Wilson, a multi-millionaire who made his fortune by supplying the oil fields with plant and machinery. He died when Harriet was young. Her mother was a prima ballerina with the Sydney Ballet Company, and an enthusiastic social climber.'

Tom had known instinctively that Harriet was from a wealthy

family, but he'd had no idea she was so well connected.

'Harriet didn't need to work in bars and clubs to keep body and soul together while she studied for her law degree. She walked into a vacancy at one of the most prestigious law firms in Sydney and has slowly been given more high-profile cases. Single, no children, owns a house in The Rocks without a mortgage, and is being pursued by one of the junior partners in her law firm, called Jeremy Prentiss. He's also single and extremely rich.'

The news that Harriet might be spoken for shook him. What chance did a copper have against a rich lawyer? He realised Belinda was watching him with amusement. 'My word,' he muttered. 'You really don't like her at all, do you?'

She eyed him thoughtfully. 'I wouldn't have agreed with you yesterday, but now I'm not sure,' she murmured. Then she shrugged. 'Harriet's OK, but the friendship we had when we were kids is long gone. We never really had much in common, and our different worlds have widened the gap.'

'What about Rosa? Still friends with her?'

She nodded. 'We come from the same background and Rosa doesn't put on airs and graces like Harriet. She's been my mate since I was in nappies. I know her moods and what she's thinking, and even though she can be a pain in the arse at times, our friendship is as solid today as it always was.'

Supper was on the table when Belinda entered the cookhouse. 'Thanks for saving it for me,' she said gratefully as she pulled up a chair. 'I'm starving.'

Harriet's smile was stiff. 'I didn't cook for Tom, but there's enough if he wants.'

'He had snags and beans with Cookie while they were fishing,' said Belinda as she helped herself to mashed potato.

'Everything all right?' Harriet asked, curious to know what had happened between the two of them. 'Tom didn't look too happy.'

Belinda shrugged. 'He has his problems, but nothing that can't be sorted.' She forced a smile. 'He just needs you lot to cut him some slack,' she said. She turned to Rosa who was concentrating on her steak. 'Did you speak to Catriona?'

Rosa finished her mouthful and took a sip of wine. 'Yes,' she said shortly. 'Mum went walkabout and invited Tom in for a drink.'

357

Belinda accepted this excuse for an apology and tucked into her dinner. Once she'd satisfied her initial hunger, she set down her cutlery and took a long, appreciative drink of wine. She looked around the table and spoke into the silence. 'Tom probably won't thank me for telling you this, but I think you should know he had to pull a lot of strings to have me with him, because I'm not really on his team.' She looked at the others, her gaze alighting momentarily on each of them to emphasise her point. 'He admires Catriona, and is very aware of how we all feel about her.'

'Why should he care?' muttered Harriet. 'He's a copper doing his job. One way or another, he's determined to get his own way, and using you to soften her up isn't exactly fair play.'

'That's true,' agreed Belinda. 'But like it or not, Catriona has agreed to be interviewed.' She paused. 'Tom's willing to stay here for as long as it takes,' she explained. 'There aren't many cops who would do that. Catriona's a lucky woman.'

Harriet regarded Belinda for a moment before speaking. 'I agree,' she murmured. 'Perhaps now, you'll explain exactly why you're both here?'

'Can't do that,' she replied. 'Catriona made me promise.'

Harriet's expression hardened. 'You're enjoying this, aren't you?'

'Not really,' admitted Belinda.

Connor left the cookhouse and headed for his cottage, but instead of going in, he slumped down in the chair on the verandah and stared thoughtfully into the distance. His concern for Catriona was fuelled by their long history of close affection and gratitude, from Catriona's unswerving belief in him and in his sister, and her generosity to them both. He rubbed the stubble on his chin, his fingers automatically straying to the crescent-shaped scar that was his father's legacy. Catriona had been there for him when he'd needed her; now it was his turn to reciprocate.

Connor dug in his pockets and pulled out his rolling tobacco. He didn't smoke very much, but now and again the nicotine helped to relax him, and the very act of sitting in the dark and rolling a perfect smoke was usually enough to settle him. But it was different tonight, he realised. His thoughts were too muddled, his concern too deep, the memories too powerful to be blown away on a cloud of cigarette smoke. He felt the prick of angry tears as he saw himself as that little boy again. A little boy whose childhood had been knocked out of him before he'd had the chance to know anything different. Connor sat there and felt the old rage stirring, just as it always did when he thought of Michael Cleary.

He stared into the distance before leaving the chair, easing his stiff knee joint and pushing his way through the screen-door. He and Rosa had learned to trust again. Ma was the first person he'd been able to talk to about his father and feel no shame, the first person who'd offered help and practical advice and the loving affection he and Rosa had sorely missed once Poppy was dead. Belvedere had become a haven. 'Yes,' he sighed. 'We have a lot to thank her for. I just hope we can do something in return.'

Connor finally gave up on sleep, it was too hot and his mind refused to rest. Tossing aside the sheet, he pulled on a pair of comfortable old shorts, grabbed his tobacco pouch and padded outside. He wandered barefoot into the clearing, revelling in the warmth of the earth beneath his feet, and the cooling breeze that caressed his chest. It was not a night to be trapped indoors. For the magic of their journey up to the stars still lingered around him despite the memories of his childhood.

He rubbed his hand over his chest and around the back of his neck. The heat was easier now, the moon waxing brightly up above, the peace of the land surrounding him and re-affirming the love he had for this place. He leaned against the fence of the corral and watched the horses dozing in the moonlight.

'You can't sleep either?' said the soft voice at his side.

He started from his drifting thoughts, surprised, but pleasantly so by her company. He grinned, suddenly shy. 'I often come out here in the night,' he murmured. 'Gives me time to think and put things into perspective.'

Belinda's gaze raked his naked chest, strong legs and bare feet. 'They say contemplation's good for the soul,' she replied. 'And I have to admit, you certainly are a sight for sore eyes.' She grinned as the heat rose in his face. 'But I reckon you already know that.'

He grinned at her, his eyes teasing. 'I see you haven't changed, Belinda.'

'Can't fool you, can I?' she replied, the laughter sparking in her eyes.

359

'So why can't you sleep tonight?' he asked.

'Restless,' she muttered. 'It's been a long time since I've been out in the Never-Never, and I want to keep hold of that magic for as long as I can.'

'Don't you miss Derwent Hills?' he asked as he leaned against the corral and began to roll a smoke. 'I couldn't imagine being anywhere but here.'

'Neither could I for a long time,' she replied. 'But there didn't seem much point in hanging about. I realised there was a big, wide world out there to be explored, so I joined the force.' She grinned back up at him. 'The rest, as they say, is history.'

Connor watched the different expressions flit across her face and in her eyes. She was lovely to look at, and easy to get along with, and he still couldn't get over the shock of seeing her after so long. He also discovered he no longer felt awkward in her company, even though he was half-naked. 'But you do miss it out here, don't you?' he persisted.

'Yes, dammit,' she sighed. 'And it's at times like this I miss it the most.' She turned and leaned back on the corral fence, her hands in her pockets, her gaze on his face. 'The journey tonight brought it all back,' she said softly. 'Do you remember when we were kids? Billy was supposed to be looking after us while Catriona was away, and he used to hypnotise us and leave us up there for hours, safe in the knowledge we'd come to no harm.' She giggled. 'I suspect he just wanted to keep us occupied while he went walkabout.' She accepted a drag of his cigarette and slowly let the smoke drift into the breeze.

'Were you never afraid?' he asked. 'I remember my first experience of flying. I was terrified of falling and crashing to earth. Then, when I realised I couldn't move at all, or come down if I wanted, I was terrified of being left up there for ever.'

She nodded. 'Me too. But you soon learn it doesn't last. The magic of the whole experience wipes away all logical reasoning eventually.'

They smoked the rest of the cigarette in silence, each of them occupied with their own thoughts. Each aware of the proximity of the other.

'She's out there chatting up my brother,' grumbled Rosa as she dropped the curtain back over the window and climbed into bed.

'Leave them alone,' muttered Harriet as she tried to find a comfortable spot on the pillow. 'She's been after Connor for years, and this is probably her last chance of snaring him.' She pulled the sheet to her chin. 'Besides,' she added. 'She probably can't sleep, and I don't blame her. Your snoring's enough to keep the whole house awake.'

'I don't snore,' retorted Rosa.

Harriet gave up and emerged from beneath the bedclothes. 'You do,' she replied. 'And very loudly.'

'Kyle always complained about it,' Rosa admitted. 'But I just thought he was exaggerating so he could start a fight.'

Harriet raised an eyebrow. Rosa rarely mentioned her ex. 'What made you think of Kyle?' she asked.

Rosa sat up and hugged her knees. 'Don't know,' she admitted. 'Maybe it's because I suddenly feel very old and very single.' She propped her chin on her knees and stared into the gloom. 'I'm nearly thirty, Hat, and there's not even the glimmer of Mr Right on the horizon.'

Harriet frowned. Rosa had never expressed the need for Mr Right before, and she wondered what had triggered this line of thought. 'You always said you enjoyed your freedom.'

'I do, most of the time,' she murmured. 'But coming home has made me realise how empty my life is.' She ran her fingers through her spiky hair, bringing further chaos to the disorder. 'I have work, which I thrive on, and a good social life, but there's no one special. No one who would really care if I dropped out of sight and disappeared.'

'Bloody hell, Rosa. That's deep, even for this time of night.' Harriet climbed out of her bed and sat crossed-legged on Rosa's. 'I'd care,' she said softly. 'So would Connor and Catriona and the dozens of men you've been stringing along for years.' She reached out and touched the tightly clasped fingers. 'You're just being melancholy. You'll feel better after a good night's sleep.'

Rosa grimaced and shrugged. She reached for her cigarettes and screwed up her eyes as the bright flame lit the tobacco. Exhaling a stream of smoke on a sigh, she grinned. 'I expect you're right, as always,' she said. 'Kyle was a mistake – a marriage made in lust rather than love – and I don't intend to go down that road again. I'm better off on my own.' She glanced through the window as Harriet opened it to let out the cigarette smoke. 'I had high

361

hopes of you and Connor getting it together, but it looks like Belinda's going to get her wicked way at last.' She grinned. 'But you were never interested, were you?'

Harriet hugged her knees and grinned. 'Not at all,' she said brightly. 'But that's not to say I don't like him, Rosa. He's just not my type.'

'Mmm,' sighed Rosa. 'I agree you have little in common, and the strong, silent, Alpha Male can be an awful pain in the arse when you want to get some kind of reaction out of him.' She grinned, the wicked impishness sparkling in her eyes. 'Perhaps you should re-consider the attractions of Jeremy Prentiss. I've only seen him in passing, but he's rich, handsome and obviously smitten, and your mother would think she'd died and gone to heaven if you married him.'

'Leave my mother out of this,' muttered Harriet darkly. 'And Jeremy too, for that matter. I admit I probably make him sound worse than he is, but that's purely my defence mechanism against Mum's matchmaking.' She chewed her lip, then sighed. 'He's actually a really nice man, but there's just no chemistry.'

'At least you've got a choice,' sniffed Rosa as she stubbed out her cigarette. 'Tom Bradley's waiting in the wings.' She fell silent as Harriet glared at her. 'Mind you,' she murmured. 'I wouldn't mind getting to know him a bit better now I understand where he's coming from. He seems nice, and if Mum likes him, then that's good enough for me.'

Harriet looked at her in amazement. 'Leave the poor man alone,' she spluttered with laughter. 'You've done nothing to endear yourself to him since he arrived. Give the bloke a break, Rosa.'

Rosa lifted a delicate eyebrow. 'Methinks she doth protest too much,' she muttered. 'And judging by the way he is around you, I reckon it would be a shame to miss out on all that sexual tension.' She eyed Harriet with a quizzical grin. 'But if you really aren't interested – and why should you be, he's only a copper – then you should stand aside and let a real woman show you how it's done.'

Harriet belted her with a pillow. 'Go to bloody sleep and stop talking utter nonsense,' she said firmly. Rosa's laughter rang out as Harriet climbed into her own bed and pulled the sheet over her head. Really, she thought, Rosa was impossible. As if she, Harriet Wilson, could possibly find someone as mundane and ordinary as Tom Bradley sexually attractive. The idea was ludicrous.

Chapter Twenty-Five

Catriona eyed the telephone and pulled out the jack again. No doubt the reporters would try ringing, and she had no wish to be bothered by them. Her favourite radio programme would have to be sidelined this morning, she decided, for the news was probably on there as well. For the first time in years she was glad the newspapers were only delivered once a month.

She was already dressed despite the early hour, and although it had been a disturbed night, she felt strangely energetic as she fed Archie and tucked into a bowl of cereal. The reason for this new release of energy was the knowledge that in just a few hours she would be free of the burden she'd carried all those years, and as the long night had drawn on, she'd come to realise it was what she had been subconsciously waiting for since she was thirteen. It was a chance to finally tell someone what had happened to her – and know she would be believed.

Archie followed her into the lounge and wound himself between her legs as she approached the trunk. She looked down at it for a moment, deep in thought, then sighed. She had wanted to go through the things she'd stored away in there, wanted to share some of the secrets she'd hidden for so long, but the time wasn't right, not now Tom was here. Deciding to leave things as they were for the moment, she quietly left the house and went for her morning ride.

Tom realised he would be spending enough time today in the company of women and chose to eat breakfast in the cookhouse. Like all male bastions, it was noisy and cheerful, the laughter uninhibited as the stories flew and the day's work was discussed and

363

apportioned out. He felt at ease, despite the hostile glances, and he tucked into steak and eggs and fried potato and washed it all down with hot, fragrant coffee. The food was better than in the police canteen, he decided, and the company less uptight. There was no thrusting ambition here, no cow-towing to superiors or back-stabbing as far as he could see. The men of Belvedere appeared content with their lot, the mate-ship a strong bond.

'G'day,' said Connor as he dumped his loaded plate on the table and sat down. 'How was it in the tent?'

'Yeah, good,' Tom replied, wincing as he scalded his tongue on the coffee. He was in need of the caffeine fix before he faced the day. He glanced at Connor who was in deep conversation with one of the drovers. It appeared the man had decided to bend a little, and for that he was grateful. All he had to do now was get Catriona to tell him what she knew and he could get out of here.

He closed his mind to the cheerful chatter going on around him and thought of Harriet. He'd dreamed of her last night, a stupid, puerile thing to do seeing as how she had a boyfriend already and was way out of his league, but that didn't alter the fact that just the thought of her did strange things to his insides or that he was looking forward to seeing her again this morning. His pleasant musing was interrupted by a gruff voice at his shoulder.

'So what you here for then, mate?' The man who sat next to Tom had a face leathered by the elements which creased into a network of deep fissures as he spoke.

'Just visiting,' Tom replied, shooting a warning glance at Connor.

'I 'eard it was more serious than that,' drawled the man sitting opposite. 'Something about a murder.'

Dead silence fell as all eyes swivelled to Tom and Connor.

The shock of those almost casual words sent Tom's pulse into overdrive. Surely the news hadn't leaked this far so soon? He forced himself to remain calm under the fierce scrutiny of those around him. 'Murder, eh?' he muttered, with as much nonchalance as he could dredge up in the circumstances. 'Why would you think that?'

'Heard about it on the radio this morning,' drawled the man, his very blue gaze pinned firmly on Tom's face.

Shit and corruption. Of all the *flaming* luck. He'd known it was a mistake to keep this quiet, should have resisted when Catriona made him promise to keep it to himself. This might be the

Outback, and thousands of miles from anywhere sensible, but radios, phones and all the other paraphernalia of the modern world meant the Outlanders were no longer cut off from civilisation. He gritted his teeth, shoved the chair from the table and stood. He was aware of the silence, of the upturned faces and the accusing eyes of the men of Belvedere. Catriona was more than just their employer, he realised suddenly. They loved and admired her, and he got the feeling they regarded him as her nemesis.

'You shouldn't listen to gossip, mate,' he said. His tone was firm, despite the rage against Wolff churning in his gut. 'The press are always getting it wrong.'

Cookie was standing with his arms folded over the barrel of his chest. His expression was grim. 'Can't of got it that wrong,' he growled. 'There's libel laws, and they would have made damn sure of their facts before releasing the story.'

Tom had no answer to that and was, in fact, surprised at Cookie's knowledge. It just proved you couldn't take anything for granted.

'So you're the mongrel sent out 'ere to arrest 'er, eh?' The grisly individual scraped back his chair, his stance aggressive. 'Reckon we might have somethin' to say about that – mate.'

Tom acknowledged the threat and watched as the rest of the men rose from their chairs and stood in silent condemnation. The mood was ugly, and it would take very little to spark off trouble. Why couldn't the flaming press keep quiet? Why the hell did they have to shoot their mouths off before he'd had time to sort things out? 'No one's going to be arrested,' he said firmly. 'Unless one of you decides to try and take me on.'

Connor rose slowly from the table and stood squarely beside him. 'I reckon you'll have to fight me first,' Connor said quietly.

There was a shuffle of heavy boots on the floor and a hum of muttering as Connor kept his gaze firmly fixed on their faces and spoke quietly to Tom. 'We need to talk,' he said.

'Yeah,' Tom replied. 'But not here.' Tom didn't know whether to be relieved that Connor appeared to be supporting him, or whether to brace himself for a punch in the mouth.

'So there ain't no truth in it then?' persisted the drover. 'This mongrel ain't 'ere to arrest the missus?'

'Why's he here then?' came another voice. 'He's a cop ain't 'e?'

'Yeah. She ain't done nothing wrong, and I'll punch any bloke here who says she did.'

'Shut up, Sweeney, and get on with your tucker,' growled Connor at the young jackaroo who was obviously itching for a punch-up. He glared at the rest of the men. 'There's a pile of work waiting, and the day's half over,' he barked. 'Ma won't thank you for wasting daylight, so get your backsides in gear.'

Connor strode out of the cookhouse, Tom close behind him. He rounded on Tom the minute they were out of earshot of the men who'd come spilling out of the cookhouse to rubber-neck. 'You'd better have a bloody good explanation for that conversation back there,' he said with deadly calm. 'Or I'll punch your flaming lights out.'

Harriet shuffled into the kitchen and noticed the telephone had been disconnected. Still half asleep, she didn't question why, and jammed the jack back into place before making coffee. The telephone rang almost immediately, and she answered it. It was her mother, and Jeanette was in no mood for pleasantries. 'Have you seen the papers this morning?'

'Hardly,' she replied as she opened a window and tried to garner some of the fresh breeze that had sprung up. Rosa's cigarette smoke was making her eyes water.

'Harriet? Are you there? I can't hear you?' demanded her mother.

'Well, it's a long way from Sydney,' replied Harriet as she looked out of the window at the glorious view. The sun had just crested the distant mountains and the paddocks were being gilded with red and orange.

'Don't be flippant,' snapped Jeanette.

Jeanette's voice was like an angry wasp in her ear as Harriet watched Tom and Connor march out of the cookhouse and become engaged in a long and obviously heated conversation. The other men were hanging around, trying to listen in, and she was curious to know what was going on over there. Her mother's voice droned on, and she looked at her watch, frowning when she realised how early it still was. 'You're usually comatose at this time of the morning,' she said, interrupting the flow of words. 'What's got you all steamed up?'

'Are you with Rosa?'

Harriet glanced across at her friend and frowned again. 'I told you I was,' she quietly. 'What about it?'

366

'There's trouble brewing out at Belvedere. It's in all the papers.'

'Bloody hell,' Harriet breathed. 'That was quick.'

'What?' her mother shouted in her ear. 'What did you say?'

Harriet pulled her thoughts firmly into line. 'Nothing, Mother,' she said hastily. 'What exactly do you mean by trouble?' She shot a glance at Rosa and lifted her shoulders in reply to her silent question.

Jeanette's high-pitched voice sang down the telephone airways as she did a rapid precis of the news reports. Harriet was chilled by her mother's words and horrified at the predicament Catriona had found herself in. It explained a great many things, but the leak to the press had obviously come from a close source, certainly too close for comfort.

She peered out of the window. The two men were shaking hands, and appeared to have come to an understanding. But had their argument been about this leak? If so, perhaps Rosa's initial distrust of Belinda and Tom had been justified. Yet Connor seemed happy to shake his hand. It was a puzzle.

Her thoughts were in turmoil as she turned from the window. 'Does this report give any clue as to where the story came from?' she asked as her mother finally came to the end of the article.

'None.' Jeanette's tone was flat.

Harriet chewed her bottom lip. She'd known the question was a shot in the dark. Reporters always kept the identity of their source well hidden, and only an Act of Parliament or a court order could change that. But her mother's reaction to that news item had her even more puzzled. 'It's unlike you to be concerned for Rosa's family. Why the sudden change of heart?'

'I couldn't care less about Rosa,' retorted Jeanette. 'It's you I'm concerned about. If you're together, and you get involved in this murder enquiry, it could be the end of your career and any chance you might have had with Jeremy.'

Knowing how Jeanette would react, Harriet kept her opinions of her career and Jeremy to herself. Frankly, there were more important things to worry about. 'It's nice to know you're so concerned, mother,' she said dryly. 'But you've no need to worry. I'm quite capable of looking after myself.'

'I'm glad to hear it,' Jeanette retorted. 'And I hope that means you'll be coming home. Mud sticks, and you should distance yourself from that awful family as quickly as possible.'

Harriet could feel the temper rising as it always did when her mother took this particular stance. 'Catriona's my friend,' she said coldly. 'I'll stick by her for as long as she needs me, and if that involves offering my professional services, then so be it.'

'You wouldn't *dare*?' Jeanette's horror fairly hummed over the airways.

'Goodbye, mother,' said Harriet. She cut the connection, and turned back into the kitchen, where she was greeted by raised voices. Rosa had obviously overheard enough to confront Belinda.

'Well, it had to come from somewhere,' snapped Rosa.

'If you'd only shut up long enough to give someone else a chance to speak, you might actually realise it would not be in our interest to do something like this,' stormed Belinda.

Harriet eyed the two protagonists and, despite the seriousness of the situation, couldn't help but smile. Rosa was swamped in Connor's pyjamas, her hair standing on end, her expression that of a petulant child. Belinda towered over her in shorts and a T-shirt, hair wild, eyes stormy. 'If only you two could see yourselves,' she said. 'You're like a couple of bloody kids.'

'It's not funny,' snapped Rosa. 'You should hear the latest piece of news.'

'I have,' she said mildly. 'Care of my devoted mother, who thinks I should distance myself from all of you at the earliest opportunity.'

'I wish I could,' said Connor as he and Tom came crashing into the kitchen. 'You lot have been nothing but trouble since you arrived.' He held up his hand as Rosa opened her mouth to protest. 'Shut up,' he said firmly. 'This mess can be explained.' He glanced at Tom. 'Go on mate, and hurry up. I don't like the gleam of battle in my sister's eyes.'

Harriet listened as Tom explained his reason for being here, and Catriona's demand that the press-leak should remain secret. The relief she felt was immense, for she didn't want to believe he could have been so underhanded. He had a pleasant voice, she realised, and she liked the way he moved his hands to emphasise a point. Those hands looked broad and capable, the nails clean and unbitten.

She looked down at her own hands as wayward thoughts distracted her. There was no denying it, she admitted silently. Tom was an attractive man. She liked the way he took charge so easily, becoming the focus of everyone in the room, calming heated tempers and soothing damaged egos, and she rather suspected that under that calm exterior lay a harnessed strength that could be unleashed at a moment's notice to stunning effect.

More wayward thoughts made the heat rise up her neck and she dipped her chin, allowing her hair to fall around her face. This is ridiculous, she thought crossly. He's just a man, an ordinary man who seems genuinely upset about the turn of events, and deeply concerned over the effect it might have on Catriona. Why on earth should that make her go all unnecessary? Pull yourself together, she berated herself silently, act your age, and remember Catriona needs you. Tom was obviously sick and tired of the whole damn affair – and who could blame him – but it seemed that he too would need their support. For she couldn't dismiss the fact that he'd gone along with Catriona in keeping the leak a secret, and she suspected that decision had cost him dearly. For she had the distinct impression Tom Bradley was an honourable man, a man who didn't relish keeping secrets, a man for whom the truth was top priority, no matter how harsh.

Catriona had enjoyed her ride, the weariness of the long night had been swept away and she was ready to face the day. She heard the shouting as she approached the homestead, and stood on the verandah listening in as Tom held sway. Her secret was out.

'Thank you for being so supportive,' she said as she entered the kitchen, dropped the riding crop on a chair, poured a cup of tea and turned to face them.

'Morning, Mum,' said Rosa. 'Thanks for keeping us in the dark.'

'Sarcasm doesn't suit you, dear,' Catriona said sweetly. 'And for goodness sake stop scowling. It makes you very ugly.'

Rosa grinned, unable to keep the dark mood for long. She kissed Catriona's cheek. 'Why didn't you tell us?' she asked. 'Don't you trust us?'

'I simply wasn't ready to share this with anyone,' she said. She smiled at the three girls. Rosa was a breath of youth, a cool spring breeze that wafted in and out of her life and gave her joy. Harriet too was young and attractive, her long legs enhanced by beautifully cut trousers. The thick blonde hair was lustrous, making her want to reach out and touch it. She was a beautiful young woman; no

369

wonder Tom Bradley couldn't take his eyes off her. As for Belinda, she could still see that little hoyden in her eyes, the lust for life, the down-to-earth honesty that shone through – hopefully Connor would see it for himself and make his move before she returned to the city and out of his life forever.

Connor strolled across the room and kissed her cheek. 'Next time,' he warned softly, 'don't keep things to yourself.' He grinned. 'You might have known you couldn't keep a secret for long out here.'

She nodded before turning to Belinda and Tom. 'I suppose I'd better get on with it, then,' she said firmly. 'No doubt the reporters will be making up their own stories by now, so you'd better hear the truth from the horse's mouth, rather than tittle-tattle.'

Leading them into the lounge, she settled back into the couch, Archie on her knee. She waited until they were all seated. Her moment had come.

'The others have heard my life's story before, Tom,' she began. 'But the tale I'm going to tell you now is one which I have never spoken of before. It was a reasonably short episode in my life, but it has lived with me ever since.'

Tom sat and watched the shadows playing across her face and knew how painful it had to be for her, to tell such a tale. He wished, with all his heart, he could have left things alone. Yet, as he listened, he realised she needed to purge herself of the evil that had been with her for most of her life, for in her day there had been no back-up support systems in place to deal with those kind of situations.

He glanced across at Belinda and saw the same thoughts reflected in her eyes, but there would be no turning back, and any regrets would have to be dismissed. Catriona was well aware of what she was doing, and actually seemed to be garnering strength from the confession. Her strength of character and her determination was admirable, and if she hadn't been made of such stern stuff, he realised, the events of that time would have destroyed her. Yet, here she was, as strong as ever. She had won against all odds and made a success of her life. She was a survivor.

He swiftly checked the tiny tape-recorder and renewed the tape and the batteries. Catriona had been talking for over an hour, and should have been exhausted, yet she sat there, head held high,

370

almost imperious in her disdain for the story she was telling.

Tom set the recorder and placed it back on the arm of the chair. Dipping his hand into his pocket, he touched the small plastic bag. It was a vital piece of evidence, but so far it didn't seem to fit the story Catriona was telling.

Her breath escaped in a long sigh as the story came to an end and her rage was finally spent. She dipped her chin. 'It was over,' she said softly. 'Kane was dead and buried.'

The silence was profound and she looked at her audience. What she saw broke her heart. Rosa's face was white, her eyes stricken with horror as she covered her mouth with her fingers, the tears coursing through them. Belinda and Harriet were fighting their own tears, their faces ashen. Tom's eyes were dull, his mouth a grim line as he folded his arms and began to rock back and forth. Connor's chin was sunk to his chest, his elbows resting on his knees as his broad hands clasped the back of his head. His silent tears fell softly to the floor. 'Don't grieve for me,' she begged. 'He's dead. He can't hurt me any more.'

Rosa raced into her arms and held her just as tightly as Velda had done that awful night. Her words were almost incoherent as she sobbed on her shoulder. Connor stood and looked at them for a long while, his face grey with pain and streaked with tears. Then he turned and determinedly left the room.

Catriona soothed Rosa and watched him go. He would find his own way of dealing with the horror of what she'd told him, he was strong like his grandmother, and Poppy's genetic heritage would see him through.

Belinda and Harriet rushed to her, enfolding her in their arms, their embraces telling her more than any words. She kissed them both, then gave Rosa her handkerchief and ran her fingers lightly over the short, spiky hair. The love she had for all three girls was so powerful it was almost overwhelming.

Once calm had been restored, she sat down and turned to Tom. 'There you have it, Tom,' she said softly. 'Not a pretty tale, is it?'

'Catriona, there are no words to express how I feel about what you must have gone through.' Tom had moved to make way for Rosa on the couch; now he was standing by the fireplace, his expression oddly out of kilter with his words. 'And of course there will be no charges brought against you for the murder of Kane.'

'I should think not,' she retorted, her spirits revived.

'But I have a problem, Catriona.' He shuffled his feet, glanced at Belinda and looked down at his boots.

'Well, spit it out, man,' she snapped. 'I want to finish this and get on with the rest of my life.'

'Catriona,' he began. 'When I telephoned you a few days ago, you seemed to know exactly why I needed to come and talk to you. You knew there had been a murder up in Atherton, and that the body had been discovered during the renovations.'

Catriona's patience was wearing thin. 'Yes,' she hissed. 'And I've told you exactly what happened and where it was buried. I don't see your problem.'

'It wasn't Kane's body we found,' he said into the silence.

Chapter Twenty-Six

'Don't be ridiculous,' snapped Catriona as she shot to her feet and glared at him. 'Of course it was Kane.'

He shook his head, his expression regretful. 'I'm sorry, Catriona. The body we found had been hidden behind a false wall in the cellar. The airtight conditions meant the body was well preserved, almost mummified. The victim showed no sign of being bludgeoned to death.' He swallowed and took a breath. 'In fact,' he went on, 'he'd been strangled by a wire noose.'

Catriona winced at the graphic image those words conjured up. 'But I don't understand,' she whispered. 'Who could it . . .?' Her words tailed off as a dreadful suspicion dawned.

Tom reached into his pocket and drew out the small plastic evidence bag. 'We found this in one of his pockets,' he said softly.

Catriona's mind went blank. The necklace was a perfect replica of the one she always wore. She sank back into her seat, her gaze fixed on it. 'Demetri didn't desert me after all,' she breathed. 'He was there all the time.' She reached out and felt the ring's warmth in the palm of her hand, closed her fingers around it and held it tightly. She had no fears for where they'd found it, no aversion to touching this memento of the past, just a deep sorrow that he'd met such an end. 'Where is he now?' she asked, her voice breaking with emotion.

Tom squatted in front of her, his warm hands covering her fingers, his expressive face full of kindness. 'He's in the morgue in Cairns,' he said softly. 'We were unable to positively identify him, and although the autopsy gave us the time and method of his murder, we had only suspicions to work with. My grandfather's original missing persons report has been a part of our family history for three generations, and when this body was found, I realised only you could have the answers.'

She stared back at him. 'So you didn't know about Kane?' she breathed.

He shook his head. 'I had a body, that's all. I didn't know who it was, but had my suspicions it was probably Demetri Yvchenkov. After doing a lot of research, I finally realised you were the only one still alive from those days.'

She shook off his hands and stood. 'You should have said,' she snapped. 'You should have made it clear as to where you'd found this body.'

His face flushed scarlet. 'When I first talked to you on the phone,' he reminded her, 'you said you knew why I wanted to speak to you, and didn't deny your knowledge of the unidentified body we'd found. As you could only have been a child at the time of the murder, I never suspected you could have been involved. And because I've always admired you, and wanted to cause you as little embarrassment as possible, I thought it best to come out here and let you tell me about the events in your own way.'

'So you let me dig a big hole for myself and watched me fall right into it.' Catriona snapped. She was furious, the heat rising in her face as she glared at him. 'I didn't have to expose my family to all this, didn't have to tell you anything about Kane's murder, did I? All this soul-searching and heartache was for nothing.'

He sighed, shamefaced as he dug his hands in his pockets. 'Believe me, Catriona, I had no idea we'd been talking at cross-purposes. You seemed so sure of your ground, so certain you knew the identity of the victim and the manner of his death. How could I have known you were describing a different murder altogether?'

Catriona's glare faltered and she finally looked away. 'You're right,' she muttered. 'I took it into my head you'd found Kane, and although I didn't want to rake up all those awful memories, I suppose I should thank you for setting me free.'

'I don't understand,' he replied.

She looked back at him. 'I've already served a life-sentence for that man's murder,' she said coldly. 'There hasn't been a day when I haven't thought about what my mother and I did all those years ago. But retelling the tale has freed me, has given me a new lease of life. I've finally managed to bury him in here.' She tapped her head. 'He's gone. He doesn't have the power to hurt me any more.'

'At least some good has come out of this,' he sighed. 'I'm sorry, Catriona. I never meant to cause you such pain.'

'I know you didn't,' she said as she dredged up a smile. 'But if you'd told me about the necklace right from the start, we wouldn't be having this conversation now.' She cocked her head. 'Why didn't you?'

He licked his lips and fidgeted, the toe of his shoes nudging at the carpet. 'There was a cock-up,' he admitted. 'When the paper-work was sent down to me, the necklace wasn't with it. I phoned one of my colleagues up there, and he told me the evidence bag had somehow become separated from the rest of the stuff and no one could find it.'

Catriona stared at him, and he couldn't quite meet her eye.

'The man was snowed under with work and had given the file to a rookie cop who got it muddled up with several others they'd been working on at the time.' He stared at a spot somewhere over her shoulder. 'It was found in amongst the last effects of another murder victim. Luckily the victim's husband was honest enough to point out it didn't belong to her.'

Catriona's expression was grim as she looked at Rosa. 'Aren't our policemen wonderful?' she said with deep irony. 'One can always count on them to make a mess of things.'

'Fair go, Catriona,' blustered Tom.

'Never mind all that,' she said sharply. 'I want to know what you've done about solving Demetri's murder.'

'From what you've told us, I can only hazard an educated guess,' he said as he glanced across at Belinda. 'I reckon he suspected Kane was up to something, probably not the abuse. I think he would have acted swiftly by calling in the cops, if he'd thought you were in danger. Kane knew the man was capable of killing him if he found out what he was up to. He was probably terrified you'd tell him what had been going on, which was why he tried so hard to break up the friendship.'

'If Demetri even suspected what kind of man Kane was, then why didn't he look after me properly? Why didn't he say anything to me or to Mam?'

Tom shrugged. 'Who knows?' he sighed. 'It's an emotive subject and not one easily discussed with a young girl who might not even understand what he's trying to say. He was an uneducated stranger in a strange land, whose family had been wiped out in the

375

Russian pogroms. Then you came along, reminding him of the daughter he'd lost. He grew very fond of you, and protective. Perhaps he thought Kane wouldn't dare do anything to hurt you if he knew Demetri had taken you under his wing.'

'But Kane was already abusing me and wasn't willing to take the chance I wouldn't tell Demetri,' said Catriona as she picked up the threads of his supposition. 'He was growing impatient, wanting to take the abuse further. Demetri had to go.'

'It's ironic,' said Tom softly. 'From what you've told us, you gave no real clue to anyone about what was already happening. Kane had manipulated you too well, so he was probably going to get away with it anyway.'

Catriona nodded. 'He made me feel as if I was the guilty one. That it was me who'd led him on and encouraged him. It took me years to realise that of course I wasn't, but at the time I thought I could make people see what was happening by being rude and disobedient and moody.' Her smile was sad. 'Silly really, because nobody took a blind bit of notice until it was too late.' She slipped the necklace over her head and felt its weight. 'I want Demetri to have a decent funeral, Tom. Will you make the arrangements for me?'

He nodded. 'Of course. Do you want to attend the service?'

Catriona thought about it. 'No,' she said softly. 'I'll always remember him, and grieve for his passing, but the dead should bury the dead, the future is what matters now.' She smiled up at him. 'What of my future, Tom?'

'The case will be closed. Demetri has been identified and his death will be judged to have been by person or persons unknown. We have no proof Kane did it, despite our suspicions.' He let out a long, slow breath as if he'd been holding it for too long. 'We'll have to dig up the ground under the shed, and bag and tag any remains we find. But I doubt there'll be much left after you poured acid all over the body.'

'Will I face charges for his murder?' She eyed him keenly, watching the different emotions flitting across his eyes.

He shook his head. 'Your mother killed him and she's dead. You were a child at the time and although it could be argued you aided and abetted in the concealment of his body, I'm going to make sure your name stays out of this.'

'And how will you do that? Surely it would be bending the truth?'

376

'Probably,' he said, and grinned as he and Belinda exchanged a conspiratorial glance. 'But then only the people in this room know why the murders took place, and we're not telling anyone – are you?'

She grinned back. 'You're a naughty boy,' she teased. 'But I'm not totally convinced. What about that little tape-recorder you've been using all day? It must all be in there.'

He reached out and eyed it with mock regret. 'Do you know?' he breathed. 'I do believe I forgot to switch it back on when I changed the tape and the batteries.'

After a short conversation with Tom, Belinda wandered across the yard in search of Connor. Her thoughts were still mired in the story she'd heard today, and she knew Connor would be suffering. As she stood by the railings and looked out at the land, she sighed. Catriona's story wasn't unusual; she'd heard versions of it before when she was working in the Child Protection Team. Yet those tales never failed to affect her deeply, and she knew she would have nightmares over the next few days. There was something dark about working with child victims, something that made her feel dirty and ashamed of being a part of the human race. Yet she knew she'd been part of the support system for those children; the one person who listened, the only person who had the power to make it stop. It was a gruelling and often frustrating task, and she'd discovered there was only so much she could take, which was the reason she'd applied for a transfer into the drug squad. Drug-dealers were easier to stomach than perverts.

'Are you staying on at Belvedere for a while?' asked Connor as he came to stand beside her.

'Just for tonight,' she replied. 'Tom and I will be going up to Cairns tomorrow to tie up the loose ends and finish the paperwork involved. Then it's back to Brisbane for a debriefing by the boss.'

'Oh.'

It was a small word, but Belinda could hear the emotion behind it. She had waited so long for some sign that he might actually miss her if she went away again, and she knew she could no more walk away from this man than fly to the moon. She needed to tell him so many things but how to find the right words? She'd never been very good at hiding her emotions and often went off the deep-end without thinking, but this was too important to mess up.

377

As they stood in the sultry heat of the late afternoon, Connor kept glancing across at her, and Belinda knew from his demeanour that, like her, he was just as frantically trying to find something to say that would prolong this conversation. They were so engrossed in their thoughts they didn't hear Catriona come up behind them.

'For goodness sake, you two, don't stand about looking half-witted. If you've got something to say to each other then get on with it.' She kissed Belinda and gave her a hug before turning to Connor. 'It isn't as if you're strangers,' she said with asperity. 'And if I was Belinda, I'd give you a boot up the backside for being so slow on the bloody uptake.'

Connor and Belinda watched as she strode away. He turned back to Belinda, his eyes speaking volumes. Belinda slipped her hand into his and felt her pulse do a hop, skip and jump. 'I don't have to leave yet,' she said, her voice unsteady. 'And I'll be back for a visit very soon.'

'When?' His eagerness was clear in the hope that sprung so brightly in his face.

'Soon,' she promised. She licked her lips. 'Look, Connor,' she began. 'I know I said some pretty stupid things in the past. And I know I was a pain in the bum when I was a kid, so I wouldn't blame you if you never really wanted to see me again, but ...'

He put his finger against her lips to stem the flow of words. 'No worries,' he murmured. 'We were kids back then. It's different now.'

She closed her eyes for an instant, revelling in the touch of his finger on her mouth as she swayed towards him. Her breath was ragged as she spoke again. 'You blow me away, Connor,' she confessed. 'You bring out feelings in me I never suspected were possible, and that scares me.' She looked up at him then and saw such tenderness in his expression it made her want to cry with joy. 'Do you think you could possibly feel the same way?' she whispered.

'I reckon you've finally worn me down,' he replied with a twinkle of humour in his eye. 'But you live in Brisbane and I'm here, so how do you think we'll ever find a way of seeing if this will work?'

'We'll sort something out,' she murmured as they drew closer. 'Now will you please stop talking and kiss me?'

His lips were demanding as they captured her mouth. His arms pulled her close, so close she could feel the drum of his heartbeat against her chest, and in that single moment she realised the dream she'd held since she was six. It wouldn't be long before she left the city behind and returned to Belvedere for good, for this was the man she adored, the man she was determined to make her own.

Catriona had wandered down to the Coolibah tree. She needed some time to herself, so she could digest the outcome of today's dramas, and put them in perspective. She was deep in thought when she caught a glimpse of Harriet through the trees. She was carrying her case as she ran down the steps and slammed into the car.

Catriona was about to call out, when the car roared off down the track. Where the hell was the girl going? And why take a case? Was she leaving without saying goodbye? She bit her lip as she stood there uncertain of what to do. There was no sign of Rosa, and she wondered if perhaps the girls had fallen out over something. It could be the only explanation for such a hasty departure.

Deciding to play it cool, she slowly walked back to the house. There had been enough dramas for one day, and she didn't intend to spark off another. 'It's amazing what a day of drama will bring about,' she said as she slammed into the hallway and kicked off her boots. 'Connor and Belinda have finally realised they're in love.'

Rosa was furiously smoking a cigarette as she banged pots and pans and crashed cutlery in the sink. 'It's about time Connor showed some sense,' she snapped. 'He was in danger of becoming an old woman.'

'Nothing wrong with being an old woman,' retorted Catriona. 'You wait. You'll be one some day.' She folded her arms and eyed Rosa who was obviously in a terrible temper.

'What's the matter?' she asked calmly.

'Nothing,' snapped Rosa.

Catriona eyed her for a long moment. 'You know, Rosa. You can be extremely irritating at times. Leave that and tell me why Harriet has just stormed off and you look as if you're about to explode.'

Rosa turned from the sink. 'She had to get back to Sydney,' she snapped.

'Why?'

Rosa ran her fingers through her hair and sighed. 'Beats me,' she muttered as she stubbed out her cigarette and lit another one.

Catriona's mouth twitched as the girl glared back at her. Rosa was incapable of carrying on the charade for very long. She would soon tell her everything, she always did.

As the silence grew, Rosa gave in. 'OK, OK,' she said, lifting her hands in submission. 'Harriet and I had a fight. We both decided it would be best if she left and gave us both some space.' She dropped ash on the floor and smeared it into the wood with her boot. 'Besides,' she said with studied nonchalance. 'She has things to sort out in Sydney that can't wait.'

Catriona dipped her chin. She was beginning to understand. 'Really?' she murmured. 'And I suppose you wouldn't have any idea what these "things" might be?'

'I couldn't say,' replied Rosa, avoiding her gaze. 'Harriet's affairs are none of my business.'

Catriona snorted. 'I might be old and past it, dear, but please don't treat me as if I've lost my wits.'

'I've never thought of you as old, past it or witless,' stormed Rosa. 'Harriet and I had a row. It was over something I said in the heat of the moment, and let's face it, the atmosphere is so charged after your revelations, it's easy to say the wrong thing.'

Catriona dug her hands into her pockets. 'I agree today has been difficult. But it had to be a very serious falling-out for Harriet to leave without saying goodbye.' She paused and licked her lips. 'You don't fool me, Rosa,' she said softly. 'I know what you've been up to.'

Rosa raised an eyebrow and tried to appear innocent, yet the colour in her face gave her away, and her inability to meet Catriona's gaze was the final proof she was guilty. She lifted her chin in defiance, prepared to fight her corner until the bitter end. 'And what exactly is it you think I've done?'

'You've been meddling in things that don't concern you,' countered Catriona. 'I hope you're prepared for the consequences, Rosa. Because nothing is ever as simple and straightforward as it first appears. Harriet's departure is proof of that.'

Rosa bit her lip as doubt swept away the anger. 'What do you mean?'

'I think you know exactly what I mean,' replied Catriona.

*

380

Connor looked down at the girl standing beside him. She was wearing jeans and a shirt, and there was a sweater loosely tied around her waist. Her mop of hair was flowing around her shoulders and her face was naked of any make-up. His thoughts turned fleetingly to the cool, sophisticated Harriet, and he couldn't help but make comparisons. He'd been attracted to her, what man wouldn't be, but apart from being one of Rosa's mates, and a sight for sore eyes on the back of a horse, Harriet couldn't hold a candle to the girl standing next to him.

'Looking a bit thoughtful, there, mate,' said Belinda. 'Something on your mind?'

He reddened as he looked down into the dark, sparkling eyes. It was as if she could read his thoughts, and he realised he'd have to watch himself, otherwise he was in danger of becoming as much of a fool as Tom Bradley. 'It's getting late,' he said gruffly. 'I should be sorting out the men.'

Belinda smiled at him and leaned back against the railings, her fingers buried in her damp hair as she yawned. Connor couldn't help but notice the ivory curve of her breasts that were exposed by the gape in her blouse. He reddened again as she caught him looking, and her deep, throaty giggle made him all too aware of the effect she was having on him.

'Nice to know you like the view,' she said, her face alight with humour.

Connor studied the ground. She was flirting with him, and he wasn't sure how to take it. He decided to fight fire with fire. 'Reckon it beats looking at a steer's backside,' he muttered.

She tipped back her head and roared with laughter. 'Thanks,' she spluttered finally. 'I think. I suppose that was meant to be a compliment?'

He grinned, feeling like a kid again. 'Reckon it was,' he drawled as he stamped out his smoke.

'You aren't so bad yourself,' she said as her gaze trawled over him. 'Almost better looking than Max, but then he's got something you haven't.' A smile twitched the corners of her mouth, and her eyes glittered with fun.

'Max?' He knew he shouldn't have asked, knew this was a game, but he couldn't help but play along.

'He's my partner,' she said, the laughter bubbling in her throat in a deep, sexy gurgle.

'Oh,' he said, his spirits plummeting. 'I didn't think you were already involved with someone.'

Her laughter was uproarious. 'Poor Connor,' she said. 'I shouldn't tease you, should I?'

He looked at her in bewilderment. He would never understand the workings of a woman's mind, but he did wish they wouldn't talk in riddles.

'Max is my partner at work,' she explained as she turned to face him. 'He's clever, loyal and the best friend I'll ever have.' She paused, looked at his face and gave him a sweet smile. 'Max is a German Shepherd, with a cold, wet nose, too much hair and a tendency for hating cats and villains, not necessarily in that order. So I don't think he's any threat to you,' she finished softly.

The relief was overwhelming. 'That's all right then,' he said, wishing he could have thought of a more witty reply.

She smiled back at him, her eyes dark, her expression enigmatic as the silence grew and the electricity hummed between them. 'It's been one of those days,' she said finally. 'What do you say to going for a ride?'

Connor thought it was a bonzer idea, but, ever cautious, he decided to play it cool. 'I would have thought you'd have work to do,' he said.

She shrugged. 'It can wait until tomorrow. There's not much I can do before I get to Cairns.' She tipped up her chin and eyed him solemnly; she was closer now and he could smell the scent of her hair. 'So, what about it? I am supposed to be on my vacation and could certainly do with the exercise and fresh air.' Her hand was on his arm. It was soft and warm and sent tingles up his spine. 'Come on,' she breathed. 'Let's get out of here.'

The sun was low, cresting the mountains, as they kicked their horses into a gallop and headed out into the grasslands. The fire of the evening sky bathed the Outback in a warm glow and set light to the tips of the peaks, throwing deep shadows over the forest of pines which clung to the mountainside.

Connor exchanged smiles of pleasure with Belinda as she rode beside him, her hair streaming in the wind, her face alight with the sheer joy of being free in the wide, empty spaces that surrounded Belvedere. He no longer felt ill at ease with her, was no longer shy and awkward, for he knew that this was the woman he wanted to share his kingdom with.

382

The sky blazed with orange and purple, the birds returned to their roosts and the kangaroos and wallabies emerged from the bush to begin their night grazing. Deep shadows spilled across the grasslands as the trees were silhouetted against the glorious sky, and the night-scents of the wildflowers drifted with the pine and eucalyptus on the cooling air. As darkness fell with the swiftness they had come to accept, they slowed their horses into an easy walk. There seemed little need for conversation, for they were easy in each other's company, and a nod and a smile was enough. It was as if they were in tune with the land around them, and in harmony with one another.

Connor looked out at the land that had come to mean so much to him, and realised how much more beautiful it was when he had the chance to share it with someone who appreciated it as much as he. He glanced across at her and found she was watching him.

'What?' he asked, almost defensively.

'You really love this place, don't you?' she asked quietly.

'Better than any city,' he replied.

'I agree,' she murmured. 'I love it too, and can understand only too well why you'll never leave it.' She sighed and he thought he heard a world of regrets in that sigh. 'I wish . . .' she began.

'What do you wish?' he asked as they approached the line of soft hills they'd ridden through the night before.

She sat taller in the saddle, her shoulders square as she looked across at him with a grin. 'I wish I was a man,' she said finally. 'Then I could have stayed at home and run Derwent Hills and told my brothers to rack off.'

He was extremely relieved she wasn't a man, and that it was dark, for as she smiled at him the heat rose in his face and his pulse rate jumped. 'Women have been known to run stations very successfully,' he said as he tried to maintain an outward composure. She was having a powerful affect on him, and all he could think about was finding an opportunity to kiss her again.

'Yeah, too right,' she replied. 'But those women don't have four brothers who actually want to run a station. Trust me to be the only girl in the one family that really loves the way of life out here.' She sighed. 'But the place just isn't big enough for all of us, so what else is a girl to do, Connor?'

Connor realised she wasn't really expecting an answer, and probably would have been horrified if she could have read his

383

thoughts at this moment. He led the way through the silent, majestic hills and drew to a halt at the foot of a narrow path which led up to an ancient cave and a grassy plateau that was all but hidden by a tumble of rocks. Swinging down from the saddle they stood side by side and he could almost feel the bolts of electricity jump between them as they looked at one another.

Belinda was the first to break eye-contact as she turned away and looked up at the steep track in the grass. 'What's up there?' she asked.

Her voice was husky, sending ripples of pleasure through him. He cleared his throat.

'The best view in the world,' he replied. 'Ready for a bit of a climb?'

'I am if you are,' she challenged with a smile. Before he could reply, she was running, her legs and elbows pumping as she raced up the dirt track and out of sight.

He grabbed a couple of things from the saddle-bag and set off after her. A long time later he arrived at the plateau sweating and out of breath to find her calmly waiting for him.

'What kept you?' she teased.

He bent over and rested his hands on his knees, the sweat streaming down his face as he fought to catch his breath. 'Where'd you learn to run like that?' he finally gasped. 'Jeez, you must've broken the four-minute mile.'

'Police training,' she replied with a hint of smugness. 'Cops have to be fit.' She lay back on the grass, her arms behind her head as she looked up at the stars. 'Besides,' she murmured. 'I'm a lot younger than you.'

Connor was about to protest when she turned her head, looked him straight in the eye and giggled. 'But for an old bloke you haven't done so badly,' she teased.

Connor plumped down beside her and drank deeply from the water-bottle he'd brought with him. He ignored her outstretched hand and replaced the cap before planting it out of her reach. Two could play that game, he thought. 'Old blokes remember to bring water and tucker,' he replied as he bit down on the laughter bubbling in his throat and unwrapped the pack of sandwiches he'd grabbed from the cookhouse. 'But being so young and fit, of course, you won't be hungry or thirsty.'

She jabbed him in the ribs. 'Give me a drink or I'll show you

384

just how bloody fit I am,' she snarled dramatically.

'Oh yeah?' He bit into a delicious chicken sandwich and munched contentedly. 'You and who else's army?'

She jabbed him again and the remains of the sandwich went flying.

Connor grabbed her wrists as she tried to snatch the water-bottle and within moments he was sitting astride her squirming legs. 'Drink?' he teased, as he opened the cap and dribbled water over her face.

'You bastard,' she spluttered as she battled with laughter and hurt pride. 'Just you wait, Connor Cleary, I'll get you big-time for this.'

'Yeah, yeah,' he laughed as he pinned her firmly to the ground. 'Heard it all before.'

She became still suddenly, and he froze, unsure of what she would do next. Belinda was anything but predictable. The silence grew as they looked at one another in the moonlight, and Connor was certain she could hear the rapid hammer of his heart.

'What are you waiting for?' she asked softly. 'You know you want to kiss me.'

Connor hesitated. There was a wicked gleam in her eyes, and an impish smile on those tempting lips. She was teasing him again. Yet it was impossible to resist such an offer. He dipped his head and, after a moment of hesitation, warily feathered a kiss against her cheek.

'Is that the best you can do?' she teased. 'For an old bloke you don't know much, do you?' She wrapped her arms around his neck and pulled him closer. 'Let me show you how we do things in the city,' she murmured.

Her lips were warm, moving against his, drawing him into a vortex of pleasure that sang in every fibre of his body. He felt her fingers running through his hair, and the fullness of her breasts pressing against his chest. The breath caught in his throat as all his senses soared. She smelled of fresh air and grass, of horse and hay and all the good things. He kissed the finely crafted nose, the dark-winged brows above her eyes, and the peachy softness of the skin that pulsed so deliciously beneath her ear.

He heard her sigh as she pulled his shirt up and ran her fingers up and down his back like a virtuoso violinist who knew exactly the right strings to play. He realised she was aware of his arousal,

385

by the way she pressed her hips tightly against him, and although it was the last thing he wanted to do, he knew that soon he would be at the point of no return, so he drew back from her.

Her hands pulled him closer, her legs wrapping around his, holding him firmly. 'Don't stop,' she breathed. 'Please don't stop. I've waited so long for this.'

Encouraged, Connor slid his hands up her neck and buried his fingers in her hair as he kissed her. He could taste her tongue, could feel the desire rising in his chest, his whole body on fire with the need for her. He wanted to possess her, to make her his own, to consummate his feelings for her here in the night, beneath the stars and the moon of the Never-Never.

Their fingers were clumsy as they fought with buttons and belts and tightly fitting jeans and stubborn underwear. Then, suddenly they were naked – pausing, breathless in that electric moment of sheer ecstasy before they gave in to their yearning.

Connor saw her beauty in the golden light of the moon, his fingers tracing the delicate path from her belly-button to the valley between her breasts. Her breasts were creamy, firmly rounded and voluptuous, her nipples dark, engorged with desire. He took one in his mouth, teasing it with his tongue as he heard the deep gurgle of pleasure rise in her throat. She tasted sweet, her skin as scented as flowers.

Her hands moved over him, exploring, teasing, drawing him ever closer as the tracery of her fingertips stoked the heat in him and her need grew. Connor's need was just as great, but he understood enough to realise this lady was special; this lady deserved the very best he could give, and that meant giving her time, giving them both time to explore and enjoy one another at leisure.

He stroked the firm columns of her thighs and discovered that her skin was like silk, soft and gilded by the moonlight. Her dark bush glistened, and he buried his face in it and breathed in her musk.

Belinda gasped and wrapped her legs around him as he brought her to climax. Then she drew him up so she could kiss the mouth that had given her so much pleasure. A moment of electricity, an instant of almost intolerable pleasure and then they were finally joined.

He felt the velvet texture of her surrounding him, clinging to him, drawing him further into her until all he could feel was the pulsating need to take this magical journey to its natural conclusion. They moved, skin on skin, sweat intermingling, dancing in time to the age-old rhythm that was as natural as breathing. He scooped her up in his arms until she was straddled over him, his hands clasping her neat bottom as they hungrily devoured each other and soared towards that final, glorious explosion of pleasure.

They had finally fallen asleep on the hillside beneath the stars, and when they awoke sometime later they reached for one another again and made slow, sensuous and achingly tender love beneath the makeshift blanket of their clothes. Sated, they drifted between sleep and wakefulness as they lay tightly enfolded in one another's arms and watched the moon traverse the sky and begin to dip below the far horizon.

Connor smiled as he looked down at her. Her voluptuous curves felt so right within his embrace, her flesh against his flesh, her soft breath stirring the hairs on his chest. She looked young, almost vulnerable, in her sleep, the thick eyelashes curving against her cheek, the generously drawn mouth smiling as she dreamed. Who would have guessed at the hidden fires in that voluptuous body, at the passion she'd wrought in him?

He feathered his lips over her brow, tracing the curve above her eyes and down to the tip of her nose; the urge to protect her was overwhelming. He had never felt like this before, had never experienced such a sense of belonging, of knowing that what they had shared tonight was right.

Belinda stirred and opened her eyes. She snuggled closer, her legs and arms tightly encircling him as she kissed his lips with sleepy contentment. 'We'd better go,' she said regretfully. 'Soon be dawn, and I've got an appointment in Cairns.'

Connor kissed her again, fearing to lose her, jealous of the sunrise that would part them. He wanted this night to last forever, wanted to shut out the rest of the world and remain here in her arms beneath the stars, but of course that was impossible.

Belinda seemed to share his thoughts, for when they stopped kissing to catch their breath, she eased from his embrace and looked at him squarely. 'I'll never forget tonight,' she said softly. 'It couldn't have been more perfect, and I wish I didn't have to leave.'

'There can be other nights,' he said as he ran his fingers through the wild curls that drifted like a dark halo around her head. 'And days too. Don't go back to Brisbane, Belinda.'

Belinda swiftly kissed the tip of his nose and began to dress. 'I have to, Con,' she said through chattering teeth as she pulled on her jeans and sweater and struggled into her boots. 'But it won't be for long.' She glanced across at him and smiled. 'I've waited too long for you to let you go now.'

Connor kissed her cold cheek and swiftly dressed, his emotions in turmoil. He was a man who rarely showed his true feelings. A man who had always been wary of trusting anyone, who had shied away from words like love and commitment – he knew where they led. Yet Belinda had torn down those barriers, and he'd allowed her to breach that dam of resistance and look into his heart. She'd released the little boy within the man, shown him the light and the warmth of a love he'd been searching for, for so long.

He glanced across to her, as he fastened the buckle on his belt. How could this beautiful young woman still love him after so many years? She was a miracle, and he was terrified of losing her. 'Belinda,' he began. 'Belinda, if I ask you something, will you promise not to laugh?'

She turned and faced him, the moonlight casting shadows across her face, silvering her eyelashes and enhancing the curve of her cheek. He was suddenly afraid to speak, to say what was in his heart for fear of rejection, for the lessons of his abusive father were firmly entrenched.

'I promise to take whatever you say with great seriousness,' she murmured. She stepped into his arms and held him, giving him the courage to speak.

'Will you marry me?' There, it was said, there was no going back.

'Eventually,' she replied, looking up at him with a smile of joy. 'Whatever gave you the idea I wouldn't?'

Chapter Twenty-Seven

Catriona watched as Tom and Belinda were flown away to Cairns. Woody would bring the Cessna back tonight, and although she probably wouldn't get much sense out of Connor today, she was relieved that at least something good had come out of all this. Their overnight stay out in the bush hadn't escaped her, and she was heartened by the glow of happiness that radiated between them as they'd kissed goodbye.

She left Connor standing in the doorway as she stepped down from the verandah, and stood for a moment in the morning sunshine, relieved the worst was over. There was still the fight between Rosa and Harriet to sort out, and that was upsetting. Yet she had the feeling things would be patched up sooner rather than later. For, after all, the girls had been friends since childhood, and although this latest spat had obviously been serious, she was sure their friendship was strong enough to withstand it.

Catriona put all thoughts of arguments to the back of her mind and looked out at the buildings that were scattered around the clearing of home yard. She sighed with pleasure. It hadn't changed so very much since that first time she'd seen it from the hills – and she took comfort from the sight of the familiar trees that looked so beautiful as the sun touched them, their silver bark glowing as if on fire. She drank in the sights and scents of home, restoring her faith in the life she'd made for herself on Belvedere. She could smell the heat in the earth and the dust, could hear the call of the birds and the barking of dogs and the sibilant hiss of a million insects in the grass and the stands of trees. The northern flatlands of Queensland were all very well, but despite the vibrant colours and the verdant green of the rainforests, she preferred these more gentle colours of home, the soft tans and ochres, the pale tissue of a sky bleached by heat.

The heat here was different too, she was reminded. It didn't smother you, or drain you of energy, making you feel as if you were living in a sauna. It was an honest, blazing heat that evaporated the sweat from one's skin and dazzled the eyes. The light was brilliant, so clear and sharp it threw the slightest deviation in the landscape into focus, and even in the dappled shadows she could see the still, watchful figure sitting cross-legged beneath the trees.

'Are you coming in for breakfast, Ma?' called Connor.

'You go on,' she said as the Aborigine got to his feet. 'I need to speak to Billy Birdsong.' She watched him walk towards her, his long, skinny legs looking frail in the shimmering oasis of heat that swirled around his feet. The sun was at his back, low in the sky, turning him into a tall, thin silhouette that reminded her of a rather stately black and white Jabiru, an increasingly rare Australian stork.

She smiled as she waited for him to approach. The description was rather apt, seeing as his mother had seen one of these birds just as she had her first birth pain. She had believed in the traditions of her people and from that moment on, Billy Birdsong's totem had been the Jabiru.

'G'day, missus,' he said as he came to stand before her.

'G'day, Billy,' she replied, the fondness for her old friend clear in her voice. She noted how he'd forsaken the shirt and trousers he usually wore for the sacking loin-cloth, and how his dark skin was stained with the tribal markings of white clay. With an overwhelming wave of sorrow, she realised this would be the last time she would talk to him.

He drew one long leg up and rested the callused foot against the knee joint of the other leg, his balance assisted by a slender stick he'd honed into a primitive spear. 'Reckon you see bad spirit alonga you, missus. Good missus have spirit to fight 'im.'

Catriona smiled back at him. His ability to understand things never ceased to amaze her. We must make a strange sight, she thought. An old Aborigine doing his Jabiru impersonation, dressed in little more than rags, and an ageing white woman in designer trousers and a silk shirt, standing in the middle of the great emptiness, having a chat. It wasn't something that could be seen often. And yet, to both of them, it was quite natural. She and Billy had

390

shared many confidences and through this wise old man she'd learned the mysteries of the land surrounding them, and had come to understand why she'd been so drawn to it. 'The bad things are gone away, Billy. It was the right thing to do.'

His ancient face creased into numerous lines and crevices. 'You should'a been black fella missus,' he said with a grin that showed his lack of teeth. 'You make good lubra – you strong spirit.'

She tipped back her head and roared with laughter. 'Billy,' she said finally. 'You are a crafty old so-and-so. I reckon if I was a lubra, I'd give you a run for your money, and no mistake.'

'Reckon so,' he murmured. 'You plenty fiery missus. Dem white fellas wanna watch out.'

She grew serious as she looked at him and saw the ravages of time that had stripped him of his vibrant youth, yet his proud bearing had not been bowed. Billy was the last of his tribe who still adhered to the old ways, and she knew as they stood there regarding each other that he was preparing to go on his final walk-about. 'I will miss you old friend,' she said quietly.

He nodded, the tangle of grey hair catching the rays of the sun. 'Spirits sing, missus. I hear 'em. Soon alonga Billy Birdsong up and up to stars.'

Catriona looked up to the heavens and remembered the times he'd taken her out into the night to the top of the hill where she could be lifted into the arms of creation and carried along the Milky Way. Those journeys had replenished her soul, and given her the strength to live with the past. 'Reckon that will be some journey, Billy,' she said with soft regret.

His amber eyes studied her carefully. 'When you alonga here first time, you very sick, missus. Reckon you find good spirits now,' he said, nodding as if to confirm this pronouncement. 'G'day, missus,' he said as he dropped his foot back to the earth.

She wanted to reach out and touch him, wanted to stop him from leaving her. They had been together on Belvedere for thirty years – however would she cope without his friendship and wisdom? And yet she knew it would break every taboo if she was to try and stop him, or even to follow him. This was his sacred and final quest in search of his ancestors. Billy would walk until he could walk no more, then he would find somewhere to sit and wait to die. His wife and the women of his tribe would make clay caps and mourn him, and he would eventually become dust and return to the earth

391

– the earth he believed fervently that no man owned. His time of safe-guarding this land of the Dreaming was over and his spirit would fly up into the sky and become a new star.

Catriona watched as he turned and slowly walked away from her. His long, slender figure seemed to shrink as the distance grew between them. Then it was obliterated by the dancing heat-haze and Catriona's tears. 'Goodbye old friend,' she whispered. 'God speed.'

Rosa was trying to drag the trunk out of the lounge. 'Don't just stand there, Con,' she snapped. 'Help me get this out of sight before Mum gets back.'

'I don't see why we have to,' he muttered. 'She asked me to get it down from the attic in the first place.'

Rose rested back on her haunches. 'She's been through enough this past twenty-four hours, and having this here is just another reminder.' She grasped the leather strap. 'Out of sight, and hopefully out of mind. Come on, let's get it out of here.'

'Leave it be, Rosa.' Catriona stood in the doorway, her eyes red from her tears.

'But I . . .' Rosa began.

Catriona waved away her objections. 'There's nothing in there that can hurt me any more,' she said. 'Not after yesterday.' She marched into the room. 'I'm not saying I haven't any regrets for the mistakes I've made during my life, there are certain things I wish I could change, but I've come to accept that all the wishing in the world won't make it so.'

Rosa took her hand. Mum looked tired. 'I think you've been through enough,' she said. 'But if you don't want the trunk removed, then, fair go.'

Catriona nodded and began to fix a gin and tonic. She poured one for each of them. 'Here's to Demetri,' she said as she raised her glass. 'And to Billy, bless him.'

Connor dragged the trunk over to the far corner of the room. 'What were you and Billy talking about?' he asked. 'You both looked very serious.'

Catriona took another sip of her drink. 'He came to say goodbye,' she said softly. She glanced up and realised that although Connor understood, Rosa had no idea what she was talking about. 'The Aborigines who still believe in the old ways

392

of the Dreaming are in touch with the rhythms of their bodies and the world they live in,' she explained. 'They call it "singing", and when they hear this singing, they know it's time to begin the last, long journey back into the Dreamtime. He believes he will meet his ancestors, witness the creation of the world and be made to confess any wrong-doing he has done during his time as a Keeper of the Earth. After he has confronted the spirits of good and evil and proved he is ready to be received, he will then be met by the Sun Goddess and carried up to the stars and become as one with the Milky Way.' Catriona sighed. 'I rather envy him that belief.'

'It's not that different to what we learned in Sunday School,' muttered Rosa. 'Personally, I doubt there's a next step. It's all a big con; because people can't stand to think they are so insignificant that this is all there is, they make up an afterlife, a paradise, and even that's elitist.'

'Oh dear,' sighed Catriona. 'You're too young to be so cynical,' she said fondly as she ruffled Rosa's spiky hair. 'But I'm far too busy to get into a religious argument with you now, I'm off to finish arranging the food for the party tomorrow, and then I've got to sort out where everyone will sit for dinner, and arrange for the band's sleeping arrangements.'

Tom and Belinda climbed out of the police car. The Scene of Crime Team would be here within the hour, and they wanted some time alone to explore the house Catriona had described vividly the previous day.

The wrought-iron gates looked forbidding, despite their age and decrepitude. They stood open, leaning precariously from their rusted hinges, tethered to the ground with creeping lantana, ivy and clumps of grass. The great chain that had once held a padlock was broken, and drooped in rusting loops through the scroll-work. Belinda shivered. The dark and mysterious rainforest surrounded them. It was strangely silent, as if it was watching them, waiting for some reaction. She noticed how the overhanging trees threw deep, almost menacing shadows over the neglected driveway; and beyond the drive was the house. It loomed out of the surrounding forest like a malevolent presence, beckoning her, drawing her closer, taunting her with the terrible secrets it had kept for so many years.

'Are you OK?' Tom's voice startled her.

'Yeah,' she lied. 'But this place gives me the creeps.'

'We won't have to stay long,' he said. 'Come on, let's explore.'

Belinda reluctantly followed him up the crumbling stone steps. Looking up she saw a stone lion's head set in the pediment of marble that projected over the huge, carved doors, and was supported by two pillars that were entwined with ivy. It was covered in lichen and half its face had crumbled away. She stood back as Tom leaned on the door and forced it open. The groan of the rusting hinges echoed through the vast hallway and up the remains of the grand staircase to the decaying roof.

'Come on, Belinda,' coaxed Tom. 'There's no such thing as ghosts.'

Belinda wasn't so sure. Catriona's story had made it all seem so real, and coming here only emphasised the horror of what had happened. She stepped into the hall. There was little left of the opulence Catriona had described. The walls were bare, stripped of the paper and paintings, and the marble floor was covered in building rubble. There was no furniture, no chandelier or bronze figure at the bottom of the stairs, only the cold ashes of a long-dead fire in the great stone hearth.

She followed Tom as he moved through the ground-floor rooms. The humidity had crept into the walls, leaving its moist green fingerprints everywhere, pervading the atmosphere with its musty odour. Dust motes danced within the rays of sunlight that pierced the broken masonry and reflected on the remains of the ornate stained-glass windows. Broken furniture had been thrown aside, wallpaper had peeled from the walls, and the once beautiful floor was scarred and scratched. The velvet drapes at the long, elegant windows hung in tatters, black with mildew.

'I've seen enough,' Tom muttered. 'Let's go and find the shed.'

Belinda was glad to be outside again. The house was evil, she could feel it emanating from the walls.

'It's like a bloody jungle,' complained Tom as they pushed their way through the solid advance of the surrounding rainforest.

Belinda picked her way through the overgrown shrubs and the weed-strewn flower-beds which must have once been quite magnificent. The broad, square lawn had returned to its natural state, the grass reaching almost to her waist, and the stone urns and flights of shallow steps were black with slime. 'How long has this place been empty?' she asked.

'Since nineteen thirty-four,' Tom replied as he inspected the damage that was being done to his expensive shoes and grimaced. 'It was a popular place for courting couples evidently, and for the occasional backpacker or itinerant. During the war there were soldiers billeted here for a while, but since then it's just been left to rot.'

They came to a halt so they could catch their breath. 'To all intents and purposes Demetri had left the district and disappeared. There was no record of his death, so this place couldn't be passed on to his heirs – if there were any – or even sold.' Tom grinned. 'Even the tax man couldn't get his mits on it without proving first that Demetri was dead, and they lost interest during the war years and seemed to forget about it.'

Belinda stood in the long grass and looked back at the crumbling ruin. The stone was green with lichen and damp, and there were plants growing out of some of the crevices that had been created by the crumbling masonry. It looked dark and forbidding in the shadows. She shivered. 'It's not some place I'd want to do my courting in,' she muttered.

Tom grimaced. 'Me neither, but if you're desperate . . .' He didn't need to add anything more. Belinda was a modern woman; she understood.

They carried on walking. 'If the owner couldn't be found, then how come someone was renovating the place?'

Tom grinned. 'I was wondering when you'd ask that,' he said. 'It seems one of the local builders couldn't stand to see all this land going to waste, and moved in his contractors. He simply took it over, hoping that the owner or his heirs would remain in ignorance. He was actually in the process of claiming squatter's rights when his men began clearing the wine cellar, knocked down the false wall and discovered Demetri.'

He grinned. 'Poor bastard,' he said without a trace of regret. 'Thought he was going to make his fortune with all this free land, had even put in plans to build a luxury complex of houses up here. But now Demetri's shown up . . .' He laughed. 'He can kiss goodbye to this place. There's bound to be a will somewhere, and if there isn't then the tax man will sell it, probably for a fortune. Land's expensive up here on the Tablelands.'

Belinda clambered over a rotting tree trunk that was firmly in the grip of lantana and ivy. 'Serves him right,' she muttered. Then she caught her first glimpse of the shed. 'Bloody hell,' she

395

groaned. 'It's going to take forever to get through that lot. I wish now we hadn't called SOCO and just left him there.'

Tom shrugged. 'He'd only turn up sometime later and cause trouble again. Better to dig him up now and get rid of him once and for all.'

They stood in the shadows of the dark rainforest and looked at the thick vines that had crawled in and out of the fabric of the old shed. The roof had caved in, the windows were broken and the door had rotted on the big iron hinges. The rainforest had crept into every corner and crevice and the wooden shack had slowly sunk beneath the onslaught.

'I doubt we'll even find anything,' muttered Tom. 'It's been too long.' He rammed his hands in his pockets and sighed. 'But when I get back to Brisbane I'm going to do some digging of a different nature. A man like Kane always left a trail, and I'm curious to know who he really was.'

Catriona hadn't realised just how tired she was, and as her birthday celebrations came and went, she finally had the opportunity to rest and sleep. It was healing, restoring the mind and the spirit, and offered solace. The guilt she'd carried for so many years was banished, swept away in the realisation she'd actually been the victim. How simple it was, she thought, to look back on things and see them for what they really were. Yet, at the time she'd believed Kane when he told her it was her fault, that she'd led him on, had wanted him to do those things to her.

Catriona slammed the kettle onto the hob. She wouldn't allow those insidious thoughts to spoil the healing process. She was clean, unburdened and whole again. He was dead and buried, his sins rotting his soul. He could no longer touch her.

As she waited for the kettle to boil, she listened to the sounds of Belvedere. The old house creaked and whispered and groaned, and the possums were making their usual racket on the roof. She could hear the men in the yard, the low of the milk cows and the soft, fussy cluck of the chooks in the pens. A dog was barking somewhere and Woody was hammering and drilling, probably doing the repairs on the barn; they were long overdue. She heard footsteps on the verandah and the whine and slam of the screen door. Looking at her watch, she realised it was four in the afternoon. Rosa must have returned from her ride.

'How y'goin'?' Rosa's cheerful face appeared around the door, her cheeks glowing with fresh air and sunshine.

'Good,' replied Catriona as she poured them both a mug of tea, and prepared for a long gossip. Rosa smelled of sunshine and horseflesh, a poignant reminder that Catriona hadn't been out riding for over a week. 'You look as if you enjoyed your ride. Did Connor go with you?'

Rosa plumped down in the chair and ruffled her hair; it was damp with sweat and stood on end, which appeared to be the way she preferred it. 'Yeah. The old bludger's finally decided there's more to life than cows,' she said with a grin. 'We rode up to the old place and had a look around; it felt odd seeing it again.'

Catriona smiled. 'It's always strange going back to our childhood haunts,' she said. 'They seem so much smaller than we remembered.'

Rosa pulled a face. 'Smaller, shabbier, I can't believe there were five of us living in there. No wonder our lives were in such chaos.'

'Your father didn't help,' replied Catriona.

'I was lucky he left when he did,' said Rosa as she plucked at a loose thread in her shirt. 'I don't remember him at all.' She licked her lips. 'Poor Connor,' she sighed. 'He still bears the scars, you know. In here.' She touched her head.

'He's much more confident than before,' said Catriona. 'The years have seen to that. And since he and Belinda have come to their senses, I think we'll see him blossom.'

Rosa grinned. 'I hate to think what his phone bill's going to be. They're always talking to one another. Ain't love grand?' Rosa jumped up from the table and searched in the larder for some biscuits.

Catriona wandered over to the window. She could see Connor's confident stride as he loped across the yard, the damaged knee appearing to give him less discomfort now his mind was easier. His very demeanour spoke of renewed confidence in himself and in his life, and Catriona prayed fervently it would remain so.

Rosa cut a slice of cake for each of them. 'I baked it this morning when you were over with Cookie,' she muttered as she eyed it critically. 'It looks OK, but I don't know what it will taste like.'

Catriona nibbled the chocolate cake and lifted an eyebrow. 'It's delicious. I didn't know you could cook.'

'I can if I want to,' she retorted. 'It's just I can't be bothered.

Woolworths and I have this arrangement. They make the cakes, I buy them.'

Catriona looked at Rosa and realised what was behind all this domesticity. 'You must be bored, darling.'

'Not bored,' she replied. 'Just restless. I've got a lot of work piling up back at the office, and my boss is beginning to make disgruntled noises.' She put down her cup and looked back at Catriona. 'I'm going to have to leave, soon, Mum. My two weeks are nearly up.'

'I'm going to miss you dreadfully,' said Catriona as she reached for her hand. 'Just promise you won't leave it so long before your next visit?'

Rosa nodded. 'I'll do my best to visit regularly.' She grinned. 'If only to keep track of Connor and Belinda's romance.'

They finished the tea and cake and Rosa left to have a shower whilst Catriona finished preparing the shepherd's pie. As she worked, she thought about their earlier conversation. It had surprised her that Rosa and Connor had gone back to the old house. It wasn't exactly somewhere that evoked pleasant memories. Yet, she had returned in her mind to Atherton to lay ghosts. Perhaps Rosa and Connor needed to do the same?

Catriona sang to herself as she laid the table. The kitchen was warm and filled with steam as she bustled about with pots and pans. Connor had come in from the yard and was sitting sideways on at the table, his injured leg stuck out to ease his knee as he read through the latest farm catalogue. 'Thinking of new ways to spend my money?' she teased.

He put down the catalogue and leaned back in his chair. 'Rosa and I went out to the old place today,' he began with a certain degree of hesitancy.

'Rosa told me,' she said, wondering where this was leading.

'It's been left to rot, and it's a shame. Could be a bonzer little place if it was done up again.' He fiddled with the catalogue. 'I was thinking Belinda and I could live there,' he finished.

'That's a wonderful idea,' she said warmly. She placed an enormous plate of food in front of him. 'I'm just a little surprised you want to use it again. The memories of that place can't be pleasant,' she said finally.

Connor fidgeted in his chair and rubbed his knee. 'What happened there is in the past. This is for me and Belinda for the future. The manager's cottage won't be big enough for when we start a family.'

'Bloody hell, Con,' groaned Rosa who'd finished her shower and was now in search of food. 'Putting the cart before the horse, aren't you? Give the girl a chance.'

He blushed and grinned and carried on eating his dinner, and the rest of the evening was spent making plans. Catriona finally went to bed as Connor was excitedly discussing the ideas with Belinda who was still in Cairns.

The dawn chorus was at full throttle when Catriona pushed back the covers and clambered out of bed. She'd slept well, and although this would be Rosa's last full day here, she had plans for making it special. It had been lovely to hear her singing in the shower, even if her voice could frighten a crow at nine yards. Yet it would be too quiet without her, for this short, but traumatic visit had invoked memories of Poppy. How alike they were in their colourful enthusiasm for life, and in their endearing personalities. It was as if Poppy's spirit lived on in her granddaughter, and for that she was blessed.

She showered and dressed and stood at the window for a while, watching the smoke curling from the cookhouse chimney and the men standing about having a cigarette and a yarn before they got on with the business of the day. She felt content, at ease with her home, her family and her surroundings. And now the spectre of Kane had been banished, she could get on with her life and look forward to the arrival of the next generation.

She smiled with pleasure as she watched the birds. They were swarming in great clouds of colour against the pale blue of the early morning sky and as she followed their flight, she realised she would never tire of the glory of these creatures for they were free of all earthly troubles, free to come and go as they pleased.

The sight and sound of the birds took her thoughts to Billy Bird-song. Had he found the freedom he'd sought, was he back in the Dreamtime amongst his ancestors? She suspected he was, for she'd heard the keening of his women and most of the Aborigine men had left to go on walkabout three days ago. There would be a mourning ceremony followed by a corroboree, which meant they would probably stagger back here the worse for wear after the grog they'd drunk.

399

Catriona turned from the window and headed for the kitchen. The Aborigine's ability to sense things never ceased to amaze her, for there was no logical way they could have known Billy was dead. Yet, perhaps by their very nature, they had preserved the ability to tune into their sixth sense – for unlike their brothers who lived in the cities and had different cares, they still lived here and mostly adhered to the tribal customs – perhaps this was what had enhanced their ancient instincts and knowledge.

Rosa was still asleep, curled up in bed with Archie. The ginger tom hadn't appreciated being kicked off Catriona's bed during the night. 'Silly old bugger,' she muttered as he opened one cold, reproachful eye and glared at her. 'You can sulk all you want, but I bet you're hungry.'

He leaped off the bed as she walked down the hall and wound himself around her legs, threatening to up-end her in his eagerness for food. Cupboard love was all very well, she thought as she opened the tin and forked the smelly meat out, but this was taking things too far.

Rosa padded into the kitchen. 'You spoil that cat,' she said through a vast yawn. 'He weighs a ton and kept me awake half the night with his snoring. You should put him on a diet.'

Catriona eyed Archie and he eyed her back. Neither of them thought much of the idea, and decided to treat the suggestion with the contempt it deserved.

Catriona put the kettle on the hob and bread in the toaster; she was excited about the plans for the day, but it might be an idea to check that Rosa hadn't made any of her own. 'What do you want to do on your last day, Rosa?'

Rosa sat at the table, her hair standing on end, her face still bleary with sleep. She yawned again. 'I'm going to have to ask the mechanic to check the oil and water in the Station ute and make sure everything's right for the long drive back tomorrow afternoon,' she said. 'Then I want to go back to the old place and consolidate a few ideas for the furniture and the type of kitchen and bathroom they'll need. Once I've got the measurements, I can order it all in Sydney when I get back.'

'I think Belinda might prefer to choose for herself,' Catriona said with gentle reproach as she filled the teapot and placed it on the table. 'After all, she's the one who'll be living there.'

'I suppose so,' retorted Rosa. 'But surely she wouldn't mind if

I helped get the place straight?'

Catriona sat down and took her hand. 'I'm sure she'd love to have you help, but she must be the one to make the house a home for her and Connor, so be patient and wait to be asked.' She smiled at Rosa to take the sting out of her words and was once again reminded forcibly of Poppy. Rosa and her grandmother shared the same impatience and impetuosity, the same zestful enthusiasm for life, although at this moment it was sadly lacking in the yawning Rosa. 'I've got a better idea,' she said. 'It will give us a chance for some fresh air, which might actually wake you up.'

'Sorry,' Rosa said. 'It's that bloody cat's fault. I wish he'd go back to sleeping with you.'

Catriona walked around the ravenous Archie who was gobbling his breakfast, and sat down at the table. 'Archie's sulking,' she said. 'He'll come back to me when he's ready and not before.' She folded her hands on the table and smiled at Rosa. 'I think we should get the old wagon out of the barn,' she said. 'We could get one of the older, quieter horses to pull it, and go off exploring. It will be quite like old times.'

'Are you totally insane?' Rosa looked at her, fully awake, eyes wide in horror. 'It's likely to fall to pieces the minute it's moved out of the barn. And besides, aren't you a bit old to be jigged about?'

'Thanks,' she said dryly. 'I might be over sixty, but I'm not ready for my coffin just yet.'

Rosa blushed. 'Sorry,' she muttered. 'Me and my big mouth.'

'It would help if the mouth and brain were co-ordinated,' she retorted. She lathered golden butter on the hot toast and bit into it. Having demolished the first slice, she buttered the second. Her appetite was as undiminished as ever, and with it came a burst of energy and enthusiasm for the coming day. 'When we've finished here,' she said finally, 'you can go and tell Connor to get the men to pull the wagon out of the barn and put old Razor in the traces.'

'Connor won't like it,' said Rosa with a waspish stubbornness.

'Connor doesn't have to come with us,' Catriona retorted. 'Just do as I say, Rosa. It'll be fun, and we can take a picnic like we used to when you were kids.'

Rosa heaved a great sigh, finished her mug of tea and, muttering to herself, stomped out of the room. Catriona grinned. Despite being in her late twenties, Rosa sometimes behaved as if she was still twelve.

An hour later they were standing in the yard watching the wagon being slowly drawn from the barn. Catriona looked around her and was hard-pushed not to make an acid comment on the lack of work being done about the place. The men had turned out in force to watch and none of them seemed remotely inclined to earn their wages.

She soon forgot her audience as she stood beside the picnic basket and ran her hands along the wagon's green and gold paint. She was remembering the long, sunny years of her childhood when this had been her home. It looked much smaller than she remembered, and rather battered, despite the new coat of paint and smart wheels. Yet there was a certain majesty about it and she couldn't wait to climb on board.

Connor was standing at the horse's head, holding onto the bridle and Catriona went to stand next to him. 'There's no need to hold him so firmly,' she said quietly. 'He's too old and fat to bolt.'

'Razor might be old and fat, but he's not used to pulling wagons,' he grumbled. 'He doesn't know what he's supposed to be doing, A bit like you, really,' he added glaring down at her.

'We know exactly what we're doing, don't we, boy?' she retorted as she patted Razor's grey muzzle. 'We just need a little bit of time to remember how, that's all.'

Connor muttered something which didn't sound complimentary, either to her or Razor, and she chose to ignore it by moving away to the side of the wagon. It would be impossible to climb up to the buckboard, she realised sadly. She no longer had the strength in her arms to pull herself up, or the power in her legs to balance on the hub of the wheel and swing over the lip, and she wasn't about to make a complete fool of herself in front of everyone by trying. 'I'll get on at the back,' she said imperiously. 'Someone come and help me.' There were murmurs and a lot of shuffling of feet. 'Quickly,' she ordered, her impatience making her sharp – it was like being back in the theatre.

With Rosa pushing from behind, and Cookie hauling at the front, she finally managed to get inside. She stood for a moment in the gloom of the wagon to catch her breath. The forgotten scents of long ago drifted back to her and she was lost in the memories of those seemingly endless days and nights she'd once spent in here. She could smell turpentine and cedar wood, fresh paint and a hint of perfume. When she closed her eyes she thought she could hear

402

Patch yapping and Poppy calling out, thought she could see the sparkle of sequins and the colour of her mother's eyes.

'Are you right, missus?' The anxious voice was at her shoulder.

Catriona turned and was faced with Cookie's bulk. He seemed to fill the enclosed space. 'Of course I'm right,' she retorted. 'Help me on to the buckboard.'

Cookie eyed her thoughtfully and before she could protest he'd swung her up in his arms and was carrying her through the wagon to the wooden bench at the front. Having deposited her rather too firmly on the seat, he backed away and scuttled off. 'Well, *really*,' she breathed.

Connor and Rosa clambered up beside her, uninhibited by age and infirmity, and Connor took the reins. 'Where to?' he asked, his mood obviously only slightly improved.

'The old house first, and then out to the waterfall. I want to see as much as possible.'

Razor began to plod across the yard and Catriona grabbed hold of the seat until she'd once again grown accustomed to the sway and jolt of the wagon. She heard the rattle of the wheels and the jingle of harness, and it all came flooding back. Her mother and father were with her, she was sure of that. And in the ghostly wagons that followed them so silently along the outback tracks, she could hear the laughter of the comedian and the chorus girls and the high-pitched yap of the little terrier called Patch.

As the day wore on and the sun climbed higher in the sky they roamed over the pastures and beside the billabongs. They watched an eagle hovering above them and saw a mob of kangaroos bound away into the bush. The pine-covered mountains were in sharp focus today, each tree clearly marked, as were the great stone monoliths which lay like beached whales in the wavering heat of the deserted grasslands, and the tall, rust-coloured termite mounds that poked through the scrub like so many grave-stones.

Catriona breathed in the scents and sights and sounds of this land called Belvedere, and was content.

Tom yawned and stretched and collected the statements into a pile. He'd found it difficult to sleep since hearing Catriona's story, haunted by the images she'd invoked and the reality of the forbidding surroundings in which it had taken place.

He and Belinda had been in Cairns for ten days. It had been

confirmed that Wolff had sold the story to the press, but instead of instant dismissal, he'd had his wrists slapped and been sent back to Sydney. Tom wasn't looking forward to facing his boss after that debacle, but he was impatient to return home and get his life back on track.

Tom shunted the paperwork into a folder and picked up the rest of the documents on his desk and dropped them into his briefcase. Following Catriona's statement, he'd managed to delve deeper into the life of Demetri Yvchenkov, and these documents would have to be handed on to his heirs. His digging into Kane's past had also been successful, and now he had to decide how to relate his discoveries to Catriona.

It had taken three days to uncover the remains beneath the shed and another two to determine the cause of death. The acid Catriona and Velda had poured over him had done its work, yet there was enough for forensics to work on. The remains would be released for cremation today, and the simple ceremony would be paid for by the state. He doubted there would be any mourners for such a man.

'Are you ready?' Belinda was standing in the doorway.

Tom plucked his jacket from the back of the chair and put it on. 'You're looking smart,' he said as he took in the black skirt and jacket and the neat white blouse.

Belinda pulled a face. 'Thanks,' she said. 'I went shopping especially. Thought I should make the effort, but I'll never get used to wearing a skirt, or heels.' She grimaced again as she slipped one foot out of the low-heeled pumps and massaged her toes. 'Bloody things are crippling me.'

Tom grinned as he straightened his tie. Belinda would always be a tomboy, even in a skirt and heels. 'I'll hand these in, then we can leave straight after. I've booked the five-thirty flight.'

'Have you had any luck yet tracing Kane's background?' she asked as they left the chief's office.

'Quite a bit, actually,' he said as they descended the stairs. 'He arrived here in nineteen twenty-two and lived in Sydney for a while before he dropped out of sight. I managed to trace the ship he came in on, and that gave me an address in England. His real name was Francis Albert Cunningham, and he was the second son of wealthy landowners.'

'Catriona was right then,' said Belinda as they paused on the stairs. 'He was a remittance man.'

Tom nodded. 'There was a scandal involving the very young daughter of one of the estate workers. The father was paid off to keep him quiet, and Kane was put on the first boat for Australia. His parents paid him a handsome allowance to stay away.'

'Were there other children?' Belinda asked softly.

Tom nodded and sighed. 'There were rumours about several children, but he always seemed to disappear before charges could be brought. That's probably why he chose to live a wandering life. He must have seen the travelling players as a godsend.'

'Sounds as if your search has been pretty thorough.'

'I've got a mate who works at Somerset House. Once we'd got his identity proven it was easy to fill in the spaces of his life before he came here. The time he spent in Sydney was easily researched, and another mate of mine managed to track down someone who actually remembered Kane. He was an old boy, but his memory was as sharp as a knife.'

They reached the foyer and paused. 'What about the money his family sent? Can it be found and put to use somehow?'

He grinned. 'All taken care of,' he said. 'There were two years of payments which hadn't been collected before the family stopped sending it over. It came to quite a sum and I've donated it to the Children's Aid Agency.'

She grinned back. 'Very appropriate.'

He nodded. 'I thought so.'

'Will you tell Catriona all this?'

'Yeah. She has a right to know.' He rubbed his fingers through his hair. 'But she's wise enough to realise a man like that would have had many victims.'

'At least he didn't get the chance to hurt any more kids,' said Belinda with a grimness that startled him. 'The bastard's dead and good riddance. It's a pity the law doesn't allow us to do away with the others. They don't change and can't be cured. They should be put down.'

Tom was inclined to agree with her and they left the building in silence.

The heat was fierce, the sun glancing off the windows and glaring on the pavement. They donned their sunglasses and climbed into the car their colleague, Phil, had waiting at the kerbside. It would take the best part of an hour to return to Atherton and the Tablelands.

The tiny cemetery was the final resting place for the men who'd built the Kuranda railway, and the pioneer families which had made their homes up in the cool flatlands of this northern outpost. It was laid out behind the Protestant Church, a small wooden building that had stood in this quiet oasis since the middle of the nineteenth century. The timber was bleached almost white, the corrugated-iron roof was as red as the earth that surrounded it, and the simple stained-glass windows and wooden cross gave it the aura of a different age.

As the three police officers walked along the cinder path that led to the cemetery, they saw that the pastures spread away to the back of the graveyard and were swallowed eventually by the rainforest. It was a peaceful place, the soft, warm wind whispering in the long grass, accompanied by the chatter of birds and insects, and in a distant paddock there was a chestnut horse and a tiny Shetland pony, grazing on the verdant grass, a pastoral scene that could have come from a picture book.

Tom stood between Phil and Belinda amongst the gravestones as the vicar intoned the words of the service and Demetri Yvchenkov was finally laid to rest in the rich red soil that had made his fortune. There would be a marble headstone to mark this place, but for now there was just a wreath of the most perfect red and white roses which Catriona had ordered. When the service was over, Tom looked at the accompanying card.

Demetri, my friend,
In death we are parted, but in my heart you will remain with me
always.
Sleep easier now, and know you are loved.
Kitty. x

'I was surprised she didn't want to be here,' murmured Belinda after they'd thanked the vicar and were walking back to the car.

'I don't see why,' Tom muttered as they set off back down to Cairns. 'She can do no good coming all this way to bury a man who's been dead for over fifty years, and was wise enough to know that. His memory lives on with her though, and that's all that really matters.'

They sat in silence for a while, each with their own thoughts as Phil drove them swiftly down into the valley so they could catch their flight to Brisbane. Tom looked out at the scenery and thought of Harriet. He wondered if she had returned to Belvedere, or whether she'd remained in Sydney. He hadn't had a chance to say goodbye, and the reason for her leaving had been a mystery. Either way, he thought sadly, he probably wouldn't see her again.

They said their goodbyes to Phil and walked into the airport terminal. Their flight was on time and they only had fifteen minutes before boarding. Tom bought them each a coffee and they stood by the large windows and watched the planes landing and taking off. There was something about airports that excited Tom, and he wished he was flying somewhere rather more interesting than his home town. Bali would be nice at this time of year, he realised, or Fiji. He felt in need of a change, a restless yearning to leave the constraints of his job and explore. Yet he realised that all this edginess had more to do with thoughts of Harriet than it did with his job or his lifestyle. He wanted to be with her, to talk to her and get to know her properly.

'I'm handing in my notice when I get back,' said Belinda.

Tom, roused from his day-dreams stared at her in shock. 'Why? I thought you enjoyed the job?'

'I like working with you and most of the other blokes, but I've had enough,' she said firmly. 'I can't work with men like our boss, knowing he'll do nothing to get rid of scum like Wolff. It wasn't why I went into this job.'

'Nor me,' he admitted.

Turning from the window she looked at him squarely. 'The trip down to Belvedere made me realise how much I've been missing the Outback,' she said.

'But you said you couldn't wait to get away from it,' he protested. 'You said you liked living in Brizzy and that there was nothing for you at home.'

'I know,' she admitted. 'But after all that business over Wolff I just can't hack it any more.' She took off the jacket and hung it over the back of a chair. 'I'm a fish out of water, Tom,' she explained. 'I've tried my best, but I'm just a country girl at heart.' She looked up at him. 'I want to go home.'

He didn't really know what to say to her. She was a good officer, a loyal, hard-working girl whom he'd come to admire and rely upon. Yet, as he looked down into those brown eyes he realised there was nothing he could say that would change her mind. 'It's Connor, isn't it?' he asked finally. 'You're going back because of him.'

She nodded. 'Gotta give it a go,' she said. 'Blokes like him don't come around that often, and I've waited years to get him to notice me.'

'You could commute,' he said hopefully.

'Nah.' She shook her head, making the dark curls swing around her face and shoulders as she undid the clips. 'Absence might make the heart grow fonder, but I'm not prepared to risk my future on an old wives' tale.' She pulled a slip of paper out of her jacket pocket. 'I got this today,' she said as she waved it under his nose. 'It's confirmation from Police Headquarters in Queensland. I take up my new post in Drum Creek Police Station in a month's time.'

Chapter Twenty-Eight

The picnic had been a success, the crisp white wine, fruit, cheese and cold chicken salad laid on a blanket spread beneath the trees. They had eaten their fill, and afterwards she'd pulled up her trouser-legs and joined Connor and Rosa as they splashed in the rock-pool. The drought had depleted the fall into a mere trickle, but it was pleasant all the same, and reminded her of when they were children, skinny-dipping in the pool, shrieking with laughter as they splashed one another and caught yabbies in the mud. Lovely days, she thought happily as they approached home yard.

Connor drew Razor to a halt by the barn and helped Catriona down from the wagon and set her on her feet. 'Thanks, Ma,' he drawled. 'Reckon it was a good idea after all. I hope you enjoyed the day as much as we did?'

'It was the best day I've had in ages,' she replied with a smile. The day had somehow refreshed her spirit and renewed her energy, although she'd probably ache tomorrow from all that jigging about on the buckboard. Rosa had been right about that, perhaps she was getting too old for such thing? She decided to ignore this insidious thought and patted Connor's cheek before turning to Razor and patting him. He was a good old boy and even he'd seemed to enjoy himself once he'd got used to pulling the wagon; there was quite a spring in his step as Connor released him from the traces and set him loose in the corral.

Linking arms with Rosa who was carrying the depleted picnic basket, they strolled back towards the homestead. The sky was traced with ribbons of scarlet and orange as the sun began to dip behind the hills, and this warm wash of colour gilded the trees and the earth as the birds swarmed once more before they roosted for the night. Catriona smiled with pleasure. All was right with her world.

As she looked towards the homestead she saw a figure standing on the verandah waiting for them. 'She made it back then,' she said softly. 'I knew she would.'

Rosa gripped Catriona's arm. 'Mum,' she began. 'Mum, there's something I've got to tell you.'

'And there's something I've got to tell you too,' she replied. 'But all that can wait for a while.' She waved at Harriet. 'Been here long?'

Harriet waved back. She looked slender and cool in the linen trousers and crisp white shirt, her straight, thick blonde hair curled beneath her chin and brushed her shoulders. 'All afternoon,' she replied as they reached the bottom of the steps. Her glance flickered coldly over Rosa before returning to Catriona. 'Where on earth have you been? I was beginning to get worried.'

Catriona smiled up at her. 'We've been out in the wagon,' she said as she climbed the steps. 'Such a pity you didn't come earlier, you could have joined us.'

Harriet returned her smile and took her hand. 'I would have liked that,' she said. 'Perhaps next time?' They kissed one another on the cheek and Harriet held the door open. 'I hope you don't mind me letting myself in? But there was no one about and I was gasping for a cuppa.'

Catriona smiled up at her. 'Since when did you have to ask permission?'

Rosa made a noise in her throat and Catriona ignored her. There would be plenty of time for airing grievances once she'd had her say. 'You two can make a cuppa, I'm going to rest my skinny backside in a soft chair in the lounge.' She watched them go off to the kitchen. If the atmosphere had been any frostier, she thought, she'd have been in danger of hypothermia. As she sat in the comfortable chair, she could hear the rapid conversation going on between them, and although the words were indistinct, Catriona could discern anger in their voices, the barely harnessed venom of two cats about to scratch each other's eyes out. 'Oh, dear,' she sighed. 'Such a waste of energy.'

The girls came back into the room followed by Connor. Darkness had fallen and work for the day was over. They sat in the lounge drinking their tea and making stilted, polite conversation. Connor seemed unaware of the atmosphere. He was relaxed, deeply ensconced in the chair, his legs stretched out before him. Harriet and Rosa kept glancing at one another – and Catriona sensed their edginess. 'It's nice to see you back, Harriet,' she began. 'I hope it wasn't something I said that caused you to go off like that?'

'No.' Harriet put down the cup, her hand unsteady, rattling the china in the saucer. 'I think you were very brave to dredge all that up again. I don't know if I could have.'

Catriona shrugged. 'You don't know what you're capable of until you're tested,' she said with little emotion. 'But I survived the catharsis, and now I'm almost free.' She fell silent and looked across the room at the trunk. 'I say almost, because I wasn't Kane's only victim.'

'Men like him have a history,' muttered Rosa. 'He abused you, he'd probably abused before.'

Catriona nodded. 'You're probably, sadly right,' she agreed. 'But that wasn't what I meant.' She took a deep breath. 'You see, when someone goes through what I did, it has a knock-on effect. It distorts their life and the lives of those they love. My mother never really recovered from that night, not mentally, and even my marriage was destroyed by what Kane had done to me.'

'How could that be?' asked Connor. 'Kane was already dead.'

'Kane was dead, but his legacy lived on,' she replied. Leaning back in the chair, she took a moment to collect her thoughts, staring up at her mother's portrait before she told them about their flight from Atherton and what followed.

The silence deepened as she walked to the trunk and took out the baby clothes. She took the tiny dresses and hats and bootees, and buried her face in the downy softness of the shawl she'd secretly been knitting while her mother was occupied with her office work. 'I couldn't bear to part with them,' she explained. 'It would have been like giving my baby away all over again.'

'Did you ever try to trace her?' asked Harriet as she put the packet of letters on Catriona's lap.

She looked down at them, her fingers plucking at the ribbons which tied them together. 'My mother wouldn't tell me where she was, no one would. It was years before I had news of her.'

'None of this could have helped your relationship with your mother,' said Harriet.

Catriona shook her head. 'She was unforgiving, certainly, and

411

adamant in her refusal to discuss my baby. But I've realised since that there was a lot for her to take in. She couldn't forgive herself for not realising what Kane had been up to. Couldn't forgive me for not telling her, and certainly couldn't cope with the idea of me having Kane's baby at the age of thirteen. She couldn't understand why I wanted to keep it, and I suppose, now, I can see her point. The baby would have been a constant reminder, and she couldn't bear it.'

'God,' breathed Harriet. 'What a mess.' She stood for a moment, her hands deep in her pockets as she looked up at the portraits on the wall, before returning to sit next to Rosa. 'What happened then?' she asked.

Catriona told them about Peter Keary and his betrayal of her love and trust as she twisted the rings around her fingers. The decaying petals of her bridal bouquet reminded her how ephemeral happiness was.

'But you found her eventually, didn't you?' prompted Rosa.

Catriona nodded. 'As the years passed and the laws changed, I was finally able to put all my research to use. She'd become a mother herself, you see, and I thought she would understand my need to get in touch with her. I broke all the rules and wrote to her. My letter was returned; it was the only one that she opened. I tried again and again, hoping she would be curious enough to read them. But she never did.' Catriona stared into the darkness beyond the window. 'My daughter had turned her back on me, just as I'd turned away from her. How could I blame her for that?'

'Where is she now?' Harriet's voice was soft as she came to sit on the other side of Catriona and took her hand.

Catriona smiled and gave her fingers a gentle squeeze. 'I suspect she's back in Sydney, Harriet,' she replied, her voice thick with emotion. 'I'm sorry she's still so bitter that she couldn't come with you, but at least my granddaughter seems to have forgiven me. Thank you for coming home, Harriet.'

'You knew all the time, didn't you?' Harriet gripped her grandmother's hand.

Catriona nodded as she smiled. 'From the first moment I saw you standing there in your school uniform, waiting for the chauffeur to unload your trunk.'

'But how? How could you possibly know who I was?'

Catriona smiled. 'I'd spent years searching for my daughter. I

412

discovered eventually that Susan Smith had changed her name to Jeanette Lacey. It was easy to keep tabs on her then, to follow her career as a dancer and take an interest in her husband and daughter.'

'That's why we always went to the ballet when we were in town,' said Rosa. 'And I thought you were just trying to instil a bit of culture into me.'

'It was the only way I could see her,' she replied. She took a deep breath. 'When Harriet came here for that first school holiday I was overjoyed. At last I could get to know my granddaughter, even though I could never tell her who she really was.'

'Why didn't you say anything?' Harriet could feel the onset of tears and she blinked them away. This was an emotional moment, but she needed to remain calm and focussed.

'It wouldn't have been right, darling,' she replied. 'Your mother wanted nothing to do with me, and you obviously didn't have a clue. I was happy to let things be.'

Harriet nodded. 'It explains a great many things,' she said. 'Mum's attitude for a start. I couldn't understand why she resented me coming out here and being friends with Rosa.' As Catriona opened her arms, Harriet sank into her embrace. Her emotions were running high as she clung to her, for she had spent a life-time waiting to feel part of a real family, had yearned for this moment of love and warmth.

When they finally drew apart, Catriona gently smoothed the hair from Harriet's face, her expression infinitely sweet. 'Why don't you tell me how you found out about me?' she encouraged.

Harriet glanced across at Rosa and remembered their awful row. 'I didn't know any of this until the day you told us about Kane,' she said bitterly. 'It seems I was set up by my so-called friend, Rosa.'

Rosa leaped from her chair. 'That's not fair,' she shouted. 'I explained everything to you – you just wouldn't listen to reason.'

'Reason?' Harriet whirled to face her. 'You wouldn't know the meaning of the bloody word.'

'Fair go, Hat,' growled Connor.

'You stay out of this Connor Cleary,' yelled Rosa. 'It's none of your flaming business.'

'Too right,' snapped Harriet. 'This is between me and Rosa.'

'Shut up,' shouted Catriona above the noise. 'Calm down, all of

413

you.' She watched as they glared at one another and sat down. 'I think you'd better explain, Rosa. And I want the whole story, not just the bits you think will put you in a good light.'

Rosa glared at Harriet, looked to Connor for support and realised she wouldn't get it. 'I read the letter,' she snapped. Catriona's expression was stony and she hesitated before carrying on to tell her about her night forage into the trunk. 'I wanted to do something special for you,' she said softly. 'You've been so good to me and Con, and I wanted to make you happy.' She sniffed and lit a cigarette. 'I didn't know how or when, and it wasn't until we went to high school that I saw my chance.'

'She deliberately made friends with me as soon as she found out who I was,' said Harriet bitterly. 'She went out of her way to be nice and to trick me into thinking she really did like me.'

'That's not true,' snapped Rosa. 'I admit I sought you out in the beginning, and I'm sorry I was so devious. But we became real friends, much closer than I'd ever expected. And as time went on I realised I could never tell you what I'd done, because I knew you'd never forgive me.'

'So why pick now?' Harriet stood with her arms tightly folded around her waist.

'It was a traumatic day,' admitted Rosa. 'The atmosphere was so charged I couldn't keep my secret any longer.'

'But can't you see what damage you've done?' persisted Harriet. 'I've always trusted you, always told you my secrets. That trust is gone now. I doubt it will ever return.'

'I think it's time for all of us to calm down,' said Catriona as she began to pour them some wine. She handed round the glasses. 'Rosa, I know you meant well, but really, darling, I do wish you'd think before you go leaping into the dark.' She smiled at her and touched her face before turning to Harriet. 'If it wasn't for Rosa you would never have known who I was,' she said softly. 'Is it such a bad thing to have me for a grandmother?'

'No.' Harriet moved to her and took her hand. 'Of course not. It's just the underhand way Rosa's gone about things that has upset me.'

'That is something you must both come to terms with, but I believe Rosa meant only the best of intentions, so try not to be too hard on her.' Catriona smiled her encouragement as Harriet glanced across at Rosa.

'I'm sorry,' muttered Rosa.

414

'So am I,' said Harriet with a sigh.

Connor raised his eyes to the ceiling as the young women embraced and burst into tears. 'Strewth, Ma. Now we've got the bloody waterworks. Talk about drama.'

'I wouldn't expect you to understand,' Catriona said with a smile. 'But just be thankful the storm is over and that I have a granddaughter.' She poured another glass of wine and waited as the girls made their peace and dried their tears.

When they had settled once more, she turned to Harriet. 'Did you never question your mother about her family?'

She nodded. 'I began to ask when I was still a little girl,' she replied. 'Other kids had grandparents and aunts and uncles, and I wanted to know why I didn't have any. Dad explained he'd lost both his parents in a car crash when he was nineteen. He'd been the only child, but he had photographs of his parents and their siblings, and lots of stories to tell about his own childhood. I never got to meet any of his family as they'd passed away long before he married Mum. He was quite a bit older than her, you see.'

Harriet bit her lip, and Catriona could hear by the tremor in her voice that she needed a moment to control her emotions.

'Mum refused to talk about her childhood before ballet school. She had no photographs, no stories to tell, and every question I asked was met with a wall of silence. As I grew older, I realised she was an unhappy, bitter woman, driven with ambition for herself and in turn for me. It seemed as if she was determined to prove she was better than other people's expectations of her, determined to erase her past and re-invent herself. I began to probe more deeply, but there were no photographs or diaries, no letters or mementos from those early years, nothing to point me in the right direction.'

'And you, Rosa. How did you manage to find out so much from a single letter?'

'I had a name and an address. I'd read the letter, so I knew that Jeanette Wilson was your daughter.' She paused as she looked at Harriet and they exchanged a smile. 'It blew me away when I realised we were in the same class at school.' She took a drag of her cigarette. 'The only trouble was, I had all this information and didn't know what to do with it. You didn't know I'd read the letter. Harriet didn't know she was related to you, and her mother seemed determined to keep it that way.' She lifted her shoulders. 'I was stuck.'

415

Catriona laughed and patted her hand. 'My goodness, Rosa, what a devious rascal you are,' she said fondly.

'Devious? Downright conniving, if you ask me,' muttered Connor. 'I can't believe you kept all this to yourself, Rosa.'

'Actually,' admitted Rosa. 'I feel utterly ashamed about the whole thing. It's just that I was so desperate to do something special for Mum. I hadn't really planned how I would go about it and although the contents of the trunk put some of the pieces of the jigsaw together, there was one vital element missing. And without confessing what I'd done, I could go no further.'

Catriona nodded. 'And that missing link was Kane. He was the progenitor and founder of all the misery that has beset me and the following generations, and if Demetri's body hadn't been found you probably wouldn't ever have known about him.' She turned to Harriet. 'It isn't something to be proud of.'

Connor rose and poured them all another drink. 'Welcome to the family,' he said, raising his glass to Harriet.

Harriet sighed. 'Mum warned me not to meddle when I asked about her family but I always had the feeling there was something missing, something I should know about.' She grinned. 'And now I have a ready-made family.'

Rosa raised her glass. 'Here's to Hat, sort of sister and best mate.' She downed the drink in one and risked setting fire to herself by lighting another cigarette.

Catriona's eyes were bright with tears. 'I'm only sorry Jeanette couldn't forgive me,' she said. She turned to Harriet. 'Did I hurt her so very much?'

Harriet stood and walked over to the window, her hands deep in her trouser pockets as she remembered the awful confrontation with her mother. Jeanette had been almost incandescent with rage, pacing the floor of the luxury apartment, her face taut and cold.

'I told you not to have anything to do with that family,' she snapped.

Harriet watched as Jeanette lit another cigarette and sucked in the smoke. 'It was certainly one hell of a shock,' she replied. 'And you'll be pleased to know Rosa and I have fallen out over this big time.' She took a breath; she didn't want a fight. 'But I had a right to know who I was and where I'd come from. Surely you can understand that?'

416

Jeanette's eyes blazed as she whirled to face her. 'Rights,' she spat. 'And what about my rights, Harriet? Do my feelings count for nothing?'

'Of course they do.' Harriet reached out to her mother but her hand was ignored. 'Please, Mum,' she tried again. 'Give me a chance to explain why Grandma gave you up – then perhaps you'll see she didn't do it lightly, or willingly.'

Jeanette glared at her, the corners of her mouth turned down in a sneer. 'I see she's turned your head already,' she hissed. 'Grandma, indeed.' She turned her back and stared out through the window over Circular Quay. Her shoulders were stiff, her stance defensive as she silently smoked her cigarette.

Harriet watched her for a moment, the barrier Jeanette had thrown up between them as efficient as the Great Wall of China, yet she knew it must be breached if their relationship was to survive. She began to talk, hesitantly at first, then more fluently as the story unfolded, aware of the pain this was probably causing her mother, but knowing the moment must not be lost.

Jeanette remained silent throughout, her arms wrapped tightly around her narrow waist. Harriet wondered at one point whether she was even listening, for there was no outward sign of any reaction, no lessening of the tension in her stance. With her back turned, Jeanette's expression was lost to her and she could only imagine the thoughts that must be racing through her mind.

'Catriona spent a life-time searching for you,' she finished. 'And when she found you, you rejected her without giving her a chance to explain. She wants to make peace with you before it's too late, Mum. Can't you find it in your heart to accept what happened and forgive her?'

Jeanette turned from the window, her face ashen, eyes bright with unshed tears. 'It's a bit late to play happy families,' she snapped.

'I'm not asking for instant cosiness between you, I wouldn't expect it and I doubt Catriona would either. But a phone call or a letter would mean so much to her.'

The shadows played across Jeanette's face as she eyed Harriet, her thoughts hidden behind a mask of indifference. 'It's very obvious where your affections lie,' she said coldly. 'But after this betrayal, what more should I expect?'

'I'm not going to ignore Catriona because you're unwilling to

417

build bridges,' retorted Harriet. 'She's my grandmother, and I've come to love and admire her.' She tamped down on the rising impatience and grasped her mother's unresponsive hands. 'But that doesn't mean I don't love you, or think any less of you. You're my mother, I'll always love you.'

'How can you, now you have your new family?' Jeanette retorted. 'You won't want to have anything to do with me once that bitch has her hooks into you.' Despite her cruel words, Jeanette's reserve broke and she collapsed into the soft couch, her face buried in her hands as she sobbed. 'I can't forgive her,' she said through the tears. 'I just can't. And now I'm going to lose you as well.'

Harriet sat next to her, the anguish in her heart almost unbearable as her mother sobbed on her shoulder. How could she make Jeanette see there was so much to rejoice in, and how easy it was to build those bridges she was so frightened to erect? All Harriet could do now was reassure, console and comfort the mother who had, before now, always been so strong and sure of herself.

Much later, when the emotions had waned and the tears had been dried, Jeanette fell into an exhausted sleep. Harriet gently kissed the tear-stained cheek and covered her in a light blanket before leaving the room. As she turned in the doorway and watched her sleeping mother she knew it was up to Jeanette now to make her reconciliation with her own mother.

Harriet returned to the present and realised Catriona and the others were waiting for a reply. 'It was the most difficult thing I have ever experienced,' she admitted softly. 'Mum was almost incandescent with rage when I told her what Rosa had discovered. She could barely look me in the eye, could hardly speak. I've never seen her like that before, and it scared me.'

'You told her everything?' asked Catriona.

'I skimmed over a lot of it. I didn't see the point in telling her the whole gruesome story of Kane's abuse, it served little purpose. I told her you'd been raped and forced to give her up for adoption. I also told her you'd been searching for her ever since.' Harriet sighed. 'In the end it didn't make any difference to the way her mind was set against you. She's too bitter to see reason, or look beyond her own pain.'

She looked across at the portrait of her great-grandmother. Velda smiled down at her, the violet eyes warm and encouraging in the flawless face, and Harriet recognised something of her own mother in her expression. 'Mum is a strong, determined woman who has lived her life according to her own agenda. Which is why her reaction to all this frightened me.'

Harriet turned from the portraits. 'She fell apart. Broke down completely and begged me not to leave her, not to stop loving her. I realised she was terrified of being left alone, of being unloved and condemned because she couldn't accept her link to you. There were powerful emotions in that room and it took a great deal of time to reassure her that despite my affection for you and the joy in knowing who I really am, I would always love her no matter what happened.'

'Poor Jeanette,' said Catriona, the tears rolling unheeded down her cheek. 'If only I'd been there to comfort and console her.' She pulled out a handkerchief and mopped up the tears.

Harriet went to her and held her. 'It will take her time to digest the things I told her,' she murmured into her hair. 'She's been in denial her whole life, so it won't be easy for her to adjust to the truth.' Easing from the embrace, Harriet looked into Catriona's eyes and felt the warm glow of a love far stronger than she'd ever felt before. 'I believe she will come to realise how much you loved her, and what it cost you to be parted from her. It could take time, but we mustn't give up hope.'

'I've been hoping for years that she'll forgive me,' said Catriona. 'I'm prepared to wait for as long as it takes.'

Harriet smiled. 'We've all learned something from this, Grandma,' she said with soft relish for the lovely word. 'I've come to realise a mother's love is the most powerful love in the world. Velda killed because of it, you lost your marriage and spent your life searching for your lost child because of it. My mother loves me, more than I realised, and one day, probably quite soon, she'll want to know what it's like to feel the warmth of her own mother's love. For without experiencing this special gift we are never whole.'

Epilogue: A Year Later

Harriet swung the powerful car through the archway and noted that the long driveway up to the homestead had finally been metalled. The engine purred as the tyres hummed over the smooth surface and she began to relax. This was a home-coming, one she had made twice over the past few months, and as she drew the car to a halt on the crest of the hill she looked down at Belvedere and smiled.

The homestead had been given a fresh coat of paint for this very special occasion, and the roses were clambering in bright profusion up the verandah posts and over the roof where they mingled with the bougainvillea. The paddocks stretched away into the distance, a peaceful green backdrop after the rain which contrasted sharply with the bustle surrounding the homestead, and outbuildings.

Harriet sat in the car and looked down on the confusion of cars and utilities which had been parked off to one side of the great barn. The sun glinted on chrome and glass and danced over the bright colours of the women's dresses and hats, and even from this distance, the sounds of laughter and music were carried up to the hill.

Having taken her fill of the view, Harriet slowly drove down the hill, the sense of excitement growing as she approached the homestead. Belvedere never failed to enchant her, but today it was as if a touch of fairy dust had been added and she could hardly wait to be a part of it all. She followed the worn track to the far paddock and parked in the makeshift car park. It was mid-winter, but the heat was still intense, and as she gathered up her hat and bag and stepped out of the air-conditioned car, it struck like a hammer blow. She was reaching into the boot of her car for her case when she was startled by a familiar voice at her side.

'Looks like you might need some help with that. Trust a woman to bring everything but the kitchen sink.'

She whirled round, the smile of pleasure already on her face. 'Tom,' she breathed. 'What are you doing here?'

'I was invited,' he drawled, his eyes warm with affection. 'And I couldn't give up the chance of seeing you again.' He smiled his slow smile and took her hand. 'Telephone calls are no comparison for the real thing,' he said softly. 'You sure are a sight for sore old eyes.'

He didn't look so bad himself, Harriet thought as she took in the smart suit, crisp shirt and silk tie. She felt the blush spread from her neck to her face. The warmth was echoed in his touch and the electricity of the moment. 'I agree about the phone calls,' she replied, her voice muted by the sudden onslaught of shyness that was so unfamiliar she didn't know how to deal with it. 'It's probably cheaper too, if my phone bill is anything to go by.'

'That's the penalty we must pay for living so far apart,' he said, his gaze travelling slowly over her face as if he was trying to imprint each one of her features in his mind.

They stood and gazed at one another and Harriet realised she'd forgotten the bustle and the noise and the milling crowds. It was as if they were alone, and needed only one another. 'I'm so glad you came,' she murmured.

'So am I,' he replied. 'Because now I know I've made the right decision.'

She cocked her head to one side and laughed up at him. 'What decision?'

'I've jacked in the force,' he said as he lifted out the case and slammed the lid on the boot. 'There's a job waiting for me with a security firm in Sydney. I've got a few weeks to sell up in Brisbane and find a new place, but I should be down your way in about a month.'

Harriet could feel the quickening of her pulse as she realised what this meant. The telephone calls over the past months had changed in tone and Harriet had wondered if it was her imagination that they had become warmer and more intimate, or whether it was purely wishful thinking. Now it seemed the feelings were reciprocated and she couldn't find the words to express her delight.

'You don't mind, do you?' he asked as he heaved the case from one hand to the other, his expression at once concerned.

'How could I mind?' she murmured, her eyes bright with a

421

teasing light. 'Anything to save on the phone bills.'

He took her hand and tucked it in the crook of his arm. 'That's all right then,' he said with a smile. 'Now, come on, Catriona's been waiting for you all morning and she's getting impatient.'

Catriona left the house with Archie and sought sanctuary from the noise and bustle indoors for a few minutes peace on the back verandah. The house was too small for so many people and it was a relief to escape. She sat down in the old cane chair, and with Archie purring on her lap, she closed her eyes and said a silent prayer of thanks for all the blessings she'd been showered with over the past few months.

Tom's discovery of Demetri's will at the solicitor's office in Darwin had come as a double-edged sword for Catriona. The surprise and delight at his legacy was tempered with a deep sadness that she had doubted him and thought he'd abandoned her. Yet, as the months had passed she saw his gift as a way of benefiting not only the next generation, but of keeping his memory alive in other ways.

Demetri's house had been demolished, the land sold to a developer for a king's ransom – it was ridiculous the way the property market had swung out of control all the way up the east coast, but at least the dark ghosts of the past could finally be dismissed and they could all look to the future. Connor and Rosa would of course be more than comfortably off once Catriona died and passed on her own legacy, but Demetri's money would ensure they were secure until then. Harriet's share had been instrumental in setting up the Demetri Yvchenkov Scholarship for gifted, but impecunious law students so they could attain their degrees.

With an overwhelming sadness she looked out from the verandah and wished Demetri and Poppy could be here today. She would have liked to thank him for his kindness and Poppy for the gift of her grandchildren. Yet, as she sat there in the shadows she thought she could feel their presence at her shoulder, watching over them all, delighting in this happiest of days, and was comforted.

She sighed as she looked at Belvedere in the winter sunshine. Here were Harriet's dreamscapes, shimmering in the heat, humming with life and the promise of even better things to come. The homestead had been spruced up for this very special occasion with a fresh coat of white paint on the clapboard and green on the shutters and doors. The verandah had been decorated with flowers and ribbons, and potted palms and spring flowers lined the stretch of scarlet carpet that ran from the steps at the front to the lawn at the back of the house. A bower of flowers had been erected on the lawn, and lines of gilt chairs had been placed on either side of the scarlet carpet that would serve as the aisle for the ceremony. It was a perfect day, with the Jacarandas dripping amethyst, the flowering gums bursting with scarlet blossom and the wattle's citrus yellow buds fairly bursting with exuberance.

'Are you all right, Grandma?'

The soft voice stirred her from her pleasant thoughts and she smiled. 'I'm good,' she said. 'What about you?'

Harriet sat down beside her and smiled. 'Very happy,' she said on a sigh. 'It's always good to come home, but today seems to have a magical quality I wouldn't have missed for the world.'

Catriona gave her a hug and a kiss. 'You're very late,' she grumbled. 'What kept you?'

'A ton of work at the office, and a long chat with Tom.' Harriet smiled at her, her face alight with happiness. 'You should have warned me he was coming.'

Catriona laughed, delighted her plans were coming to fruition. 'I always think surprises are such lovely things,' she replied. 'Why spoil the moment with forewarning?'

Harriet grinned. 'You're naughty, you know that, don't you?'

Catriona nodded. 'And why not? At my age I've earned the right to meddle a little, and I thought it was about time you two came to your senses.' She regarded Harriet for a long moment. 'Has he told you about his move to Sydney?'

Harriet laughed. 'Nothing much passes you by, does it?'

'Not much,' she agreed contentedly. 'How do you feel about having him in your home town?'

'Oh, I think I'll like it just fine,' she replied, the happiness radiating from her like the sun.

Catriona looked over her shoulder. 'What have you done with him, then?'

'He's over at Connor's.' Harriet giggled. 'It's some sort of last-minute bachelor thing the best man's organised.'

'They'd better not be drinking too much,' muttered Catriona as she dumped Archie from her lap and brushed his hairs from her expensive silk dress. 'The guests are practically legless already and the men had quite enough the other night,' she said fiercely as she glared out at the milling crowd pouring from the beer tent.

'Where's Rosa?' asked Harriet after a moment. 'I haven't seen her for weeks, and I wanted to catch up with the gossip.'

'Off somewhere with her young man,' replied Catriona. 'I must say, he was quite a surprise. Rosa's men are usually highly suspect.'

'Not nearly as much of a surprise as it was to me,' laughed Harriet. 'I still find it hard to believe Rosa and Jeremy Prentiss are an item. They must have crossed paths many a time, though I know they never actually met. But one look at each other at my firm's summer party and bam, it was the whole nine yards including the earthquake. I don't think they've spent a night apart since.'

'Life is full of surprises, my darling,' replied Catriona. 'Who would have thought you'd end up with Tom Bradley? I seem to remember you didn't like the look of him at all when you first met.' She winked to take the sting out of her words, for she actually liked Tom very much.

'True,' Harriet conceded as she watched Tom walk across the yard. 'But you know how it is, Gran. He sort of grew on me.'

Catriona noticed the way Tom's face lit up as they smiled at one another. What a lovely day this was turning out to be, and how glad she was to be alive and a part of it. They sat in companionable silence for a while, watching the passing cavalcade of guests until a signal from the house told them it was time for the ceremony. Harriet took her arm. 'Come on,' she said softly. 'The bride's ready to make her entrance, and I can see the groom is on his way. We'd better go and sit down.'

'Let me escort you,' said Tom as he met them at the bottom of the steps. 'It's not often I get the chance of showing off with two lovely ladies.'

From anyone else Catriona and Harriet would have considered his remarks verging on the obsequious. Yet they saw the teasing light in his eyes and accepted his offer with good grace. 'You're a rascal,' teased Catriona as she took his arm and accepted his kiss on her cheek.

'So are you,' he murmured.

Catriona watched as he and Harriet smiled at one another. She wouldn't be at all surprised if there wasn't another wedding on Belvedere very soon, and maybe even a third if things continued in the same vein with Rosa and Jeremy. Her heart swelled with love and happiness as she let Tom lead her down the red carpet to the front row of seats. It was proving to be an emotional day and she hoped she didn't make a fool of herself by bursting into tears and making her mascara run.

With a nod and a few words to Pat and John Sullivan and their friends, she sat down next to Rosa and Jeremy. Rosa looked very well, she thought as she took in the scarlet dress, the cap of dark glossy hair that curved to her elfin chin and the gypsy earrings which sparked gold in the sun. The very handsome Jeremy Prentiss was obviously having a remarkably good effect not only on Rosa's penchant for rainbow hair, but on her dress-sense. She turned from Rosa and smiled at the groom. Tears were already threatening; goodness only knows what state she'd be in at the end of all this, she thought happily.

The vicar had let them borrow the portable organ from the church in Drum Creek, and the organist began to play the first rousing chords of the bridal march. As Catriona stood, she thought of Poppy and her presence seemed so real she thought she could see the bright peroxide hair and hear the laughter of her dearest friend. How proud she would be to see their handsome Connor on his wedding day. How overjoyed to know that Rosa had at last found someone who loved her. She turned with the others and watched as the bride was escorted by her father up the red carpet to the bower of flowers.

Belinda looked radiant. Her hair framed her face in a cloud of dark curls beneath the coronet of yellow roses, and the diamond earrings flashed in the sunlight as she walked slowly down the aisle. Her dress was a sheath of ivory silk which clung to her hourglass figure, and the yellow roses in her bouquet were still dewy from when they'd been picked from her garden that morning. The tomboy had become a beautiful young woman, Catriona realised.

She looked across at Connor, so handsome in his dark suit and white shirt, the yellow rosebud in his button hole matching his tie to perfection. His face was as radiant as Belinda's, his eyes bright with emotion as he watched his bride approach. Catriona felt the tears run down her face and dabbed them away. How proud Poppy must be as she watched from above. Her precious boy had put the terrors of his childhood away and was willing to begin again with the girl he loved.

She sniffed and blew her nose as Belinda arrived by Connor's side. She was being a sentimental old fool, she realised. But Connor was the boy whom she'd loved and cherished from the day he and his sister had come to live with her. He was her son and she had a right to be proud of him, a right to feel this great heart-swell of emotion as she watched him marry the girl who'd brought a new sense of light and life to Belvedere. They would be happy, she knew that, and soon, if fate was kind, there would be another generation to love this place.

All too soon the ceremony was over and the happy couple were posing with their guests for the photographs that would grace many a special album. Leaning on Tom's arm, Catriona slowly made her royal progress through the happy, chattering group and took her place for the family photo.

'I reckon we could be having another wedding soon,' muttered Harriet as they shifted around to the orchestrations of the photographer and tried not to step on Archie who seemed determined to take centre stage in front of the bride and groom. 'Rosa and Jeremy seem to be joined at the hip and I've never seen her so calm and happy.'

Catriona grinned up at her before winking at Tom. 'You never know,' she said. 'But this is certainly a perfect setting for a wedding should anyone want to have one.'

Harriet blushed and Tom put his arm around her shoulders, pulling her close so he could drop a soft kiss on the top of her blonde head.

Catriona smiled. There was something about weddings that brought out the romantic in the most hardened cynic. Dear Harriet, she'd been so determined not to marry, so convinced her career was all that mattered, yet here she was aglow with a love she probably hadn't had time to realise she possessed. She ducked her chin and hid her smile in her handkerchief. Love had a way of creeping into your heart when you least expected it.

'What a happy day. I'm so glad to be a part of it all.'

Catriona turned to the elegant woman next to her and put her arm around her narrow waist in a swift hug. 'So am I, my darling, darling girl,' she said fervently.

Jeanette Wilson dabbed her eyes. 'Thanks for everything, Mum,' she whispered as they gripped one another's hands and turned to face the photographer.